PENGUIN BO

A BEAUTIFUL EVIL

A BEAUTIFUL EVIL

BEA FITZGERALD

PENGUIN BOOKS

PENGUIN BOOKS

UK | USA | Canada | Ireland | Australia
India | New Zealand | South Africa

Penguin Books is part of the Penguin Random House group of companies
whose addresses can be found at global.penguinrandomhouse.com

www.penguin.co.uk   www.puffin.co.uk   www.ladybird.co.uk

First published 2025

001

Set in 13.25/19pt Adobe Jenson Pro
Typeset by Six Red Marbles UK, Thetford, Norfolk
Printed and bound in Great Britain by Clays Ltd, Elcograf S.p.A.

The authorized representative in the EEA is Penguin Random House Ireland,
Morrison Chambers, 32 Nassau Street, Dublin D02 YH68

A CIP catalogue record for this book is available from the British Library

HARDBACK
ISBN: 978-0-241-62433-3

INTERNATIONAL PAPERBACK
ISBN: 978-0-241-74495-6

All correspondence to:
Penguin Books
Penguin Random House Children's
One Embassy Gardens, 8 Viaduct Gardens, London SW11 7BW

[Dedication to come]

AUTHOR'S NOTE

A Beautiful Evil is a work of fantasy fiction, inspired by many things, among them experiences and concerns drawn from our world. At its core, this is a romantic comedy about the power of hope – and my own hope is that it is a fun, enjoyable and uplifting read. To enable that, I wanted to highlight some topics within these pages that might be difficult to engage with, depending on your own lived experience. This is a book about being true to yourself, so if these topics aren't something you feel comfortable reading about right now, know that I appreciate you listening to your own heart. Please take care of yourself, and consider that this may involve talking to a loved one, a trusted adult or a doctor, or referring to another resource as needed.

- This book contains discussions of and references to rape culture and sexual assault. There are no graphic scenes of this content.
- An arranged marriage, within the context of a fantasy world, is featured and centred.

- This book touches upon war and its aftermath.
- Content includes blood, gore, surgery and other medical treatments.
- Ableism, fatphobia and misogyny are explored.
- This book features emotionally manipulative, coercive and abusive familial relationships. There is no physical abuse.
- There are specific mentions of suicide.

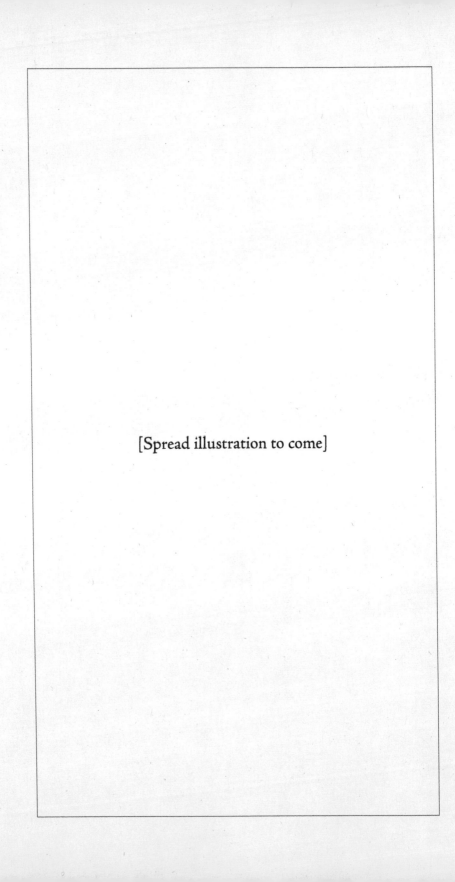

[Spread illustration to come]

[Spread illustration to come]

CHAPTER ONE

T HE KING OF THE GODS demanded a beautiful evil – and so
I was born.

They're reckless things, words, especially on the lips of
gods. Beings have been created from less – from blood and
flesh, from seed and soil, from hopes and wishes. A good
handful of the pantheon spewed forth from errant thoughts.
And there I was: a command.

Kalon kakon. A beautiful evil.

Words made me, ones issued by Zeus himself – but then . . .
hands, careful and precise, and I became more than the furious
venting of an impetuous god. I wasn't supposed to *be* yet, and
I knew even as the gods crafted me that I ought to hide myself
away until they declared me whole. They would be so much
happier to believe I owed everything to them.

I was the first human woman – and this was to be my
foundation: smile, keep my mouth shut, and listen.

The gods bickered among themselves as Hephaestus
worked, carefully carving out each individual tendon in my
hand, chiselling each freckle and mole.

'Make her hair longer, give him something to hold on to.'

'Oh, come on, you can go bigger than that with the breasts.'

'Are you serious? We're going to need to reinforce her back at this rate.'

'You've got good hips there. Give her thighs to match – yes, just right with the stomach! She looks so delightfully soft.'

'Soft? She's made of clay.'

'Well, she's not always going to be, is she? She'll be a full-rounded woman, flesh and blood, with a belly to lay a head down upon and thighs to bury yourself –'

'Yes, yes, I get the point. Are you sure about the nose, though? Looks a little too upturned.'

'He's not going to care about her nose with ankles as enticing as those.'

I didn't know them all, but one boy arched a coy eyebrow in a way that identified him, with an instinct drawn from whatever forces had conceived me. He was mischief incarnate – Hermes. Now cutting a half-amused sneer at the man who had just spoken.

'Her *ankles*, Poseidon?'

'Yes. What's wrong with admiring a nice shapely pair of ankles?'

'At this point, I'm beginning to believe that if it turns you on, it's intrinsically wrong.'

I didn't like it, the way they picked over me piece by piece, like I was deficient if I did not align with their ideal – one they couldn't even settle on themselves, each one shouting their preferences. No sooner had Hephaestus made an adjustment than they changed their minds, like my form would be an ever-racing thing, chasing after their whims in a competition I could only, inevitably, lose.

But as much as Hephaestus indulged their wishes, he alone seemed more considered: the god of blacksmiths creating me to be more than the sum of my parts – and I realized as he inflated my lungs and pumped blood through my heart that he was pouring something else into me, too. A sort of resolve, solidifying with each chip of vertebrae down my spine.

Love.

He was creating me with love – the sort of adoration an artist has for their creation, and I did not care that to him I was just another thing he had made. Because it was a thing one step removed from the intentions that had birthed me. And soon there was so much love within me that the words Zeus had spoken – whatever they were – slipped clean from my newly formed mind.

'She's a bit young, isn't she?' a woman asked, something about her painful to look at, though I didn't understand why until she brought her hand to my temple, filling me with thoughts of longing and desire. *Aphrodite.* The name was the barest whisper of sea foam against waves. Goddess of a trickling array of responsibilities, yet *beauty* sang loudest. Looking at her triggered lust and envy in equal measure. I wanted to tear my gaze away, the embarrassment too fierce – but it would have been worse to reveal that I was conscious for my own creation. Indecent, somehow.

'Epimatheos has only just reached adulthood,' Hephaestus said, the first words he'd spoken, as he stepped back to review his work. Throughout, he would chip away a piece just to brush it back over, or carve out a little too much, then pat clay back on – rounding me out, smoothing me down, not resting until each aspect of me was exactly as he demanded. And now, finally, he gave a satisfied nod. 'She's perfect.'

Another woman approached. She did not wear her famed helmet but those piercing grey eyes, shrewd and dissecting, labelled her as Athena, goddess of wisdom. She began draping cloth around me, clasping it in place with delicate gold filigree pins. They had just quibbled over my every part and now they covered the mound of my breasts, the gentle rolls of my belly, the curve of my hips right down to my supposedly covetable ankles. When my body was art, it was a thing to be admired. But to become flesh, it was layered in rules of decency and modesty. It was a thing to shield.

With each fold of the sheet, Athena whispered in my ear – words so quick I could not work out their individual forms. But my mind filled with images of the loom and threaded needles until my fingers itched for them, to prove this talent I felt burgeoning inside me.

Aphrodite stepped forward to touch my face again, let her slender fingers run down my cheek, and I shuddered, hoping no one saw. It was the first movement of my body – and suddenly it was all I wanted: to touch and be touched, to feel desired, to find someone who might adore me in every way I suddenly craved.

'There,' she said. '*Now* she's perfect. She'll be irresistible.'

'We'll see,' Hermes answered, stepping up to take her place. He stared hard into my eyes, and I wanted to run, to hide – to pretend I was never here at all. He whispered into my ear and his words sank through my skin and slid down my throat. There they solidified into long cords, giving me voice – language that could be a disguise. Words that could be wielded as weapons. I wanted to take all I was and every precious thought I had and hide it from view, to twist it into something else and declare it to the world, like the truth would only be safe concealed from the light.

I'm not sure what he did to me, exactly, only that afterwards I didn't want to let them do what they wanted to me any more.

More women entered the room, carrying jewels which they layered about my throat on long golden chains. They tucked flowers into my hair until they ringed the golden diadem Athena had placed there, and studded them through the embroidered veil that brushed down the back of my neck.

I felt beautiful – and somehow also ashamed of the fact, even though I knew any beauty I had was the intentional work of these gods. Anything of mine was theirs. And still it seemed my shame to bear, like I ought to apologize for my own existence.

When the women were finished, Hermes hummed, tilting his head this way and that. 'I think she'll do.'

He entered then, loud steps clashing with the immediate silence that fell upon the gods about me. His words were so distant to me now that I didn't recognize him as the man who had spoken them and demanded my invention.

'This is her?' he asked – his voice a harsh crack, like a lashing whip, like thunder wrenching apart the sky.

'Yes, Lord Zeus,' Athena said assuredly when no one else made any indication to speak. 'Is she to your satisfaction?'

Zeus took another step towards me, his eyes narrowed like he was taking aim at a target. He ran his eyes over my face, my body – and even though I was now clothed, it felt so much worse than the scrutiny of the other gods. I had no doubt that if the answer were no, that I did not suit his purpose, the gods would simply scrap me and start again.

And I liked who I was now, all the things they had made me: a girl who hoped for love; who enjoyed working the loom and could spin lies that were just as pretty; who feared the hunger inside herself as much as she longed to satisfy it.

'She'll be the ruin of them,' Zeus said at last. 'I name you Pandora.'

Oh.

A piece of me I did not know I was missing.

A name.

A summary of all that I was and all I might be.

With it, Zeus makes me whole. I had existed, but now I come alive, clay softening to warm creamy skin, eyes blinking, and I am stretching my hands out before me, moving through the empty space, part of the world I glide through, marvelling at the feeling of the cold air, of the heavy metal jewellery draped about my throat.

I am Pandora.

CHAPTER TWO

GODS, I NEED TO TAKE this dress *off*.

I'm trying to process the world around me – the gods and the crowded room full of sharp-edged tools and cluttered workbenches – but I keep tripping over my thoughts, hurtling right back to how hideous this cloth feels against my skin. I am not sure which is worse: the constant discomfort or the way I cannot move past it – a thoroughly infuriating loop.

But the gods are watching me, and instinct forces a smile.

'Ah . . . hello?' I try.

Everyone's gaze pivots from me to Zeus, like they're waiting for his judgement. Athena's gaze feels pointed, eyes boring into mine and then back to Zeus, like she's trying to tell me something.

But I don't know what, and clearly I should. I taste bile, and there must be something wrong with the way Hephaestus moulded my lungs, they aren't working properly and –

Zeus.

The king of the gods. Ruler of the Heavens. Conqueror of the Titans. Master of thunder. Wielder of lightning. Bearer of the

Aegis. That once-instinctive recognition is blown beyond all reason. Once the names start they do not stop, epithets tumbling and swirling, titles he himself must have insisted they plant within my mind.

As the script finally slots into place, I blurt, 'My lord,' and dip into a low bow.

'Pandora.' He draws the name – *my name* – out into a long, questioning hum, like my existence is a thing to query. 'How do you feel?'

Like I'm going to scream if I don't get a change of clothes. The fabric is the wrong weave, wrong heaviness, seams sewn in the wrong places, and I am excruciatingly aware of it all.

But oh, they worked so hard.

I don't want them to feel bad, or to imply I'm unappreciative of all they've done. I watched them chip away at me for hours, saw the thought and consideration they all put into my creation. I can't diminish that over some fabric that doesn't sit right.

'Delighted! By the Heavens, look at this dress!' I twirl, letting the dove-white linen flow outwards before settling back into perfectly pinned drapes. I clutch at the necklaces I'm wearing. 'And these jewels. Oh, thank you! Thank you all!'

So *that's* how it works, this deceptiveness Hermes rooted in me – a need to please that morphs so easily into a readiness to lie. But I want the world to be a soft, kind thing – and if words can birth me, then surely they can do that?

I take Athena's hands – who looks a little taken aback at the gesture but pleased enough – before turning to the three women who adorned me with the golden chains. They beam at me, my cheer contagious, until all four of us squeal at the beautiful garments. And there is some truth to that: the clothes are lovely, finely stitched and made with such care. And these girls, the Graces, are all so welcoming and bright and so thrilled at my adoration of everything that suddenly it's not an act any more.

I am a collection of gods-given gifts and I'm so thoroughly overwhelmed by that generosity that I'm not sure where to turn, who needs my thanks next.

'Of course,' Zeus cuts in with a derisive sort of mirth. 'Well, you certainly did as I asked. Perhaps a little *too* well – it's not as though we needed another woman to fawn over clothes and trinkets.'

I'm confused for a moment – because his words are scathing and dismissive but it feels as though there's a sort of fondness there too. Like he would not waste his time sneering at me if he did not also want something from me. And I know I'm not the only one to notice, because a couple of the goddesses stiffen.

But the gods created me, and they inscribed a love for pretty clothes into my mind – or at least the idea that I *should* love pretty clothes. So how can they also fault me now for celebrating that? They have marked out a space as mine and then dismissed it as flippant, like it is not one of the few joys made available to me.

Still, the women's reactions to my compliments imply I have not stepped out of line – nor do Zeus's comments, really. He seems pleased to have had his apparently low expectations satisfied.

'Well, let's show off our newest gift, shall we?' Zeus doesn't wait for a gap in the conversation, his voice simply carries over everyone else's.

And he doesn't wait for a response, either, just turns and stalks out.

Everyone follows – even Hephaestus, who seems far less interested in me now that I am complete. He does not place much weight on one of his legs, instead leaning on a cane with every step – a cane now flecked with clay. I imagine him later – washing it clean, scraping the mud off, specks of it flaking where he walks. Fragments that could so easily have been a finished part of me, now just discarded dirt to be shed.

'Oh, please don't lust after that old fart,' Hermes says as he lingers beside me, offering his arm.

'I . . . I wasn't,' I rush. Flustered, I feel my cheeks warm, a sensation I feel equally embarrassed by.

Hermes laughs. 'Sure.'

I run through the things I know of Hermes – knowledge that flows as readily as air to my lungs or blood through my veins – *god of roads, thieves, merchants, conveyer of souls to the Underworld and the messenger of the gods.* An overarching theme of transportation, then – and is that why they have left me with him? So that he might bring me wherever we are going?

I take his hand though I'm not sure why we're leaving, or where we might be going. This place seems perfectly lovely, though I realize it cannot possibly be Hephaestus's main forge; there are no fires, no workers, and only a limited array of tools. Sturdy pliers and sharp carving knives, bright-hued paints and a large potter's wheel I hadn't noticed I'd been standing on until I step off it.

In front of me, in a large amphora, are bulky lumps of clay. After a moment, I understand what I'm looking at: a hand, chiselled and moulded but the nails not quite finished, and an eyeball, slightly too oval in shape; a mass of hair thinner than my own; a breast lopped off at jagged edges. The parts of me that did not make it.

I think of the clay drying on Hephaestus's hands.

My eyes sting – but new instincts surge, ones that make me a woman and tell me how to survive it, insisting that now is not a good time to cry. That it will be a weakness. That I must press through to the end.

As Hermes and I leave the room, I am blinded by white marble pillars and a floor of bright, shining gold, reflecting the light of a dozen chandeliers.

I fall still, taking a moment to admire it all – the twinkling lights and the sharp colours, the smell of peonies in the air and the way my shoes tap against the metallic floor.

'It's beautiful!' I exclaim.

'This,' Hermes says slowly, 'is a corridor.'

He guides me on and I realize the gods must have made me in some back-end room of the palace. And as we pass several heavy doors, bolted shut, I wonder what other projects they are working on.

I wonder if the door to my room was bolted shut too.

I nearly stumble over the threshold of the Great Hall. Its ceilings arch so high I have to squint past the flickering lights strung from the rafters to see the marble above. The stone walls are etched with layered art, stories within stories – spear-wielding figures drawn in the wild tresses of centaurs and whole myths in the spiralling patterns of Athena's shield. And not paying attention to any of it are the hundreds of gods milling around, dressed in explosions of colour and swaying to the lilting chirps of panpipes.

But as my excitement soars into something thoroughly *delightful* it crests too high, keeps climbing, and all at once it's too much. It's so loud – so many gods, all chatting, the cups clinking, footsteps heavy on the lacquered floor.

Ahead of us, Zeus has joined a huddle of gods. He gestures to me and heads turn in my direction. Conversations drop to murmurs.

Hermes leans close and conspiratorially whispers: 'They'll sate their curiosity and move on quickly, I'm sure. So I'd enjoy the attention while you have it.'

Enjoy? I cannot stand all the faces turning towards me and their chafing whispers.

A god pushes through the crowd to reach me. His blonde hair glows as golden as the rest of the room, with its metallic floor and flickering candle-lights. His chiton slides from his shoulder, baring tanned skin, and I feel that warmth again, that flush. Something enticing about it even as looking feels shameful.

'Apollo,' Hermes introduces. '*Very* quickly sated by all accounts. Most would say too quickly.'

'At least they're talking, Hermes. Funny how we never hear rumours about your conquests, no matter how much you try to spread them.'

Hermes starts to retort but Apollo is already ignoring him, reaching for me, hand clasping mine, bringing it to his lips.

He's beautiful – and there's something entertaining in the way he tosses Hermes' wit right back at him.

'Now, who is *this* lovely creature?' he asks.

'Pandora,' Hermes answers before I can – though the question sounds like it was addressed to him in the first place. 'The first human woman.'

Apollo squints, confused, and Hermes rushes on. 'And she's reserved, I'm afraid.'

'That hardly matters, I can –'

'Prometheus.'

Those nearest fall silent, and I realize only then that they have been listening in.

They share worried glances, and Apollo's face drains of colour.

'I don't understand,' he says.

'That does not surprise me in the slightest.'

Apollo's lip curls. 'Well, what's she doing here, then? Being paraded around, dressed like that, when she's already taken? Why are you letting me waste my fucking time?'

He doesn't wait for a response, turning and stomping back into the crowd.

'You were right,' I say so only Hermes can hear. 'He finished disappointingly quickly – and made no effort to ensure I was sated in return.'

Hermes' answering snort of a laugh blares loudly. I'm not sure I find it funny – I think I'm actually rather upset by the whole thing – but a need to be liked seems to have taken over and plucked the thing that might most endear me to Hermes from the options planted within my head. From the fond smile that settles on his face, it appears it – I – was correct.

The encounter with Apollo had distracted me from how busy the room is, how loud. Now all I can process is the loud buzzing and, gods, this awful dress, scratching my shoulders, my hips, touching all the parts of me I'm sure Apollo was dreaming of.

Someone should inform him of the amphora of my potential pieces. I'm sure he'd find it just as enticing.

Another god comes over offering distraction and this time I seize it.

'Dionysus,' the man introduces himself before Hermes can. He's beautiful too – in a different sort of way, all curling locks and soft boyish charm. How much beauty can there possibly be in this world? The very corridor brought me to a standstill, and now every god that crosses my path has me enamoured a little more with existence.

Dionysus catches me looking around and cocks his head to the side, an easy smile unfurling. 'Ah yes, I remember my first visit to Olympus too. Here, this might help.'

He hands me a chalice, something dark and red glistening inside.

I take it and ask, 'You weren't created here, then?'

It hadn't really occurred to me that I was somehow unique in the manner of my birth.

He smiles. 'Well, sort of – but I couldn't see much from within the thigh my father stitched me in once my mother died. Then, once I was born, I spent most of my time on the lands below – still do, gallivanting around and getting into trouble. So many parties. So many vintages.'

I blink. 'I have questions. A lot of questions.'

Dionysus arches a brow. 'Where would you like to begin?'

So I let them spill out, my reservation shaken free by nervousness, and the questions come one after another, each answer I get only eliciting a dozen more.

'Your curiosity is rather charming, Pandora.' Dionysus eventually catches his breath, chuckling to himself. 'I almost don't want her to go,' he addresses Hermes, like I'm not the one beside him. 'She's nothing like these boring bastards. Any joy in this place tends to have an edge of cruelty to it.' He looks back to me. 'It's a relief to see it . . . unencumbered. You'll have to find some time in amongst all the grand plans they have for you to visit Naxos. I have to introduce you to the maenads – they'll love you. And there's a lot more of *that* to be found.'

He nods at my now empty cup. *Wine*, apparently. I like it – the heavy sweetness, and the way it dulls the edges of how overwhelmingly *bold* everything in this room is.

'Absolutely! And you have to let me join one of your revelries, they sound so fun!'

'And the orgies,' Dionysus adds.

I'm taken aback. Had we been *flirting*? Or is this just the sort of thing he says?

I start to make some bawdy joke in return – like with Hermes, I'm certain it will land well. But Athena slides into the space beside him and what actually tumbles from my lips is an awkward mumbling of, 'Well, I don't know about that.'

'Interesting,' Hermes says, watching me with a shrewdness that reminds me of his gaze while I was being created, like he could see everything inside me, even the parts I wasn't aware of.

'Yes?' Athena asks him, and Dionysus chooses this moment to disappear back into the party.

'She's irresistible.' Hermes cocks his head at me. 'It varies from person to person. But it appears she's quite adept at finding it.'

'Why, thank you,' I say, laughing to disguise my discomfort. *Smile, smile, smile. Be pleasant. Be fun. No one else is struggling so don't let them sense that you are. Become whoever you need to be and figure the rest out later.*

'Hmm, I'd like to see that. I'll accompany her, now,' Athena says. So she does, Hermes nodding farewell and joining a circle of gods in the corner.

Athena introduces me to more gods, each as interesting as the last. They tell me of their domains and origins and I lose myself in their stories and gossip.

I push my fear aside and lean in, until the shiny projected veneer of my confidence becomes all I am. I drink more wine. I dance. I laugh so hard I fear my sides might split like clay in an over-hot kiln.

'Charismatic,' Athena finally declares, and soon she's glancing around the room as though she's looking for another god to take over as my chaperone — bored, apparently, now she has solved the puzzle of me.

I look away, if only to hide the embarrassment of her sudden and evident disinterest in me. My gaze catches instead on a mural of her etched into the walls, sword aloft, plumed helmet towering above the men cowering before her.

Something about it tickles a memory, something the gods want me to know . . .

I dart quick looks at the other carvings, and there I see it again and again: victory. *Their* victory. This place is a temple to their might.

'Ah yes. Our defeat of the Titans,' Athena says, like she can hear my whirring thoughts.

It rushes through me like my mind is still settling in place: *the gods' predecessors, led by Zeus's father, Kronos. The Titans had done abhorrent things: torn their parents limb from limb and devoured their own children. So the gods had overthrown them in a long, brutal war . . .*

The gods saved us. Their might prevailed. They are brave and worthy heroes.

The thoughts jolt me – because surrounded by the gods of this world I have not yet felt much reverence. Is that what they're all waiting for? For me to fall to my knees, in fervent worship?

But the ideas slip away as soon as they occur, like they cannot find ground upon which to set down their roots.

Beside me, Athena is fixated on the etching of herself, her grey eyes distant. 'My birth.' She nods at the mural, her sword held high. 'Kronos wielded time itself. He warped it about the battlefield like a distilling plague, and the gods found their own magic to fight it, like a fog fights the horizon. Yet even in those colliding torrents of moments, where minutes unravelled and years coiled tight, still nothing quite as strange as *me* had yet occurred in its midst. I was born fully grown, plated in armour, and leapt into the fray from the skull of Lord Zeus itself. Which is to say –' her lips press into the barest hint of a smile – 'that I understand what it is like, to suddenly *be* and to be thrust into the frenzy.'

She glances back at the room, and I realize she hadn't been looking for another god to abandon me with, but rather attempting to see it all through my freshly rolled eyes.

'Personally,' she says, 'I'd choose the battle over this.'

I don't know what to say. Everyone else had wanted something from me, and I had flowed to fill the mould they requested, but this attempt to cut to the heart of me like she might find kinship there has me stumbling, and before I can find my footing, she says: 'I think that's enough now. Come.'

She strides towards Zeus and I hurry to follow. He is surrounded by other gods and does not even look at me as we approach, just turns to the gods at his side: Hermes, Aphrodite and now Athena.

'Well, you might as well take her down.'

'What? Take me down where?' I interject before I've thought through what I'm doing.

Every one of them pivots to glare at me.

There is a difference, I realize, between being part of a conference with the king of the gods and attempting small talk with him on a dance floor. My voice is not welcome in the former, and raising it when it was not asked for goes against everything they've instilled in me.

Hermes rushes to break the silence before it can turn on me. 'To Colchis. To your husband.'

'Don't worry, Pandora. You'll love him,' Zeus says, flashing teeth. 'It's the very purpose of your existence.'

CHAPTER THREE

A GODDESS PASSES US, HER tumbling curls tangling in the lyre strung across her back, and it's enough to distract Zeus, who follows quickly after her without another word.

'Well, I suppose I'd better make the delivery,' Hermes says cheerfully.

Athena turns a stony gaze on him. 'I will come as well; this is too critical to risk.'

'My postal services are a risk?'

Aphrodite laughs. 'My letters to Adonis took two weeks because you were distracted ferrying souls to the Underworld.'

'The passage of mortal souls is more important than the erotica you two spew back and forth.'

'I guarantee you it is not! Besides, Adonis is in the Underworld too; it shouldn't have taken so long! And on the topic of spewed erotica, I'm coming as well. I want to see these sparks fly in person.'

'Why? So you can let your jealousy ruin the moment?'

I feel myself fading out as they squabble, like the whole world is just happening around me. By the time Hermes loops his arm through mine, I'm no longer sure what's going on, or where I'm being led. I blink and suddenly I'm in a chariot, Athena at the helm with Hermes and Aphrodite crammed in too.

The chariot charges forward and I would be tossed out if Hermes didn't hold me in place, his hand clamped firmly on my wrist like I might choose this moment to run away.

I shut my eyes, wincing against the cold as we fly through the sky – and that's it, I've left Olympus.

My skin burns as the air tears at us, my hair knotting around the clips that hold it in place. My stomach churns and, gods, I really ought to have drunk less wine.

I'm waiting for it to be over, but as we start to slow I risk peeking over the edge.

I'd expected glorious views – all that's surrounded me since my eyes first opened is unparalleled beauty. But all I can see are clusters of trees, distinguished only by the hills rolling beneath them. With dusk descending, they're too dim to find much depth or detail, just dark shards forming an impenetrable mass.

As we draw closer, the trees cut to an abrupt halt, revealing grey dust speckled with grass. Ahead, cliffs drop into a dark thrashing ocean. And between the two are the orange-tiled roofs of what must be our destination.

Colchis. My husband.

I shut my eyes again, and pretend it's the wind that forces me.

By the time we land I feel like I've been churned up and resettled, like the gods dragged me back to the workshop to push me into some new shape.

I wonder what my husband will think of it. Of *me*.

Athena dismounts but Aphrodite turns to me, heaving a deep and wistful sigh. 'You are so lucky, Pandora. To be made for love. How glorious. There's nothing more powerful in the world.'

'How's it worked out for you?' Hermes scoffs, leaping to the ground and abandoning us in the chariot.

Aphrodite ignores him with a pointed hair-flip. 'Don't pay him any attention. Love is joy, it is completion. Many spend their whole lives searching for it, and here you are getting it hand-delivered!'

My unease settles a little, diluted by a weak spark of hope. The goddess of love herself is telling me happiness awaits — how could I doubt it? This man I'm to marry *must* be perfect, if Aphrodite approves the match. *My* version of perfect at the very least, as suited for me as I am for him. Two halves designed to fit together in seamless harmony. I wonder if the gods made him, too — split our clay into parts, and are now bringing us back together to become whole.

Still, my concern lingers — and how utterly infuriating, that these churning emotions do not listen to the logic of the gods' will.

Aphrodite gestures for me to dismount the chariot. So I leap, my thin-soled shoes not offering much protection from the hard-packed dirt my feet slam into. It's not particularly high, but it feels like I've jumped from Olympus itself.

The trees look sparser from this angle, long thin trunks with leaves that fan out above. Still, past the edges they cluster so tightly that I cannot see far through the forest's depths. I stare a little too long, and I know, really, it's to avoid looking in the other direction.

'Come along,' Athena calls.

I turn to her, and – *Olympus above* – the house.

Tall white walls and thick wooden-framed windows. Cobblestone path winding up to its slatted door. It looks tiny, settled among so much nothing, but imposing too, ominous almost in its very existence, here where there's little else to be found.

As before, there is only one way to dull this anxiety: I must press through to the end.

I feel every stone through my sandals, each step painful. I think of the smooth, shining golden floor of Olympus. I think of ripping the shoes off. I want to tear the dress off, too. I think of being naked before the gods' gaze, before I thought to think anything of it, and I think of the fact they designed me for whoever I'm being led to, but every man in that room wanted me to be perfect for them, too, like they could only want something if another man wanted it as well, and –

We're at the door.

Hermes is lifting a big iron loop and letting it fall heavily against the wood, and it rings and rings. In each of the house's windows I see lights flickering to the rhythm of its chimes and I can't get the sound out of my ears even after it stops. My heart chimes too, shrill vibrations against my ribs, like it might chip away at me every bit as much as Hephaestus's chisel ever did.

A key scratches at the lock.

A boy flings the door open almost recklessly, no care for

who might be on the other side. No peering through a crack first, like he might wish to know who he is opening up his home to.

I feel like I am racing through the sky once more, hurtling forward quicker than I can comprehend. I can only take in snatches of him: thick, bold brows arched over eyes that remind me of the forest – oak-brown at the edges, spiralling into impenetrable darkness; himation thrown carelessly over his chiton, slanting across his shoulders; gold cuffs encircling his ears, his hair a mess of sleek black curls that look so thoroughly tactile . . .

'Well, what an absolute delight,' he says, voice like a warm forge. And then he flashes a brilliant smile – straight white teeth, creases in the corners of his eyes, actual dimples etched into his warm brown skin.

There was no furnace for me, no kiln to harden the malleable clay. Is that why I suddenly feel so unstable? As though I am still unset within? One glance at that smile and my insides melt, my heartbeat staggering in flux.

The boy's gaze falls on each of us in turn and as he reaches me he adds: 'To what do I owe the *pleasure*?'

That last word on his lips, the way he meets my eyes as he says it . . .

He leans against the doorframe, and even angled he looks down on us all. Athena is straight as a javelin beside me and she just about scrapes his eyeline. How is he standing so casually – so *calmly* – when I feel so thoroughly dazed?

'Might we come inside?' Athena asks, a forced innocence to her voice that snaps me from my frazzled lust.

The boy – my husband? – doesn't seem to notice the threat,

he just smiles once more and opens his arms wide. 'Of course, come right in!'

He steps back, welcoming us all through. One by one we step forward and I'm excruciatingly aware of passing him, the fear I might be too close, that I might brush against him.

The door opens into a large courtyard, the rest of the house set in a wide arc around it. Utility mixes with comfort: there are long, low lounge chairs and a deep-set well, finely tended flowers beside fruit-bearing trees and half-filled pithoi of crushed, fermenting grapes. In a corner is a sundial that cannot possibly work, with the way the house must shade it entirely each morning. Athena smirks as she considers it, perhaps thinking the same.

In the twilight, everything is enchanting, lit by the flames of a brazier at the courtyard's centre.

A dog races towards us from inside the house, though there is something odd to it, a shape rearing from its back. And as the flames illuminate it, the dog shines. I gasp. It is metal, pure and shining gold, tiny gears glinting beneath its chin and behind its ears.

Hephaestus's hand is clear in this and when my mind whispers *an automaton* it is as though one creation of his can recognize another.

Now the shape on its back becomes clear: a tray balancing cups and an oinochoe of wine.

The dog sits, neatly sliding the tray to the floor beside us, then races to nudge the lounge chairs invitingly closer to the fire, its tail wagging just like the real thing.

'Thank you, Korax,' the boy says, reaching to pick up the tray.

'Korax?' Hermes loudly whispers. 'You can't name a golden dog *Raven*, surely?'

Athena shakes her head. 'He's thanking a metal dog, Hermes. I think the name is the least of his issues.'

Our host gestures for us to sit as he pours the wine out.

'It's so lovely for you all to visit,' he says, handing a cup to Athena. 'I can't recall the last time an Olympian blessed me like this.'

'I wonder why,' Hermes says, glancing around and not bothering to conceal the curl of his lip. As beautiful as this home is, its quaintness apparently does not appeal to the opulent tastes of the Olympians. 'Remind me what it is you do here?'

'Um, live?' the boy says, then rushes to continue at Hermes' derisive snort. 'Forage, make wine, care for the forest –'

'Yes, yes, how very exciting,' Aphrodite says, taking the next cup from his hand before he can offer. 'Now, shouldn't we make a toast? Especially on a day like this?'

The boy rushes to pass me a drink, only half filled, but better than nothing for an apparent toast. He barely has time to splash anything into his own cup.

'Yes,' the boy says. 'How wonderful it is to drink with friends.'

Aphrodite rises to her feet. 'And a glorious day to celebrate young love.'

Now he frowns. 'I don't under–'

'You have been given a great gift by Zeus himself,' Aphrodite continues. I'm so distracted watching him – enjoying the way he looks at each person talking so intently, following the words on their lips like each one is a thing to be treasured – that I don't even notice Aphrodite as she comes to stand behind me, placing her hands on my shoulders. 'He rewards those loyal to Olympus. And you have always shown great loyalty to those who deserve it, and cast aside those who do not. Isn't that so?'

The boy's expression darkens, ever so slightly, but his words are jovial. 'Yes, of course. I fought for Zeus to claim his rightful throne, and it pleases me to see him rule so justly.'

Aphrodite gives a warm, tight smile. 'I'm sure it does. And just as he punishes those who betray him, those who please him he rewards. Pandora here has been created just for you. And given every gift the gods can bestow. Zeus hopes you enjoy her.'

Enjoy me.

Is that all I am? Something to be received and revelled in? Some kind of bribe for future loyalty?

It shouldn't matter, should it? If this arrangement makes everyone happy, then why question the decisions that led us here?

But something's not right – and I think it's the way they've chosen to draw this out into some grand reveal. Like they want to linger on his surprise. Or like they want to trick him somehow.

The boy steps back, knocking the tray to the floor where it clatters against stone. He doesn't even flinch. I'm not altogether sure he notices.

'Oh, that's very . . . kind. Of course. But I'm not –'

'I know you don't refuse a gift of the king of the gods, Epimatheos,' Athena interrupts – and for a second I'm shocked.

Epimatheos – after wisdom – as a name, it means *afterthought.*

A guest does not insult their host in their home, not when bound by the hospitality laws of xenia. It would be foolish – and Athena certainly isn't that. Which means she isn't insulting him, at least not beyond the actual name itself and whatever the giver of it intended.

Athena continues. 'Nor would you refuse the gift a guest might bestow upon their host, surely.'

She's bound him twice now, first through the threat of Zeus and then by xenia. That's why she asked to come inside – but why would she *need* to bind him? Aren't we supposed to be perfect for one another? Didn't Aphrodite say I was made for this man's love? Does this mean –

But Epimatheos stills any concern I might have had by crossing quickly to my side, his smile so blinding I have to look away from it, glancing up into his eyes which capture mine with their intensity.

'Refuse? Rivers of Hell, why would I refuse? Pandora, I believe?'

I nod, too surprised by this turn of affection to say much at all. He takes my hand and I rise, stepping forward to close a little of the distance between us. He's at least a foot taller than me, lithe-limbed and towering. I can't look away until he does, his gaze raking down me, slowly, and I am suddenly so aware of every inch of my skin.

His eyes meet mine again. 'You are the single most divine creature I have ever laid eyes on.'

'Careful, Epi, that's sacrilege,' Hermes warns, but there's an amused lilt to his tone and he lazily swirls the wine in his cup as he speaks.

Epimatheos blanches. 'Oh, I didn't mean to . . . forgive me. I am just so overcome by Lord Zeus's generosity.'

'It's quite understandable.' Aphrodite nods.

'This is . . .' Epimatheos shakes his head and he can't stop smiling. Neither can I. It feels like my heart might burst. 'This is beyond anything I dared hope for. I know my family have betrayed the king in the past, and I have lived with the bitterness of that fact for so long. I cannot stress how much Lord Zeus's forgiveness means to me. And to be rewarded, too? With a woman like this? This benevolence is an honour.'

'Yes, that's Zeus.' Athena stands. '*Benevolent*. Well, perhaps we'd better leave these two to become better acquainted. After all, we just led a procession to your door. I believe, by the customs of the minor gods and nymphs, that makes you officially married.'

'Yes!' Aphrodite calls behind her as she makes to leave. 'You have a wedding night to enjoy!'

Epimatheos turns to me and winks. 'Oh, absolutely we do.'

My lungs, my heart, my *knees*, apparently! How many parts of me did Hephaestus make weak to this boy?

Hermes downs the rest of his wine in one lung gulp. 'Rivers of Hell, no one needs to stick around for that. If it's anything like the last wedding procession I was a part of, I'll never get the horrifying sound of all that moaning out of my head.'

The wine I drank earlier feels like it has completely worn off, not a single part of me dulled to Epimatheos and the effect his lingering gaze is having on me.

They leave and I barely notice – I am too busy trying to still my racing heart and freewheeling mind.

Epimatheos says nothing, just piles the cups back on to the tray. Athena's chariot darts into the sky, and he scowls as he looks up to it, though the expression vanishes as he turns once more to me. Smile back in place like it never left.

'Let's go inside, shall we? Away from prying eyes.'

Even this still-horrendously annoying dress isn't distraction enough from the thoughts that flood my mind: all the things we might do inside, all the things couples do on their wedding nights – knowledge of which Aphrodite has blessed me with, but the actuality I fear I am definitely not ready for. Part of me is screaming yes, while the parts that supposedly make me irresistible – shyness, demureness, maidenhood – are busily deeming that desire despicable. The contradiction of myself inflames, spirals – yet none of it is enough to stop that longing . . .

'Right,' I manage. 'Yes. Let's.'

Did Athena herself not declare me charismatic? Then why am I not currently capable of full sentences?

He takes my hand, his skin so warm, and I look up into those deep dark eyes.

He draws me forward, stepping across the threshold of his – *our?* – home.

I can't cope with all this, and yet . . .

It's the purpose of your very existence.

I have to trust in the gods who sent me here so I turn, ready to throw myself into it. To flirt with my husband as much as he has been with me. To assert that I am just as thrilled to be gifted to him as he is to receive me.

The door slams shut and Epimatheos towers over me, pressing his arm to the wall above my head, trapping me in place.

All trace of his happiness is gone, that devastating smile not even a memory in the sneer that is etched in its stead.

'Now, what the hell am I supposed to do with you?'

CHAPTER FOUR

'M LEANING BACK, PRESSING MYSELF into the wall, trying to create some distance. He's so close, and now is not the time to notice the woody scent of him, the aniseed tang. It's all merging: confusion and arousal and a tinge of fear until words are tumbling from me – incredibly foolish words when a boy has you pressed to a wall like this.

'I was literally born this morning and even I know what you're meant to do on your wedding night. If you don't, then I'm not sure I can help you.'

Oh no. Oh gods, no. I know immediately that I've got it wrong – snatched to put on the same front I wore for Hermes and Dionysus and presented it to Epimatheos instead. But what else can I do? That same instinct not to let anyone see my confusion or, worse, my *hurt* is reaching for the first shield it can find – and apparently it's one of unbothered snark.

But his instant glower tells me that bravado isn't going to help me here.

'This is not our wedding night. We are *not* married.' His voice is low, the letters so sharp and crisp that I feel them vibrate through my bones – feel my spine straighten in response.

'But the gods said –'

'The gods lied. Repeatedly. You will find it is what they do. So, *Pandora*,' he sneers my name – and I'm not sure I can blame him. If my name meant *afterthought* I'd be resentful of someone named *all the gifts* too. Even though he's being awful, I find I can't even *think* of him as Epimatheos – it feels too cruel – so, short of something better, I simply drop the insult. Matheos – *thought*. That ought to do. 'What exactly are you doing here?'

'I assume you don't mean up against this wall? Because I was hoping you might enlighten me on that one.' I suppress a wince. This version of myself is sticking, then, I suppose. At least it hides the rest of me away, lets my feelings cower until they're safe.

Irritation clenches his jaw so tight he growls through his teeth: 'What is it you *want*?'

Gods, what a question.

I think about it for a moment. My bafflement is a blurry thing – I don't know the rules of this world, am unsure where I've gone wrong. But there is a gnawing in my gut at the thought I've trespassed on some taboo or other.

'Right now? I want to be led somewhere I can rip this dress off.'

When his narrowed eyes widen with alarm, I realize how what I've just said sounds.

'I'm not sleeping with you,' he snarls.

'Pity.'

'Pandora.'

'I'm joking! I don't want to sleep with you, either, when you're going to such lengths to make your disgust of me this clear. I mean, this is hardly scintillating foreplay,' I lie – it turns out being pushed against this wall with his face so close to mine is indeed doing *something* to me. 'If you don't want me that's fine, I am more than happy to go back to Olympus –'

'You're not going anywhere.'

His words land heavily, and though he doesn't move, the space between us feels like it's contracted even further. Like the walls are closing in.

'Excuse me?'

Matheos steps back, the arm that had blocked me in place falling to his side. But the way he's regarding me makes me feel no less trapped.

'The gods sent you to me for a reason. And I intend to find out what it is.'

The gods have been incredibly obvious about why they sent me here. It's *his* behaviour that's unclear!

My throat tightens with the confusion of it all. The hurt I can keep at bay, the rejection a thing to postpone thinking about. But the feeling of the ground vanishing beneath me? Of the fragile rules I have built the outlines of this world with paling to hazy marks? It is too fundamental, disconnecting something within me until my responses spill without thought, Matheos's every action sudden and jarring and every breath a thing I must fight for.

Only one thing is clear: that this is not a place to let my emotions show. They are a vulnerability; the very existence of them is to lose. But I can already feel a stopper loosening and everything threatening to burst free.

I need to get out of here.

'This is ridiculous,' I dismiss it, taking a step towards the door. But another metallic creature appears in front of me. This one with *very* sharp teeth. Some sort of big cat – a panther or lion. It cocks its head at Matheos, cogs twirling in its eyes like it's waiting for permission.

I swallow. The threat is obvious but whatever Matheos means by it doesn't land as it should. Despite everything, I really, truly cannot believe Matheos would risk injuring a gift from the gods. The automaton waits, and I wonder whether Matheos summoned it somehow or whether this situation – a gifted girl in his home – is so common that the beast has a programmed response. It, too, is clearly a creation of Hephaestus – so did the god send it here for a purpose, presumably one other than keeping me trapped within this house?

I blink, startled at my own distraction, and return to the matter at hand.

Matheos regards me with the same curiosity I directed at the automaton. I realize now how he played the gods – with his baffled nods and ditzy acquiescence. He probably chose his name himself to drive its point home. Surely he would not undo all his efforts to persuade the Olympians of his unthinking obedience by destroying the thing they so clearly want him to have.

I'm on the cusp of taking another step when he speaks again: 'What's your plan, Pandora? Going to wave at the sky until they send another chariot for you? They won't come. You aren't a god. *We* aren't gods. We're nothing to them.'

Obviously he's not *nothing*, or they wouldn't have engineered all this.

But I am.

Didn't they make that plain every time they spoke like I wasn't there? Every time they did something to me and I didn't even think to protest – took me to Earth, handed me over to a complete stranger, and I never even thought about saying 'no' because they'd made it so clear that wasn't an option.

'If you aren't a god, what are you?' I ask, because he's blatantly not human either – not if he looks eighteen but apparently sided with Zeus in a war that happened centuries ago.

For the first time, his disgust falters. It's replaced with a strange sort of hesitance – perhaps even reluctance.

And then, levelling his gaze at mine, the challenge within clear, he says: 'I am a Titan.'

I can't help my sharp intake of breath. The murals on the walls of Olympus: Kronos consuming babies, ordering his armies, their vicious blades wielded against the gods, the ichor they gleefully shed, golden lacquer painted on to the marble friezes like the wounds still wept . . .

'Not one of those ones, obviously,' he snaps and I realize I've made this situation so much worse by reacting with the fear he'd obviously anticipated. 'And though you may be loath to believe it of a Titan, I'm not going to hurt you. I'm just –'

'Imprisoning me?'

'Keeping you where I can see you,' he corrects, brows drawn low over a piercing glare. 'I'm going to uncover every lie you're trying to tell me. Every ruse, every manipulation, every falsehood. I will find you out, Pandora. I won't give you the chance to fulfil whatever purpose you were created for.'

Loving you, a voice in my mind answers. *That's all.*

Matheos snorts, like he can hear my thoughts and thinks my answer weak, my purpose only worthy of disdain. Like love must hide an ulterior motive.

And when he speaks again, it's a clear and blunt dismissal: 'Stephanos here will show you to your room.'

CHAPTER FIVE

T HE HOUSE IS BRIGHT AND cool, more orange tile under foot and rough white walls surrounding me as I walk. The air is tinged with lemon, and my footsteps echo loudly in the stairwell, and then even louder in the large room it leads to. There's a scattering of low reclining chairs and a few barren tables but certainly nothing to fill it, or stop any sound bouncing in the sparse lounge.

It seems Matheos doesn't get many visitors. So how lonely am I about to become?

An empty house full of creaking automatons. An angry boy and a girl made of clay. Impenetrable forest all around, the sharp drop of the cliffs . . . We are at the edge of the world, in a place the gods forgot – or they will, at least. I'm sure of that now – their plan complete, a task marked off, a girl made and delivered . . .

Stephanos trots out of the only door, and we emerge on to a wooden walkway, shaded by the low slanting tiled roof and lined with doors and curtained windows. It stretches the length of the house and looks into the courtyard below.

I am taken to the very end, and Stephanos stares at another door expectantly. *Stephanos. Circlet, wreath* – and my eye catches on the melded metal mane about its neck. Did Matheos name it? But the lion nudges the door impatiently so I push it open. I take in the bed, the chest at its foot, the small table and chairs in the corner. Everything wooden and roughly hewn. The linens the colour of the sand outside. It's all just as simple and paltry as everything else.

The door shuts behind me.

I immediately fumble with the ties to yank this dress from my body.

I find fresh chitons in the trunk. They must be spares or cast-offs – left for guests who might have need of them. The new fabric is softer, and I'm thankful the sheets are folded to fit because I'm considerably shorter, fatter and – frankly – *bustier* than Matheos. Even so, the dress stretches across every curve and bump he doesn't have – a little too tight on my hips and riding up where it gathers above my backside.

Why is every chiton in this world determined to spite me?

It's difficult to knot in place, and I think of Athena delicately tying each one on my previous outfit, and all the love the gods poured into my creation, abandoned the moment I became real.

Maybe the idea of me was preferable to the reality.

Which is the thought that finally undoes me, my body caving and the tears spilling fast.

Maybe the gods liked me better still and silent and under their control.

Still, even if that's true, at least they liked me in *some* regard – not like the man I was supposedly moulded for. The cruelty of it is inescapable now, searing and caustic: his every barb, the utter hatred with which he spat each word, the threats he wasted no time in levelling against me.

It just doesn't make sense. My heart was not made for this sort of break. I should be locked in an embrace right now, sweet whispers in my ear, hands on my skin.

I wasn't just born to love; I was meant to be loved in return.

I'm failing at the very purpose of my existence.

I dive beneath the sheets of the bed, hoping the weight of the blankets and the darkness they douse me in might be the only place where my tears are safe.

Instead, every hope the gods adorned me with begins to spiral.

Some are too hazy to recall, some so clear their sharp edges cut: *irresistible, temptress, charming, 'a bit young'* – because *Epimatheos was young, too, and each shred of me was an intention for him* – 'reserved, I'm afraid' . . .

I throw the covers from the bed.

Prometheus.

That was what Hermes had said. Not Epimatheos.

I frown.

Afterthought and *forethought* – brothers, perhaps? One the clear favourite, with names like that. All right, all right . . . I stand and begin pacing, hoping the answers might flow as quickly as my harried steps.

Hermes hadn't necessarily meant I was 'reserved' for Prometheus instead – it was just the name he'd used to shut down Apollo. So I suppose the real question is *why* build me for Matheos? They'd said I was a reward for loyalty, that Matheos had stood by Olympus when others had not . . .

Others like Prometheus, maybe?

It is, of course, just a theory. I'm still discovering the way my mind works but it seems primed to shield me from despair, so maybe this puzzle is just another distraction to latch on to. But it would make Matheos's hostility if not *reasonable* then perhaps *understandable*: I might remind him of whatever betrayal Prometheus committed, or he might doubt the gods are truly here to reward him, or maybe that name of his and the long years in this lonesome house have convinced him he doesn't deserve an offering like me.

Interesting. I suppose I wouldn't need all the gifts the gods gave me if gaining Matheos's love were easy. Maybe they knew I would have to wield the talents they awarded me to win him over. Maybe they knew it would take time, and skill and devotion.

It may not be as easy as I had expected, but won't love be all the sweeter if it is a thing accomplished rather than instantly given?

The gods do, after all, enjoy nothing so much as a testament to their power.

And maybe that's what we're destined to become.

What felt impossible last night feels simple in the bold light of morning – I am going to make Matheos love me. That is, until the moment I open the door and find the golden dog on the wooden walkway, sitting opposite me and watching. I step forward and the dog is immediately on its feet, moving to block me.

'Oh, really?' I sigh. 'A guard dog now, are you?'

I contemplate barging past it, but it's a metal machine and I imagine it can stop me. Or at least bark loud enough to wake Matheos.

I ransack what I know of this thing.

Korax. Automaton. Built by Hephaestus. A servant of sorts. A guard.

A dog.

I scratch its ears. Its tail wags. I reach down, feeling around for a groove or latch, something to allow for maintenance.

I find one beneath a ridge on its back – a lever held to one side. But I hesitate before switching it, my curiosity warring with reluctance. I want to know what it does, but don't want to risk the harm it might cause.

Korax's jaw opens, almost like it's smiling, as I continue to scratch.

Oh, fine.

Besides, if it's reacting like this then it will probably act like a dog in other ways, and so my curiosity latches on to that instead.

'What if you showed me the kitchens? I bet there's lots of lovely treats – meat, a bone, maybe?'

Korax's ears prick, alert once more and holding firm. It cocks its head at me like it can't believe I even tried that.

Automaton. 'There's probably lots of very nice oil, too?'

Its tail wags far more enthusiastically.

'Come on, then, and if you're good there might even be tummy scratches available.'

At this it bolts off and I rush to chase it, making a mental note to ask Matheos how often he oils his pets if Korax is this excited about it. I pass locked door after locked door, down the steps and past still more doors until the dog stops at one and gazes up at me with big black eyes that suddenly look incredibly sad. *And pleading.*

'Yes, yes, I'll get it. Good dog.' I give it another pat on the head – which it doesn't look like it appreciates, eyes darting pointedly towards the door like now is not the time for affection but treats – and then I twist the handle.

I don't know what I was expecting on the other side, but it wasn't a dozen golden birds. They flutter through the air in glittering streaks, shimmering with every flap of their delicate wings. Utensils are clutched in their beaks, grain pouring from tilting talons, and the kitchen knives remain untouched as sharp claws slice berries apart.

I look down at Korax. 'Are you telling me that the horrible man who imprisoned me yesterday has a household staff of adorable bird automatons?'

The dog barks.

'Yes, alright, I get the point. I'll find the oil.'

The moment I finish the sentence, a bird stops before me, wings buzzing as it hovers in place. The handle of a lekythos is clutched in its beak.

'Ah! Thank you.'

I take it and turn to Korax, who nudges a bowl forward. I fill it with oil and the dog doesn't even wait for me to finish before it begins lapping it up. I straighten, and the bird is hovering before me once more, waiting to return the jug.

I hold my hand out and the bird obligingly perches, so small its talons curl round a single finger. It's exquisite, the workmanship fine as needlework. The gold is seamless, like it's been poured into a mould rather than seared together. Behind its glassy eyes I can make out cogs and gears, small pins and latches that allow it to move.

I have a sudden urge to fetch a mirror, and examine myself for evidence of machination like this. I was sentient for my creation. I know that I am clay with anima poured in, the will of the gods shifting earth to flesh. But still, I cannot help but wonder.

The bird allows my inspection. It's so beautiful, so delicate. And part of me wants to tear it apart, to dissect its every coil and spring. To understand it.

So I hand over the oil before I can give in to such instincts and watch as the others continue preparing food – and then I catch the errors. Eggshell poured into a pan, carrot tops missed, seeds unplucked.

I can do this, I realize, these mistakes cataloguing in my mind. And an itch to lay my hands on all of this myself. *Interesting.* The gods have automatons or servants – they do not cook themselves. But they filled my head with the knowledge to do so – so they must want me to. If my purpose is to find love with Matheos, is this how I achieve it? Or is it simply a first step? Perhaps all my gifts will be necessary to win him round, my days spent showcasing talents until he sees the wonder of what the gods have given us both.

But when I step up to the pan it's not because of the questions chasing one another in my mind. Beneath them all is a simpler fact: I *want* to. The birds make way almost happily – if automatons can be happy. Though judging by the way Korax is still gurgling oil, I suspect they can. I call out ingredients and tools and the birds deliver.

I'm making something. *Me.* A creation, creating something else.

And the kitchen is wonderful. The tiles are a dark, earthy green and dried herbs line the walls, which make it feel cosier than anywhere else I've been. The hearth is warm and inviting and I feel powerful, controlling the temperature and the ingredients, mixing batter with my own hands, the birds fluttering at my call.

I'm good at this.

Maybe I didn't fail the gods after all.

'I had no idea flour could be so upsetting.'

I startle, grain scattering into the air.

Matheos stands smirking in the doorway, watching me like I am a scene playing out before him. How long has he been there?

Then I register his words, swipe at my cheeks, unaware tears had spilled until he pointed them out. *Callously*, I might add. They'd actually been happy tears, born of excitement at all that I can do. But here he is ruining it, snide comment readied like he might see me low and seize the opportunity to bring me lower.

Korax finishes licking up the dregs of the oil and jerks as it turns, just as surprised to see Matheos as I was.

Matheos snorts. 'Some guard dog you are.'

Korax barks.

'Yes, okay.' Matheos shakes his head. 'Run on, then. I saw some seagulls out there in need of a good chase.'

I frown. 'You understand the dog?'

'Korax is not a dog, it is an automaton,' Matheos says – the sudden chill in his tone making clear how much more warmly he'd spoken to the not-a-dog than to me. 'And you've clearly worked out its weaknesses if you managed to bribe your way out of your room with oil.'

'Don't be grumpy just because you're an ineffective jailer.' I force a smile, a quick laugh. Like none of this is serious. Like he can't get to me. That shield springs back into place – though it doesn't feel quite like the others I wore for the Olympians. If I am made for Matheos then maybe who I become around him is who I truly am: smiling bright no matter the slight and faking a confidence I certainly don't feel.

'Cloth, please,' I add and a bird drops a length into my hand so I can withdraw the bread from the oven.

'And what exactly have you done since you wormed your way out?'

'You're looking at it. Now, I've made an olive relish but would you prefer honey? Or cheese?' The birds summon each item as I list them, clunking them on to a large, intricately painted dish. 'An assortment it is.'

Matheos's gaze lingers on my lips as I speak, and I feel a knot in my gut tightening.

'You've . . . been making bread.'

'Yes, I believe they call it breakfast.'

'For me?'

'Well, I can't get through it all myself, you see. And I thought it might make a nice change for you to eat something edible.'

Matheos looks at the fluttering birds. 'Yes, they're better at cleaning than cooking. Go on, then,' he calls to them. 'It seems everything is in hand here and if our guest is awake I assume there's a bed to be made.'

They swoop out of the window before he's even finished speaking.

'You seem far fonder of Korax. No need to play favourites with the automatons – they might get jealous.'

Matheos glowers. 'My ears were damaged in the war. So not that I particularly care to listen to what you have to say, but it's easier for me to hear when the birds aren't in the room. Their wings make too much interfering noise and I have to lip-read more.' Ah, so perhaps it wasn't my gods-gifted wiles that had him staring at my mouth.

'Oh, well, thanks for letting me know.' I pick up the platter, the bread still steaming and, Olympus above, it smells so good. Surely this makes it very clear just how much better Matheos's life is with me in it. 'Shall we?'

He goes to speak, and I can tell from the sardonic tilt of his smirk he's about to utter another scathing dismissal – but then his eyes drop to the bread again.

'Fine, but I have a busy day ahead. I can't stay long.'

'Of course.' I nod sweetly. 'I wouldn't want to take any time away from what I'm sure is a packed schedule of brooding, moping and sulking.'

'Precisely.' But he holds the door open for me, and I carry the plate through, ducking under his arm and trying to pretend I don't hold my breath as I pass him, like if I don't draw a breath I don't have to notice the way it catches around him, or the way my heart thunders.

'And practising scowling in the mirror – can't forget that one,' I add.

'Indeed, it's quite time-consuming.'

'You'll have to write some good insults too, or –'

'I assure you, this bit of yours is nowhere near as funny as you seem to imagine.'

'Now see what you're like when you haven't had enough practice? That hardly even stung.'

He rolls his eyes and squeezes past me to open the next door, too, and I take the food out to the courtyard. It's lovely this morning: a salt sea breeze, sweetened by all the flowers blooming in beds around the edges, sun-soaked air cooled by the shade to a relaxing warmth, birds – real, rather than metal – singing in the forest beyond. I place our breakfast on a low table and settle on the reclining seat beside it. It creaks as I do and I scowl at the scant furnishings dotting the courtyard.

'We should get more furniture out here,' I say. 'So we can take meals properly.'

'*We* will do nothing of the sort.'

'Ahh yes, I forgot that the gods sent me here with the evil intent of outdoor dining. I can't believe you foiled me so quickly.'

He throws a shrewd glare at me. 'Hermes was involved in your creation, I assume. Athena too. Artemis?'

I try to think of all the gods and goddesses who flitted in and out, the gifts they bestowed. 'The first two, yes. I'm not sure about the latter. It was hard to keep track. Why?'

'Just trying to work out whose voice I'm hearing when you speak. Tell me, is it the same god responsible for the baking or is there a room of Olympians somewhere pulling your strings?'

My knife skids through the bread, tearing rather than sawing.

He's doing this on purpose, I remind myself, *don't let him get to you. It's what he wants.*

But it doesn't change the fact it does get to me, and I'm not sure why when I know I am picking myself apart at every visible seam. But I hadn't been, not right then. The teasing came so easily that it was the first time in my existence that I'd started to feel like a *me* and not just a mirror of someone else's desire.

But he thinks that cannot exist? That nothing *can* be 'me'. That all I am is an echo of the beings who made me. Or perhaps not even that – like I'm little more than a shadow the gods are casting upon this world.

Is that true?

'I think Hephaestus gave the most to me,' I say without missing a beat. 'So that would be – what? Incredible skill and absolute genius?'

'Hephaestus?' he asks – and there's something new in his tone. *Fascinating.* I left the door wide open for another insult but, instead, I get curiosity. Maybe he doesn't care for the easy shots.

I take some bread and wave for him to help himself. He wastes no time sprinkling olive oil across a slice, clearly hoping to get this over with quickly.

'He's . . . an acquaintance,' Matheos continues.

'Oh?'

'He provided the automatons. These too, when I asked him to.' He taps the gold cuffs latched about his ears, delicate filigree with vines etched through them. 'They help me hear. And when my brother . . . Well, Hephaestus is an acquaintance, as I say.'

'Sounds like a friend.'

Matheos – shockingly – scowls. 'I don't have friends.'

'Is it because of your sunny disposition?'

This sparring is, surely, an odd way to go about winning his approval. But the quips keep rolling to my tongue and there's something enticing about the rhythm of these back-and-forths. *She's irresistible . . . it varies from person to person* – that's what Hermes said. Let us hope that *irritating* is what Matheos longs for.

'Sure, let's go with that,' drawls Matheos, tearing the bread he holds to pieces. His hands flex, tendons sharp. 'Is this why they sent you? Is my punishment eternal annoyance?'

'And good bread.'

He glances down, seemingly realizing he hasn't actually eaten any yet, and takes a bite as though determined to prove me wrong about that, too.

'Don't worry,' I say as his brows quickly lift – followed by a deepening scowl. 'I'm not going to think you're in love with me just because you like my cooking.'

His eyes meet mine, deep and dark, and I can't hold his gaze, have to look away. But I feel it on me all the same. 'Isn't me loving you your endgame here?'

'I don't . . . I don't know,' I start, but he's glaring with such disbelief that I throw my bread back down on to my plate. 'Alright, fine, yes. I suppose it is. No, stop that,' I scold, as a smirk unfurls on his face. I'm not sure if it's for being proved right or my desperation for his love, but either way it's thoroughly unbearable. 'I didn't think making breakfast for you would make you love me. But I'd hoped it might make you less repulsed by the idea of it – or at least the mere idea of me being here. I was made to be perfect for you, Epimatheos.'

The name sticks in my mouth – and it's not just the insult of it. It's the fact that it's not how I think of him, the intimacy of knowing I have a private name for him that makes his actual name difficult to speak.

His smirk falls. 'Trust me, that's not what the gods made you for.'

'Why can't you even consider the possibility that the gods wanted to reward you for not doing as your brother did?'

'Don't you dare,' he growls, slow and deliberate, like he would linger on the menace of each and every word. 'Do not speak about him again.'

I swallow as dread settles into my stomach and I might as well be cowered against that wall once more. So much progress made – not towards love, perhaps, but towards inoffensiveness and harmlessness . . . and one misstep has ruined it all.

But still, a small part of me is satisfied – he did not correct me. Prometheus *is* his brother. And he betrayed the gods. I was right.

'Alright, I won't, I'm sorry,' I say quickly, forcing a smile, like this was a mere stumble and not a catastrophic mistake. 'But the gods are clearly grateful for you and your loyalty, so why couldn't that gratitude result in your friend Hephaestus creating me?'

'I told you,' he insists. 'I don't have friends.'

'Charming.'

We both jump – not just in our seats but fully scrambling to our feet, like we've been caught in some salacious act.

A woman strides through the door, each step purposeful and assured, her back straight and head high. Her long black waves are tied back with a ribbon and razor-sharp shells hang in spirals from her ears. Another person hurries behind her, carrying a large canvas sack. They have so many bangles stacked on their wrists that they jingle as they walk, the gold warm and bright against their deep-brown skin.

The woman fixes a cold glare on me before shifting it to Matheos. 'What is she doing here? You never should have accepted anything from the gods, Epimatheos – I thought you knew better than that.'

A stony displeasure sets in his face, though he doesn't answer.

'Agree to disagree,' the other person laughs, dropping the bag they're carrying and offering me a quick wave. 'Hi, I'm Ione, so lovely to meet you! Epimatheos, here's the grain you asked for. Also there's a deer outside, but I'm not sure if –'

'I'll get it,' he says quickly, seizing on the distraction. I'm not sure what's so interesting about a deer, unless an increased likelihood of venison for dinner is particularly thrilling.

But instead of moving away from me, he steps closer, expression twisting with distaste.

'One thing you would do well to remember,' Matheos says, voice a low, chill vibration. 'You're wrong. You weren't made to be perfect for me. You were made to be perfect for the man I *pretend* to be.'

This time I flinch, and that smirk returns in earnest.

'The man I actually am could not possibly care any less about you.'

CHAPTER SIX

PIMATHEOS STALKS OFF, AND I'M reeling, his words resounding. What cruel irony, to prove that the gods certainly wove some form of compatibility between us, some ability to read each other – because Epimatheos always manages to cut me where it will hurt the most.

And these other people are still standing here.

In my house. *Xenia.*

'Please, do help yourself to bread; it should still be hot. And I'll get some more refreshments.'

That seems to only increase the ire of the woman who was so scathing earlier.

'We don't want your "refreshments". You shouldn't be here. You know you shouldn't. Whatever danger you bring, take it to another door.'

Ione tenses by her side, looking between the two of us like they're not sure what to do. 'Kerkeis, please . . .' they say softly.

'I . . . I don't have anywhere else to go.'

'I fail to see how that's Epimatheos's problem.'

I try to regain some footing, square my shoulders and channel every bit of resolve the gods gave me. 'I'd like to think my husband would have something to say on the matter if I vanished.'

Kerkeis's eyes flash. 'I think your "husband" just made it very clear he'd like nothing better.'

I'm currently failing at my gods-given purpose – so how does this woman's hatred even touch me? It is so minuscule, so incomparable in scale. And yet it feels like another fracture in my being. Irresistible? Well, apparently not to Matheos, and not to this woman either.

In fact, whatever talent I'd possessed on Olympus to become whoever I needed to be feels far beyond my reach right now, worn down by the relentless barbs until there is only this: my own desperate floundering, my own despair, *me* – tired and hurt and on the cusp of admitting defeat.

'You don't know me,' I say, despising the way my voice wavers.

Kerkeis laughs – high and dismissive. 'In the sea we trust no tide, no jet stream, no current – any of them could be a god trying to pull you under. I certainly won't trust a girl they've spat up on the shore.'

'Alright, my love, I think you've made your point.' Ione touches Kerkeis's wrist, a gentle plea for restraint.

Kerkeis nods her agreement. 'Fine. Let's go.'

'I'll stay a while.'

'Ione,' groans Kerkeis.

'You know that by this evening you're going to feel guilty about how mean you were. Now imagine how much better you'll feel if I do a bit of damage control.'

Kerkeis flicks a quick glare at me. 'I won't feel anything.'

Ione hums. 'Of course. You're too vicious. Iron-hearted. The menace of the Euxine Sea, whose unyielding tongue leaves no room for regret.'

But Kerkeis just rolls her eyes and stalks off, muttering something about keeping her unyielding tongue to herself from now on.

Ione smiles fondly after her until the door swings shut, then they spin to me with shrewd focus and an intensity that pins me in place before finally declaring: 'Well, you don't look evil.'

I'm pathetically relieved to hear it. 'Thank you?'

Ione continues. 'Then again, most creatures that look evil are actually very sweet, so I suppose you never do know. I'll have to make my own mind up, I suppose.'

They fall into the nearest chair but I remain standing, my fingers toying with one another like they might find the grip my mind is lacking. 'I don't really know how to prove myself "not evil". If I did, then I wouldn't be in this predicament.'

Ione leans forward. 'I don't *really* need you to prove anything. In my experience the gods often create strange and wonderful things just on a careless whim. I couldn't imagine the ocean without all the hippocampi swimming around, so why not you?'

'Is that what I am? A strange and wonderful thing?' I repeat, startled into a half-laugh. It ought to be insulting, I imagine, to be compared to half-horse, half-fish creatures — but Ione says it with enough delight that I do not doubt it is meant as a compliment.

Ione shrugs but they're smiling. 'Maybe. At the very least I'm open to the idea you might truly be here as a gift for Epimatheos. And a lesson to the others — punishment for those who disobey, rewards for those who follow? That certainly makes sense to me. But – as you might have gathered – Kerkeis and Epimatheos distrust the gods. It's not *you* they're sceptical of, it's them.'

I'm not sure that's true. But for once Matheos's opinion of me is not at the forefront of my mind. It's the blasphemy, spoken so casually. I half expect a thunderbolt to strike Ione down.

But nothing happens.

So perhaps the gods aren't paying attention to me right now. And I don't know how I feel about that. I'd assumed they were just as invested in the outcome here as I am.

Have they already given up on me?

'They don't trust the gods?' My voice is scarcely audible over the howling wind.

Ione's smile falls. 'Ah. Forget I said that.'

'I won't tell the Olympians,' I rush. I do not even consider that I wouldn't know how, even if I wanted to – scrape some food into a fire and send a quick prayer, hoping it finds listening ears? 'I just don't understand.'

Ione arches a brow. 'Well, that's interesting, isn't it? That the gods made you capable of keeping secrets from them?'

I blink. 'I suppose. But they made me to love Epimatheos, so maybe not doing anything that would put him in danger is simply etched into me.'

'Did those etchings say anything about protecting my salt-blooded girlfriend?'

'Um, no, I suppose not. Salt-blooded? Is that an insult among the nymphs?'

Ione snorts. 'No, not an insult. Literal. She's a nereid. I'm a naiad – the freshwater equivalent. Pretty hard to find somewhere we can both live but the Euxine is brackish so she left her distant ocean and I left the Nile and, well, here we are. But anyway, back to the point at hand: the gods made a girl who would not betray a mere nymph's distrust in them?'

'I don't want to get anyone in trouble,' I say, wringing my hands in the folds of my dress. 'Maybe it's just part of whatever irresistibility they planted in me – a desire to be liked but, *apparently*, if these conversations are anything to go by, not the means to make it happen.'

Ione laughs. 'If the gods knew how to be likable, they'd start with themselves. Besides, there are far more interesting things to be.'

'And Epimatheos? What would he find interesting?'

They consider. 'I'm not sure. He's not really around enough people for me to know what he likes. I'm *fairly* confident he enjoys our company but even then he seems to express it in blunt assertions and ever-ready glowers.'

I smile. 'Well, maybe I'm not so far off, then.'

Ione barks a laugh, and it's that which settles the gnawing fear in my gut, enough that I finally take a seat opposite them.

Maybe this is what I need: someone who can help me understand the man I'm supposed to be in love with. If the gods anticipated our struggle, it seems they didn't predict all the things I would need to overcome it. If only they'd cut some of those epithets they planted in my mind and replaced them with *a lesson in grumpy boys who'd rather sulk than communicate* or *what to do when isolating on the edge of civilization is someone's chosen mechanism to cope with trauma.*

'It makes sense that he doesn't trust the gods. When I arrived he told me they were liars. And when I tried to ask him about his brother just now he . . .'

I don't finish because Ione is already wincing. 'Oh, yes. He wouldn't like that.'

I'm starting to feel like Matheos's hatred of me has very little to do with me at all.

'So what happened? What did Prometheus do?'

Ione glances around, like they too would avoid upsetting Matheos by speaking about it. 'Honestly? I don't know.'

I give them a look and they half laugh, protesting: 'I don't, I swear!'

Even more intriguing. The gods did not tell me anything about Prometheus. And Matheos hasn't spoken about his brother's crime with the closest thing to friends he has.

I don't need to know all the details, I remind myself, just whatever it is Matheos fears so I can assure him I'm not it. He's made it clear that asking directly will only make him hate me more, so here I am, scurrying around, putting all those gossiping skills Aphrodite blessed me with to work.

'I think the gods hurt Epimatheos,' I say, giving voice to a theory I didn't know I'd been puzzling over. 'Unintentionally, I'm sure. But enough that he doubts they would send him someone like me with good intentions.'

Ione shut their eyes like if they're not looking at me they're not betraying Matheos by telling me. 'He never speaks about it. But I know that his father and two of his brothers sided with the Titans in the war. His father's incarcerated in Tartarus. Menoetius was killed by Zeus's lightning bolt. Atlas was rounded up when it was over and forced to bear the weight of the sky for all eternity in punishment. But . . .' Ione's eyes open and they lean forward before lowering their voice. 'He was always closest with his brother Prometheus. His mother's an oceanid but she lost corporeality when he was young – became one with the currents, as we say. I think Prometheus practically raised him. Together, they fought against their own family in the war and afterwards, when we all thought the horrors were over, Prometheus did . . . *something*. I don't know what, only that the gods punished him greatly for it and Matheos came here, alone, where he's been ever since.'

So it was just the two of them against their family – a family the gods killed and punished. And then, when it should have been over, the gods took Prometheus from him? Whether deservedly or not, no wonder he's locked himself away. No wonder he doubts all this.

I nurse a new thought.

Maybe I'm not the *reward* the gods declared me.

Maybe I'm an apology.

CHAPTER SEVEN

IT'S NOT EVERYTHING I WANT to know but it's enough to work with. Enough to formulate a plan. First, let Matheos lower his guard. Wait out his hostility, make myself quiet and unobtrusive and useful. Don't rise to his hatred, just smile through it, and treat it like the ridiculous thing he will soon, surely, realize it is. Give him time to understand just how much better this house is with me within its walls. Then, once his rage and suspicion have faded, endear myself to him, build a friendship and then, finally, let him consider the prospect of something more.

I'm tested almost immediately. He steps through the front door, looking tired. Blood specks the cloak thrown over his chiton.

'Epimatheos,' I chirp happily, like his return has delighted me and not made my anxiety spike. 'I wanted to speak to you about earlier, I –'

He heaves a sigh – or perhaps it's a groan. 'I'm not doing this again.'

Then, before I can continue with *I'm sorry I mentioned your brother* or *If I did anything to upset you* – he reaches up and unlatches the cuffs hooked around his ears.

I gawk and he arches a pointed brow as though daring me to say something. I don't, and I swear as he walks away I hear him chuckle softly to himself.

I grit my teeth and remind myself of my plan. If he wants to ignore me, that's fine – I can find something else to turn my attention to. Tasks unfurl before me in a long, gloriously distracting list. I begin with the kitchen, exploring its every nook and cranny, taking stock of every sack or amphora in its pantry. Then I head to the washroom – a wide, deep tub, stacks of linen cloths, olive oil soap and washbasins arrayed with jars. A long pipe connects to a box and when I turn a dial on the side, hot water pours out. It's extraordinary. It's magic. It's . . .

Hephaestus.

I roll my eyes. Some 'acquaintance' if he's designing Matheos's bathroom.

Soap. Candles. Salts and scents to add to the water. I index them all in my head, these things we need that I could make and provide. Ways in which I could be beneficial.

In the corner, I spot a familiar green cloak, covered in flecks of blood.

I practically seize it.

It takes half an hour to get the stains out – cold water and salt, and so much scrubbing.

I find some rope and tie it between the chairs in the courtyard to hang the cloak to dry.

'What are you doing?'

How does he always manage to sneak up on me? And in the shock of his appearance, all thoughts of *quiet* and *unobtrusive* quickly vanish from my mind.

'Does that truly require an answer?'

I don't even turn around, focused on pinning the cloak in place so it doesn't fall to the dusty floor or flutter into the fire.

'I don't need you washing my clothes.'

'Is *thank you* really so difficult?' I turn and my words catch in my throat. Matheos wears only a chiton, and the fabric bends around the blades of his hip and slopes off his shoulders. I can see every line of him, the slants and angles with which he holds himself – and then I catch the dampness to his curls, the crisp clean scent of him. The cloak in the washroom. The blood.

The thought of him in there, moments before I was . . .

I race to cover my hastily slipped-out words, and now I'm speaking even more quickly when I say: 'Come on, try it with me. It's really not hard, we can even do it together: *thank you* – no? Just me?'

'Stop it,' he snaps. 'Enough with the cooking and cleaning. I was fine before you got here and –'

'Oh yes, by all accounts you were perfectly happy.'

'I don't get to be happy,' he says, more vitriol lacing those words than any he's yet thrown my way. 'But I was *fine*. I don't need a wife and I certainly don't need a servant.'

'I'm just being nice, Matheos. People do that. I'm sure even you are capable of it if you really put your mind to it.'

'You have a truly astounding ability to issue an insult in a way that's practically cheerful.'

'See, that's a start! Now see how I respond: *thank you*.'

He groans, hands curling in his hair, head thrown backwards so all I can see is the long stretch of his neck and the sharp line of his jaw.

'You are infuriating!'

'Yes, *I'm* the unreasonable one here,' I say with a shake of my head. Gods, waiting out his suspicion is going to be painful. 'Now, is there meat to prepare?'

'What? No, no, of course not,' he says – as though me offering to perform the job (one I had very much *not* been looking forward to) is offensive. 'Stop trying to –'

'Stay busy? But that's all I'm able to do, dear husband. You've made it quite clear this isn't going to be the happy marriage I was made for. That's fine. I don't want your love if you don't want to give it. I think I would enjoy your friendship, but if I have to settle for "someone I happen to live with", that's fine with me. And in that vein, instead of the happiness I was promised, I will gleefully settle for "not bored".'

He frowns. 'You expect me to believe you doing all this isn't some misguided ploy just to get me to like you? To trust you? That you actually *want* to do it?'

'Well, maybe I don't get to be happy either,' I snipe, partly because *yes, that is indeed the plan and how does he keep seeing through me?!* But also because that life he's dismissing is the only one he's currently presenting me with. That I might plan, might use every tool the gods gave me and still end up with nothing but this resentment for the rest of my life is not a pleasant thought.

He looks at me like perhaps he is seeing that long, forced future together spilling out before him, too.

I take a breath, meeting his hesitant gaze with my own. I force a smile. 'Now, is that all? Or can I return to the scintillating thrills of laundry?'

I spend some time exploring the rest of the house, cataloguing all the ways I might busy myself in this barren space. I spend hours weaving on a rickety loom Kerkeis and Ione must have brought at some point, because the wood is half rotted with salt water and the weighted stones have been polished smooth by harsh waves. It doesn't hold the threads down properly and my weaving is rough and jagged until I give up on any hope of weaving something new and stick to repairing what I can find – clothes and towels and seat covers. Small patches, the loom and then the needle. I find myself scraping a little extra food into the fire that night, sending a quick prayer of apology to Athena for the quality of my work, though if she truly wanted me to utilize her gift of weaving she might also have considered sending me better equipment.

Matheos continues to lurk and scowl, tossing the odd insult and suspicious remark my way until they're as easy to tune out as the hum of the bird automatons' wings.

Ridiculous man.

But I'm finally forced to pivot from my plan of strained coexistence and seek him out when he refuses the food I've cooked for the dozenth time that week. So this time I knock on his door, and I don't stop until he answers.

'What?' he demands when he finally opens up.

'Good evening to you, too.'

'*Pandora.*'

He says my name like it has edges, like it is something to be ground out.

This really is ludicrous. I have very successfully left him to his own devices, and am only interrupting now because I seemingly cannot stand the thought of him suffering – going hungry! – because he wishes to avoid me. And somehow I am the one at fault?

'Can you at least tell me why you're annoyed with me this time? Because your vegetarianism I quickly figured out, but still, my meals keep being sent back. I've considered a range of allergies and intolerances, and not only have you refused everything, you're now treating these honey sesame pancakes like they might be the gods' vengeance incarnate.'

'*You* are the gods' vengeance incarnate.'

'So the pancakes are fine?'

'It's not the food I object to,' he says – rather predictably.

It takes me a moment, but I finally note his appearance. 'You're wearing the chiton I patched up.'

A muscle at his jaw twitches. 'I asked you to stop, and you didn't. Me wearing clothes you've repaired doesn't mean I appreciate your continued efforts to worm your way into my good graces.'

'The same could be said about eating the food I've cooked – it won't make you like me, I get that. I'm not expecting it to. I just don't like worrying about you going hungry, so can you please just eat something?'

His nostrils flare. 'You aren't going to seduce me with cake.'

What did I *just* say?

I'm so angry, so tired – why be given a voice if it does not matter what I say?

Fine.

I cock my head to the side. 'Epimatheos, Aphrodite herself breathed seduction into my head. If I wanted to seduce you I wouldn't be scurrying around this house trying to stay out of your way. I'd be finding excuses to touch you.' I let my fingers trail to the edge of the patch of cloth I sewed, across the chest of his chiton. I feel a hint of muscle beneath – lean and slight but hard all the same. Matheos pulls away so sharply his arm catches on the doorframe. He doesn't even wince.

I shift my shoulder as I draw my hand back, letting the linen slide off it, revealing a sliver of skin. His eyes follow the falling fabric. 'I'd let you find me, lounging somewhere. My skirt a little too short. Chiton a touch too loose, like it might be better to come off entirely.'

I watch with satisfaction as he swallows, the way he forces himself to look up, his eyes locking on mine.

I ignore the way my own mouth dries at the intensity of his scrutiny.

I lean forward, voice warm in an intimate whisper. 'Or I'd remind you just how good it felt to have me pinned against that wall.'

His jaw clenches, eyes flicking up towards the Heavens, like he's cursing the gods who sent me to his door. But he can't look away for long, which I expected. Olympus above, if all I wanted *were* to seduce him, I wouldn't have a problem.

A beat passes, and then another until he finally hisses: 'I don't want you.'

That is demonstrably false. He simply does not want to want me – evidently sees it as another sign the gods are manipulating him.

'Which is why I'm not trying to seduce you,' I say, jolting my shoulder so my dress neatly falls back into place. 'Just being nice.'

I thrust the tray into his hands – and he must be thrown because he takes it without question.

I flash a smile Aphrodite taught me too: equal parts innocence and temptation. 'Eat the food, please. You look *hungry.*'

CHAPTER EIGHT

THE INSULTS STOP, BUT ONLY because I have apparently terrified Matheos into avoiding me altogether.

He keeps out of my way, haunting these halls rather than inhabiting them. He is a series of echoes: his footsteps down a corridor, the creak of a nearby floorboard, a closing door in the room next to mine. He always slams the doors a little too harshly and I wonder if it's pointed or whether he just doesn't hear it as acutely as I do. I almost begin hoping for the former – that it might be *about* me because that would mean he notices me at all.

I trace him only from what he leaves behind, the dirty plates and creases in chairs that I start to cling to, anything that lessens the sense of total isolation that is beginning to suffocate me.

The days drag, lightened only by the occasional visits of Ione. Mostly it is hour after hour of me trying to stay busy, listening for Matheos's footsteps and holding my breath before I open each door, as though he might be on the other side.

The last conversation I had was with Korax, and it was distinctly one-sided.

Then, for the first time in days, I catch an actual glimpse of his wine-dark chiton whipping around a corner. And another voice – Kerkeis. Scurried footsteps and the familiar solid clunk of his study door closing.

Before I can think about it I am already standing in the hallway, staring at the smooth wood between us. They *must* be discussing me in there – else why not chat out in the open?

I creep forward, my curiosity no longer an itch but a desperate, demanding need. I press my ear against the wood for any indication that this stifling loneliness is worth it, that my plan is working, that he is thawing.

'You need to do something,' Kerkeis says. 'You can't just ignore her and let her run around the place free. Who knows what she might do?'

'What's your alternative? Send her to the mortals where she can do real, actual damage? Or are you proposing I return her to the earth they made her from myself?'

I flinch back, reaching a steadying hand out for the tiled wall. He said it scathingly, like it was an absurd suggestion, but still . . . the gods sent me to a strange man's house, and it's never occurred to me before that there might be a risk to my safety.

I turn sharply. There is a light thump as my hand hits the wall and though I'm certain they can't have heard it, being found listening to them isn't something I care to risk.

Still, I do not leave quickly enough to miss Kerkeis's next words:

'You know what you need to do – you need to talk to your brother.'

I am still turning Kerkeis and Matheos's conversation over the next day, down on the beach with Ione and admittedly distracted as they try to convince me dents in the sand are proof that sea goats are not only real but have clearly clambered on to our shores.

Kerkeis thinks Matheos should speak to his brother about me.

The mystery of Prometheus, now further bound up with my existence.

But that's not all that's haunting me.

'What do you know about humans?' I ask Ione – because more and more, I am thinking about them too. Even more, possibly, than the other mystery before me. This is a haunting, lonely place where I am never quite sure of my role or the rules or who I need to become. But there are more people like me out there. I might be the first human woman, but there are human men who populate this earth.

So maybe a long dreadful existence here isn't my only backup plan.

Ione shrugs. 'I've visited them a few times. I'll be honest: you're the first interesting one I've met. They're very wrapped up in their lives. Rarely stopping to look at the sea goat tracks in the sand, you know? Nice, though, some of them. I was at a town a few days ago and a woman was –'

'A woman?' I repeat, startled. 'What do you mean? I'm the first human woman and I've only been alive . . . what, three weeks? Four?' Gods, time is really beginning to slip with each dragging day. 'At any rate, definitely not enough for there to be more of us.'

Us. Olympus above, I'm part of an us.

'Oh gods, sorry, Pandora. I assumed Matheos would have explained . . .'

'In our famously lengthy conversations?'

They flash a bashful grin. 'Right. Sorry. Okay, well, to fill you in – Colchis was a prominent battleground in the war between the Titans and the gods. Both sides were manipulating powers of time so it settled a bit strangely here. It moves more slowly in some parts than in others. Which is why the centuries since the war have only felt like a few years to Matheos.'

I blink. 'Of course.'

How long have I truly been here, then? If centuries can become a handful of years?

'More women have been popping up in the years since you arrived,' Ione continues. 'More than that, actually – you're not just the first woman, you're the first *other*. Before you, the race of men was, well, a race of men. Now look at them. So many new genders and ages – though personally I find the babies quite annoying. Mortals finally have the variety the rest of us have.'

My head is spinning. I look to Ione, who smiles gently and adds: 'I don't think your purpose was ever confined to a boy's love, Pandora. Look at the impact you've had on the world, and you weren't even trying. Imagine what you could achieve if you were.'

Back home, I lie across the long low sofa, staring at the roughly hewn ceiling, trying to get my whirring thoughts to still enough to make sense of them.

There is a whole world beyond this house.

One that's racing by while I make soap and mend linen and try to convince a boy not to hate me.

But he's not just 'a boy', is he? He's my husband. He's the purpose for which the gods made me. He's a lifetime of promised love and happiness.

Except that hasn't exactly worked out so far.

He's keeping things from me. He's plotting against me.

And I heard him leave the house two hours ago.

I am on my feet. I am down that hall again. I whistle and one of the bird automatons flies to my side.

'I need you to keep a lookout,' I say. 'Kick up a fuss if you hear anyone coming.' It makes the sort of high-pitched hum I often hear them singing to each other, which I take as affirmation.

I suppose I might be worried that the automatons will give me away, but having bribed Korax on my first day, I know they're not quite the watching eyes and ears Matheos would have me believe. Besides, I've earned their loyalty. I give them oil, talk to them, even sit with parchment, observing their behaviour. In addition to Stephanos, Korax and the birds, there's a wolf that mostly comes out at night to patrol the outer walls and a cat whose purpose, as far as I can make out, is to behave like a cat.

The bird positions itself down the hall, and I twist the handle to Matheos's study.

It's not even locked. I could have come in here at any time. Maybe it's because there's nothing here. But it stings, too – that here is evidence Matheos does not truly see me as the threat he claims. He can joke about *murdering me* – but isn't concerned enough to lock his damn door.

Inside, the walls are a dark clay red, the room small and surprisingly cosy, given it's just as sparse as the rest of the house.

Chitons have been piled on a chair – the same messy heap that I recognize as 'this was deposited by the birds' – a large desk which is a mess: scrolls unfurled, wax tabs half wiped, and even ink on a comb tossed hastily on top of it all. A kline in the corner is little more than a place to sit and relax but it's covered in a tangled mess of sheets and, oh gods above – the comb, the clothes, the sheets.

He's living in here.

And I realize, with dawning horror, that I have not seen another bedroom on my wanderings.

Just the one that I am in.

Before I arrived, it must have been his. So it's his bed I sleep in. His chitons I'm wearing.

Of course they are. Why would he have spare living quarters or clothes? It's become distinctly apparent he does not have the sorts of guests who stay over.

I feel warm but also like I might be sick. With no time to waste dwelling on those distressing thoughts – Olympus above, I am wearing his clothes! – I hasten to tear through those scrolls scattered on his desk.

Migration patterns of buzzards.

Hibernation habits of marmots.

Dietary requirements of jackals.

'What on earth is this?' I breathe, turning the last over anyway, like it might finally be the one that says: *what really happened to my brother and why it's preventing me from loving my wife.*

But no, it's about squirrels.

The bird automaton outside gives a flurry of chirps, and I scurry from the room, making sure the door is properly shut behind me. I pass Matheos outside the kitchen, ducking my head so he can't see the guilt there – and so I can't look up into the sharp planes of his face and his downturned lips and all that beauty and think about the fact that the fabric resting on my skin once sat upon his.

CHAPTER NINE

I STOP MAKING NOTES ABOUT the house, and the automatons, and start making them about all the questions I keep coming back to. In particular: Prometheus. The mortals. And, bigger than the others: is this relationship with Matheos ever going to work? And what will I do if it doesn't?

But mostly, I try to stay just as busy as ever I did. Though instead of using work to distract me from my spiralling thoughts, I let them whir.

I'm piling wood into the courtyard hearth when Stephanos makes a screeching, grinding sound and its head begins snapping erratically back and forth. It looks painful, even though I doubt it can actually feel anything. The wood tumbles to the floor as I rush over. This is, clearly, some kind of deeper mechanical issue, beyond the minor ones I have fixed before. So, almost instinctively, I pull the lever behind the automaton's mane.

It shudders to a halt and a back panel lifts off.

I see the problem immediately: rust flecking some of the cogs, one so badly it has jammed mid-turn. So I fetch vinegar and begin to clean it – taking advantage of the excuse to map its extensive insides. I had known these machines were works of art, but they are nearly beyond comprehension. I kneel down to get a better view, grinding dirt into the knees of my dress and leaning back so the sunlight streaming into the courtyard can illuminate the internal mechanics. Every cog and gear is finely carved bronze, gold filigree etched into panels and quicksilver thrumming through pipes. A glistening, decadent treasure trove of ingenuity.

This is purpose. To fix what has been broken, to discover how these beautiful creatures work so that I can admire them all the more. It is accomplishment, fascination – all the things I realize I've lived these weeks without.

'What exactly do you think you're doing?'

'You really must try *hello* one of these days,' I sigh – but I'm so relieved he's gracing me with actual words that I have to crush a smile. Is this what he has dragged me to? Relief at another bickering argument? I climb to my feet, gesturing at Stephanos. 'Look, isn't it phenomenal? You have how many bird automatons – ten? And each must have exactly this attention to detail, each made with care and love and precision and –'

'And a far more intelligent hand than yours,' he snipes. 'Do not touch it.'

I laugh. 'Cleaning a few cogs is hardly going to damage it. Besides, how else are we supposed to know how it works?'

'We're not – and you're certainly not.'

'And if it breaks?'

'I will ask Hephaestus to fix it.'

'So there's no harm in me having a poke around, then, is there? If Hephaestus fixing it is an option.'

I slide the cogs back into place before Matheos combusts. I tap the lever again and the panel slides shut. Instantly, Stephanos gives a shake of its head, and bounds off to do whatever lion automatons do around here.

I wonder if I can open it up again sometime. Study the internal mechanics, figure out how it works. Maybe even make something similar. More questions spiral: how and what and why. It's glorious, thrilling, so much more than excitement. It's some desperate yearning, one that feels shockingly base and fundamental, curiosity like hunger or tiredness until it feels like I *need* to prise open that lid and discover the depths of what's inside.

'How hard is it?' Matheos demands. 'Not to touch the automatons? You've invaded my home, my life – all I am asking you to do is leave them alone.'

'You haven't given me a good enough reason not to.'

'I'm asking – is that not a good enough reason?'

'No! It doesn't make sense.'

Beneath my frustration is something harsher, something so unfamiliar to me I almost don't recognize it: anger. I've spent several exhausting, lonely weeks proving I am not dangerous, and the one time I do something that actually brings me joy in this wretched place he decides it's the greatest threat since Kronos?

'I don't want the woman forced on me by the gods rooting through the mechanics of my automatons.'

'What do you imagine I'm going to do, Epimatheos? Break them? Reprogram them? To do what, exactly?' My anger simmers, a hot sting that has me spitting out words quicker than I can think better of them. But what does it matter, anyway? Thinking my sentiments through hasn't exactly got me very far – so why not tell him exactly how I feel for once. 'You seem pretty certain I'm here to ruin your life, but what life would that be? You hide yourself away from the world, you don't talk to anyone and –'

His eyes flash. 'You have no idea what you're talking about, Pandora. Just leave me alone.'

'What do you think I've been *doing* for the last three weeks? Don't tell me I've driven myself to the brink only for you not to even notice!'

'Oh, I've noticed,' he grumbles, his voice low, with real menace. All this avoiding one another means it had not occurred to me that he might be the edge of something too, and now his fury breaks as well. 'The way you interfere with everything here, trying to make your mark on anything you can. I've endured quite enough of it. And the automatons are a step too far. Touch them again and I *will* restrict you to your room. Properly, this time.'

I scoff. 'Excuse me? You seem to think you're in some position of authority over me. But running the household is a wife's job –'

'You aren't my wife and this is *my* house.'

A dozen responses roll to the tip of my tongue – because I could protest, tell him the gods think we are married, that his house is ours.

But who would stop him?

I was built for kindness, made for love.

And this man . . .

He is not who I was made for.

And he is not my only option.

'Very well. You're right: this is your house. And I think I've overstayed xenia.'

I cross the courtyard, eyes set on the gate bolted within its outer wall. I take a step – I'm going, I'm doing this – and then:

'Pandora, stop. You can't leave.' He grasps my hand, pulling me back.

No begging, no pleading – just more of these lurching commands. Gods, he's insufferable, egotistical and thoroughly ridiculous.

'Epimatheos, I have had quite enough of you telling me what I can and can't do.' I wrench my hand free, stride forward and tilt my head to the Heavens. 'I quit! Whatever you wanted this to be, it's not happening, he's –'

But the gods never find out what he is, because next thing I know Matheos has collided with me, and I'm on the floor, his weight on top of me, hand clasped over my mouth.

His skin grazes my teeth and I bite down but he doesn't so much as flinch, not until in all our scrambling I manage to curl my fingers into his hair and give a sharp tug, enough for his hands to slip.

'What in Hades do you think you're doing?' I shriek.

'Saving your ungrateful life,' he hisses, tense and so very close. I can see every ounce of his ire burning in his eyes, that spiralling amber thoroughly hateful.

I purse my lips to a loud shrill whistle and the birds come flurrying. They fly straight at him, pecking and clawing, and I stumble to my feet, smarting from bruises I hadn't felt through the shock, and am mere inches further away than I had been when he commands: 'Not me, *her*! Inside, now!'

The birds abandon their target and suddenly they're pushing at my back, pulling at my chiton, hounding me forward and I stumble, crossing the ground so quickly my breasts heave up, nearly taking me out in the process. The automatons don't let up until I cross the threshold of the house.

I spin but Matheos is right behind me, blocking the door. The birds flee, like they do not wish to be caught between us again.

'So you *did* reprogram the automatons,' he seethes, like it is *I* who owe *him* an explanation.

'No, I spent time with them,' I spit right back, wiping at my mouth like I can still feel his hand clamped over it. 'But manhandle me again and see just what I can make them do.'

'Believe me, this is hardly my preferred approach. But you leave me little choice when you attempt to garner the attention of Olympus. Or do something as foolish as leave this place.'

'And why exactly should I be expected to stay here and suffer more of this? Of you? There's a whole world out there, other humans that might actually like me or at the very least won't despise every fibre of my being. Why are you even fighting this? We both know the gods made a mistake when they paired us together, so just let me go.'

He winces, cooling a little, and that's almost worse. His anger I can take, this edge of pity strikes harder. 'Say that again.'

'By the mercy of Zeus, really? You need me to tell you to let me leave *again*?'

'No, Pandora.' He pinches the bridge of his nose. 'The other part.'

I glare at him, my patience non-existent.

Finally he gets to the point: 'The gods do not make mistakes.'

Those words fill the space between us, heavy and choking. The world around me shifts, like I can feel each wave crashing outside, like the very ground beneath us might fall into the ocean below.

The gods do not make mistakes.

The amphora of their discarded attempts – the hand and the eye and the breast. Parts of me so carelessly wasted – so why not the rest of me, too? Another effort made, a little better than the last one, but still not quite what they're looking for. Not quite perfect.

A simple purpose: to love and be loved.

And I've failed.

'No,' I say, falling back against the wall behind me. 'No.'

He grimaces. 'We can't risk it. Fates know, if I thought we could, I would have sent you away the moment you arrived. But the last time I asked Hephaestus to repair a broken automaton he melted it down and used its parts for all these birds. It's what the gods do to the things that fail them.' His eyes lock with mine, his gaze . . . heavy. 'If you're not here, with me, then you're dead.'

No human villages. No lands far from here. Nowhere apart from this man's side. Not if I don't want to risk the gods deciding I was a failed experiment. A blip for them to erase.

'But I can't stay here with you,' I choke. Not when my options are either crushing myself to oblivion to garner his neglect or . . . or what? What exactly *is* an option here where I'm not constantly scraping for his approval? 'You hate me. Why do you even care what the gods might do to me?'

He considers me for a moment, a scowl deepening between his brows. 'I don't know why you're here. But nothing good comes of the gods. I do not wish to give them licence to destroy you, but I won't allow you to destroy me, either.'

'Destroy you? I was sent to *love* you, Epimatheos. Short of that I thought we could at least coexist. I cooked. I cleaned. I *cared* for you in every way I possibly could.'

Embers of the anger that had begun to subside flicker back to life. Matheos regards me with such intensity I can feel the heat peeling off him.

'You loved me, Pandora, in the way that they trained you to. You made yourself useful. You keep telling me you were sent to love me, that we were supposed to be perfect for each other. But do you want to be loved, or do you just want to be needed? To be of so much use to someone that they cannot bear the thought of life without you?'

'It's the same thing!' I blurt, baffled. Isn't it? Isn't that love – love in each knead of dough, in each tender stitch, in being necessary. Love is to give and give and give.

'You would bleed for me and you do not even like me!' he says, not quite shouting but his words are forceful, hatred seeped deep – but not, I realize, directed at me this time. 'How can the gods call that love? How can they claim they sent you to love me when you were made to serve them, and so they etched serving into your very bones? If I were to love you, Pandora, it would be for all that you *are*, not all you can *do*.'

I don't . . . I don't understand.

My heart hammers, his gaze not leaving mine, and it all feels too much to carry within me, this riot of feeling.

But one part lingers: *you do not even like me.*

'I don't like you,' I repeat, letting the idea land.

He arches a brow. 'However will I cope?'

'You're rude. You're horrible. And mean and ungrateful and cruel, you assume you know best and don't even deign to share why with the people involved, you're entitled and selfish and, oh my . . . I don't like you at all.'

He stares at me and, oh gods, I don't like him, and now his beauty is infuriating, the way the candlelight kisses him, makes his skin glow and hones his every angle, the way those thick eyelashes make his eyes look deeper, like I could fall into them if I linger long enough. Awful! Like the hypnotic lure of a viper preparing to strike.

'I was made to be perfect for you. Except . . . I wasn't, was I? Because if I was, then I'd like you, I'd want to be with you – and not just because that's what the gods want of me. But I can't stand you –'

'Alright, I get the point.'

'And you're right – the gods don't make mistakes. I saw them make me; they were so attuned to any error, any misstep . . . I *am* perfect. Just not for loving you.'

I am made perfect for some other purpose entirely.

He hesitates, then sighs like he is giving in, admitting something he shouldn't. 'I've suspected for a few days now that maybe you really were unaware of the way the gods were using you – and whatever they were using you for.'

'And you treated me terribly anyway.' Olympus above, I can't believe I spent so long worrying about why he didn't like me that I didn't even stop to consider whether I liked him in return. 'All I wanted was love and you made me feel like I didn't deserve it.'

'What else was I supposed to do? I can't ignore a warning from my brother in favour of –'

He cuts himself off at my pointed brow.

'What warning from your brother?' I demand.

'It doesn't matter.'

'Tell me or I'll walk back out there and take my chances with the gods. Maybe tell them everything I know about your hatred of Olympus, too.'

His eyes narrow. 'You wouldn't dare.'

'My alternative is staying here with you, dear husband. I'm being torn apart either way.'

We stay, staring at one another, the challenge taut between us.

'Very well,' he finally relents. 'But I need you to swear you won't leave afterwards. And that you'll say nothing to the gods. Put me in danger all you like but my brother does not need their increased ire.'

'Alright, you have my word.'

My word, I decide, means nothing. Not with all he's kept from me. But if he wants to put a price on information I am owed, then I will certainly pretend to have paid it.

'Prometheus is a seer,' he says carefully, like he will give me precisely what he has promised and not a sentence more. 'And the last thing he told me before they dragged him to eternal torment was that I should not accept any gift from the gods.'

Prometheus knew I would be sent here?

Matheos seems to mull his next words over, looking at me with sudden anticipation, like saying this will be difficult but hearing it will be worse. 'My brother was punished for trying to protect humanity from Zeus. And he said the greatest threat to them all would be me accepting you.'

'What?' I breathe, staring up at him, aware of how very close this corridor is, of how the greatest span between us is from his angled face down to mine.

'He didn't know what the gods would bring, just something I would struggle to refuse. I thought he meant I'd want it too much. I spent so long preparing to not be tempted, readying myself to accept whatever punishment they had in store for a man who refused their gift. But instead they brought you, and in doing so put a real human woman's life on the line. One woman for hundreds of mortals. It should have been an easy decision. But I, the ever-foolish brother, made the very choice my brother warned me against. So here you are. If the gods intend for us to love one another then trust me, Pandora, that love would be ruinous. Our love would be a curse. One that might end humanity.'

This is worse than realizing I was lied to, that love is not my purpose.

This thing I was told to want so badly, to centre my world upon, which I have fought for with every fibre of my being, could be world-ending.

'You could have told me this,' I snap. 'Why didn't you? If you had, I would never have even tried to build love between us.'

'Would you have listened if I had? You wouldn't have taken the word of a man you'd never met over the gods you were certain altruistically crafted you. Gods who, as far as you knew, could never have a vested interest in the destruction of humanity?'

He's right. If he'd told me, I wouldn't have believed him. I still don't, not entirely. Not when he's evidently still keeping so much from me.

'Well, congratulations on circumventing such a hideous prophecy. There's nothing to worry about any more. Me loving you is a distinct impossibility.'

'I'm pleased to hear it.'

Though he does not, in fact, sound pleased to hear it. He grinds the words out, like he is irate at their mere implication.

Well, at least I understand why Matheos was so reluctant to get to know me. But now, a dozen questions take that one's place. It doesn't erase the loss – the humans I'd begun to want so desperately to meet. All that variety and purpose Ione claimed I had supposedly brought them.

But it eases its sting – because there are bigger mysteries to solve here first.

Including one inside my very skin.

'I want to find out what it is the gods made me for.' I think of prising open the automatons and inspecting their gears. To take a thing apart and put it back together, just to see how it all fits. That's what I want – to work out who I am, how they built my mind to tick, my instincts to draw and work backwards to the *why* of it all. 'Don't try to hinder me. No more threats. I'll avoid you and you can avoid me.'

'What if I want to help?'

I straighten up, no longer leaning against the wall, and glare him down like even with my back rigid I'm not a foot shorter than him.

'You literally imprisoned me.'

'Badly.'

'And you were ready to try again.'

'Practice often leads to improvement.'

'It's not the quality of your imprisonment that I'm furious about!'

He laughs, a slight huff, a twitch of the corner of his lips. It almost startles me out of my anger.

'I know it was cruel,' he says. 'But I don't regret it. When it comes to the gods, impossible choices are the only ones that keep you safe.'

'I suppose I should be thankful you didn't lock me in the pantry instead,' I allow. 'But given you threatened to detain me again mere minutes ago, I'm failing to see where your sudden desire to help me discover my purpose is coming from.'

He shrugs, but instead of feeling dismissive it's almost challenging. His eyes are levelled at mine with a grave and solid intensity. 'Working out what you're here for and what it is the gods have planned is the mystery that haunts me too.'

'Sounds like you've spent a lot of time thinking about me.' I smirk. 'Which is interesting from a man who repeatedly insists he does not care for me.'

He doesn't rise to the bait, that steely solemnity unwavering. 'I want to know who you are, Pandora. But just because I think you might be an unaware tool of the gods, doesn't make you a less dangerous one. So, yes, trust that I spend an awful lot of time thinking of you – and I intend to think of very little else for the foreseeable future.'

CHAPTER TEN

COAT MY ROOM - OR rather, *Matheos's* room – with parchment, scribbled notes and scrawled ideas, leaping from one thought to the next quicker than my stylus can keep up so that half the pages are indecipherable. This is every analysis of the automatons tripled, my own thoughts recorded and detailed, and still there is more to set down – opinions, behaviours, habits, everything I have done in the last few weeks marked to be studied. There is a prophecy, and a mysterious man facing an eternity of torment, and there is me, in this room, crafted for an as-yet-unknown intent.

My fear of all that the gods might do to me if I fail them is swiftly sidelined in favour of the mystery of all that is at play here. And those questions consume me, a focus so intense the rest of the world blurs. I start writing that evening and continue long into the night, sitting on the floor of my room, only realizing how long I have been spilling my every thought in ink when my candle sputters out.

I light a new one and blink at the chaos.

Oh.

There is an order here, an organizational system that would, I imagine, make sense only to me. But I also understand as I look at it that this is not enough. Not all the answers to my existence can be found within my own head, and there is a stack of questions I simply do not have answers to: why the humans were created in the first place, why they were all men and whether the gods have ever arranged a marriage like this before.

Questions that, with all the information buried in my mind, the gods must have kept from me intentionally.

And perhaps it is only from them that I can get the answers.

Ah. A foolish idea – even more so for the god it centres around.

But her words ring in my mind: *I understand what it is like, to suddenly be and to be thrust into the frenzy.*

And I wonder if Athena had questions, too.

We are not the same – it's ludicrous to even consider it – but didn't Athena herself draw the comparison?

I do not have to tell her why I am asking – and while that feels even more foolish, to imagine I can wrest knowledge from the god of it, as soon as the thought occurs I cannot shake it. I *need* answers. And if this is how I get them, then so be it.

I take another scrap of parchment and write down this observation: *My curiosity is reckless.*

And then I go outside.

The rituals are all etched into my mind and I've been performing them out of ingrained habit, but now I actually mean them, all my hope and all my intent scraped into the flames along with the scraps of our food: the olive pits, carrot tops and eggshells. All the parts we cannot eat, sent to the gods above.

Athena, I pray. *Please, goddess of wisdom, of knowledge, please share it with me.*

I stand before the flames – unsure what to expect. She might ignore it, or might take days to respond. I certainly don't imagine she will spring forth from the hearth itself. But I stand a few moments longer anyway, and am just about to leave when an owl swoops low overhead.

A bird sacred to Athena.

So despite the fact it is the dead of night, and I am not even wearing shoes, I chase after it, out of the front gate and to the cliffs, where it coalesces into the form of the goddess.

Athena wears a simple ivory gown – no armour, no plumed helmet. She seems smaller, willowy, her alabaster skin luminous in the moonlight and her grey eyes dark as the waves below.

It's a gentle night – as far as gentleness goes here. The wind loud on the cliffs, but not as cold or forceful as usual, like the goddess of war stripped of her armour has calmed the world about her.

'We're not supposed to meet with you,' she says, casting a quick look up to the Heavens. 'But with the cover of night and the wind carrying away our words? Perhaps we might risk it.'

'Not supposed to?' I echo – hiding my relief. This may be easier than I thought if Athena will so readily hint at the gods' intentions.

'Zeus has forbidden it. We're not allowed to offer our help to you – that's what got Prometheus in so much trouble, after all.'

'Prometheus?' I repeat, trying to mask my excitement – aware only after I force the word flat that it is a tendency Matheos has ingrained in me. No joy, and certainly no implication I am prying into his brother.

She hums affirmatively, casting her gaze up like she might see a watchful eye looking back. 'Yes, Zeus hates the mortals – or at least finds them thoroughly boring. He probably made us create you for a more interesting version of them. But Prometheus loved the mortals. He made them, and then betrayed Zeus for them – and I suppose our king is terrified we might do the same for the mortal we created as Prometheus did for those he moulded.'

A more interesting version of the mortals – is that all I am? An effort to prove Zeus could do better than his traitor's attempt? But 'probably' means Athena doesn't know why I was created, she's just speculating. And then a very interesting thought occurs to me. Is *that* what Prometheus's supposed vision was? Is that what made him tell Matheos I was dangerous?

Was it that one day the gods would turn on Zeus for me? He might punish the humans, too, if that occurred. But why –

Later, I promise myself – all this rumination can come later. For now I heed as much information as I can get from the goddess in front of me. So instead, I ask: 'Prometheus made the mortals?'

Why had I not considered that before? Had I just assumed all creatures were assembled in a room in Zeus's palace? Or –

No, a better question: *why* did I not already know that? The gods filled my head with tales of their own grandeur, with the rules of their worship and an intrusive whisper to fall to my knees in supplication before them – albeit never one that permeates too far. Is that why? Because at my core, before anything else, I am human – and my being knows what the gods did to the man who moulded us, even if my mind does not?

All that knowledge about the gods, and nothing about what it means to be human.

Perhaps there is where my answers lie. Beyond the question of who *I* am: who *we* are.

Athena seems to realize what she has said. 'Not all of you. *We* made you. You're different. Prometheus's love of mortals would probably extend to you – Fates, he's probably the only one who would show you benevolence without expecting anything back – but you're not like the ones he built. You're better. Naturally.'

But she's wrong. Apparently, Prometheus does not like me at all. So why is Athena so certain he would?

'Has Epimatheos not told you any of this?' Athena asks with a steadily deepening scowl, and then adds, like it's the worst thing anyone could possibly do, 'He's kept this knowledge from you?'

'No! No, um, well, he doesn't like talking about his brother. He's upset he turned on the gods, too.'

Given my life depends on being happily in love with this man, it's probably better not to stir the gods' resentment of him.

Athena hums. 'I suppose he would be. But things are well, between the two of you, I hope?'

'Oh yes,' I say, smiling softly and ducking my head. That deceptive urge Hermes placed in my mind takes over, and I am the blushing, gleeful bride once more. 'He's wonderful. I'm so grateful to have this home with him.'

'Good,' Athena says, though her grimace suggests it's not the sort of *good* she aspires to herself. 'I admit I haven't been as attentive as I should. Last I glanced down was weeks ago when you were scrambling about in the dirt together and Aphrodite was far too overjoyed about such "evident passion" to stand. That woman's smugness is something I tend to avoid.'

At first I'm far too repulsed by the thought of what Aphrodite's supposedly been celebrating to catch the part that matters.

Weeks ago.

I didn't try to leave weeks ago – it was mere hours ago.

I know time is warped around this land – but to turn a handful of hours into weeks?

'I'm sorry,' I say. 'It's all been a lot, settling into existing – and, as you said, the frenzy of it all. I can't imagine what it must have been like to have to deal with all of this, but in the middle of the battlefield, too. There was one here, wasn't there?'

'You don't have to do that, Pandora,' she says softly, pulling her arms close about her, like she could hold her anxiety at bay. But she offers me a small smile, one that speaks of collusion. Of shared secrets. 'I made you. You can ask me what you would like to know without trying to mask the meaning. I won't punish you for your curiosity – quite the opposite. It's refreshing to speak to someone who cares to seek knowledge out, as I do. I'm used to those trying to avoid it.'

I think I startle her by laughing, and after a second she laughs too.

'What is it you truly wish to ask me?'

'Time is strange here,' I say. 'Because of the way Kairos and Chronos collided on Colchis's battlefield.'

Athena's brows knot together. 'It would make sense, I suppose, though fighting on Colchis must have been before my time. Before my *frenzy*.'

She jokes, and seems a little surprised by herself.

'How did those powers work?'

'Well, Kronos took the power from the primordial Chronos and named himself after the magic he stole, but that didn't change what it was – linear, the circular spin of Gaia herself, time made steady and relentless. He could only push it forward – speed it up but never slow it down. Kronos would accelerate the battle, so that the Titans might run about the field, striking blows, before the gods could even blink. Inventing Kairos to combat it was the only thing that stopped an all-out massacre. But Kairos is one of those large, unwieldy powers that refuses to stay tethered to any one god for long – though Caerus could briefly manipulate it, which is why we named it similarly. Aeon, too, for a while – before he distracted himself with cycles of his own. Kairos is a different sort of time power – where Chronos is steady, Kairos is erratic, personal. It is the dawn of a critical time, the lightning strike of the right moment.'

She offers me a sympathetic smile, like she does not wish to be condescending as she adds, 'I imagine you're still too new to encounter it but sometimes, in a crucial moment, it feels as though the whole world slows, perhaps even stops. That's Kairos. Chronos is time made immutable, Kairos is time made subjective. When weaponized? It gave us the upper hand over Kronos.'

'Oh, I can imagine how that might leave time shaky here. Thank you.'

'Indeed.' She nods. 'And don't worry, Pandora. It's a noble thing, the pursuit of knowledge.'

And now I wonder if, just maybe, I am not perhaps built for one purpose but many. If each god who had a hand in my creation gave me something of theirs to nurture, and this is hers.

It's such sweet, blissful relief, a satisfaction I discovered admiring the cogs and gears within Stephanos. This is the thrill of a question answered.

And, I determine, it will not be my last.

CHAPTER ELEVEN

A THENA LOOKS TOWARDS THE SKIES once more. 'I should not tarry longer.' Her stormy eyes fix on me. 'Keep up your resolve. Prometheus did not design his mortals to suffer – in fact, he did everything in his power to avoid it. But he was the only one who could pre-empt Zeus, match his wits – who stood a chance in his resistance.' She squirms a little as she lets her formality drop. 'I find myself somewhat fond of you, so please don't put yourself at risk.'

She does not wait for me to say farewell, not even to thank her again.

Instead her form shifts back into the large-eyed owl and soars into the air.

I watch until it vanishes into the horizon.

Then I turn – and nearly jump out of my skin when I see Kerkeis standing a few feet away, clinging to the cliff edge, her lower half still mist as she takes solid form from within the currents of the ocean.

'I heard you,' she says – and my heart races. Did I say anything untoward? Anything private that ought to be protected? Any falsehoods that might sound suspicious to doubting ears?

But then she adds: 'You protected Epimatheos. You could have blamed him, told her the facts of what is between you, and turned her wrath towards him, but you didn't. You lied to keep him safe.'

No, I lied to keep myself safe.

But, oh! That's something, isn't it? After weeks of putting his needs first, it was my own that sprang to mind.

'It's what I'm made for,' I answer anyway.

Kerkeis nods. 'Thank you.'

And then, just as her feet materialize, she dives off the cliff, becoming droplets again before she even hits the water.

The gate swings shut behind me, and with the gentle clack of the lock I'm home, the dim courtyard illuminated only by the hearth in the middle, throwing shadows high against the walls.

And then one of the shadows detaches itself.

'Hello, *wife*,' Matheos says the word like it could slice, with such sweet vitriol that if I hadn't already frozen at his approach it would set my every fibre on edge.

Did he see? Does he know? But I did nothing wrong – quite the opposite. In fact, if he really does want the answer as to why I'm here, then I just garnered several possible leads.

But right now, when he has only just accepted that *maybe* I'm not in collusion with the Olympians, being seen with Athena probably would not bode well.

He steps into the dim light, the fire darkening the shadows beneath his jaw, along his collar, in the hollows of his cheeks. He tilts his head as he adjusts the golden cuff on his ear, so the sharp planes of him are thrown into even sharper relief. And then his eyes lock on me. 'Do you have any idea how late it is?'

'Not precisely – the sundial doesn't work at night, you see.' It doesn't work for most of the day, either, not with the way the house throws it into the shade. But this doesn't feel like the moment to point that out.

'What were you doing?'

'This again? When it's so perfectly clear that I was plotting your demise, summoning the spirits of the Underworld and instructing the ocean to smother the world whole.'

'*Pandora.*'

And, oh gods, I know I shouldn't – it is only at best a sign of his great irritation and at worst my imminent danger – but I love when he says my name like that, the low growling rumble of it.

'I couldn't sleep, Epimatheos. That's all there is to it.'

He arches a brow, so I hurry on.

'I went for a walk to try to tire myself out.'

He runs his eyes over me and I suppress the urge to shudder – cursing the fact that whatever the gods made me for, they decided to mask it beneath a body that is far too responsive to this man. I hold my breath, wondering if the lack of shoes will prove me a liar, but his gaze softens, like he believes it to be evidence of just how very worked up I was.

'I see,' he says. And I am waiting to hear what exactly he sees when he adds: 'Tea?'

'Tea?'

'Yes. Herbs, flowers, steeped in boiling water and –'

'I know what tea is,' I snap.

He just raises that brow again, gives a half-amused huff and says, 'Well then,' before turning on his heel and stalking towards the kitchen.

I hesitate, in case there's anger lurking beneath his offer. But asking me if I want tea doesn't sound like he thinks I was just betraying him to the Olympians.

So I follow him to the kitchen, which is oddly quiet without its usual fluttering birds and the way they often sing to each other. Do the automatons need to sleep? Or at least to shut down and rest? While I'm pondering, Matheos pulls a pot from a hook on the wall.

Some instinct in me itches to take it from him and do it myself, but I force it quiet. I recognize it for what it is now, that need to be of service – and its reverse, the part that won't let someone do something for me instead.

I'll have to write that observation down when I get back to my room.

'So, did your walk clear your head?' he asks, leaning against the counter as the water boils. 'Give you any indication of what the gods sent you here for?'

My jaw clenches. 'If it did, I'd sooner discuss it with the birds.'

'They're excellent listeners. Not so good at problem solving, though.'

'I'm not a problem to be solved, Matheos.'

'Matheos?' he repeats, the question laced with something else. Amusement, maybe? Is he mocking me?

Oh gods. I'm too tired for this, so I steal his favoured line: 'It doesn't matter.'

We fall into silence for a moment and Matheos begins stirring the tea leaves through the boiling water. It's only as he eventually strains and pours it that he speaks. 'I didn't mean to imply you were a problem.'

He passes me a cup.

I take a sip, letting the flavours roll across my tongue. Lavender and chamomile, the light florals undercut by the heaviness of liquorice root.

'It'll help,' he says. 'Trust me, the chamomile was left in the wake of Artemis and her huntresses. It's gods-touched.'

Which is when I notice his curls are flattened at the back of his head, his chiton less intricate and hastily tied like he has thrown it on – and the way he adjusted his hearing cuffs as he saw me, like maybe he wasn't already wearing them, like maybe he'd taken them off because he doesn't wear them when he's . . .

'You were sleeping.'

'Trying to,' he corrects. 'Which is why I'm here.'

He raises his cup to mine, lets it clink softly against the rim.

'The tea is good,' I admit. 'Not your first time making it, I assume? You don't tend to sleep well?'

He looks at me, potentially for the first time without the harsh edge of defensiveness. Maybe he's also too tired for this. 'It's a lot. Living out here. Being somewhat happy when . . . *others* aren't. It's never far from my mind, but it's been more on it of late. I'm sure you understand what it's like for thoughts to crowd your mind if you were trekking outside to try to drown them out.'

I swallow. I don't want this closeness with him – not any more. This vulnerability from him that I spent weeks chasing.

But I do want him to know what he did to me. 'It's a big change, I suppose. I've spent most of my short life trying to stay busy to avoid thinking about the fact I was failing at the very thing I was created for. That the person who was supposed to love me hated me. To be so alone out here, so despised that mutual isolation was preferable and . . . then to find out none of it was true? That I've been in control of my own happiness this entire time – and I don't even know where to start with finding it.'

He swallows, gaze drifting up, like he might see past the ceiling to the Heavens above. His jaw tightens and, without looking at me, he says: 'For what it's worth, if the gods brought you to my door again, I'd make the same choice, however cataclysmic. I still wouldn't send you away. I hate much about this, Pandora, but I don't regret it.'

It shouldn't be worth much of anything, to know he doesn't wish he could hand me back to gods who would surely scrap me. He doesn't get credit for not wanting me to die.

But my heart warms, like the bar might truly be so low.

'Well,' I say, trying to harden myself against words I'm sure he's only saying to dig beneath my defences, perhaps to rip them up altogether. Perhaps insights into the inner workings of my mind or, worst of all, *my trust* are the pieces he believes he has been missing to slot this puzzle all together. Well, I refuse to let him know before I do – not least because I'm certain he won't deign to tell me if he does discover why I'm here. 'Perhaps you ought to think that decision through. Your brother didn't say *I* would bring about destruction, he said *your* decision to accept me would. You keep asking what my purpose is here, but what are *you* doing, Epimatheos?'

He levels me with a glare reminiscent of the rocks clustered at the cliff base: sharp, cold and lying in hidden, lethal wait. 'Whatever the gods would wish me to, I suspect.'

'Take responsibility for your own actions. The gods aren't here. It's just us.'

Incensed, he places his half-full cup on the side heavily, moving to the door like he would not discuss this for another moment. In its frame, he hesitates.

Gods forbid he shouldn't get the last word.

'Yes,' he agrees. 'It's just us. And that very well may be the problem.'

CHAPTER TWELVE

B Y MORNING, MY QUERIES HAVE split into the large – the plans of the gods, what they expect of me, how I might help – and the immediate: how to work through what is *me*, and what is their programming. Or rather, the question of *why did they send me?* ringing against *who even am I?*

They are, decidedly, not about Matheos.

Because I'm refusing to think about him.

Even if his words are the ones I keep coming back to: that I am wired simply to want to be of use.

I want breakfast that isn't inedible, and I like cooking – the experimentation, the act of creation, the transformation of it all and, of course, the delicious final product. But do I just like cooking because I should? I could make food only for myself, I suppose, but I also like sharing it. That's part of the joy. How do I draw a line between niceness and politeness and the way those two things are centred in my mind when, for others – maybe just for men – they're cursory mentions? But isn't it more a flaw of theirs if they don't care?

Thankfully, I don't have to make a decision, because just as I'm crossing the courtyard to find Korax, the gate screeches on its rusted hinges and I jump, expecting Matheos back from wherever it is he disappears to during the day.

But walking through the gate is Ione. And, behind them, tossing the hair from her face: Kerkeis.

She flashes me a haughty look, chin high, as Ione beams.

'Pandora!' Ione greets, flinging their arms about me. 'We brought honey cakes from Asparus.'

They look expectantly at their partner.

'I've decided to give you a chance,' Kerkeis says, like this is a greater gift than the cakes.

I hesitate, a part of me considering telling her that I'm perfectly fine without her approval, thank you very much. But between my husband and the gods who made me, frankly I have enough people to distrust. 'Sure, why not.'

Ione sets the cakes out and I dutifully throw a handful of crumbs into the flames, sending a quick prayer of gratitude to the Heavens.

'I still can't believe Prometheus pulled that off,' Kerkeis laughs with a quick shake of her head as she watches me.

'What do you mean?' I ask.

She glances warily at Ione, who shrugs. She weighs up her decision and, clearly, settles on actually trusting me. 'The food sacrifice. Zeus wasn't happy about Prometheus creating the mortals so that they walked upright. He saw it as a threat, so demanded reassurance that the mortals knew their place — that they'd sacrifice everything for the gods. Even their own livelihoods. He wanted a ritual, half of their food offered to him.'

'But he doesn't even need food! Not to live, at least. And certainly not as desperately as the mortals do.'

Kerkeis snorts. 'Zeus needs to feed his ego and that's enough. So Prometheus took the nicest parts of the food, and hid them beneath the worst. He took the inedible parts – the bones and gristle – and covered them in a glaze, making it look delicious.' It decidedly does not sound it – especially not with a honey cake in hand. 'Zeus wanted the best, and believed it was the latter. When he found out he'd been tricked, that he'd gone for what looked good over what was truly substantial, he was furious. But the ritual was sealed and now the humans give the gods the food they cannot eat.'

I swallow. 'Is that why Zeus punished Prometheus?'

'No, no. That came later,' Ione says.

Later? But Athena said Prometheus betrayed Zeus for the humans – and if that's not the betrayal she meant, then ... how many times did Prometheus choose to protect them? Choose us?

I'm starting to wonder if, perhaps, I was sent to the wrong brother.

I look at Kerkeis. 'You told Matheos he needed to speak to his brother.'

'You listened in,' she says, smiling a little. 'Good. The way Matheos was going on about you, I didn't think you had any interests outside of darning his socks.'

'Well, I'm pleased to know he was ranting about that,' I say. And I am, actually. If he wasn't thankful for it, at least he was annoyed. 'But *can* he speak to Prometheus? Are there ways to see him?'

Maybe ... Well, I don't let myself finish the thought. It is a big lingering *maybe* that will not shake free from my mind.

'In theory, yes. Mount Caucasus is in Colchis so it's not far, but it's pretty difficult to climb. There's a stream, though, that runs its length.' Kerkeis shudders. *Mount Caucasus* – so that's where he is. A trek, but a manageable one. 'I don't love fresh water –'

Ione feigns indignation. 'Yes, you quite literally do.'

'Okay, the love of my immortal life aside.' She rolls her eyes but there's a hint of a smile on her face, and Ione practically glows. 'My point being, I know a few naiads have been – out of curiosity, I imagine. A god might be able to climb it, or descend in one of their chariots, but the terrain is steep and dangerous. A mortal would struggle. But its danger is beyond the physical – who knows how far Zeus's wrath will reach if he would punish someone for even venturing near. I was foolish to encourage Matheos – not when he's done everything he can to distance himself from his brother.'

Perhaps.

But Prometheus is clearly at the centre of all this. And I am tired of becoming the gods' own sacrifice – picking at the inedible scraps of the information I'm given.

I want the full story.

Unfortunately, that's going to involve playing nice with my husband.

CHAPTER THIRTEEN

GET TO WORK - AND this time there is no hesitation in my mind when I head to the kitchen. Because I know why I am doing this: to get the answers I am owed. And I am going to use every skill at my disposal.

Korax is settled at my feet – though I suspect only because it enjoys the heat of the stove. It makes a gentle rumbling noise as the gears within it turn, and it almost sounds pleased. The birds flit through the air, and I have to focus on the task at hand – not letting myself get distracted by why Hephaestus programmed them with recipes ingrained, or how he achieved such a thing. Or did they learn it themselves, and are yet to work out the errors in their ministrations?

I make a veritable banquet.

I set it all up outside, light the fires and decant the wine. I put on a simple silk chiton I made from a bolt of fabric Ione brought me. It is comfortable and the deep red makes me think of heavy wine or the flames flickering in the darkness. Everything feels cosy and warm. But when I rush to the bathroom mirror – unable to arrange my dark, unruly hair without a reflection – I see that the silk hugs my figure in a way that my usual linen does not. Each drape feels intentional, and I am shown in sharp relief: my wide hips and the gentle dips as they meet my thighs, the soft curve of my belly, the swells of my breasts. Even the material, smooth and shimmering under the light, looks like it's begging to be touched.

Oh gods, no.

Matheos will think I'm trying to seduce him again. This is not how I intended to get him to lower his guard. I wanted good food and relaxing music and wine lingering on his tongue – *no, don't think about his tongue!* – and to ask the questions which might not feel as prying over soft candlelight.

But just as I make up my mind to change chitons, I hear the gravel crunch and footsteps I know instantly are his – softer than you'd expect and always a little hurried.

Well, looks like we're doing this.

'Is Ione coming over?' he asks, like he didn't storm out on me last night. Then he turns his attention from the table to me.

It's infinitesimal – not so much a change in expression as the forced lack of it, like he has frozen at the sight. Gaze steadfast like he doesn't dare take all of me in, jaw clenched tight like he might gape without effort – and then the delightfully slow swallow.

If I'd intended this, it would be a lot more fun. As it is, it's too much, like being in the palace of Olympus, smugness and embarrassment and something I can only describe as *heat*.

This is what he does to me: makes me feel too many things at once.

It's ridiculous; I am the one accidentally dressed up. He is only his usual kind of gorgeous – with the added wind-tousled look that tells me he was at the beach. It's not like I don't know Matheos is beautiful – in fact, it's probably the only nice thing I am capable of saying about my sort-of husband. But if he's always gorgeous, why are his dark eyes lingering on me making me feel so particularly flustered tonight?

Then Korax pelts out of the house, running to Matheos and jumping up at him excitedly.

I have never been more thankful for one of the automatons.

'No, no guests! I thought we could dine together,' I say, forcing a lightness I certainly don't feel. 'A truce of sorts. You asked me to let you help me figure out why I'm here and –'

'You're accepting?' Matheos asks, scratching Korax behind the ears and decidedly not looking at me.

'I'm *considering*. I thought we might try a genuinely civil conversation and go from there.' I scrape the cast-offs from the plate into the fire, sending a quick prayer to the Heavens that mostly centres on Aphrodite not ruining this for me by making me look too good in silk.

'Pandora,' he says – and it sounds like a slow exhalation, an almost wistful thing. 'Maybe this isn't a good idea.'

I straighten up a little, trying to look stern. 'Epimatheos, I have spent most of my time here having an existential crisis about what *I* want and what the gods primed me for, so much so that I can't even dip bread in oil without worrying about their subterfuge in my desire to cook. But tonight, I made an entire meal to spend time with you. So for once, could you please just sit down and eat it? Nicely, if possible.'

He hesitates only a second, and when he does take the nearest chair, it's with a sigh of resignation, like I am brandishing a knife instead of an oinochoe of wine.

'So, long day?' I ask, pouring the wine into his cup. His eyes dip only briefly, and then look downright panicked and up to the sky, and I realize leaning over him like this just gave him a view of more of my cleavage than I'd have liked.

'No more so than any other,' he replies tightly.

I laugh. 'Is that all I get?'

'Well, what exactly do you want to know?'

'What you were doing. Where you go when you leave here.'

Matheos looks at me. 'Why? Is it not enough that I leave you in peace?'

I don't think I've ever felt peace in my entire life.

'I had no idea it was such a sensitive subject,' I say.

'I just want to know why you're asking.' He shrugs but his nonchalance is forced. 'Is it simply politeness?'

Oh. He's studying me. And, of course, I'm studying him – both of us dancing around each other, our conversations surgical incisions to get at the truth. But if we can work out what that truth is – *who I am* – it may not necessarily be a bad thing. Whatever threat Prometheus believes I pose might not actually be what the gods intend. For all we know, the supposed 'threat' he sees is *his* humans becoming more like me.

But they're all just theories – or perhaps not even that. They're possibilities. Baseless ones.

'Just making small talk over dinner, Matheos,' I say, spearing an artichoke on my fork. 'Would you prefer I discussed the weather?'

'Would you like to?' he retorts almost too quickly and, Heavens above, I hope I'm more subtle in my interrogation than he is.

'It's overcast,' I deadpan. 'And you were where, today?'

He snorts a little – the way he does, I think, when I have genuinely amused him and he doesn't want to admit it. 'A whale beached itself a little way south of here. The oceanids managed to keep it alive until I got there and could help it back into the sea.'

That is absolutely not what I was expecting. So I chew a little slower, formulating a response.

'The oceanids couldn't get it back in but you could?' I ask and though it's not what I meant to imply, Matheos lets out a low bark of laughter.

'What are you trying to say about my upper-body strength?'

Frankly, nothing that needs saying.

And I find myself laughing too. Matheos is slight, his muscles not exactly lacking but spread across his tall frame so that they're not the first thing you'd note. But I like that – it's finer somehow, carved details and intricate intention.

'Politely? That it doesn't equate to multiple oceanids.'

'That I'll allow,' he grants. 'I didn't heave the whale back in, if that's what you mean.' He pauses, then relents as though it costs him something. 'It's . . . my responsibility, I suppose. Once the gods won the war, there were jobs those of us in the lower echelons had to undertake while they partied on Olympus. I was asked to distribute attributes to the animals – sharp teeth and speed, camouflage and venom. The things that let them survive. Now, when they're in trouble . . . well, they tend to find their way to me. I can draw out those gifts, still. In this case, help the whale hold oxygen longer, swim faster and give it a stern talking to that perhaps the Euxine Sea isn't the best place for it to be swimming in.'

I reach for my wine.

'What?' Matheos prompts.

'You won't like it.'

'I'm sure I've handled worse.'

'Well . . . it's very nice of you. It's frankly adorable. In fact, it's possibly the sweetest and kindest thing I've ever heard.'

Matheos narrows his eyes. 'I was expecting something more insulting.'

'You've made it very clear how much you despise me complimenting you. And I've already antagonized you into dining with me, so I don't want to push it.'

He huffs, leaning back in his chair. A slight scowl is etched into his forehead and though I'm used to seeing it, I've never really taken a moment to *admire* it before. The downturned tilt of his brows, the pressed line of his lips – the general sulky air that just makes me want to etch that frown further or break it into a laugh I know he'll be more irritated by.

It's also, unfortunately, very cute.

'So is that what you do with your days? Go around rescuing whales?'

'Whales are actually quite rare on the shores of Colchis.'

'But deer?' I ask, suddenly remembering my first day here.

'Much more common. And more often in need of rescuing.'

So that's it? That's what he's up to? Studying the migration patterns of birds and healing injured woodland creatures. It hardly seems worthy of the gods' wrath, though not exactly a feat of heroism they'd rush to reward, either.

'What task was your brother given, after the war?'

Matheos's shoulders tense, and though I don't think his guard was ever lowered, it certainly springs back up now. 'Pardon?'

'Your brother – you were asked to assign attributes to animals. So what did he do?'

I am prepared for his outrage. But I mean it: if Matheos would have us work together, then I will at least try to level the playing field. I could try to get it out of him with lies or coaxing, but Athena's right: there's no shame in asking questions.

Matheos takes a long sip of wine, setting the cup back down before he answers. 'Why do you want to know?'

'Curiosity?'

He glowers and I nearly back down in the face of it. But I'm not forcing him to answer – I'm just asking.

'Pandora,' he pushes.

I sigh. Alright, then. 'Will you tell me what he did to betray the gods? If I am here for some nefarious purpose, it would make sense that it's because of something to do with that. I don't see how we can ever figure out the gods' plan if I don't know what it is my existence is supposedly in reaction to.'

He meets my gaze. 'We?'

I hesitate – but it does seem a fair trade if I'm asking him for all the things he holds closest to his chest. Enough subterfuge. If we're working together, let's do it properly. 'Yes, we. But I need to know what you know, otherwise I don't see how I can possibly trust you. Not to mention we'd just be wasting time we don't have, while it races so quickly away from here. We literally don't have time for me to fight through gaps in my knowledge to get to answers we might otherwise have reached sooner.'

His brow furrows, cup clutched tight as he contemplates. But though he doesn't look happy about it, he also hasn't said no. 'That's a very personal thing you're asking of me, *wife*. I can't just jump to the end point. You'd need to know it all – and it's my history, too. His story is mine.'

'I know. But it's also mine, and I don't even know what it is. If you want to work with me on this, then telling me the basics is my price. If you want to help, you need to actually help.'

Matheos glowers before leaning back against the edge of the sloping chair. 'I don't like the frequency with which you're winning these arguments.'

'You'll have to get used to it.' I look up, unable to stop my half-smile. 'It's very cute when you sulk, you know.'

'Stop it,' he growls.

'Never – you make it far too fun. Now speak, you adorable man.'

CHAPTER FOURTEEN

MATHEOS HEAVES A SHUDDERING SIGH – and I'm uncertain whether it's in response to me or the tale he's about to tell me. I suspect both.

'How far back do you need me to go? I expect you don't need childhood anecdotes.'

'I would *love* childhood anecdotes.' I lean forward excitedly, propping my head in my hands and smiling at him with the sort of unnerving attentiveness that I know burrows beneath his skin. An irritation that feels intimate – like he would shed his own flesh to cast me out. 'And if you have any embarrassing marble friezes depicting you as a baby in loincloths that would be excellent.'

In lieu of such snapshots, Matheos glares like he might turn me to stone instead.

'What?' I protest weakly. 'Some of us didn't get childhoods.'

'Forgive me for thinking you might take the great mystery of your existence somewhat seriously.'

I pout. 'I'd hoped it might be fun too, but fine, I'll permit you such graveness.'

There's a slight chance this flippant tangent I'm chasing has something to do with the nervousness currently churning in my gut. How absurd – to both want an answer and fear it in equal measure. It should not require bravery to take a steadying breath and suggest: 'Why don't you start with the war? Most things seem to track back to that. So: you sided with the gods against the Titans.'

Matheos winces. 'No one called us Titans until *after* Prometheus's name was a curse on the lips of the Olympians. My father was a Titan, my mother an oceanid of the Erythraean Sea, just off the coast of India. That lineage could technically make me a god.'

Interesting – that a god and Titan might be so broadly defined. Why does humanity feel like its own distinct category, then?

And one the gods have hidden from me . . .

'My eldest brothers sided with our father and the other Titans. I followed Prometheus to fight for the gods. My brother thought Zeus was the saviour we'd been waiting for. No one was more loyal to him.'

Was . . .

It's still warm, but that breeze suddenly feels biting.

'Prometheus shielded me from the worst of the war, got me assigned to organizing rations and polishing armour. Without him I would likely have died several times over. And when we finally won, the work continued. I was given the animal attributes. My brother was asked to make humanity. What is it?'

'Hmm?' I'm startled from my thoughts.

'You are quite literally biting your lip.'

'And that's distracting?' I tease and he offers me a glare I'm growing rather fond of. Strange, to be so attuned to my own likability, and use it to revel in annoying Matheos as much as possible.

I'll have to write that down, too.

'Go on, ask whatever question is on your mind. It's your curiosity I'm trying to sate, after all.'

'How did Prometheus make the humans?'

By which, of course, I mean human men. Because even if there are more now, I was still the first human woman – and, like Epimatheos, it appears we are an afterthought to our own creation.

'He moulded them from clay.'

'Oh,' I breathe. 'They did that for me, too.'

'You know that for sure? You saw the clay?'

'Yes, I was conscious for it. For all of it.'

'Really?' He takes up his cup and leans across the table, so that the candle perched on it lights up the intrigue shining in his eyes. My stomach lurches, fixed in the confines of his gaze, his interest locked on me to the point of my own entrapment. 'That's not how my brother did it. He went to Panopeus and found clay which he mixed with tears –'

'Tears!'

'Prometheus is dramatic. And when he was done, Athena breathed life into the figures.'

Athena is part of this story? She hadn't mentioned that. She'd made humanity sound like Prometheus's project alone. Something he would do anything to protect.

But would she?

Not as blatantly, of course – Athena is intelligence and stealth. But if humanity were under threat, might she not send someone else to save it? Maybe even make someone for the job . . .

It's a stretch, and a ludicrously self-aggrandizing one at that, but I've been so desperate for any indication I might be here for good rather than evil that I latch on to that fine, shimmering thread with all the grip I can muster.

'Before she did that they were nothing,' Matheos continues. 'Just finely sculpted lumps of clay. But no god breathed life into you?'

'No ... no, someone did.' I try to sort through it all, try to remember. But the further back I try to go, the hazier the memories become. 'It centred me, made me *me*. I existed but I wasn't *alive* until then, I suppose.'

'Then maybe the gods didn't create you,' Matheos muses. 'Maybe they just gave you form. In which case ...' His gaze intensifies, like he is seeing to the bones of me. 'What are you?'

What indeed.

'They definitely shaped me; I remember that. Gifts and attributes. But yes, my consciousness was already there.'

'Alright,' he considers. 'Let's come back to that, I suppose.'

It's rather nice, surprisingly, to bounce ideas back and forth like this. To have someone musing alongside me – even if it is Matheos.

He takes a breath, and his shoulders tense, like he might flee at any moment.

'I'm sorry,' I say. 'I know this is hard.'

He shakes his head. 'I don't even know what it is. When it comes to my brother, it's all guilt and relief and guilt at that relief so I try to avoid thinking about it much altogether.'

Oh. Contradictory feelings, too many things at once – he knows it, too?

The thought that this is not merely a human thing should feel expansive, should make me feel aligned with all the gods and beings in the universe. But it doesn't. On the edge of the world, harsh waves echoing beneath the howling wind, that feeling of the gods watching vanishes. We feel so decidedly alone, like this courtyard might be the only thing to exist: these flickering flames, this wine on my tongue, this man sitting across from me. Like the world might be careening around us but we are the fixed, still point.

'Hard or not, you're right. You deserve to know.' Matheos shrugs – and I hadn't dared hope for that: him sharing not out of obligation but genuine agreement that I ought to know. 'Prometheus loved the humans. He made them to be like the gods – in form, upright, with intelligence – but bound to the Earth. Zeus didn't like that very much.' Matheos's voice is quiet, barely carrying across a wind that has grown harsher since we first settled here. 'He said nothing should be *like* the gods. So he issued Prometheus a warning and demanded reassurance that the humans would sacrifice everything for the gods. Even their own livelihoods. Prometheus devised a trick with their food that angered Zeus so much he took fire from the humans in punishment.'

'Oh no.' I bring a shaky hand to cover my gaping mouth. 'Tell me he didn't!'

Because fire – the hearth – is everything. It's safety and warmth, it's the ability to cook and nourish and heal. It is warm bread and sterile water and sharp-edged tools. It is stepping past the threshold of a door and a house becoming home. And with that stolen light, any hope that I'm here for something good fades too.

'My brother stole the fire back, hid it in a fennel stalk and returned it to the mortals. Thrice he defied Zeus, and so finally Zeus had him bound to a pillar deep in the Caucasus Mountains.' Matheos twists the rope tie of his chiton about his fingers. It is the only sign of distress as he says: 'Every day an eagle tears his liver out. And every evening it grows back so that the torture may begin again.'

'Matheos,' I say softly, but his fingers still and he looks at me not with anger, but an almost fervour, like he is clinging to something he cannot bear to let go.

'So *that* is why I am so certain you were not sent here to love me. The king of the gods tortures my brother. If he wished to reward me, he might stop that. No, I think it's clear that he's still not done with us.'

On this, I quite agree.

My mind works in details, in patterns. And here one is clear.

'Prometheus made mortals stand on two legs and Zeus demanded half their food,' I say, listing it all like it's not painful, like it doesn't inflame the vacated hole in my chest where hope lived only moments ago. 'He offered the wrong portion and stole their fire. But they get it back and Zeus settles for only punishing Prometheus? When everything prior suggests he would come for the mortals too, once Prometheus was bound? It would be his next logical step.'

'Right.'

The food remains piled between us but my appetite has vanished.

'And then he made me.'

'And then he made you,' Matheos agrees. 'But why send you to me? If he meant to make a woman so beautiful men would tear themselves apart fighting over her, why send her to the edge of Colchis? The nearest mortal village is a three-day hike through the woods, and the closest town would be two weeks, at the foot of the mountains.'

I stare at the flickering candle wick, trying to ignore the way Matheos breezes right past my beauty and on to the practicalities. I try to pretend I don't catch the way his voice lifts, the way he hurries just a little self-consciously. I'm sure it is nothing beyond awkwardness, or, at best, an acknowledgement that he finds me physically attractive, because why wouldn't he? That was never his problem with me. And wasn't every other god squabbling over me? My looks are meaningless; they're just an adornment. A disguise.

But disguising what? What dark heart have the gods created to shroud in this beauty?

'How long ago was Prometheus imprisoned?'

'Two years, right after the war ended.'

Two years in this time-addled place would be decades for the Olympians, perhaps even centuries. Would Zeus really wait so long for his next step? But then, if there was so much to sort through after the war, perhaps he was distracted – chasing after the next goddess with tumbling locks and an instrument strapped to her back, or doling out domains to everyone else.

'There's more, Pandora. My brother knew exactly what would happen to him every time he broke one of Zeus's rules,' Matheos says, his gaze fixed on his wine as he gently swirls it around his cup. 'He and his wife, Hesione, worked out their every move step by step for years. Prometheus knew what would become of him, he planned it, accepted it as the consequences of the choice he made long before he made it. I never understood why, but I suppose here I am, having done exactly the same thing. Made a choice I already knew would end badly.' He looks up, and this time he doesn't look angry or cold, he looks desperate. Like he'd do anything to have his brother here, telling him what to do, advising him on the problem before him. '*Don't take their gifts* – and here you are, Pandora. All the gifts I should not have accepted.'

I do not believe I have ever *really* considered that I might be ill intentioned. Rolled the idea around in my head, perhaps, but never truly let it settle.

And now it sinks through me, blunt and unyielding.

The horror of it, and the stupidity – the denial I had clung to despite all signs to the contrary. How pathetically self-centred to have hoped to be a force for good, when the prophecy's meaning now feels abundantly clear. I am a threat to humanity. And that is precisely what Zeus intended.

'Thank you for telling me,' I say. A quick nod. Polite, even, while I feel ribbons of myself unspooling at my feet. 'If you'll excuse me, I'd like some time to sit with this.'

Then I'm not sure what happens – it is as though reality itself detaches. Everything stops being real, least of all me. I am not scurrying away, I'm drifting – a mortal girl in a world of gods, a ghost already haunting these halls.

I make it to my room as my last hold on the present falters, and the world itself slips clean away.

CHAPTER FIFTEEN

M Y ROOM – OR MATHEOS'S, I suppose – has a small cupboard built into its wall, one which has always been empty, the chitons folded into a trunk at the foot of the bed instead.

I end up inside it, curled beneath a mound of blankets against the cupboard's corner – less the result of a decision and more of a suffocating need, to be somewhere smaller, closer, darker, weighted by enough pressure that the mental weight crushing me might shift to a physical one.

So many thoughts race through my mind that it feels like a fog, thick and numb. At some point I realize I'm staring – just sitting, wide-eyed, watching the wall opposite me, but I don't have the energy to so much as close my eyes, let alone move.

So I just wait, long hours passing until I suppose I must feel better, because when there's an incessant pecking I manage to reach for the door long enough to swing it open and let a bird automaton flutter in.

It perches on my knee, regarding me with a tilted head before shuffling closer, like it's settling in here with me.

I run a finger across its cool metal surface and, eventually, the thoughts slow, coalescing into a thick, weighty stream that I can just about decipher.

That I am likely revenge of some sort. That I might hurt someone. Maybe a lot of people. That the gods made me as a weapon.

At which point I manage to drag myself to bed, the automaton fluttering on to the table beside me, watching over me as I finally cry myself to sleep.

I wake a lot later than I normally do, the light pouring in from the curtains I forgot to shut. The bird automaton hops closer the moment I open my eyes, and I realize one of its claws is catching, moving in jagged, sudden motions.

Oh. *Oh.* Something about that – the idea that it needed someone to fix it and found me breaks through the lingering numbness and I hold it steady to open the hatch at its back.

There's a frayed thread of gold where a solid ribbon ought to turn around gears. Thankfully, another has a bit of extra give so I use the spools and scissors with which I repair clothes to cut and shape a new line. Once connected, I shut the panel and the bird flitters back, if not to life, then to a very strong semblance of it. It hums a quick tune as though to prove its returned functioning.

'You don't think I'm evil, do you?' I ask it. It chirps back – which could mean anything, but it soothes me nonetheless. In the light of morning, it's harder to believe the truth that felt so clear last night. It feels too huge, too grandiose. I'm one, lone, mortal girl. If, as the logic suggests, the gods meant me for some grand scheme then surely their plan is laughable.

Even if I am capable of some kind of large, planned evil, I am just as capable of small kindnesses like this. So then why give me a will of my own? Why make me a conscientious objector to my own purpose?

Maybe if I can explore more of *how* they wired me, I can learn how to resist whatever ill intent they created me to enact.

There's a knock at my door – or rather, the light pecks of more birds.

I open it to find a flock of them hovering. At first I expect they have come to collect their missing worker but half flit away, slowly weaving through the air while the rest swoop in behind me, pushing me forward.

I am being led somewhere, it seems.

'Really?' I mutter when it becomes distinctly apparent that the kitchen is our destination.

Something smells incredibly burnt and for a brief moment I wonder if I'm being summoned to put out a fire.

But no, it's Matheos, standing over the oven, two charcoaled, smouldering loaves on the side. He's pulling out a third – which looks marginally better – from the stove, cloth wrapped round his hands.

Oh gods, there's flour dusted across his cheek.

He startles at the door opening, and the bread would fall if the automatons didn't swoop to save it.

'Pandora,' he says, staring at me in alarm like I've caught him in some compromising position. Then he sobers, narrowing his eyes at the automatons. 'I think my instructions were rather clear.'

One of them chirps defiantly.

He's baking. He's . . . The flour? The secrecy?

I can tell I am on the verge of saying something rather stupid, so I rush to the pantry before I can, rummaging through the stores just for the excuse to avoid him.

'I'll fetch the preserves!'

'No, don't,' he says, following after me. 'You weren't meant to . . . that is, I'll get them.'

'Oh, you know me,' I say, trying to laugh, trying to find that joviality that used to come so readily. 'Just desperate to be helpful.'

I reach for an amphora on the topmost shelf, which is far too high but I've committed, and I'm so thrown by whatever is going on here that I stupidly lunge for it, catching its edge.

I watch as the whole thing teeters.

Matheos snatches it out of the air before it can fall on my head, reaching above me and so very close in these tight confines.

Where are those damn birds? Aren't they supposed to deliver amphorae for me?

Matheos hands me the jug. 'I believe "useful" was the word I chose.'

'You're making bread.' Ah, there it is: that stupid thing I cannot help but say.

'Trying to,' he answers. He turns swiftly, as though worrying the loaves might have leapt back into the flames without his supervision. But the storeroom door handle doesn't twist open.

'Matheos . . .' I say slowly.

He doesn't answer, doesn't spin back to face me, just keeps his hand on the door handle that is decidedly not turning.

'Matheos, tell me I did not joke about you locking me in a pantry only for you to actually lock me in a pantry.'

'Well, I wasn't supposed to be in here with you,' he replies, voice flat.

'Let me try.'

He shuffles aside, as much as there is space to. I have to lean around him to reach the handle, my back digging into the shelves to create even a breath of space between us, and I am excruciatingly aware of every inch of it.

Somehow, the handle doesn't magically budge under my touch.

'Can you unlock this?' I call to the birds on the other side. I cannot believe I clambered into a cupboard for comfort last night and now I'm stuck in one with Matheos. Did I tempt the Fates? Are they punishing me for thinking I can avoid the gods' will?

'Get Theron,' Matheos shouts.

'Theron?'

'The cat. It can get in anywhere. It'll be a while, though; Fates only know where it escapes to.'

Hunter. I assume of mice – and, Olympus above, the flour on Matheos's cheek and the adorable names he gives his automatons … Can he stop with these glimpses of nicety when I have finally determined my disinterest in him?

'I fixed one of the birds this morning,' I say dejectedly. 'I should have given it lock-picking abilities. Instead I just got it humming again.'

'They hum?' Matheos asks, surprised.

I turn to him and he shrugs. 'I know they creak sometimes. It makes for awful interference when I'm trying to hear actual birds call.'

'They creak because you don't oil them enough,' I mutter.

Matheos just sighs. 'I'll add it to the list. Though it's not exactly proving a successful one – as those burnt loaves can attest.' He slumps to the floor, sitting in as cramped a way as he can manage. Light filters in from a high – and very small – window and I eye the remaining space doubtfully – I'm already struggling not to brush every wall at once. But I think I can fit, if not comfortably. So I manoeuvre my way into sitting beside him, though spun to face him. The result is us pressed up against one another, my ankle at his hip, his knee by my chest.

'Why *did* you decide to take up baking?' I ask, latching on to the first question I can think of to distract from his body up against mine

He sighs, and I wonder if he's actually going to answer. But this absurd situation appears to loosen some truth from him. He stares at my forehead when he speaks – I know because I've realized I do this often, have to focus to meet his eyes, automatically gravitate upwards. But with him it feels less instinctive and more out of a form of embarrassment.

'You said yesterday that you were struggling so much with working through the instincts the gods gave you that you could only cook to spend time with me. I'm sure what I said about you being primed to be useful didn't help and for some reason I thought I could make something better than the automatons could, leave it on the side and have you imagine the birds baked it.'

'Secret bread?' I laugh.

'I didn't want you thinking you owed me anything.'

I run my nails over the pad of my thumb, fidgeting to avoid looking at him. He's right – if I'd realized I would have felt I had to repay it tenfold.

'Clearly the birds had other ideas,' Matheos says. 'I suspect they didn't want you thinking they were responsible for those burnt loaves out there so dragged you to witness it. I got distracted. Kerkeis visited. She met a nereid in the Euxine who apparently fled the Aegean Sea after a new island formed there. Kerkeis said the island used to be a woman.' His voice is detached, so devoid of emotion that it feels all the more choked with it. 'Well, actually, she told me it used to be my cousin. Asteria. She turned herself into an island to escape Zeus's pursuit.'

'That's awful. Fates, Matheos, I'm so sorry.'

'You have to understand, Pandora, that that is what the gods do. They don't create women and send them into happy marriages. They force them to flee, to turn themselves into islands. They torment them.'

Yes, I understand that now. I realize my mind is full of such stories – even the one he's just mentioned, I think. Unless there are multiple women turning themselves into islands – which also would not surprise me. The nymphs and goddesses transform in the stories, become islands and trees and flowers. *Human woman.* I wonder which descriptor is more important in getting to the root of all I am. Humanity and womanhood intertwined. Maybe transformation is important, somehow. This bending of myself, this appeasement, this irresistibility – becoming anything they want me to be.

I slip a scroll from my pocket, and mark the parchment with this latest observation.

'You're annoying, definitely,' I tell him as I write. 'But I wouldn't call you a torment.'

'Kind of you.'

We fall into silence. And then, because I cannot stand our quiet breathing or the way our eyes keep flitting across each other, I say: 'Bread, really?'

'Please, don't –'

'Think you're adorable?' I tease, smiling as he tosses his head back against the shelves with a groan.

Something in my chest flutters and – *no*, I remind myself, that's not what we're doing any more. He's horrible and cruel and mean-spirited and – only, no, we're not doing that either. Not after whatever agreement we came to last night. We're working together, right?

But I don't know the parameters of that, and the lurch from wanting him to hating him to being locked in this cupboard pressed up against him has my mind doing loops through all of the above.

Perhaps he's thinking the same because he takes the sort of breath I now recognize as one pre-empting a speech he's mulled over a few too many times. It comes a second later: 'I admit I've given you every cause to hate me but –'

'I don't hate you. Don't flatter yourself.'

'No? Because this is now the second time I've imprisoned you.'

'I don't *like* you,' I say, which feels merciless in such confines but he doesn't even flinch. 'You have traits I appreciate, outweighed by ones I do not. But they don't play on my mind. It's more like . . . indifference, I suppose. I'm busy. I agree the gods probably intended me for something awful but that doesn't mean I have to see whatever it is through, so trust that I'm too focused on figuring out the puzzle of myself to spare much thought for you.'

'Well,' he says, drawing the word out like he needs a moment longer to dwell on what I've said. 'You should note that down in your favour. The gods know little else but hatred. I do not think them capable of crafting a heart without priming disdain to seed within it. So perhaps you're right, maybe there is also a way to circumvent their plans for you.'

I scowl, trying to work out if he's teasing me. It seems too much – that he would decide I might not be complicit in the gods' intentions, and then that we could dodge them altogether, in mere days when he harboured his hatred of me for weeks.

But he seems sincere, and I'm so desperate for any indication that I might be right, and the intentions of my maker do not determine the course I will take, that I do indeed unfurl the parchment once more and add: *a heart not primed for hatred* to my list.

'Somehow I doubt you truly believe that, Matheos,' I say. 'Imagine we do figure this out, and discover I really am here to enact some kind of horrific evil. Would you actually trust me not to pursue it? Or would you sit back, itching with anticipation, waiting for the day it finally happens? Then will you stop me, with whatever means necessary?'

Would he do it then? Return me to the earth I was born from, just as he once proposed?

'I could ask the same of you, Pandora,' he counters. 'What will you do if you find out such a thing is true, after all? Fight against it, or see it as your duty to the gods who made you?'

'Matheos, I couldn't stand to see an automaton in pain without trying to fix it. What sort of evil do you think I'm capable of?' I drop my gaze to my lap, toying with my nails once more. 'I don't hate the gods, not like you do. But I think

I hate some of them. Zeus and all the things he did to the humans, certainly. But he didn't make me himself. There is altruism among the gods. I've seen it. Hephaestus carved me with utter consideration; Hermes gave me the very ability to speak and Aphrodite an aggressively hopeful heart. Athena's the goddess of war but the gift she gave me was art – not skill with a sword or a thirst for blood, just knowledge of how to work a loom. So *if* Zeus sent me for some nefarious purpose, I'd see it as my duty to the gods who gave me a whisper of kindness to fight against it.'

'And your duty to yourself?'

I look up to that familiar scowl. But not, I think, one laced with doubt. Maybe concern? It's so difficult to tell with him, when any range of emotions can be depicted with those furrowed brows.

Duty to myself is something I'm slowly beginning to consider.

'Well, that depends,' I say. 'Are you going to let me live long enough in this scenario to find out?'

'Pandora, I couldn't send you to your probable death even with a prophecy hanging over all our heads – so what sort of evil do you think *I'm* capable of?'

I exhale, slowly, not realizing I had been so tense. But I am not fully relaxed, more resigned. 'Maybe not that. But I think you'll lock me up again, try to stop me. I don't think you'll ever trust me, Epimatheos, when it really comes down to it.'

'I'm back to Epimatheos, I see.'

'Tell me I'm wrong.'

'You're wrong,' he says quietly. 'And that is the problem. If I weren't so certain the gods couldn't cross the threshold of my home without breaking xenia, I'd have thought they broke this door handle themselves. I think they know avoiding you is the only way to cope with you. But here I am, locked up even closer. My brother or Hesione would have figured you out in moments, but here I am scrambling to keep you at bay. Desperately reminding myself of the threat you pose because if I relax even for a moment you . . . whether you mean to be or not, you are risk incarnate.'

I laugh like it can disguise the way my pulse jumps, thinking about what he himself admitted: all that time spent thinking about me.

'Confirming why I'm here isn't going to make me disappear, Matheos.'

Instead of answering, he smiles a little, says under his breath: '*Matheos* once more.'

I sigh. 'Look, I know Epimatheos is your name but it's rude and I don't like saying it.'

He blinks, then stares at me a little too long before he straightens up and scoffs. 'You just said you don't like me but my name is too much to bear?'

'It's different. *You* gave me reasons not to like you. But the name you've been given is . . . it's not justified, it's just cruel.'

He snorts and goes to say something – a harsh tilt to his smirk, condescending gleam in his eyes. But he can't hold it for long; soon it fades like mist and he's left just staring at me.

Ah. Whatever the gods imbedded in me that allows me to sense who to morph into, to pick up on someone's behaviour and emulate it – here it is now: this recognition that Matheos is someone who passes off everything that hurts with a joke, or a sneering eye-roll. Recognition, too, that as much as I wish to tell him he shouldn't do that, there are small steps to take first – and I do want to embarrass him when his defences are so low.

But apparently I don't need to.

'My name is both gift and curse,' he says, gaze fixed on the wall instead of me – like any acknowledgement of what he is saying means something might be wielded against him. 'When they came for my brother, he begged me to play stupid, so that he could take the fall. My name was protection – told them I had no idea, wasn't a part of his plans, indeed could never understand a plan like Prometheus could. It wasn't exactly a lie.' He looks at me then, long and hard, and I hear what he is not quite admitting: that he *was* a part of it.

Then he tilts his head back, lets it rest against the shelf and, judging from the shadows of his lashes, shuts his eyes. 'Here is my theory, Pandora. The gods sent you knowing I would have questions only Prometheus could answer. Or maybe they thought you'd seduce me and then you'd innocently ask to see my brother. Or maybe they thought I'd be terrified and run to him for help. I think that's what they want. Me to do the one thing I haven't in years: talk to my brother.'

You're wrong, he'd said. And here he is, trusting me.

It feels foolish to trust him in return but if, pressed against one another as he reveals the cards he holds, I cannot take that risk too, then I'm not sure I would trust myself in the future either.

So, foolishly, I say: 'When I was on Olympus, Apollo tried to flirt with me. Hermes said I was reserved. And then he said your brother's name. I thought that meant whatever they sent me here for was wrapped up in his punishment and your reward for loyalty. But maybe all this *is* a way to close in on him and whatever secrets he's still keeping.'

Isn't that what Matheos himself had said? That Prometheus already knew what would happen. That he was several steps ahead? Maybe the gods want to catch up.

'He's keeping a prophecy,' Matheos says with a soft exhalation, like it is a relief to finally admit all this. My hip begins to smart where his knee presses so sharply against it but I cannot bear to move. The pressure of him is . . . reassuring. And maybe if he wasn't touching me, if there was even a breath of distance between us, he wouldn't feel he could keep going as he does. 'About the downfall of Zeus. That's what the gods want. They pressed me for it when they came for him but, well, *Epimatheos*, as I say. What would I know? No,' he says, when I go to ask. 'I don't know what it is. I don't even think he told Hesione. To keep us safe, I suppose. So that's what makes most sense to me – that the gods sent you to drive me to him in the hopes he might finally share it with me. Years of torture couldn't force it from his lips, but if he imparted it to someone he trusted, then . . .'

'Then they can torture you for it instead?'

He shrugs. 'Maybe.'

'I wanted to know about Prometheus so desperately,' I admit. 'Maybe that's why. Maybe the gods gave me this *need* to learn then kept that particular bit of information from me because they hoped it would drive *me* to go to him, and you to follow me.'

'Perhaps. Either way, we can't let Zeus get his hands on that prophecy,' Matheos says resolutely. 'My brother bleeds for it, every day. And if Zeus knows what's to come, he might be able to stop it. Our only hope of ever living free of his rule is the future unfolding as Prometheus has seen.'

This is treason.

Matheos doesn't just mistrust and dislike the gods.

He's conspiring against their king.

The door shudders open, and reveals the cat automaton sat licking at a paw like it has had nothing to do with what's just happened. The birds are perched high on the rafters, far away from it.

Matheos practically leaps to his feet. 'Finally.'

I scramble up too.

'So, we don't go,' I call, a little too loudly, like he has already moved away when he very much has not. 'We stay here. I can't be a threat to humanity if I'm far away from them. You can't betray your brother's prophecy if you never hear it.'

Matheos hesitates. His brows are drawn low – concern or bafflement, I'm not sure. His words, when he speaks, are almost too quiet to make out. 'Just you and I for the rest of eternity?'

The alternative is supposedly torture and destruction.

But I know that's not what makes me say: 'It sounds bearable.'

'I thought you didn't like me.'

How does he somehow feel closer as we stand unrestrained and facing each other, like I can feel his every breath as it rises and falls?

I swallow, my mouth dry, and say: 'You're growing on me.'

He gives a final, heavy nod which seems like it frees him – and I consider that perhaps he does not wish to know the *why* of me to be rid of me, but to free himself of the weight of his suspicion. 'I'm not much primed for hatred, either.'

He walks away, and I stand for a moment longer.

It sounds almost peaceful. To cease this unravelling, of what is gods-given and what is humanity and what is *me*. To be a whole, and not divided parts.

Just one thing I'd need to silence: that ardent, keening whisper in my mind that has spun a new mystery – Prometheus and a whole, separate prophecy. One that will upend the world and the Heavens as we know them.

And just how desperately I want to hear it.

CHAPTER SIXTEEN

HAVING SEEMINGLY EXTRACTED FROM MATHEOS all that he knows, I turn to my other resource for answers: me. Who I am, why I am and what abilities the gods granted me — in the hopes I can finally uncover what it is they're hoping to achieve with me.

Which primarily involves a lot of giving in to my every whim and interest, like I might spot an instinct and trace its trail.

I build a new loom, which is far more interesting than actually weaving — working out the bolts and weights, the traction required to hold each string taut. And isn't that fascinating in and of itself? That the gods might have granted me knowledge but not passion, like they might have given me an arsenal but something else might be at play too, something that rejects part of their conditioning while latching on to others.

This tension is something that feels intrinsic — maybe connected to me having seemingly existed before they crafted me, some deeper *me* that welcomes some gifts while deriding others.

A *me* that I am desperate to get to.

I make other things, too: a step stool for the kitchen pantry, wider chairs for the reception room, hooks for the kitchen walls so I don't have to hang everything from ludicrously high pipes.

'Do you plan on redecorating entirely?' Matheos asks dryly, while I'm adding extra bolts to the klines in the courtyard to halt their creaking every time I sit down on one. 'Because I draw the line at allowing you anywhere near paint.'

I flip my hair back as I straighten up, wiping a sheen of sweat from my brow. I thought this would be easier.

'Everything in this house, Matheos, is designed for one skinny and obscenely tall man. I'm just trying to make it a little easier for me to exist in – or are you still hoping I'll cease existing at all?'

I'm only trying to wind him up a little, and I see that battle within him – his irritation warring with the fact that he knows his irritation is my goal and he doesn't want to give it to me. At most I get a slight upward glance that might be the start of an eye-roll. 'Of course not. Korax is far too attached to lose you now. So, given that you are, in fact, existing, what can I do to assist? I can't promise I'll be much help but I did learn a few things at Hephaestus's forge.' Between us, we manage most of the adjustments – enough that I can begin thinking past *need* to *want*.

I set up a workshop in one of the disused rooms, assembling tools and materials. I pull things apart, mix things together, chase my curiosity wherever it leads. But first I make more ribbons for the automatons' cogs, in case more need replacing in future. Then, when one of the lights which flickers when someone knocks at the door begins malfunctioning, I open the whole thing up, find the tiny gears at the door which sense the vibrations of the knock and translate into the corners of every room – in case Matheos isn't wearing those cuffs across his ears. Instead of noise – light. More specifically: a scattering of oil and a sparking flame. I realign the flint so it catches the scraping metal and the light flickers back into being. I don't think Hephaestus put such knowledge and skill in my head – not the way Athena and the others did, at least. It's more like an inkling, a hunger to learn that delves deeper with each new mystery. It might even be something entirely my own.

And if there is something of my own beneath all this, is it the sort of thing that might be capable of fighting whatever intent Prometheus saw? He warned Matheos off accepting me, but if there's something behind all those gifts they gave me . . .

Maybe he'd know. Maybe talking to him *would* solve all of this and – no, I'm not supposed to be considering that. There must be other ways to find out than powers of prophecy – experimentation and investigation and definitely not risking everything by going to those mountains.

So I follow other desires instead. I bake and bake and bake, until every kitchen surface is covered in cooling dishes and Matheos stills as he walks in, looking from the trays of bread to me with slowly widening eyes.

'Do I need to stage an intervention?' he asks.

'I didn't hold one for you after you and Ione spent most of last night debating chimeras.'

'It's ridiculous – I don't understand their fascination. I gave out attributes to those the gods forgot, not those the gods keep crafting to throw at their heroes. All those gifts I awarded in careful, precise balance, spliced up and thrown together in some lion-goat-snake abomination –'

'Matheos, I do not need the encore.'

He approaches one of the loaves and prods at it. 'What's this one?'

'Cabbage and cherry.'

He recoils. 'What would possess you to try that?'

'Well, that's sort of what I'm trying to figure out.'

One day as I place a pillow on those wider chairs I created, it occurs to me that I might be able to build more furniture to fill this empty house with. I grab some parchment and I think of that uncomfortable-looking kline in Matheos's study – too narrow, too upright, too short for all that height, and the way he towers above me, those finely etched features catching the light whenever he tilts his face to mine and –

He throws open the door of my little studio and I turn the page on the design I've been drawing, wanting it to be a surprise. And because it might excuse how flustered I suddenly feel.

'Will you help me?' he asks, and I realize he's breathless. He must have run here.

He doesn't have to say anything else; I'm already on my feet. Because Matheos does not ask for help – ever.

And when he leads me outside – with me having to take three quick steps for every one of his long strides – I see the problem. A hunting dog, its muscles honed and teeth sharp, one paw twisted in a snare.

'If I hold it still, can you untangle it?' he asks. 'Or we can work the other way round. This is going to hurt. The poor thing will fight.'

'I thought we'd established some concerns about your upper-body strength,' I say, staring at it. This is not a dog like Korax, all sweet gestures and predictable rote. It's a being, a very large being with very dangerous-looking teeth.

'How dare you! I'm a trained soldier of the Olympian army,' he counters.

'You organized the food rations.'

'A vital skill.'

'Alright, fine. Hold the dog.'

So we get to work, Matheos wrapping his arms around the beast, one of his hands coming to its head which he begins to pet softly, murmuring reassurances in its ear as it whimpers.

I start loosening the knots of the rope.

'Excellent, you're so brave,' Matheos soothes.

'Me or the dog?'

His alarm jolts him so abruptly I worry he might release the animal. 'I . . . The dog, of course. I would never –'

'Joking, Matheos. Just joking.'

The dog whines.

'She is not,' Matheos tells it.

'I'm not what?' I ask, pulling at one of the kinks.

Matheos glowers, though his hand continues its soothing pats. 'Egertes here believes you're funny.'

'Wow, you were right, what an excellent dog.'

With that, I pull the final yoke free and the dog wrenches its paw out of the trap. Matheos slips the dog some dried bread from his leather bag and the animal runs off.

'Will it get back alright?'

'Oh yes,' Matheos says. 'Artemis blessed these woods. She

hunts in them sometimes. Animals in need can find their way to me, and back to wherever they need to go.'

'First Hephaestus, now Artemis?' I tease. 'How many friends among the Olympians are you hiding?'

He glowers at me, then back at the woods, like he's daring anything remotely amiable to emerge from it as he says: 'I told you. I don't have friends.'

I am pulled into a new passion for days before forgetting about it entirely, moving from weaving to sewing to painting. I delve into pottery, delighting in sculpting things out of clay, like I might be my own creator. I finish the bed, Matheos marking down numbers and holding pieces for me to nail into place, and we bicker over whether he is ludicrously tall or I am obscenely short when we have to start again because of mismeasured pieces.

The only hobbies I never tire of are cooking and engineering – always a new recipe to try, a new technique to master, or a new mystery to unravel and solve. I think mostly I like the magic of them both: combining ingredients or mechanics, the way they merge into something new. Something more than the sum of their original parts.

'Is this useful, at all?' I ask Matheos, presenting a new contraption I've been working on.

He glances up from the wine he's been decanting. The bird automatons are perfectly good at plucking the grapes and squashing them into the amphorae to ferment, and far less skilled at pouring the resultant liquid into manageable jars.

He squints. 'What is it?'

'A sort of harness.'

His eyes widen.

'For the animals, Matheos,' I scold, resisting the urge to drop it and run, out of extreme embarrassment. 'I reinforced the weave here and added some leather, then these buckles are repurposed from scrap metal but, all in, it should be strong enough to help with whatever you need – like if you need a paw lifted, it can keep the animal in place.'

'You ... made this? For me?' His expression has shifted from alarm to the same sort of vulnerable openness as when I first dropped 'Epi' from his name.

'Once again, Matheos, I have to insist that I did not make this for me.'

And this time I do practically throw it at him and dart away.

Later, Matheos finds me sketching out mechanical patterns – trying to envision what I've seen in the birds, attempting to understand how it all works. The movement, I get – how each limb twitches and every eye roams. But I'm still unsure what's forcing that momentum, what's triggering it all to come alive.

'Do you have pliers?' he asks, and when I turn I see him fiddling with one of the cuffs at his ears.

'Sure, what's wrong?'

'The fitting is a bit loose. I need to bend the loop back in. Do you want to do it?' Matheos slides the cuff off and passes it across. 'It's just that top arch, where it hooks over my ears. It should be easy – though let's hope repairing automatons means you can fix these, too, if they ever need it.'

I nod, examining the intricate metalwork in my hands. It's so detailed, like the patterns have been plucked out with a needle – golden leaves and winding vines. Beautiful as well as practical. 'Of course. Do you mind me asking what they actually *do*?' His eyes fall to my lips so I try to speak a little slower and push my hair out of my face. 'Do they make sound clearer or translate it to another sensation or change the pitch or –'

'They amplify sound by magnifying the vibrations,' he says, laughing a little. 'Though it sounds like you have some fun ideas for alternatives if I'm ever caught in a Greek fire explosion again. Hephaestus worked with Asclepius to build them for me. It's not quite like how I used to hear – they have their faults. They amplify all sound across the board, so it can be hard to pick out sounds or discern them from one another, and I guess they're not picking up on *all* sounds if you're telling me the birds have been humming this entire time – but otherwise they're brilliant.'

'Oh, interesting! I wonder how they did that.' I take up the pliers and twist the loop he points to, closing the circle a little more.

'If they ever fault, I'll ensure you're first in line to open them up and poke around,' he says. I return the cuff and he slides it back on to his ear. 'Maybe that's your purpose, actually: to leave things better than you found them.'

Matheos and I begin dining together – a new routine, alternating who cooks or sometimes managing it together, squabbling over how long to simmer grain or how finely to slice vegetables. We sit by the hearth, lingering at the table until we can no longer stifle our yawns. There's a lot of my relentless cheerfulness and Matheos grumbling but it's clear he enjoys it as much as I do.

But we've barely begun – are still carefully laying the table, gently marvelling at the easy rhythm of it all – on the night Kerkeis and Ione burst through the front door.

'Don't tell me this is about another chimera,' I mutter.

'They were –' Matheos begins.

'He's so –' Ione starts.

'No,' Kerkeis cuts across them both. 'This is actually important. It's the humans.'

Matheos rests a hand on the back of the chair like he might need the support, and I'm acutely aware of my arms tightening their hold about my sides.

'Yes?'

'Well, there have always been stories,' Kerkeis says. 'You know. Abducted shepherds turned into cupbearers and men kidnapped by the dawn itself. But . . . there are more now. So many more. With the arrival of mortal women the gods are tripling their conquests. We just got back from one of the new settlements and . . .'

'I just wanted to see what they were like,' Ione adds, voice strained. 'The women popped up after the gods made you and I wondered if, with some time to settle into themselves, they'd become more like you. Less stilted, more compulsive . . . But they're not, they're still very fixed in their ways. And the stories . . . the humans have engraved them on to the very walls of their temples, worshipping the gods who do all these horrors to them.'

Kerkeis looks genuinely sympathetic, which is alarming enough in and of itself. 'We thought you'd want to know. I'm sorry.'

'I do,' I say, nodding, but everything feels empty.

The humans. More than just a group I am a part of, they're a group I feel *responsible* for. I'm the first woman – my existence triggered theirs – and I'm safe here in this house while the gods traumatize them.

Prometheus must have felt similarly, to have sacrificed everything for them. But how is this the existence he gave it all up for?

Matheos falls quiet and, though we pick over the details, by the time Ione and Kerkeis leave we're both still sitting round the fire.

'Do you think they're trying to drive us out?' I ask. 'Going after the other mortals in the hope we try to help. Or go to Prometheus to find out how to stop it?'

'No, I don't,' he says, then sighs and buries his head in his hands. 'Like Kerkeis said, there were always stories. The gods always saw the mortals as their playthings. And given the way they treat the goddesses and nymphs, it's no wonder the existence of mortal women has those stories increasing.'

That's true. It means not all their focus is on us, that not every disgraceful thing they do is to get to me.

But it doesn't mean it isn't still connected to me. And it doesn't make it any easier to bear.

'It just makes it more crucial than ever that we stay here,' Matheos says. 'We can't risk whatever fate Prometheus saw between you and the humans. And it's too important that the prophecy Prometheus saw is allowed to unfurl. And it's not like he'd tell us what it is, anyway.'

But it doesn't look like that reassures him.

And it feels a little harder to breathe than a few hours ago, like whatever plan Zeus has intended, whatever it is we are missing, it has drawn its noose around us all and is slowly beginning to pull tight.

From there, rumours flow like the tides of the Euxine Sea: fast, timely and with vindictive violence. The gods are luring mortals into traps. They're transforming them in punishment. They're taking whole ships hostage and forcing their crews to serve in their temples because above all else the gods want one thing from the mortals: uncompromising subjugation.

'Do you think Prometheus would know how to stop them?' I finally venture to ask Matheos. He'd stopped the gods at every other turn, after all, before they took him out of the equation.

Maybe it's a mantle we could take up.

'We can't risk it,' Matheos answers abruptly, his gaze narrowing as though he suspects an ulterior motive. I suppose I do in fact have one – hoping Prometheus will not only know how to help stop such misery but also answer all those questions buzzing in my head. My patience has worn out – this is not just pressing but personal. Every day I find out more about myself, but is it really *me* or *us*?

And how can I even imply an *us* – like I am a part of something, a member of some wider humanity – if I remove myself from their suffering like this?

'I know,' I say. 'We can't go. But maybe we could get a message to him. Kerkeis or Ione could go – they said there was a stream.'

'I don't think they should risk it either,' he says. 'The gods made their play: they sent you. If they really are trying to drive us to him, then we cannot contact him at all or the gods might punish the messengers. The things the Olympians are doing are horrific but they're happening to a few, lone individuals. When they took back fire and tried to starve the humans, it was an attack on them all. I don't want to push them into that again.'

Which I must reluctantly admit is a point that I hadn't considered – that the gods' end goal, whatever it may be, might not be something we wish to rush towards.

So I try, once more, to distract myself with life here. And when we do dine the next night, we do not sit outside, on account of the howling screech of wind and cacophony of clashing waves. Matheos says it's difficult for him to discern sounds when they're that loud and the noise is coming from all around, so we perch on the counters in the kitchen instead. The wind is a distant hum, and we eat straight from the pots we cooked in.

There's something about the informality of it – the chaotic hum of the birds fluttering around us – that makes my heart ache. It's a home, really and truly. Locked away from everyone and everything else.

But that is simultaneous joy and guilt. My heart feels whole and my gut feels empty – because there is so very much we must ignore to feel such happiness.

'Are you still making notes?' Matheos asks.

He has a single leg drawn up, his knee beneath his chin, while the other trails, and his casualness, the languid ease and the way his chiton drapes around his lanky frame . . .

I picture it, cooking in this kitchen, his arms around me, spinning me to kiss him every time there is a break between ingredients.

'Yes,' I say, forcing myself to meet his eyes. This is the sort of thing I need it for, to write it all down and make sense of it. 'I enjoy exploring the way it brings all my thoughts together. I like the way my brain works.'

He smiles – and it's so easy. Wasn't it always hard, drawing those grins from him?

'I'm rather fond of it myself.'

Through all my investigations, that *want* to know the answer has been the clearest marker of myself that I have. An *I* that desires, not a passive vessel through which the gods will enact their will.

But then I look at him, and I feel that *want* I have grown to know so well.

If I am following my every instinct, then there is one in particular that I am steadfastly ignoring, a resistance that feels increasingly futile.

And that feels more dangerous than anything the gods could ever have intended.

CHAPTER SEVENTEEN

THE NIGHTMARE WAKES ME FIRST: pain and confusion, my first breath in this body, the morphing of clay to skin, now shifting again, flesh hardening, ridges rising, expanding, stretching myself so wide and thin as body becomes land, as, unable to escape, I choose to root myself in place as a solid, immovable mass. I lurch up – not an island, not clay, just flesh and blood and desperate panting breaths – and Korax barks, gruff, loud and urgent right outside my door.

Something is wrong.

I hurl myself from my bed and throw the door open, narrowly dodging the bird that was attempting to dive-bomb its way through.

'Where was this energy when we were stuck in the storeroom?' I ask, not waiting for a response because Korax is running, and I am hurtling after it.

I practically fling myself down the stairs, cannot move quickly enough for my body to keep up, and I am all flailing limbs, lurching flesh and desperately grasping hands, like I could pull myself along even faster. As I round the corner,

I see gold stains splattered across the tiles, and long slashes marked along the walls. Something that suggests haste and quick movement.

And then I remember that golden ichor pumps through immortal veins.

Blood. Our hall is filled with Matheos's blood.

I scream his name, fumbling for the door of his study, and he answers as my hand grasps the handle.

'Yes?' he calls, voice strained and taut, like spitting the word out took concerted effort.

I almost pull the door off its damn hinges.

He's propped up on the kline he once used as his bed, hand clutched about his bicep, metallic blood dripping between his fingers. He holds a needle in his mouth, is measuring thread with the other, limp hand.

'Fates, Matheos,' I say, snatching the needle from between his lips. 'What are you doing?'

'I should think that is obvious.'

'You're going to stitch *yourself* up? You didn't think to wake me?'

'I didn't want to be a bother.'

'A bother! You weren't even going to sterilize the needle! You know what's a bother, Matheos? Infection!'

I am already pushing the iron through the candle flame, the skin on my fingers beginning to burn in my unwillingness to wait even one second longer.

'Are you shouting at me for being injured?' he says, unbelievably with an amused air. 'I'm not sure I've ever heard you shout and you choose to do it now?'

'Keep pressure on that,' I insist instead of answering. I feel calm, but in a way that's almost more alarming. My mind is darting about – sterilize the wound, needle, thread, linen bandages. I prop the needle up in the flame and run to the kitchen, throwing supplies together, breathing a sigh of relief when I see the birds have already got pots boiling – water and a mix of wine and vinegar to disinfect.

I grab hold of them and run back, my pulse hammering. He'll be okay. He has to be. It is not a bad wound. I can fix this. But, Olympus above, there's so much blood.

'How do you know what you're doing?' Matheos asks almost casually, like he is not holding his own flesh together.

'The gods made sure I know how to sew.'

I push his hand away from the wound, in too much of a hurry to instruct him, washing the gash clean in careful swipes, the water shining brighter and brighter.

'What happened?' I demand.

Matheos hisses as I exchange the water for the disinfectant. Even I wince – the very mixture stings my eyes; in a wound it must burn like the Phlegethon. Gods, I wish I had willow bark or mandrake, something to numb it all for him.

'There was a bear that wasn't a bear.'

I suspected as much – the jagged edges of the wound and Matheos's veterinary proclivities had me expecting teeth or claws.

'A bear at this hour?' I ask, partly interested and partly to distract him as I thread the needle and hold his arm still. His skin is warm beneath my touch – not burning but enough for alarm – and I check him for any sign of illness I might have missed, foolishly shocked to find him so close. His eyes are tired, this pain costing him more than he wants to show.

'Hence why it wasn't actually a bear,' he says. I hold the needle up and he nods, proffering his arm. I press it in and he winces before continuing. 'Which means any power I might usually have to interact with animals was nullified. She was distressed, I thought I could help but . . . well. Evidently not. Pandora. Pandora.'

He repeats my name when I don't answer, too focused on the careful stitches. I turn to him, wondering why he's choosing now of all moments to interrupt me. His expression is heavy and insistent – with just a hint of the worry I'm feeling.

'It won't kill me. It won't even remain injured for long. I'll be fine. It's a scratch and I'm a Titan.'

He's trying to reassure *me* while I force a needle through *his* skin.

'A Titan who was bested by a bear.'

'Not a bear. I thought I was quite clear on that.'

I sigh. 'Alright, then, explain it.'

I return to the stitches, difficult now with all this blood, with how slippery the needle has become. It's getting better as I pull the skin tighter together. But, Titan or not, it's going to scar.

'Do you remember I said Artemis hunts near here sometimes?'

I hum my affirmation. I'm nearly done, can tie it off soon and bandage it up and berate him properly for letting this happen.

'The bear was one of her huntresses. Transformed. She was . . . pregnant.'

I scowl. 'Artemis's huntresses swear not to lie with men.'

'Yes.'

I let the implications of that wash over me. That maybe the goddess transformed her huntress in punishment for her transgression. Or that maybe breaking that vow was not voluntary. Or both . . .

'Oh.'

I make the final stitches in silence, then tie off the thread. I wrap the bandages around his arm and, when I'm finally satisfied, stand up from where I've been crouched by his side.

'Are we going to talk about this?' I ask.

He doesn't look at me – just reaches for the cup I'd placed beside him. I remind myself that he's lost a lot of blood and maybe now isn't the most opportune time for this conversation.

But I'm not sure it can wait.

He takes a long sip, puts the cup down and speaks. 'Firstly, I agree with the sentiment.'

'I haven't told you the sentiment.'

'The sentiment is that the gods are doing abhorrent things and you want to stop them.'

'Alright, yes, I suppose technically that is the sentiment.'

'Pandora, I don't disagree.'

There are a multitude of ways he says my name now, and this one always hits me deep, like he has reached into my chest, curled his fingers round the core of me and pulled. *Pandora* – like he is savouring it, like each individual letter weighs heavy, matters, is worth lingering on.

But it's also tinged with that reluctance I once knew so well – when each conversation with me was a thing to resist.

'But?' I push.

'They're gods. What can we possibly do?'

I've been thinking about this one for a while. In no single story does anyone fight the gods and win. Except for one – because Prometheus bested them twice. *He was the only one* who could pre-empt Zeus, match his wits – who stood a chance in his resistance.

What if that resistance could continue?

'We could speak to your brother.'

Clearly Matheos was expecting this, because his eyes flutter shut like it is a brief sting, and he shakes his head. 'We cannot do that.'

'Because it's a trap. Because the gods *want* us to get that prophecy from him, because we might give it up more readily than he has.'

'Yes, that about summarizes it.'

'But doesn't doing nothing feel like a trap too?'

'One with far less potential torture.'

'We can't refuse to act because we're scared!'

'It's not me I'm afraid for.'

My gaze falls to the wound torn across his arm, slowly clotting before my eyes. Am I truly prepared to ask him to bleed for this?

Matheos picks at the shredded edge of his chiton. 'Maybe if I thought it would fix it, I might consider it a risk worth taking. But if my brother had the power to stop this, he wouldn't be chained to Mount Caucasus right now.'

'Your brother didn't fail, he bought them centuries of peace. That's not unimportant.'

'Please,' he asks quietly.

'You can't ask that of me.'

'Don't make me lose someone else I care about to the gods' wrath. Pandora, I'm begging you; I cannot take that again.'

I still, and Matheos takes my hand, almost tentatively. His own blood dries beneath his nails, and coats the creases of my palms. He's close again, eyes big and dark and desperate. I want to soothe, want to reach out a trembling hand and stroke it down his cheek. I want to press my forehead to his and exhale against his breath, want to lean for a moment and acknowledge how hard this all is.

Is he manipulating me? Using my affection to force his will?

Did the gods intend this in their plan? A girl whose heart bleeds, to bend to the slightest push?

'I'm coated in the ichor that ought to run safely through your veins,' I say. 'What if you'd been further afield? What if you couldn't get back in time? What if I wasn't here or –'

'Pandora . . .'

'You can't insist we stay out of this when it is at our doorstep. When the consequences of the gods' will has torn into your skin.'

'This is a scratch.'

'And next time it might not be.'

He stares at me, pained in a way I suspect has little to do with the stitches in his skin. My chest heaves, the air taut with the knowledge that he is aware of each rise and fall.

We linger in that quiet a moment longer, the panting breaths, the desperate clutching.

And then I finally relent.

'I'm not rushing off tomorrow,' I say, squeezing his hand before I let go. 'We can continue to discuss it. But I'm serious, Matheos. I'm not sure how much longer I can stay out of things.'

CHAPTER EIGHTEEN

THE BIRDS SWOOP WHEN I carry the medical supplies from Matheos's room, but I shoo them off and wash it all myself, needing the time to settle my thoughts. But by morning, I'm still rattled, my mind jumping from one thing to the next without apparent link.

Matheos is gone by the time I wake so I go in search of Kerkeis and Ione and find the latter on a rock by the shore, staring out into the ocean and nervously twisting one of their bangles.

'On your own?' I ask.

Ione shrugs. 'We're fighting.'

'Oh? Not the chimera *again*? Or have you moved on to basilisks?'

I can't really imagine what a true fight between the two of them might look like. Kerkeis is sharp with everyone but Ione, and Ione so unwaveringly gentle that one firm word is often the only time Kerkeis realizes she might have gone too far.

'No, that would be far easier.' They sigh. 'Kerkeis thinks we should steer clear of mortal towns for a while – thinks it's too dangerous, that clearly the gods are looking for any excuse to cause harm and we shouldn't put ourselves in the firing line. I said if it was bad enough to need to avoid them then we should probably try to do something to help them, and she said it wasn't worth it. That we couldn't tempt the gods' retribution.'

'Ah, Matheos and I had a similar argument last night.'

Ione smiles. 'I assume you take my side – that we cannot embrace cruelty in the face of cruelty.'

'Um, I don't think I worded it quite so well.'

They laugh. 'Well, I imagine Matheos's response wasn't as artfully worded as Kerkeis's "absolutely fucking not".'

Don't make me lose someone else I care about to the gods' wrath.

I swallow. 'No, it was a little different.'

Ione continues. 'I know she's scared, and it's not like I don't get it. We were near Lipari when Apollo slaughtered the Cyclopes there because they built the thunderbolt Zeus used to kill his son. We've seen first-hand what the gods are capable of and if something happened to Kerkeis I don't know what I'd do. They're gods and we're water nymphs. There are just as many stories warning us to be careful as there are about mortal women. But are we really just supposed to cower for the rest of eternity? Surely at a certain point inaction is complicity?'

'So what do you think we should do? I assume you don't plan to personally storm Olympus?'

'No.' Ione bites at a nail, eyes flicking down. I've never seen them so dejected – and when they speak it's to their feet. 'I was thinking of using water currents – filling them with whispers, sowing seeds of rebellion. Not without risk, of course, but . . .'

'One worth taking,' I finish. I'm so tired of these arguments centred on risk, as though I haven't had the revenge of the gods drummed into my brain from the moment it was moulded in clay. *I know.* And I think we should do it anyway.

Ione nods. 'I know I'm not powerful enough to overthrow the gods, but I'm not powerless, either. I feel like I have to do *something*. And in this case, it would be all that I can do.'

'Did you discuss that with Kerkeis? Or is she just imagining open rebellion and swift punishment?'

Ione swallows. 'Probably the latter. I mean, it's not unfounded. The Cyclopes didn't even *do* anything. Fates, I should go find her. And you should speak to Matheos. I can't imagine facing off against the gods is an easy thing to consider with all that he's already lost doing that.'

I know that, too. I would not have tried so hard to be content here if I didn't. 'He doesn't have to join me.'

Ione levels me with a cold, hard glare. 'I think we both know that's not an option for him. He is with you. It's what he does: follows those he trusts into whatever depths they drag him to.'

I don't see Matheos until the sky breaks, its colours slipping apart and trickling into the ocean below. We'd planned to dine by the shore this evening, so I find him beside a pile of blankets gathered in preparation for the way the temperature cracks, sudden and harsh, the moment the sun dips behind the horizon.

He's a few steps closer to the forest, crouched beside a tur that must have wandered down from the very mountains I wish to visit, holding it still as he prises a rusted arrow from the goat's side.

I am about to offer help when he closes his eyes and I feel a shift in the air, not quite a chill, more a pressure swelling. His magic at work.

The sleeve of his chiton is rolled up, baring the wound of last night – already healed to a pale bronze line. I follow those other lines, the fine muscles of his arms flexing as he curls those strong hands about the arrow shaft and pulls. Matheos is beautiful, but there's something specific about seeing him in motion that captures a harder beauty still, the elegance of a diving fisher-bird, the anticipation of a cresting wave, and all those careful motions he makes, like every slight thing he does is considered and intentional.

The creature doesn't so much as flinch, and the wound bleeds a slow, thick trickle that Matheos quickly bandages, barely finishing before the animal has sprinted away.

This. This is what I am pulling him from – this life that means so much to him, the small made so expansive. That no creature is unworthy of his time, that each act of care is important and more divine than the gods in their Heavens.

But here I am, swept up in the larger currents of the Olympians. Perhaps even drawing him with me.

'I'm going to Prometheus,' I say before I lose my nerve. 'I'd like you to come with me but I also understand if you can't.'

Matheos turns to face me, but doing so has him silhouetted by the setting sun so that I can't read him beyond the rigidity of his every limb.

'Is this up for discussion?'

'Of course, that's why I'm here. I don't want to do this behind your back, Matheos.'

'Why do you want to do it at all?' he demands, voice low

and soft but trembling – like he is fighting to remain calm. He steps forward, out of the blinding light. He looks stricken.

'Because the humans are –'

'None of your problem! You've never met them.'

I blink at him, a little taken aback. This sudden hostility jars against the care I just witnessed – and surely I do not have to explain compassion to a man who whispers soothing refrains to injured dormice. 'Do you have to meet someone to know you don't want them to suffer?'

'No, Pandora, of course not. But to do all this . . . you need some form of proper attachment, surely. You're not proposing speaking to Zeus on their behalf, you're suggesting getting advice from a convicted traitor. Even *speaking* about this is treason. And that's before considering that we would almost certainly be playing right into their hands.'

'But maybe there's a way to bring it all forward – trigger that fated course Prometheus has imagined and hurtle towards that end point of Zeus losing power. Surely in Colchis of all places, where time itself is malleable, we might be at an advantage. Move ourselves ahead, take the prophecy not as a future to unfold but steps to enact. If he tells us what they're planning or how we can –'

'He *won't*, Pandora! Olympus above, please trust that I know my brother well enough to be certain he won't just share all the intricacies of his millennia-old plans or the prophecy he's never disclosed just because we turn up and ask.'

'But you're his brother.'

'Our other brother lies dead,' Matheos says, his frustration giving way to a cold, flat dejection that blunts his words and lends menace to his gaze. 'Another holds up the sky. Prometheus is brilliant, Pandora. He is not one to be swayed by familial ties. The only one he ever gave glimpses of his plan to was his wife and even then neither of us had the full picture because it was too much of a risk.'

He is fixed on me, his every word intent and pointed. I cannot tell whether he wishes me to give in or fight back, let him have some kind of outlet for this intensity broiling inside. But I am beginning to see how futile all of this is. We've talked and talked about this, and it's never going to be enough to undo the years of struggle and heartbreak.

'That's dreadful, Matheos,' I say, trying again anyway. 'You do realize that, right? To demand you follow his orders without explaining enough to give you a choice. That's what Zeus does and –'

'Pandora,' Matheos groans, tearing his fingers through his hair in frustration. 'This is precisely the problem. You think if he stands against the gods then he must be everything you're hoping for. Someone good and fair and just. But he's not. Which is exactly why he's effective. Keeping Hesione and me in the dark was the only reason the gods didn't torture the information from us when he refused to give it. He's protecting us and protecting the humans precisely because he does not explain. Because he can make the difficult decisions so that no one else has to face the consequences for doing so.'

'Maybe I *want* to make my own decisions and face the consequences.'

'You're an idealist. And you know nothing of this world.'

I tense. 'Well, maybe I should see more of it, then. Perhaps it'll cure me of my naivety.'

He meets my glower with his own. 'So you're going to get yourself killed to spite me?'

'Have you considered that if the gods sent me, they trust me? I can use that. I can lie to them about whatever Prometheus tells me.'

'*All* I have considered is that the gods sent you.' He steps closer, so that I have to arch my neck as he snarls: 'And right now why they did is more apparent than ever.'

We linger in loud silence, the quick rise and fall of his chest only inches away, his taut gaze locked on me – and the waves crashing about us, the wind whistling like arrows sniping through the air.

His words echo in the quiet.

All this time, as I uncovered so much complexity within myself, and he still sees me as nothing more than a thing to resist. Where I thought we might have grown to care about one another, he still suspects me, still resents me, still believes me nothing but an assigned purpose.

'That's what you think this is. The gods have just been biding their time with my brain, setting a trap, luring you in.'

I watch as he swallows, the dimple at his throat shadowing. 'Maybe. Would that be so ludicrous?'

I don't argue with him. If he still thinks I am nothing more than the gods' will incarnate, I won't dissuade him. So instead, I ask what seems so much more pressing: 'Does it make it easier for you, Matheos, to believe everything you like about me is a deceit?'

'That's not fair.' His voice is pained and I feel the tension between us like a physical strain, a pull in my chest, like one more tug and it may burst open completely. 'It's not unreasonable to doubt your motivations. I cannot ignore the facts just because I . . . ' His eyes are dark and impenetrable against the setting sun but they're locked on me with unwavering focus. 'I lied,' he says slowly. 'When I told you that you were perfect for the man I pretended to be. That I could not care any less about you.'

I know, I think, but the words die on my tongue because that does not seem to be all he wants to say.

'They succeeded, Pandora.' He spits the words, takes the sentiments and snarls them hatefully. 'And if I'm to admit that then I have to put distance between us. If I want to take the sliver of you that I'll allow myself to have, then it will always have to be tainted by this scepticism.'

The wind whips off the cliff, my hair snapping around my face, our words a sharp crack above.

'You'll allow yourself?' I repeat.

'Can't you see it? Because I can. If I let myself fall for you, I would. If they created you to lure me into a trap, I'd go. If you're here to warp my mind, it will bend. That path is *visceral*.' His words slice through the air, and, oh gods, what beautiful evil – loving words sharpened to a knife's edge. Words I've dreamt of hearing ground out like they burn, like there is nothing more horrific to him than the idea of them. They are an agony.

And still he continues, like he has a blade he needs to drive home. 'I'll allow myself only this friendship because I fear I'd lose myself in the fall.' His chest heaves, but he no longer snarls, no longer shouts, is sorrowful as he says: 'I could love you, Pandora, and that is exactly what the gods want of me.'

If I kissed him now, would it break him?

I want to. I'd love nothing more than to shatter his resolve with his own hunger.

We could, couldn't we? Just the two of us, here at the edge of the world.

But I'm used to dissecting my own feelings by now, and I recognize a sheen to my desire, that same fire twisted. Anger.

I see it for what it is. It is Hermes sneering at my supposed lust for Hephaestus. It is Apollo's lascivious smiles turning to snarls of disdain when he discovered I was spoken for. It is the agony in Matheos's voice as he declares his supposed affection – or the potential for it.

They can hate you every bit as much as they love you. They can despise you even as they long for you. They will hurt you while declaring their affection.

'You don't get to like me while wishing you didn't, Matheos. I deserve a love that isn't some man's lamentation.'

'I don't love you,' he says softly, almost wistfully. Like loving me would be the easier option. 'That's not what I'm saying.'

'And that's not what *I'm* saying,' I rebut, a little harsher than I'd intended but I am so very tired of keeping myself in line. 'I don't care to debate the semantics – love, affection, this draw between us that you wish didn't exist. Aphrodite told me I was made for love – and if this is even a semblance of it then I don't want it. I'm going. I'll speak to Prometheus, I'll find out what it means to be mortal and, best of all, I won't be *here*.'

I turn, walking away before the wound festering inside me drags its hurt to the surface. He doesn't get to see it.

'So you're just going to behave exactly as they created you to?' Matheos overtakes me, turns to face me, is clearly expecting me to stop.

I push right past him, not slowing even as the house appears. 'Perhaps! I'll send my congratulations to them once I get there.'

'Pandora –'

'No, Matheos! Maybe my actions align with the gods' wishes and maybe they don't. Either way, they are *mine*. I refuse to be a piece the gods have placed on the board. If they are playing a game against Prometheus then so be it, but I'll become a participant.'

I push the gate open, expecting Korax to run up to greet me like it always does when I return home.

But it's already busy, tail wagging ferociously as a woman scratches its ears. She turns as the gate groans open, and I take her in: a tall, lithe form, dark hair which falls in an arrow-straight sheet, everything about her angular and precise, like a nail wouldn't dare break without her express permission.

Behind me, Matheos makes a somewhat strangled sound.

The woman looks up, eyes darting between us before she pins her scrutiny on Matheos.

'So the rumours are true. I take it, then, that there is truth to everything my husband has supposedly been screaming from that mountain. I think it's time the two of us had a conversation, Epimatheos.'

Matheos collects himself – or rather, the shutters fall tight across his face and he retreats into the shadows. From within their depths, he says: 'Good evening, Hesione.'

Hesione.

Wife of Prometheus.

CHAPTER NINETEEN

ATHEOS'S EASY SMILE FALLS INTO place a moment later. Gleeful and vacant – the performance of Epimatheos, that foolish, easily dismissed afterthought.

I'd thought it was just an act for the gods. But here he is plucking it out for his own family and I don't like that one bit.

'It's been years!' he says. 'Perhaps centuries. I confess I don't really understand all the time-warping effects of Colchis.'

Hesione regards him with a steady, shrewd expression that reminds me of Athena. Like she sees him flitting about, this movement of smiles and babbling words, and is waiting for the moment she can throw her spear and pin him in place.

'Yes, well, I trust I don't have to remind you of the last time we spoke.'

Matheos stiffens – and if anything it forces the smile deeper.

'Please, have a seat,' I say, summoning up my own role. Hostess. Besotted wife. A veritable delight who was not fighting with her husband mere moments ago. 'Unless you'd rather be indoors? I'll fetch refreshments.'

Hesione turns that expression on me – sharp and piercing.

It cuts me for a moment, but she breaks it quickly with an entertained huff. 'I see.'

Matheos takes my hand, standing a little in front of me like he would shield me from her view entirely if he could. And in that moment I forget the heat of our argument, or that a part of him might agree with her suspicion and hostility, and there is only his tall body standing beside me, and his hand curled tight around mine.

'Hesione, can I please introduce you to my wife, Pandora.'

He lingers on those words: *my wife*. Like they mean something to him.

And an edge, too, a warning to Hesione's disrespect.

I clutch him a little tighter.

'Yes, I have heard what happened, Epimatheos,' she snaps. 'How could you? You accepted a gift from the gods – knowing your brother specifically warned you against such a thing?'

Matheos tenses, and I can almost see cogs turning, can imagine quicksilver flashing through his mind. 'I . . . I didn't realize,' he says, letting his gaze fall. 'I wasn't expecting the gift to be a person, so –'

'You are an utter fool. I expected many things to be your undoing but I thought even you'd do better than to risk everything, blinded by lust.'

'Hesione,' I say, her name a sharp hiss on my tongue. 'Please, *do* have a seat,' I repeat. 'You're a guest in our home.'

Matheos's hand squeezes mine and I'm not sure whether it's a silent thanks for defending him or a warning against doing it again – as though I can just stand there as she insults him.

Hesione's eyes narrow at this curt reminder of the laws of hospitality currently binding us.

A BEAUTIFUL EVIL

But she turns, struts to the chairs and plants herself within one.

'Well, my love,' I say to Matheos. He turns to me, eyes flickering with a panic I haven't seen there before, and I force a smile. 'Why don't you sit, too, and I'll fetch us some wine and instruct dinner preparations.'

'Korax can –'

'No,' Hesione calls loudly. 'Let her go. I would speak to you without . . .' She stills, unable to say any of the things she would gladly call me within the confines of propriety that xenia dictates.

'You're right, darling husband, Korax can fetch refreshments.'

Hesione's nostrils flare. 'That is not –'

Matheos gives her a blank smile like he doesn't understand why this might be a problem. 'Anything you have to say can most certainly be said in front of my wife.' He draws a chair out and a little more assertively says: 'Here, Pandora, please sit.'

Oh, so he trusts me again, does he? Unless I'm little more than another shield he's throwing up – a way to stop Hesione berating him for the plans he has supposedly ruined by preventing her from discussing them at all. Wouldn't want *risk incarnate* to hear your plans of rebellion, I suppose.

But there's something else at play here, something that has Matheos on edge, and given the way this woman is treating him, I don't particularly want to leave him alone with her, either. So I take a seat.

Korax must have overheard, or maybe it's just programmed to behave like this whenever there are guests, because I remember when we first arrived and it ran out, laden with wine. It does the same now, tray balanced on its back, oinochoe full of dark-red wine.

'So, is that what you're here for?' Hesione asks me as I pour. 'To play the dutiful housewife?'

'I'm here to love Epimatheos.'

I say it boldly, unable to even look at him as I say it. I should be all bright gleaming smiles and saccharine looks of adoration but there's only so far I can pretend right now. Skirt too close to the truth – of all the things I feel for this man and all the things I know he feels too, and all the ways we have corrupted it – and I'm not sure I could choke the words out through my closing throat.

'And what has Epimatheos ever done to be worthy of such a thing as love?'

'Excuse me?' I hiss before I can think better of it. All my pain bleeds red, and the rage – *finally* – consumes me. 'Who are you to come into our home and insult my husband?'

'The wife of the one who took the fall,' she tosses back, taking up her cup of wine and leaning back to level me with the weight of her disregard. 'And I am here to remind him that instead of shouldering any of that responsibility, Matheos is traipsing around Colchis with some hapless harlot who threatens the very people my husband bleeds to protect.'

'Hesione,' Matheos says, voice calm and measured. 'By all means continue to berate me – I certainly deserve it. But please leave Pandora out of it – she did not ask to be involved in this.' She goes to speak but he rushes on: 'I assume you did not come here after all this time solely to insult us both.'

She takes a breath and seems to remember herself. I can see it all, the hurt and grief, the desire to find someone to blame, someone she can scream at because she cannot fight Zeus. I catalogue it, the need to become a mirror, to be irresistible. But I don't care, I don't sympathize, I want her gone.

And then she speaks.

'The humans. You must have heard, even out here, what's going on. The things the gods are doing.'

Matheos and I glance at each other. That unspoken agreement to play the roles the gods assigned us: foolish Epimatheos and his dutiful wife, crumbling like weatherworn cliffs against a harsh gale.

'We've heard rumours,' Matheos says carefully.

'Prometheus has sacrificed everything for them,' Hesione says, voice strained. 'We can't let them suffer like this. We can't let it all be for nothing.'

Matheos nods. 'But what can we do?'

She presses her lips together, thin lines puckering around them, and I note that they spider from her eyes, too. She looks exhausted. 'We may not be clever enough to think of a solution.'

I have never met Prometheus, and am unsure I hold him in much regard, but I've been told enough that I hear what she is not saying: *but he is.*

'But he said we were to remain here until –'

My head snaps to Matheos. *Until* has never once been uttered – not in any of his insistences that we stay put.

'The plan needs to change,' Hesione says, cutting him off with an anxious glance in my direction. *The plan?* All this time working out why the gods sent me when this subterfuge was underway? If the gods knew – or suspected – and gave me above all else a curiosity that could not be stilled, then wouldn't this be their intent? To send a spy disguised as a wife to discover the scheme at work?

'The plan can't change,' Matheos says with resolute firmness. 'Not while Prometheus is still bound, how could we –'

'Just trust me, darling brother, please.' She sets her cup down and leans forward, and I'm glad his hands are clasped in mine because she looks as though he might take them. 'I've travelled to a dozen oracles and examined the threads in countless shroves and shrines. All I can discern is that destiny is diverting from the path we've worked so hard to ensure is fated. And the only thing that's changed in that time is . . . her. You've jeopardized everything and now I'm asking you to set it right. Prometheus wouldn't trust anyone else with something like this – only you.'

'Not you?' I interject, tempering my anger. To come here and insult Matheos then demand his action. I may have begged him to go but I certainly wouldn't manipulate him into thinking all this – everything the gods are doing – is his fault. And I was always planning on going with him. I would not let him shoulder this danger alone.

But she would have him take this risk on her behalf.

'It's too precarious,' she says. 'I'm his wife. They're always looking at me. Even coming here took several misdirections. I could not get anywhere near that mountain.'

'And you think Matheos can?'

She arches a brow at the name, and I curse myself for my carelessness. I do not want her to gauge anything of the truth of us, only to pay attention to the roles we are playing.

'*Matheos*,' she sneers – and I hate it, hate the way she takes that kindness and laces it with disdain – 'has, by the very nature of his cravenness, made himself invisible. No one pays attention to him.'

Matheos does not even flinch; it is as though he expects it.

'Well, evidently not, or I wouldn't be here,' I counter. 'You think they sent the thing changing the future to a man who doesn't matter?'

'Pandora,' Matheos says and when I turn I see he's not looking at me but at her. 'I think perhaps Hesione was right and it would be better for us to speak in private. There are things you cannot know. So would you mind leaving us for a brief while?'

My protestations die in my throat. Because of course – why should this surprise me when he just stood by the ocean shouting that he still cannot trust me?

What does it matter, anyway? I have come to my decision; all this is a distraction.

I don't care to persuade him any more. I'm going to Prometheus.

Hesione is forcing the wrong hand.

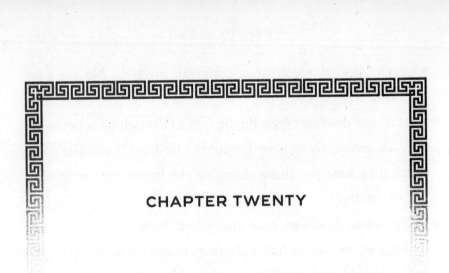

CHAPTER TWENTY

CALL TO KERKEIS AND Ione, and after a few moments they pull themselves from the water, shimmering as their liquid forms solidify.

'Hello, sorry, we were at a party, got here as fast as we could,' Kerkeis says, reaching over to adjust the pin holding Ione's dress together. Given the frizz mussing up Kerkeis's normally sleek and shiny hair, I suspect a party is not what I interrupted and while I'm somewhat apologetic for that, I am at least relieved to know they've made up.

'Sorry, I didn't mean to cause any urgency.'

'Well, it's not often you call.' Ione shrugs.

It's a strange sort of dark by the ocean at night, the deep impenetrable. Yet where the light shines on the water – the stars and moon and their reflections – it could burn almost brighter than the sun.

It's enough to see the way their faces fall when I say: 'I want to visit Prometheus. And the humans. Can you tell me how to get to them?'

They share a look I can't decipher.

'Epimatheos knows how to get there,' Kerkeis says slowly, like she's solving a puzzle with each word. 'So I assume he is not a part of this? Is he at least aware?'

I nod, my stomach tightening. What if they don't help? Do I just walk in a direction and hope for the best? Surely I'd reach some semblance of civilization eventually?

'Yes, he knows. He disagrees but I'm going anyway. I told him as much. He's not happy about it, obviously, so I don't think he'd give me directions.'

Kerkeis shakes her head. 'It's so dangerous.' She looks at Ione and my guilt doubles. 'Why can't you just stay out here and be thankful you're safe? Being hurt by the gods isn't going to make the humans suffer less. And you can't possibly believe you're going to make the situation better.'

'Kerkeis,' Ione says gently. 'Sometimes you still have to try.'

'That's idiotic.'

It is a little, I suppose. 'I think a great deal of the gods' power comes from convincing us they have all of it, and we have none. But I don't think they'd see us as such a threat to be stopped if we were actually so inconsequential.'

Kerkeis looks stricken. 'Why us? There are so many people in this world, why should we be the ones to fix it? Do you think witnessing the way Prometheus's skin knits itself together, the way the flesh weeps, will give you the strength to stop them? It will break you. It's not wrong to cower in the face of all that hideous might. It's certainly not wrong to do all you can to protect those you love from the same fate.'

'It is not a matter of simple right or wrong,' I say. 'It's far more complicated than that. But I also know myself – after all, isn't that what I've spent months trying to unravel? And I think

I have to do something. Aside from anything else, they're human. I'm human. They're *my* people the gods threaten.'

Ione crosses over to me and wraps their arms around me, not letting me go until I break the hold myself – which I take some time to do.

I might not have Matheos any more.

But I am so thankful not to weather this alone.

'I can't encourage this, Pandora,' Kerkeis says almost desperately. 'Please, please, don't do this.'

'Maybe we can't encourage it,' Ione replies, squeezing my shoulder in a way that suggests they, at least, are indeed encouraging it. 'But we don't get to make that decision for you. Do you have parchment? We only go by the ocean and rivers, but I think we know enough of the directions to give you a steer.'

I take my rough-hewn map and I sit with them for a while. When I tell them Hesione's visiting, Kerkeis hisses, 'That fucking woman,' but won't elaborate further – though having met her for all of a few minutes I can't say I disagree.

I wait until I'm certain Matheos must have finished speaking with her before making my way back. I'll pack a bag, and set the automatons making rations. Hard, dense grain loaves, jars of pastes and preserves, dried fruit and pouches of nuts. The sort of thing that can last a long time – and if I make the batters and mixtures, it will not be too awful to let the birds finish it. I'll gather supplies – maybe borrow a chlamys from Matheos to drape over my silk chitons. I'll go straight to bed after, and set off in the morning, before Matheos wakes and thinks to stop me.

But I can hear Korax barking long before I reach the house, and when I rush into the courtyard, the automaton nearly trips me from where it stands on the other side of the door.

Hesione sits alone, picking at oat biscuits I made earlier in the day.

'Where is Epimatheos?' I ask, forcing my voice calm when everything in me insists that something is very wrong.

'Gone,' she says, taking another bite, chewing slowly and turning her hand over to examine a nail that must be far more interesting to her than the girl she claims has ruined everything she's ever worked for.

'What do you mean?' I snap. 'Gone where?'

Did she work him up so much that he stormed out? Is he just off somewhere looking for animals to save while he calms down?

But then why would Korax be barking like this?

'Where do you think?' she scoffs. 'I told him where to go and he went.'

My face blanches. 'He wouldn't go. He's spent the last week refusing to even discuss it.'

'Yes,' she says, pulling apart another biscuit. 'He didn't want to take the risk. Or, apparently, he didn't want *you* to take the risk.' I catch the edge of her eye-roll. 'But I've made him see sense. He's going to his brother, and you're going to wait here.'

I stare at her. 'He said that, did he?'

'No, I'm saying it. He didn't really say much at all, just packed a bag the moment you left and set off. He told me to keep you safe. Epimatheos is a wonderful boy, but if you think you can take advantage of his kindness and gullibility, know that he has his family behind him.' She finally looks at me, and her eyes are vacuously cold. 'And we are not so easily swayed.'

I don't stay to hear more of whatever she has to say. I do not fetch supplies, do not remain to bake rations, do not do anything at all sensible.

I just think of how far he might have got in – how long? One hour? Two?

I hold the door open for Korax.

'Come on, let's go get him.'

CHAPTER TWENTY-ONE

KNOW MATHEOS WELL ENOUGH to know he won't be clinging to the cliff edge like I do. He is at home in the forests, trusts the trees the way I trust gears and levers, that one cog will turn after the next.

But it feels too dangerous to abandon the natural path of the coast and plunge into the depths of the woods.

Not that this is much better. Korax's eyes glow softly to illuminate a few feet ahead of us. The coastline thins as we move north, the trees encroaching, the cliff edge drawing sharper. And the wind howls so ferociously I worry it might haul us right off the side. Hair lashes my face, the cold bite of the air churned off the ocean – perhaps we need the trees to shelter us from it. But even clinging to the forest's edges feels too great a risk, thinking of that bear, and the chunk it tore out of Matheos's arm.

I draw my own arms in, trying to keep myself from shaking. It's cold in a way I've never felt before, the chill rising from the heavy night air and the plunging ocean, a cold that cuts straight through the weave of your chiton, slices through your skin and into your very bones.

I did not think this through and it might kill me.

'We have to go in, don't we?' I ask Korax, who just looks at me with tilted head, waiting for instruction.

'I don't suppose you have some sort of compass attachment? Your tail always points north?'

Korax is not forthcoming, though, to be fair to it, I got lucky enough with the torches in its eyes. Anything further would truly be pushing it.

I know this is incredibly foolish – I might never find Matheos in there. He might even have stopped and I have overshot him. Though if his subterfuge is any indication, he has to at least suspect I'll come after him, or else why try to get such a head start?

'Okay, we're going in but we can't lose sight of the stars. That bright one ahead? That's what we're following.'

Korax barks in agreement.

At least, I assume it's agreement.

The forest is startling, the way we are mere moments away from the ocean, but seconds after we enter its depths the sound of sea colliding against rough rocks ceases.

And then other noises take over: snapping twigs, scuttling in the undergrowth, distant bird calls and rustling leaves that make me jump at regular intervals.

Korax's light hardly penetrates this dark and the stars flicker in and out of view above the foliage. It's a little warmer but the cold feels irreversible, the damage done. I feel like I might submerge myself in flame and still never be warm again.

We keep walking, eyes forward, not daring to look when the

occasional fox darts across our path or something slithers in the branches above.

There are wolves in these forests, I know that for sure. Bears too. Maybe worse – the monsters Ione has gleefully described, cast out into these far reaches.

Then Korax begins barking, leaps in front of me, bends low and growls.

Ahead, a large cat-like creature prowls out of the darkness.

My fear bites, strong and acidic, and I clutch at Korax, letting my fingers trail along its back like I am trying to soothe it rather than myself.

Korax bares teeth and the lynx stops, looking at it almost curiously. It tilts its head to the side, then without warning leaps up, scuttling into the trees and – hopefully – away.

I do not let go of Korax as we set off again and I wonder about Matheos in these woods. His abilities with animals had reassured me that he would be fine. But what if one pounced on him when he was unaware, before he could make clear who he was? I think of the slick of his blood, the resistance of his skin as I pierced it with a needle. The desperate need to fix him.

And then, almost as though I have summoned him, he crashes out of the patch of forest in front of us.

His face is thunderous, and he stalks forward, ripping his cloak off as he does. 'What the hell are you doing here?'

He practically throws his cloak around my shoulders – which is all very disconcerting, to be yelled at and warmed at the same time – so much so that I spend a good moment gaping at him before scoffing: 'I might ask you the same question!'

'You know exactly why I'm here.'

'No, Matheos, I don't, actually. I'd know why you were here if it were tomorrow, in the bright crest of a new day with a perfectly sensible packed lunch swinging by our sides. I'd know why you were here if we'd settled in this spot to take a nice break from all the walking. But here? Charging through the forest to stumble upon me because you stormed off in the dead of night after making me think I was not privy to some conversation so you could sneak off alone? No, that I don't understand at all.'

My hand closes around the cloak, fist curled tight to draw it closer to me, and when I feel my nails press through I realize the full extent of my anger.

Olympus above, he left me! He tried to cut me out of my own plan, decided my will was not as important as his.

'Firstly, I didn't stumble upon you; several animals began discussing a strange glowing dog. A lynx reported your whereabouts to me and I had to trail back and, I might add, considerably to the east of where we are supposed to be.'

'*Firstly?*' I choke. 'You abandon me in the middle of the night with your sister-in-law – who's awful, by the way – and you think that is the first point that needs rectifying?'

Matheos takes a breath, his chest heaving, and he's close, looking down from all his height, his chiton just a touch too thin.

'I was worried,' he confesses, voice breaking with the immensity of his apparent concern, his newfound relief.

'Well, I was too,' I say. 'When I got back and you weren't there. When Hesione said you'd come out here alone.'

'I am fine in these woods.'

'Perhaps. But if you're foolish enough to betray me and sneak off like this, who knows what danger might otherwise befall you.'

'Betray you? I was trying to save you!' he fumes. 'To take this awful risk instead of you.'

'I don't need saving, Matheos. And I certainly don't need you making decisions for me! I told you I was doing this. I said I refused to be a part of the games and wished to become a player. And you decided you'd go instead? When you wouldn't even consider coming with me?'

'Hesione said to go. That changes things.'

'That's not an answer.'

Matheos takes another breath. He seems thoroughly exhausted – and even though I'm sure it is partly just the late hour, it seems likely a bigger part of it is the way our arguments seem to spiral.

'It is possible my family has a predilection for self-sacrifice,' he says at last. 'I'll try to work on it.'

'Try quickly, because I'm here and I'm going to those mountains.'

Matheos glowers. 'I'm going to be angry about the danger you've put yourself in for at least the rest of the evening. And that's not even taking into account the fact you went into the forest alone at night. Did you bring *anything* with you? You look freezing.'

'I am,' I admit, then straighten up and lift my chin. 'Someone panicked me into running out the door before I could pack.'

'You're blaming *me*?' he asks, sliding his bag from his shoulder and pulling open the ties.

'It might have been somewhat foolish of me,' I admit.

Matheos draws out a thick, woven blanket and drapes that about me too, his hands lingering on my shoulders.

'Thank you,' I say but, now we're standing rather than moving, my body begins shaking quite violently.

Matheos sighs. 'We'll camp here, then. We'll have to share a tent, and, well, I only brought the one blanket.'

'Are you asking me to cuddle for warmth?' I tease though my heart picks up its pace.

He arches a brow. 'You're the one who's cold – I'd consider it more that I am offering my services.'

'Your services as a hearth are greatly appreciated.'

Korax barks, and looks at Matheos expectantly.

Matheos sighs and pays it some attention, scratching at the latch behind the scruff of its neck in the spot Korax seems to enjoy.

'I like that it waited until after we were done arguing.'

Matheos scowls. 'We weren't arguing. It was ... mild bickering. I can't believe you brought Korax with you.'

'Someone was irritated mere moments ago about me venturing into the woods alone. I thought you'd see bringing the dog along for protection as a brilliant move.'

'A dog, I might agree. This hunk of metal?' He cuts Korax a look of disdain, though doesn't stop scratching it.

'It's here because it was worried about you, and here you are, being horribly mean to it.'

'I am simply saying that we are on a journey on which we should be trying our utmost to hide from the watching eyes of the gods, and you brought an invention Hephaestus can probably track.'

'Well, the same could be said about me.'

Matheos looks at me sharply. 'You aren't an automaton.'

'Are you sure about that?'

'Yes,' he says decidedly, not leaning into the joke for even a moment. 'And for the record, I'm not trying to pick you apart because I suspect you of being some mindless tool of the gods. I was told not to accept a gift from the gods and I did. My brother warned me against you, Pandora. I do not believe it is because you are biding your time to betray humanity. It's me. I'm the one who's the risk. Just like I let you through my door in the first place, maybe I'll make the wrong choice again, blinded by my affection. Maybe they'll leverage our love somehow – I do not know what the gods are working towards or *how* love would damn us, only that it will if we choose it.'

I feel my heart in my throat. 'Your brother warned you against accepting me. That was the decision that would undo us – not whatever we might become after it. He said nothing about us. He certainly said nothing of love.'

'You cannot take my brother's words so literally. That's not the way things work with prophecy. His meaning was quite clear. And besides, even if we take all that out of the equation, if we're right, and going to my brother is what the gods want us to do, then we are once again falling into whatever trap they have laid. If they told you we were to fall in love, then resisting that is the one place we might claw back a shred of power. The threads of fate are complex: even the slightest variation can have an impact. And in this instance, denying the gods this one thing might be the key to preventing a thread forming where Zeus clings to power for the rest of time.'

I clutch that blanket tighter and try not to look right at him, because I don't want to see the intensity of his gaze when I, reluctantly, agree: 'Alright, on that you have a point. Strategy-wise, it's the only aspect of all this we can remain in control of. I suppose, regardless of *what* exactly he said, your brother didn't want me crossing that threshold for a reason. And maybe you're right. Maybe it's because he knew our love might undo us all in the end. And that *maybe* feels too big a thing to risk.'

Matheos nods but he doesn't look particularly relieved I am agreeing to this. 'I just need you to know that you were right. You deserve someone who wants you, who thanks the Heavens every day for the opportunity to love you, and I —' He cuts himself off, then heaves a deep sigh as he realizes he's come too far to back down. 'I'm *not* thankful for you. I'm resentful. My every thought of you is a wish that I felt nothing, because it's the only way we might all survive this. But . . . just know that when I question you, when I turn your every word over again and again, it is only because I cannot get them out of my mind.'

I reach for him, my hand on his arm, because it's near, because it's all I can let myself touch.

'Matheos,' I say quietly, lured in despite myself.

I risk glancing at him and . . .

He is handsome in the moonlight — his usual delicate precision enhanced by the shadows clinging beneath his jaw, in the planes of his cheeks, the hollow of his throat. His eyes shine beneath the glow of the stars, seem all the more intent on me, like we have captured one another in our gaze.

'Please don't,' he whispers. 'If you tempt me right now, my determination will falter.'

'Maybe I should let it.'

I want to clutch him to me, want to curl my hand into his chiton and pull him down to me, to press my lips to his, to trail them along his jaw, his neck, anywhere I can reach.

I deserve more than this, but this – *this!* – oh, I could so happily settle for this. After all our worry and stress, all the fear of where we are going and what we face, why should we resist when we could lose it all? Why hold ourselves back?

Except, of course, for the many reasons we've just discussed as to why we shouldn't. I remember Aphrodite's fingers trailing down my face, filling me with such desire. The gods wanted this, made me chaste and wanton in equal measure. He's right: this does feel like a trap, or at the very least like a vulnerability. Something for them to exploit, a crack to prise open the rest.

And that other reason, the one I do not want to fully acknowledge but which is there all the same: could I do this to him? The gods have taken so much. And this is dangerous. The gods truly might punish us for going to Prometheus or devise tortures to rinse information from us if they think we have it. It is one thing to push Matheos away so they will not hurt him in order to pull truth from me. Another to push him away so they will not hurt me to get to him – not for my own preservation, but because he has built a fortress of miles of barren land and leagues of emptiness between him and Olympus, because his heart is fragile. I do not want to be the thing that breaks it. I do not want to be another thing for him to lose.

I should shut this off before I become another pain for him to bear.

And yet . . .

'I agree that we shouldn't,' I say. But I don't let go.

'We can't.' His eyes dart across my face, like he is looking for an out, like he needs me to stop this.

'We can't,' I echo. My mouth feels so dry.

Korax barks.

The moment shatters into laughter, both of us catching our breath.

'Oh Fates, you brought a chaperone,' Matheos chuckles.

'Apparently.'

I take up the long poles Matheos has strapped to the side of his bag and together we build the tent. My fingers are too numb to thread the rope through the holes in the hemp sheet so Matheos takes over. It takes longer than it should – it's late and we're both so tired, our limbs heavy with exhaustion. Now the cold begins to subside I'm aware of how sore my thighs are, the way they chafed as I walked, and all I want is to clamber somewhere warm and rest until everything stops aching.

When we're done, Korax settles like a guard outside the door and we fall inside, Matheos drawing the blanket up around us. He's right: his warm body beside me is a good source of heat.

I wish we weren't lying like two parallel lines, as far apart as we can possibly be beneath the blanket. Though, still, it is not all that far – a shift in the night and we will be pressed together – and somehow that is even worse than if we were to touch right now. With so little distance to traverse and the impossibility of remaining still, our coming together is weighted with inevitability, like each second might draw us a little closer.

'How long a journey is it?' I ask, staring at the canvas stretched above.

'Two weeks.'

'Fourteen nights.'

'Thirteen after this one.'

'That seems doable.'

'Absolutely,' he says. 'What could possibly go wrong?'

'Possibly, referring to us being together as "going wrong"?'

'Well, we need a backup for when the dog doesn't interrupt us in time. An argument certainly hasn't failed us before.'

'A fair point.'

'Goodnight, Pandora.'

'Goodnight, Matheos.'

We fall asleep clinging to the hope that we might get through this. A thought that feels, almost certainly, like a lie we are praying to believe.

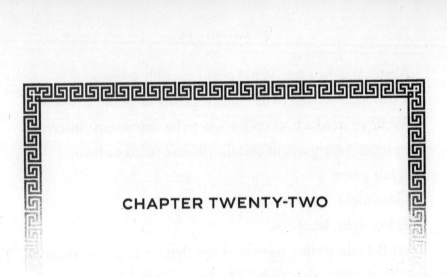

CHAPTER TWENTY-TWO

MY NIGHT IS DIVIDED CLEANLY in two. There is the first half, me ultra-aware of every slow breath Matheos takes, his body beside mine, the way he tosses and turns and – crucially – the way I am sure he is not sleeping either. The other things, too: the sound of the forest around us alive and moving, the rough ground that our thin sheet cannot soften, the questions running through my mind, the way it simply will not still. And then the second half of the night: when sleep closes over me like an abrupt and sudden blow.

I do not dream. I do not stir. I am so thoroughly exhausted my mind must have shut down in protest. Until all at once I am jerked awake to a snapping twig.

Low heavy breaths, slow footsteps, a general sense of being surrounded.

It is all so quiet as to be uncanny, yet thoroughly unmistakeable.

'Matheos,' I whisper.

Has something happened to Korax? Though it's not exactly the best guard dog, not in my own experience.

It seems absurd that the gods might surround us in the forest when they could have crossed to our door whenever they liked, if they had merely deigned to, but it is the only explanation I can think of.

The golden light of morning filters through the canvas, enough that I can see Matheos sleeping soundly across from me, peaceful in a way I have only rarely managed to coax from him – softening features and deep breaths. I hate to disturb it but I whisper his name again and then, remembering the way he removed the golden cuffs from around his ears and set them gently aside before he slept, I reach over and give his shoulder the slightest shake.

He jerks starkly awake. 'Wha–'

He cuts himself off as I raise a finger to my lips and nod towards the door – or rather, the flap that passes for one.

Shadows move across the canvas and he snatches up his shoes, clips the ear cuffs on and draws a long, sleek dagger from his bag.

It is only the confident fluidity of each of these movements, the way he makes them as a matter of course, like arming himself is just another part of his morning routine, that stops me from shouting or at the very least yelping and surely alerting our assailants.

My plan, other than waking Matheos, was more along the lines of having a conversation.

Matheos pulls himself into a crouch, his head brushing the canvas roof, and then he peeks out, his dagger held behind him like he would keep it in reserve.

'Oh,' Matheos says with only mild surprise, something that verges more on intrigue. He steps outside and I rush to follow.

A few dozen animals ring us, predators beside prey, all sitting, waiting almost patiently.

Korax leaps to its feet, tail wagging, and comes dashing over for its morning affection.

'It seems maybe they weren't all finding their way to the house,' I say, eyeing the broken limbs, the injured paws, the wounded eyes.

'Apparently so,' Matheos agrees. 'I can't . . . I mean, I can't leave them, Pandora.'

'I wasn't going to ask you to.'

'But it will delay us.'

'I know, so let me help.'

It takes most of the morning. For all my jokes about knowing how to sew a wound shut, it appears my knowledge actually runs deeper. I prise out thorns, I disinfect, I apply stitches and bandage wounds. Some need more. There are limbs that need amputation, wounds so infected I'm not sure life is salvageable, at least several that need poultices and herbs and sustained treatment.

But those Matheos manages, and he works his strange magic and off they go.

He's incredible to behold. The care and attention, the soothing tone every time he speaks, the way he holds each creature valuable.

If the gods really do intend to lead this man into a trap, to find some excuse to punish him as they did his brother, then I will topple Mount Olympus itself before I let them get anywhere near him.

When we're finally done, we set off once more and Matheos

falls into a quiet I might not have noticed – because he is so often withdrawn, his mind a concave thing, reflecting inwards, sharing only what he must with the world – but this silence feels laden.

I cannot tell if it is the thought of where we are heading or what we have left behind that haunts him. And I have so many questions that I'm not sure where to start.

'You're brilliant, Matheos,' I finally manage. I accused him of not caring enough, and here it is evident that quite the opposite is true: he is a man who cares so deeply it will consume him, break him, tear him asunder. I know shadows of what that is like – my time on this planet has felt like an open wound, my heart an amphora I cannot stopper.

I thought it an aspect of mortality, to feel so potently it scares you. But I see it in Matheos, too: to fear that cavernous expanse of your heart so greatly that you might run to the furthest reaches of the world to hope you never hurt again, to convince yourself it is better to slice a flower at the root than watch it sprout and wither. And to still cultivate gardens anyway.

'You're just . . . you're really brilliant.'

Matheos looks at me askance. 'Is this the set-up for a wildly creative takedown?'

'No, I'm quite serious.'

'Oh. Well, may I ask what's prompted such a sentiment?'

'A lot of things, honestly. More than I think I can list right now. But seeing you this morning, watching you do what you love and be so incredibly good and talented at it? It was amazing and, well, from the way Hesione spoke to you, I just don't get the impression you've been told much how wonderful you are.'

He doesn't answer immediately and I worry I might have gone too far.

'Hesione was compatible with the parts of my brother I didn't much like. They've only got worse, since his incarceration. She has some minor healing powers so I think she blames herself – knowing she could help him but can't. So she lashes out instead. Still, I can't blame her for what she said. She's right, even if I don't love her delivery.'

'I didn't . . . I don't want to overstep –'

'Step wherever you like, Pandora. I know you don't do it from malice. Besides –' a small smile plays at the edges of his lips that catches me off guard – the quiet happiness of it – and I nearly trip over a twig – 'I know what you're like when you're trying not to ask questions. Distracted, irritable, a pained expression on your face. I'd hate to see you suffer like that.'

'I'm not that bad!' I protest. He gives me a look that has me caving immediately. 'Alright, fine. But when I asked you why you came here, you said it was because Hesione told you to. You were so against going before, so I can't help but wonder . . .'

He takes a moment, staring straight ahead as though this open path might fork. 'I wouldn't have come just of my own volition, if that's what you're asking.'

'You trust them,' I say, hesitating. This feels so delicate a conversation, like a weave that must be unpicked thread by thread to avoid damage to the whole. Cautiously, I add: 'More than you trust yourself.'

Matheos kicks at a stone as we walk – only lightly, like he just wants to see it skitter across the forest floor. Like he needs to see his impact on *something*. 'When Prometheus and I sided with the gods, they wanted to put me in one of their camps with the other boys for agoge, to train as one of their soldiers. Prometheus kept me from that – pulled strings to have me packaging nectar and ambrosia. I was safe but, Olympus above, Pandora, it was so boring. So lonely.'

'I can imagine,' I say – because I think Prometheus knew that too.

'An opportunity came up – repairing armour and weaponry with Hephaestus. I wasn't great at it but I liked the company. He was kind, Hephaestus. But I lasted a little over a month before the Titans attacked the forge. There was an explosion. Greek fire. I was hurt. I spent a while drifting in and out of consciousness and, then, at some point: there was Prometheus. He was terrified, and furious. And he was right – I wouldn't have been injured if I'd just done what he said and stayed put.'

'I don't think that's the conclusion to draw,' I say.

Matheos shakes his head. 'No, that's not what I mean. It's not like I felt if I didn't listen to Prometheus bad things would happen. It's more . . . I don't think I'd really recognized what war was until that moment. Prometheus hadn't just been trying to keep me alive, he'd been trying to keep me from the horror and brutality of it – all while he faced it. Because that's what he did: walked into danger to keep me safe.'

This is so very warped and twisted, and I think the worst part is all the glimmers within: the love and care, wound around control. Should I even dare pull this apart, knowing that losing one might destroy the other?

'Immortals can heal from most things – but there are limits. Damage too extensive, or taken too young – like when Hephaestus was thrown from Olympus. For things like Greek fire and Stygian blades you'd need a god of healing. Asclepius was summoned for those of us caught in the blast. He set my bones and tended to the other injured but he was rushed to the next battlefield before I woke up and ... everything was so *quiet*. The world felt different, dizzying, and by the time we could finally get Asclepius back it was beyond even magical healing. We're not entirely sure what happened – whether it was the volume of the explosion or when I hit my head as I fell, or maybe even some other substance in Hephaestus's lab that spilled on to me when I was unconscious. All we know is the sensory lining in the inner part of my ears was damaged. Without my cuffs the world sounds muted – muffled. And as I told you – even with them it's not quite as it was. Even if Prometheus had allowed me to stay at the forge I imagine it would have been ... overwhelming. Especially while I was trying to get used to it.

'So I went back to the rations and Hesione joined me to keep me from running off again. I'm not oblivious to what they're like. Hesione and Prometheus expect my blind loyalty and trust me with nothing in return. They berate me until I bow to their will. They are so focused on protecting humanity and fighting the gods that they'll say and do whatever they need to, no matter how hurtful it may be. They're good people but they're also cruel and calculating. I know that. But, honestly, maybe they're right to cut me out of their schemes.'

'Matheos ...' I reach for him but his eyes have fluttered shut, and I'm not sure that he's seen so I let my hand fall, and wait for him to continue.

He takes a breath. 'My gifts – the way I got this name. Zeus charged me with distributing the attributes among the animals. And, well, so the story goes, strange boy with more curiosity for the world around him than for the gods on their thrones. He did not realize that he was running low, did not stop to think about which one he was giving to what, just gave them all out without care.'

I greatly doubt that – Matheos does nothing without care.
'The story?'

'Yes,' he says, pushing a branch out of our path and gesturing for me to pass. 'It tells that when the last gift was given, the boy realized he had saved nothing for humanity. And surely animals with teeth like razors and claws like blades would shred these defenceless humans to pieces. How brilliant: the problem of Prometheus's special race destroyed by the thoughtlessness of his foolish brother. How utterly wonderful to teach someone with foresight a lesson, especially through kin who could not think so far ahead as the end of a bag of gifts. The gods do so adore irony.'

I can see it, vividly, and worse is the tension in Matheos's voice. The way he's trying so desperately not to still be hurt by it. And how he so clearly is.

He looks at me, like he is leading me towards a conclusion but fears my reaction. 'So that's why Prometheus stole fire for the mortals. I left them with nothing. After everything Prometheus had done for me and all he had suffered, all he wanted was for this one creation of his to be safe – and I prevented that. So you see, it's my fault Zeus bound him to that pillar.'

'Matheos –'

'I appreciate it, Pandora, whatever argument you're about to make. Your ability to believe the best of people is truly astounding. But please know it's not you that I need absolution from.'

I consider. I could argue – I would like to. I have plenty to say on the topic of Matheos's self-flagellation. But something about the tale gives me pause – and then I realize it is exactly that: a tale.

'Is there anything the stories leave out?'

Matheos laughs – one of his soft, gentle huffs of pleasant surprise. 'Yes.' He takes a breath and then his voice falls again, the amusement vanished. 'I knew that there weren't enough attributes for everyone. It was a trap. And just as now, I walked into it willingly. I could have left an animal out, given humans the speed I gave falcons or the teeth I gave lions. But then those creatures would have been vulnerable instead. I knew Prometheus would act, knew he would not leave humans defenceless where he would happily leave the animals. So I chose to leave them nothing.'

Oh. That guilt he feels, compounded. No accident but a decision – with consequences.

But still . . . 'That's sweet.'

'Sweet?' He looks genuinely baffled. 'My priorities are wrong, the choices I make deadly. The very way my mind works is at odds with the world.'

'It's beautiful,' I insist. 'You couldn't bear the thought of leaving animals defenceless. You're probably the only person in the world who would make that decision and I –'

Love you for it.

I am sure I do not mean it profoundly. Not in the way my heart was crafted for. But in a way that feels all the more expansive for it, like I had no idea you could find affection in so broad a manner until presented with all the myriad ways I think I could love Matheos – and some of the ways I already do. I thought love a single thread, connecting two lovers, and instead I find it is a tapestry whose detail surprises me.

'That's not all the stories leave out,' Matheos adds. 'Prometheus didn't do it alone, Pandora. I provided the stalk that hid the fire. I stood guard while he stole it. And when Zeus came, my brother insisted I act as though I knew nothing about it. I protested, but not as much as I should have. Prometheus swore that he had prophecies, that all this needed to unfold in a certain way, that in this plan of his he would one day be free and then the next step would come, we simply had to wait. So you see, I cannot fault Hesione for despising me. She's right: I am craven. And I have a long record of letting my brother take the blame.'

'No,' I say.

'No?' he repeats, a hint of a laugh. I love that, too: when no matter how melancholy he is, I can still startle him just enough that amusement slips in.

'No, actually. And I don't care if you don't need absolution from me, you're getting it because it doesn't sound to me like you let Prometheus take the blame. It sounds like your brother wanted to control the situation, and pushed you into obeying his plans with the threat of an unknowable future and the fear of a violent past. You may have noticed, Matheos, but I'm rather in support of people making their own decisions instead of others deciding they know best and forcing them to fall in line.'

Matheos shrugs, his eyes dropping to the forest floor. 'I suppose.'

I know my words won't change his mind – at least not quickly. But I'll happily continue to remind him.

'And it sounds like neither your brother nor Hesione holds anywhere near the respect for you that they should.'

Matheos says nothing, just looks ahead and keeps walking.

His hand brushes mine.

And then it takes it, twining the fingers through and still not glancing at me, still remaining silent.

I set my gaze on the forest ahead as well, and I let my words fall silent too.

Anything more and we'd have to reckon with what we are doing. We would have to untangle our fingers, make hurried apologies, claim it an accident.

If we don't acknowledge it, we might enjoy it a moment longer.

So, hands firmly clasped, we continue into the forest, and we do not say another word.

CHAPTER TWENTY-THREE

THAT EVENING WE RISK A small campfire. The smoke, the warmth, the smell of the eggs we scavenged frying in an iron pan. Surely the gods must be too familiar with the sacrificial fats and bones the humans cook to turn their heads towards our plates. It cannot be much of a risk, yet it feels it. Enough that we shuffle closer together, like sitting a little nearer might gift us the bravery we seek.

'Do you have those herbs?' I ask, shifting the eggs in the pan.

'What herbs?'

'The ones you've spent all day foraging?'

He's been plucking at the undergrowth as we've walked, tying bundles to his bag.

'Oh,' he says, rolling one such bunch between his fingers. 'They aren't for us. Well, I suppose they could be, but that wasn't my intention. Foraging food would probably have been smarter.'

'Matheos,' I say, before he can keep rambling. 'Would you like to tell me what the mystery herbs are for before I assume an unsightly ailment somewhere you'd rather I not see?'

Matheos glowers. 'I don't have any ailments.'

'That's precisely what you'd say if you did, so I'm not sure I can simply take your word for it.'

'*Pandora.*'

Delight thrills down my spine at that: the ire I can draw from him, the way it feels so excruciatingly intimate to know just where to press to get a response.

'They're for the animals,' he says with the sort of tone that tells me he decidedly does not think me amusing. 'I thought making some poultices would be helpful in case more wounded creatures find us in these woods. It would be quicker than me working my magic.'

Oh. He's been thinking of them as we walked? Not of the horrors potentially waiting for us or the brother whose words work their own sort of magic on Matheos?

'Show me,' I say. 'I'll help.'

So we sit before the fire, shredding herbs and grating seeds, mixing up fine pastes to disinfect, ease and heal.

'I should have brought some jars,' he says, pushing the concoctions into a spare water skin. 'The plants are medicinal enough but I could have enchanted the poultices further. Bronze and gold hold magic best, but even clay can be imbued. A water skin, though? Any power will probably fade long before we need it.'

'Excuse me, I'm clay imbued – are you telling me I could be even better if they'd smelted me from metal instead?'

I feel myself unfurling before the warm flames, relaxing my tired muscles. My calves feel unbearably taut, unused to so much walking and, without thinking, I lean my head on the shoulder Matheos has just been massaging himself, also taut from a night spent on the forest floor.

He's so tall that it's not much of a lean, almost a solely horizontal movement. It's not the most comfortable. So why do I feel no desire to move again? Why do I feel like the branches could snake up our feet and bind us here, transform us into a part of the forest itself and we would be content?

Matheos stiffens at my touch, and then, with a breath, he relaxes once more.

'And you'd be even worse if they'd stitched you from leather,' he says, his weight shifting like he is leaning back against me, too. 'Olympus would quake at the very thought.'

More animals gather the next day, but as we tend them we hardly talk at all. And as we set out, the silence lingers. We are too tired, our limbs too heavy. We do not hold hands, not like yesterday. And when we settle for the night again, Matheos is clutching at his shoulder like his hand is all that's keeping his arm in place.

Korax is pulling supplies out of Matheos's bag, a hard loaf of bread clutched between its metal jaws. I suppose that answers what we'll eat tonight.

'We'll reach the nearby village tomorrow,' Matheos says. 'We can pick up supplies there that will last us until we reach the bigger town of Tarsuras at the foot of the mountains.'

Humans. Tomorrow! It is almost too exciting – and too terrifying. To meet others like me and learn more about myself in the process, to explore the range of us and find the specifics of me.

'Yes, okay – oh, will you please stop, you're probably straining it more. Here, can I?'

I swat at the hand which had been reaching far too low at his shoulder blade, probably risking hurting the other one. I press the spot he'd been aiming for, immediately feeling the strength of the tension in the muscle beneath.

He hisses.

'Sorry,' I hurry, lightening the pressure. I run gentle circles into the skin, my thumb pushing at the knots I find.

'You don't have to do this,' he says, even as he relaxes into my touch.

'It's fine, I feel responsible – I made you too nice a bed and now you can't cope with sleeping on the floor.'

'Apparently so. I'm sleeping through the night, though, so there's that. My mind feels calmer, out here.' He pauses, and then perhaps because he is not facing me it is easier for him to add: 'With you.'

I did not realize a knot had coiled in my gut until it tightens.

'Thank you for doing this,' he says, arching against my pressing fingers.

'Well, it's not like there's much else for us to do. Though the massage would be much more effective if you were to strip off.'

'Pandora,' he growls, jerking away.

'I'm joking!' I protest, pulling him back. 'Sort of. I mean, don't get me wrong: I am very, *very* much not averse.'

'I am not going to let you keep touching me if you're going to continue flirting so shamelessly.'

'Would you like me to flirt with more shame? Wow, Matheos, I had no idea you subscribed to those archaic notions Hera's trying to push so –'

'Pandora!'

'Stopping, stopping,' I mutter – because if my efforts are to ease the tension in his shoulders then inflicting stress myself probably isn't useful.

The knots seem a little more stubborn than they were mere seconds ago.

'Matheos,' I start. 'Are you alright? You're –'

'No, no, obviously not, because now you've put it in my head all I can think about is that, yes, this would be a lot more pleasant if there were less fabric between us.' He says this quickly, then jolts sharply away and turns to face me, pulling his already firmly tied chiton tighter, like my efforts might have drawn it loose.

I sigh.

He sighs.

Korax pushes the bread at us.

'Shall we eat? Then once we've both cooled off maybe we can try again.'

So we do, and when we finish he nods quietly for me to begin, though he looks distinctly uncomfortable. But he was still rubbing his shoulder while we tore into the bread so I imagine it's the pain that forces his hesitant acceptance.

This time I keep my mouth closed, and, slowly, he properly relaxes.

I try to keep my movements intent and mechanical. This is just another automaton with quicksilver built up in the vessels, needing to be heated and kneaded out. This is dough, a stubborn stain, a thing to be massaged that's definitely not Matheos's skin, his lithe muscles, the expanse of his back mine to trail my hands along.

I wonder if he'll need such massages every day that we travel.

I wonder if I'll eventually need them too and, oh gods, that's the thought that undoes me – the idea of his hands trailing along the shape of me, light touches and gentle pressure, the care of it, cautious and considered and *lingering*.

Matheos rushes to bed not long after I finish.

And I sit, staring at the dying embers, wondering whether we'll ever satisfy this yearning, or if our lives will just be one slow, torturous longing.

We walk for only a few more hours the next day, the sun all but hidden behind the thick foliage overhead. Korax's torches shine even in the daylight, illuminating snags and snares in the path ahead. Then all at once the forest halts, lurching us into a clearing without warning.

An expanse of tangled weeds, moss-soaked rock, and tumbling ruins of stone and mud.

I take a step forward, the ground soft and spongy underfoot. Evenly spaced stones litter the floor – their tops worn and weathered.

'This is the village?' I ask, taking another step. If I hadn't expected a settlement, I'd have thought it a meadow and taken no notice of the marks where houses might once have stood.

'I . . . I don't understand,' Matheos says.

'Time?' I ask. Because these ruins are old. Centuries at least, hundreds of years of decay.

'It must be. But this is drastic . . . whole centuries to pass in this place while decades pass outside? Only three days away from a house where only two years have unfurled?'

'You haven't been to the nearest village since you settled in Colchis?'

I turn to him, but he is steadfastly watching Korax, who hurries around the clearing with its nose pressed flat to the ground, snorting great heaving sniffs.

'I didn't know how close an eye the gods were keeping on me. The last thing I needed was them thinking that I too had an attachment to the humans my brother adored.'

I glance around the clearing. 'And it was definitely here? You haven't led us to some other clearing.'

'It was here.'

'Colchis must be more time-scarred than I imagined.'

I knew time dragged here – but had not understood that it might vary even within the land. How long will have passed before we return home? How long has Prometheus spent on that mountain?

I explore the ruins – the rusted tools and crumbling bricks half buried in the dirt. But, for our purposes, my main finds are a well of rainwater and the remnants of an orchard in the back, most trees shrivelled without tending, peppered with the stones of long-rotted fruits. But I find an overgrown blackberry bush still bearing fruit, and an apple tree that has some under-ripe offerings that might work cooked and stewed.

'Well, I think those are the only things of use,' I say once our bags are full. 'Shall we be on our way?'

Matheos nods. I take one last look at the worn stones and the barren land where people once walked. It would have been home to them. It would have been their world.

And now it's nothing but ruins – no clue even to what made

it that way. Another question, another puzzle, in an ever-growing list.

We rise early the next morning, trying to get a head start on the gathering animals. When only a small group of them remain, the ones whose injuries are complex and in need of Matheos's magical touch, I leave him to it and go in search of breakfast. I scour the surrounding forest for nettles to stew, delighting in finding a small patch of wild garlic instead. I found a whole bushel of flowering portulaca yesterday, which should make a more exciting salad than most of what we've been eating – a thought that is apparently so thrilling I do not notice the owl diving through the boughs above until it coalesces into the goddess standing before me.

'I do not have much time,' Athena begins, the second she no longer has a beak. 'The gods do not know you're headed to Prometheus yet but they will the moment you pass through Tarsuras. Your presence there will alert them.'

It is a collision – this sinking horror that the gods, even just Athena, know of our plan, and the rising panic that we really might be headed into a trap. Together, they clash so quickly my mind falters, the very-big-all-too-much feeling pushed aside, shelved for later, and then there is only this clarity – the precision of the goddess before me and all the practicalities of trying to deal with what she's saying.

'Should we avoid the town?' I ask, but I do not even finish before she's shaking her head.

'No, quite the opposite. I think you should convince them your intent is *only* to visit the humans.'

I consider. 'Is that the lesser crime?'

'They'd be suspicious, I'm sure. They might worry you give your allegiances to the other humans rather than the gods. But I think they'd be curious, too, to see how the human we made pairs with the ones Prometheus created. Perhaps curious enough they'd miss your visit to Prometheus entirely – especially if you were to leave your husband in town. They'd be just as interested in Prometheus's brother's reaction to the mortals, alert for any betrayal, that they might miss you entirely. I can think of no better distraction and they'd never suspect a weak mortal girl would venture off alone. It wouldn't even occur to them.'

I look at her – the way she arches herself towards me, her quick words and darting gaze, like we might be observed. Like I am in her confidence.

And I wonder if I can trust it.

'I can't leave Epimatheos behind. Prometheus is his brother,' I say – because it is the natural protest to what she has suggested.

'And so all the more noticeable.'

'Is this . . . is this what the gods want of me? Why they made me? To drive Epimatheos to that mountain?'

Athena sighs, and glances quickly about her. She steps closer to me and drops her voice to a whisper – as though everything she's said isn't just as treasonous. 'Honestly, I don't know what they want of you. And it's not *they*, anyway. It's not *the gods*. It's Zeus who demanded your creation and I'm not sure why. I've tried to work it out.' Her voice becomes a low, frustrated growl. 'I can't stand a mystery.'

'Me neither.'

She flashes a quick smile and I think about all those months ago, on Olympus, when she said she knew what it was like to suddenly be, and to be thrust into the fray.

I wonder if she queried her own existence then, too. Whether she still does.

'Is that why you're going?' she asks. 'For the mystery?'

Is it? Matheos is going because Hesione told him to, and when she or his brother tells him to do something, he does so without query. But me? I'm going because Prometheus sacrificed everything for the humans and now they're suffering, so if he can't help them himself, maybe he can tell us how. And because there is a prophecy I want to hear – plans I wish to be a part of. I want to know how Zeus will fall so I can ensure it happens. An active participant and not a piece in a game, caught in this fight between Prometheus and Zeus with both sides withholding the information that might empower us enough to threaten their carefully laid plans.

But, with Athena before me and that simple suggestion – the mystery – it is a little harder to ignore the sheer strength of the drive within me pushing me towards that mountain. The way I fixated on Prometheus the first time the mystery of him arose, the way all of this seems to revolve around him. And I am not sure which is stronger, or if maybe they're the same: my curiosity, and whatever seeds the gods planted in my head telling me to go to Caucasus.

'I'm going because I don't know what else to do,' I admit. Because that, really, is what it boils down to: nowhere else to go, nowhere else to ask for help.

Athena is quiet a moment. And then, voice low, she says: 'I do care about the humans, you know. The life I imbued them with lingers in every breath they take. And I care about *you*. I am fond of my creations, Pandora. I would fight for every town that bears my name, for every person within them, and for you too. The mortals craft, they build, they strategize – they give me purpose.'

She hesitates – seemingly debating whether she should continue before finally letting her eyes flutter shut and confessing, 'And I think you *should* meet Prometheus. It would be good for you. I was never able to meet my mother, and he is the closest thing to a maker outside of the gods that you might find. I want that for you.'

I smile – a reflex, a way to hide my grimace. That is decidedly not what I am looking for with Prometheus, but if Athena is helping us out of some hope she might live vicariously through me or fix her hurts by not allowing me to suffer similarly, then I will take it.

'What if he's not willing to help me?'

'He'll get past his distrust. He'll be too curious not to.'

Oh. Perhaps that is where I get it from, if this curiosity is a core part of humanity.

'I've gone over it so many times,' she says. 'Trust me, I am goddess of strategy in war. There is no easy, safe option here. But I believe this is the route that will serve you best. And if nothing else, it will keep your husband safer, too.'

And that's what does it – because I dragged Matheos into this, and I don't want to be another person who makes decisions he will end up paying for.

She places a hand on my shoulder. 'I can't stop the gods from hurting the mortals like they have been. I've tried. But I can help you and . . . if I can't save them all, I would like to save just one. Go to that mountain alone, Pandora. Do whatever you can to stay safe.'

*

I return to Matheos, mulling over how to broach this new information. I cannot mention Athena – any hint that the gods want us to keep taking another step forward and he will haul us back home without another word.

I don't like it – it feels like exactly what I have raged against: withholding information to get my way. I'd tell him if I thought he might simply head back himself. But I wouldn't put it past him to drag me with him and I *need* to keep going.

So, guilt churning, I choose my words carefully.

'If the gods do see us, they'll be more likely to punish us for visiting Prometheus than the humans, right?' I ask and when Matheos nods I continue. 'So maybe we can distract them from that.'

He scowls. 'We can hardly hide hiking up a barren mountain.'

'No, but one person is easier to hide than two. Especially if one of us is being big and loud and obnoxious with the humans at the same time.'

'Pandora,' he says carefully. 'Please tell me you're not suggesting –'

'You know what I'm suggesting. You avoided the humans for years. You know the gods will be particularly interested in how you spend time with them. I think it's you they wanted me to drive here – otherwise why send me to you? If I have any purpose, it's to force your hand somehow. They probably won't pay any attention to anything I do when it's not in relation to you. So if I were to sneak off, I could probably get the prophecy without them even realizing.'

Matheos stops walking, takes my wrist, and I let him guide me off the thin path, like we need the cover of the trees to mask our discussion. He stands close, looking down at me.

Thick stubble has grown while we've been in these woods, and the dark bristles highlight the sharp blade of his jaw – at this angle it begs to be touched, to have my finger glide gently along it. I wonder how it would feel against my skin, perhaps even beneath my lips.

Matheos does not let go of my wrist.

'Do you have any idea how dangerous what you are proposing is?'

'Yes, I think you've made it perfectly clear once or twice. I know what the gods might do. I know what they *have* done.'

'No,' he says almost fiercely. 'I should take that risk, not you.'

'Why?'

'Excuse me?'

'Why?' I repeat. I'm having to arch my back to look up at him, his face above mine. 'I am just as capable, just as susceptible to pain and just as competent in weighing up the odds and making a decision.'

His eyes narrow. 'You are mortal.'

'That makes me lesser?'

'It makes you more finite,' he hisses. 'You are too valuable. I might survive their tortures, where the thought of you experiencing them would be the worst suffering they could concoct.'

I place my free hand on his chest, can feel the steady pounding of his heart beneath my palm.

'And if I feel the same?'

'You can't,' he insists, staring me down like he's daring me to argue.

'And yet.' I can taste the words, the bite to my refusal.

His growl catches in his throat, and he releases me, stumbling back like being close to me is dangerous. Which, I suppose, it is.

A thought occurs. 'This isn't . . . this isn't because you think I'm tricking you? That the gods sent me to get the prophecy and I'm trying to cut you out to fulfil that brief?'

His eyes meet mine and they are pained, like even looking at me is an echo of an agony he cannot bear to face again.

'No, Pandora, in this instance it is because I care about you.'

He turns, stalking off into the forest like he might vanish behind the thickets forever. I glance at Korax, who looks at me in a disapproving manner that is almost human, and then we follow after him.

We discuss it for days: our options, our ways around it. We do not venture near the one I have suggested again, though it remains firmly on the table. It came from Athena herself. It is the best idea. And I think he knows it, and every time we refuse to think about it, it becomes even more glaringly obvious.

One night the temperature plummets, and though we fall fitfully asleep pushed against our usual sides of the tent, I wake pressed against him, my leg hooked over his, head bent into his shoulder, his face buried in my hair, his arms clutching my waist tight. Both of us holding fast.

I close my eyes and pretend I haven't noticed, let myself drift back off, and when I wake, there we are, in our two corners again, until I am half certain I imagined the heap of our tangled limbs.

The next night, after a particularly treacherous and miserable day as the heavens opened and the forest floor turned to slick mud that halted our efforts to wade through it, we find a dry enough place to make shelter beneath the boughs of a dozen trees. But we can't risk a fire beneath them catching and spreading.

Matheos ties his damp cloak to a pole of the tent like it might dry overnight, and I do the same with the chiton I've been draping about myself – one of Matheos's, as he was the only one to pack properly, a thicker weave that's not quite the same as a cloak but worked perfectly well as one until this downpour.

And then we don't even discuss it, just climb into the tent and bury ourselves beneath the blanket. His arm falls across my waist, the weight of it a heavy, comforting press that I feel through our thin chitons. He nestles his face into the crook of my shoulder and breathes, low and deep, like he would take all of me in. I turn my head so that his hair tickles against me, the smell of rain and earth that clings to him.

I don't risk breathing, in case it drives him away.

But after a moment I cannot take it.

'What are we –'

'Don't,' he says softly, sleepily. 'If we think about it we have to stop.'

And I don't want it to stop, not the warm press of him against me, or this baring of himself, like all his guards fell away the moment that rain hit. We fit together too perfectly to ever let go.

So I enjoy it, and I put off sleep so I can enjoy it for longer.

And when I wake, I have a few moments more before he

stirs and we separate, pretending it never happened, and I, at least, am hoping that if we do not talk about it, it might happen once more.

I'm grouchy in the morning. I hardly slept, the rain pounding on the canvas sheet. The accompanying thunder that struck sometime in the early hours.

Matheos is positively spry.

'You're showing off,' I grumble, as he plucks a thorn from a rabbit's paw – our final waiting patient of the day. He started whistling three animals ago.

I didn't even know he knew how to whistle.

I certainly never imagined he'd be inclined to.

'You know I rarely sleep well – permit me to be pleased at discovering a storm can't interrupt me when I do. I'm adding it to the list of benefits of hearing loss: sleep through storms and your wife's incessant snoring.'

'I do not snore!' I protest, thoroughly indignant. I'm too sleep-deprived to be teased; I would like to go back to soothing cuddles and perhaps, if I'm really admitting what I *actually* want, a few gentle kisses to my forehead as I fall gracefully back to sleep.

He chuckles. 'You do. I rarely sleep well, remember?'

'I'm handcrafted by the gods to be perfect. I doubt that includes snoring.'

'You're handcrafted by the same god who made these,' he says, tapping one of his cuffs. 'Trust me – this is the sort of detail Hephaestus would find hilarious.'

I have no rebuttal to that, and short of harrumphing in discontent, I shoot him a look. 'Would you care to return to *why* you slept so well? Because I was awake, Matheos. You didn't let go of me once.'

His brow furrows, that scowl etching deep. 'Ruin my good mood, why don't you? On that, Pandora, you'll find I have no comment. And nor will you if you want it to happen again.'

We are nearing the end of our journey when the distant rush of a river sounds, muffled by leaves and detritus, and growing louder with every step we take.

Korax runs forward before we can stop it, leaps and splashes in loudly before propelling itself across.

Matheos arches a brow. 'Maybe *that's* the distraction we need. We can leave Korax to wreak havoc in the mortal towns while we visit my brother.'

The bank is further away than I'd like, but Korax hauls itself up and barks as though summoning us.

'I'm sure we could tell it to come back,' I say somewhat nervously, worried Matheos is about to say we should follow it.

'We should follow it,' Matheos says. 'The water is shallow, just wide. We should be able to wade across.'

'What if I can't swim?' I ask.

'Can you?'

'I don't know! I've never had cause to find out.'

The last and only time I tried, I dipped a single toe in the Euxine Sea, screamed at the cold and abandoned all thoughts of following Kerkeis and Ione in.

He looks at me, quirking his head to the side in a way that makes me squirm.

'What?' I demand at his examination.

'Just assessing whether wading across hand in hand is too much of a risk or if I should carry you.'

'You are *not* carrying me!' I practically squeak the words out.

'Well, if you insist,' he says, and offers me his hand instead.

I hesitate only long enough to glower at him before I take it, and pull him towards the river before he can decide carrying me is indeed the better option, leaving us to wrestle with the *very* fun question of whether he even can with the way I am likely heavier than him. I'm still not sure if those comments about his upper-body strength were a joke or if he has some sort of Titan leverage. Either way, this doesn't seem like the most opportune moment to handle that potential situation, so I pull him forward until my toes hit the river's edge.

The water is cold, though not as unbearably so as the ocean, and we slide down the muddy riverbank until we are waist high in the rushing water. The currents push against us, but not so firmly that I really need to hold Matheos's hand.

Then I stumble, and it is not merely his hand in mine but my other latching on to his arm to keep me steady as his low rumble of a laugh sounds.

'This is foolish,' I fume.

'Only when you lack coordination.'

Which is when he is whipped beneath the surface.

The grip of his hand in mine lurches me down too, and I dig my feet against the rocks, leaning back, trying to anchor us in place, but my foot comes free and we skid down the river. Matheos surfaces, gasping, and the water is so deep here I can't even reach the ground to gain a footing.

I am barely keeping my head above water. Matheos's arm hooks beneath mine, hand across my stomach to hold me close as he tries to swim us both to the bank, the currents churning off the ground and swirling around us, trying to tug us under. I try to kick, try to help, but we're being dragged further along, and I try to take a breath just as I am sucked under and then I am choking, reaching – grabbing at a low-hanging branch, and my shoulder sears in agony at the sudden pull of my body and his.

Matheos scrambles for it too as I cough and gag. The moment he has a hand on the branch he fumbles at his ear cuffs with his other.

'Are they –'

'Fine,' he assures me, perhaps reading my panic because I can barely hear *him* above the roar of the water. 'They're waterproof … just … worried one might have … been knocked loose.'

He can barely catch his breath. He hauls me and I haul him, both of us trying to pull ourselves up until we finally collapse on the bank, gasping for air.

'Are you alright?' he demands, reaching for me though he has only just let go, hand on my forearm, leaning over me. His hair is wet, curling in damp ringlets over his face. His chest heaves as he draws breath, chiton clinging tight, almost transparent.

I see him take a similar assessment of me, his eyes meeting mine, pupils swollen.

My heart still pounds, adrenaline like fire in my veins.

'Remind me why we aren't doing this?' I say, letting my gaze fall to his lips, parted and panting, now closing in one slow gulp, the rise and fall of his throat …

'I cannot recall.'

His lips meet mine with nothing short of starvation, a kiss ferocious in its need, and I am just as desperate, fingers curling into his chiton, pulling him closer. He tastes of the river. *We* taste of the river. His hands slide along my waist and I shiver beneath his touch, catch his parted lips with my teeth, and he groans into my open mouth, kisses me with more urgency, like we are still tumbling beneath the currents and this is our last desperate escape.

He pulls away and my heart lurches, but it is only to moan my name, so close to my own lips I can taste the sound. Then his lips close on mine again, the scratch of his stubble against my cheeks, his fingers threading through my hair, drawing me to him.

I am aflame, *wanting* even as I have, more and more, needing him closer still. I am so aware of myself, of him, of the ground beneath us and the sky stretching far above, of the rustling of the trees and the pounding of our hearts. He makes me feel *everything*.

'Pandora,' he says again, this time like his throat is closing. 'We shouldn't.'

'Illogical, thoroughly illogical,' I mutter, running my hand down his chest, the damp chiton fine as thread over the planes of his stomach.

He pulls away, scrambling further up the bank like being anywhere near me is too great a temptation.

I make a strangled noise of frustration. My skin is hot, my heart pounding, and I would very much like to scream. 'Very well, Matheos, why shouldn't we do this?'

'The prophecy . . .' he says, trailing off vaguely, like he can't quite remember why, either.

'If what your brother intended was to warn us apart, haven't we already failed? We like each other! If the gods wished to use us against each other now, it would work. Kissing won't change that. Sleeping together won't change that! So why shouldn't we, if we think we may be days from oblivion? Why not take what pleasure is left?'

He shakes his head as though at a loss. 'It feels foolish. I just . . . don't trust myself to make the right decision here.'

'Then make the wrong one, Matheos. But at least make a decision. At least stand by it rather than waiting for someone else to tell you how to think. Don't keep telling me how much you want me and then turning cold a moment later.'

I climb to my feet, dusting off my chiton, though the mud clings to the damp fabric. He steps closer, tries to take my hand but I snatch it back.

'*You* are my decision,' he thunders. 'Whatever keeps you safe, whatever ensures the gods do not target you. The only thing I've ever wished for more than not wanting you is to be free to be able to. And if I'm not, then I will like you from within the confines they have placed me in and do all that I can to guarantee they do not put you in them too.'

My racing heart does not slow, and this time when he reaches for my hand I let him take it.

'They won't come for me because you kissed me. And not kissing me won't keep me safe.'

'I disagree,' he says. 'The gods have a history of harming the people I love.'

I feel what it is they say about these lands: that time warps, stills, manipulates. I feel caught in its riptide, everything slowing down and hurtling forward all at once.

It is nothing we have not already confessed – that we care for one another, that there is love here, between us. It is not necessarily the type of deep and heady love the gods created me to seek.

But my lips are swollen, and I can still feel his fingers pulling at my hair and those words feel weighted.

'They already think we *do* love each other,' I say. 'The only way we could use that belief against them is if we did not actually hold any affection for one another. But we do. If they want to use me to get to you, they will do it regardless of how much we hold back now.'

We tried, didn't we? As though resisting temptation might have allowed such temptations to fade.

But it didn't.

It won't.

And I don't know how he can kiss me like that and not have this agonizing, burning need to do it again.

'You're right.' He nods. 'You're right. Still, can you . . . give me a moment for my mind to catch up with that reality? I've spent the last few years convinced that all my actions have caused horrors, that none of my choices can be trusted. I want to choose you without any reservation.'

I want him *now*, want my curiosity sated, want him to hold me and kiss me and make me forget everything waiting ahead of us.

But is this not also what I have wanted? The gods placed me here to serve, and I refuse to be the girl sent to his door to heal him, to be his tool for self-betterment. Is it not better for him to work through his hesitations and come to me when he has?

Do I not deserve love in abundance rather than snippets?

'Alright,' I agree. 'But I won't wait forever, Matheos.'

We do not have forever, after all, and my mortal heart slows like it must preserve each one of its beats.

But whatever time I thought I'd given Matheos to ponder *us* falters – not even five minutes walking through the trees, and the forest clears.

Because, of course, a town will settle by a river.

And unlike the village in the forest, this one is bustling, busy and thoroughly swarming with people.

CHAPTER TWENTY-FOUR

T HE TOWN REMINDS ME OF home – *home*. Oh, I had not realized how I missed it in the forest, not until I see all these white stone walls and terracotta roof tiles, the smell of ageing oak and fresh herbs, birds swooping on abandoned crumbs. Like our home but so much more.

Our home? Is that what it is now?

I step towards the town, entranced.

And everywhere, all around: *humans*.

People. Like me.

So many of them hurrying about, women hauling bundles of fabric or baskets of food, men dragging carts or struggling with amphorae, children trailing after their parents, imitating them like they too are busy at work. Everyone moving with purpose.

Matheos steps up beside me. 'So, what is our plan?'

'I want to explore. Immediately.'

'Very well.'

So we do, wandering the streets aimlessly, passing people and buildings, tanners and blacksmiths, bakers and merchants.

No one even looks at us, they're all so fixated on the tasks at hand – eyes dead ahead, exchanges brief and curt.

For a while it is delightful – the smells, the sounds, the sheer quantity of it all. And then we pass into a busier street, and someone brushes past me, their shoulder to my shoulder, another at the back of my hand, my hip. Electric sparks at each point, signals flaring, the gears of my mind churning, not connecting, not making enough sense of it to do anything but be excruciatingly *aware*.

Then a man grabs my waist to push me aside, muttering, 'Excuse me,' but behaving as though I am not a person but an obstacle in his path. I'm not so easily moved, and his hand just presses into the flesh of my side and he scowls, like he expects a woman to be a pliable thing, and I do not even think, just startle at his touch and shove him away from me.

He staggers back, and at once those stilted conversations erupt into uproar, dozens of people around us begin shouting, only fragments of it reaching me: *calm down* and *there's no need for that* and *control your wife*.

But I'm still caught on the earlier loop, the touch at my waist and *why? Why would he think it was all right to touch me? It was intentional, wasn't it? And why* there, *if he absolutely had to, why my waist and not my arm? Would he touch a man there? Would he touch a man at all?*

And they're still shouting, and it's so loud and I don't know why what I did was wrong when clearly it was the other person's fault. In fact, the man in question is blinking, furrowed lines forming between his brows.

'Sorry,' he whispers, that frown deepening like he is confused by his own response. But then someone else jostles him and he moves on and no one else seems to hear his sort-of apology, they're still shouting about propriety and each yell is like another flare in my mind, and I am blinded by the continuous, erupting flashes.

'Pandora.' Matheos tries to touch my hand and I flinch, so he steps back, nodding, sticking his arm out wide to keep anyone else from getting close. 'What happened?'

'I need to get out of here,' I gasp.

My vision feels obscured, tilted, like nothing before me is real. Certainly not the dozens, maybe even hundreds of people surrounding us who suddenly, immediately, fall silent and leap to the sides of the road, pressing close together to clear a path for us.

'What?' Matheos asks, scowling at them, but I can barely register myself and my own body, let alone what they are doing. I am dimly aware of Korax at my other side, trying to form a buffer between me and the silent, watching people. Matheos shakes himself and gestures forward, still not daring to touch me, and says: 'Come on, let's get somewhere quieter.'

Everything jolts, flashes. If my mind were quicksilver, it would not be smooth fluid to be poured but fragmented shards, each thought disconnected from the next, jumping into place or tumbling through.

We escape into a courtyard and then, somehow, I am sitting on the ground of it, clinging to the cool press of the stones beneath me.

By now I feel as though I cannot even see, though I can. I am aware of what's around me, know there are images before me, but my mind cannot process them into actual understanding. I might as well be blindfolded.

I draw my legs up to my chest, rubbing the pad of my thumb over my nails, pressure to hold on to.

It takes a while, sitting there in the haze of my own thoughts. But slowly I become aware of more – of the birds flittering overhead and Korax curled up at my feet and Matheos, sitting beside me, offering me a flask of water.

I take it, the embarrassment striking as soon as I begin to feel well enough for such thoughts to penetrate.

'I'm sorry,' I say, twisting at the stopper of the flask. 'I don't know what happened. I just wasn't expecting someone to touch me and –'

His eyes flash. 'No one should be touching you if you don't want them to. Do you want me to –'

'No, no, it's fine. It was just so busy and I was already a little overwhelmed and it just ... made something snap. I'm sorry.'

'There's nothing to apologize for, Pandora.'

'But my reaction –'

'Was natural,' he says firmly and then his gaze softens, anger ebbing as concern resumes its place. His hand flutters, like he had gone to reach for me before second-guessing himself. 'And again, nothing to apologize for. Are you feeling any better now?'

'Yes, yes, I think so,' I say, and rise to my feet, dusting the dirt off. I offer a small smile. 'So much for a gleeful first meeting with my people. I just ... didn't expect it to be like that.'

'Me neither – I've *never* seen people behave like that before,' Matheos muses. 'Humans so uniform and synchronized? They felt more like automatons.'

'How do you mean?'

He looks pensive. 'I don't know. There was just no . . . chaos, I suppose. The people Prometheus crafted were never like that crowd – constantly in action, each of them just focused on their individual tasks. It was like one of Dionysus's theatres, like they were all just *acting* being humans. Even when they began yelling it was only because you weren't doing what, to them, you were supposed to: ignore being touched and not make a fuss.'

I huff. 'That doesn't sound all that different from what the gods expect of the goddesses.'

'No, and I suppose that was always part of the problem. Prometheus modelled his mortal men on the gods – that's why Zeus was so furious. My brother tried to keep them safe by building in all these contingencies to prevent Zeus from seeing them as a threat, and I know a strict adherence to rules was one of them, to keep them from stepping out of line. But they never behaved quite like *that* – and I never saw anything like when they all lined up as they did, quiet and immediate. That was like someone had pulled the same string on every one of them all at once.'

His concern is alarming, but from the way he keeps bringing it back to his brother, I suspect a part of it may simply be all the anxiety of being so close: to him, to his creations – and hopefully to the secrets he guards so fervently. But it must be a lot – with Matheos's years of isolation, I can't even imagine what it's like being here, let alone with the added mystery of the humans' strange behaviour on top.

'Well,' I consider, trying to reassure him, 'it's been a long time for them – maybe they've learnt some different habits. And Ione did say the mortals had changed since the gods created me. Maybe we're seeing some sort of merging of behaviour from the two – your brother's humans, and the sort the gods moulded when they made me. Or maybe being so near your brother has them behaving differently to other humans?'

Matheos smiles a little. 'Of course, you already have theories.'

'Shall we test them?' I ask, wrapping my arms about myself like it might better hold me together. 'As long as . . . as long as it's not like that again.'

Matheos smiles and my heart squeezes – he's being so good, so unbearably good, and all I want is to fall into his arms right now, to be comforted and held. But after kissing him mere hours ago, I'm not sure that's a sensible idea.

'I don't particularly love busy places either, you know,' he says. 'The more people making noise, the harder it is for me to discern. So I tend to rely on lip-reading, which only gives some clarity and isn't ideal when most large gatherings involve low lighting, hurried movements and people talking through mouthfuls of food. Frankly, it's exhausting. So I'm more than happy to avoid the crowds. We could start with the temples, maybe? It would be a gamble – the gods might not yet know we're here. But if we want to convince them we're here for the town and not the mountains, it could work.'

He nods at the buildings surrounding us, and I see that what I had mistaken for larger homes have spiralling columns, porches facing into the courtyard and statues perched in their centres.

I scrutinize him but can't get a read – unsure whether he is truly interested in going or just trying to distract me from the shame of fleeing the crowd. But maybe he's right, maybe my reaction was nothing to be embarrassed by. And isn't it more interesting than anything? The way my mind works?

I think it's beautiful sometimes, but right now I feel thrown by it, like I have missed a step and lurched to the next. I know there's beauty in that, too, and I hope I find it. But for now, I'm happy to take a distraction.

We start with the Temple of Zeus, imposing and monumental – and the largest, of course. All that time toying with the automatons, wondering if I could build such things too. But actually seeing them? It makes me think that maybe I could. With enough practice and the right tools, maybe I could make things that seem impossible a reality.

But then I remember the mortals have built this incredible thing in honour of the gods, at the foot of the very place where Zeus has bound the one god who actually cares for their well-being. And suddenly they feel less like monuments than tombs.

'You lead,' I whisper. 'I'm not sure I can manage kind words about my creator right now.'

'Excellent idea. I am so known for my adoration of the gods,' Matheos mutters, pushing the door open and holding it wide for me.

We are barely a step through when a priest rushes over to us, almost dwarfed by the draping of his chiton, his gangly limbs darting from beneath outrageous folds.

'What are you doing here?' he asks hurriedly, gaze darting around like there might be a thousand other people to attend to.

Matheos bows his head. 'We wished to pay our respects to the great Lord Zeus.'

I cover my laugh with an unconvincing cough.

The priest's brow furrows. 'This is his home; we do not allow anyone to simply walk in.'

'I'm not anyone,' Matheos says, holding out a hand. 'My name is Epimatheos.'

The priest does not take his hand, merely looks at him with mild bafflement and faint irritation.

Matheos sighs like this is something he encounters often and adds: 'My brother is Prometheus.'

I'm not sure what I'm expecting – gasps? Outrage? Something more than the understanding nod of the priest.

'Ahh, you're an immortal. Very well, I'm sure that's fine, then. But please do be quick, I have to clean the altars, pour libations and polish the busts . . .'

I blink. That's it? How many immortals do they get in here?

But I'm immediately distracted, catching sight of the burning hearth at the centre of the temple. 'That's odd, isn't it?' I ask the priest. 'Zeus taking fire from humans, but expecting one to blaze in his own temple?'

'Oh yes, thank you. *And* I need to sweep the embers from the hearth.'

That appears to be the only answer he plans on giving.

'Sorry, just out of curiosity, why did you choose to work in *this* temple? Why Zeus?'

'Because the temple needed priests,' the man says, a frown forming between his brows. 'There are tasks to be done, jobs to be worked and at the top of that list is to worship the gods.'

Is that it? Do the humans simply do things by rote and out of necessity? I do not even *like* Zeus and I'm sure I could summon a more devout justification for his worship. Where is the passion I feel blazing in my heart, the vibrant need I'd thought so gloriously human?

'I believe you misunderstand the king of the Heavens,' the priest declares with sudden zeal, that very fire I was pondering on lighting his eyes. 'He is just. He is harsh but strong. You cannot expect the gods to abide by some fragile mortal vision of morality. He is the very thunder in the sky, listen – through it can you not feel the pulse of the gods in this world? Their mark on every wonder we exist within?'

He speaks quickly, growing more fevered with every word, spittle flying from his lips, gasping for breath like he might choke on the words in his need to speak them.

'Zeus in his clemency left us with fire to remind us that he did not abandon us, did not leave us in the cold. He took it in his anger, and allowed it to be returned. Punished the traitor and forgave humanity because he is merciful.' The man is so frantic his words vibrate with the force he is snarling them with. They ring in the air around us, and I can barely keep up with his diatribe.

Matheos suddenly takes my arm and pulls me away from the priest. 'Thank you, we'll make our prayers and offerings now.' As he leads me away, his voice drops. 'When I said "make a scene" I did not mean "imply we have ill will towards Zeus in his own temple".'

I'd been so distracted studying the man that I hadn't even thought about us being studied in turn – and now I rush to recover: 'Oh, I am so sorry, dear husband, if it sounded as though I was questioning Lord Zeus. I meant quite the opposite. I wanted to ensure his priests harbour the respect and adoration he deserves. What a glorious temple this is!

Aren't humans wonderful, honouring the gods just like we are supposed to!'

Matheos's glare suggests my lies might not be particularly convincing. But I trust they sound persuasive to ears that know me less well – after all, Hermes gave me this treacherous tongue for a reason.

We pour libations before Zeus's statue and make offerings to the fire. It is all very perfunctory, going through motions and hoping we appear devout.

'We have journeyed a long way to thank you, my lord,' Matheos says quietly, giving a quick nod to the temple. 'We are grateful for our union. Your benevolence is unparalleled.'

It is not particularly heartfelt but something feathers in my chest. To hear that fragile line we tread given voice: enough to give us cause to be here, a brilliant excuse for our journey, but not enough to convey any depth of affection, withholding the implication that they might use us to harm each other. *Afterthought.* But here he is, the truth of him, thinking everything through so carefully, maybe a little too much, mulling things over so long they paralyse him.

Things like me.

And that tender thing fawning over Matheos's genius shatters with the ache of all he has suspended – the question of *us* which feels so very urgent, yet requires a patience that might break me.

We traverse the rest of the town, taking our time to browse market stalls and stroll through quiet alleys. The mountains tower above us, appear to stretch so high I can almost understand why the humans are seemingly indifferent to

Prometheus's suffering – even right beneath it, it feels so very far away.

I run my fingers across silks at a market stand, delighting in the soft feel of them and all their wonderful colours. Further down, a whole stand sells jewellery – wide-linked chains and smooth hammered gold. Behind it are tools, and I reach out – pliers, a small angled hammer, fine wire saws. Most are in bronze, and I think about what Matheos said, about bronze and gold holding magic well. The fact that humans wield the same tools as the gods feels like magic in and of itself.

'They're available, too,' the man behind the stall says, looking up from the chain he has been linking. 'If you have something to offer.'

I smile and shake my head, then turn to Matheos as we continue to walk. 'What did he mean by "offer"?'

'I believe the gods have only just begun sharing the concept of coins with the cities they favour,' Matheos explains. 'When Kerkeis and Ione bring goods they normally have to barter for them.'

'Well, what do *they* offer?'

'Pearls, shells, treasures from sunken ships . . . It's why they don't let me pay for anything – they just pick things up off the ocean floor and trade them.'

We move on to the next stand, laden with bolts of fabric of the kind Ione has occasionally brought me – soft and finely woven.

'Finest in Tarsuras,' the woman smugly declares, her fingers still dancing over a loom set up behind the stall – no one here pausing in their work even to trade their wares.

'They look it,' I agree, reaching for the nearest and its feather-soft weave. 'I'd love one but I'm afraid I don't have anything to trade for it. I'm sure the next –'

'You should take it!' she squeals. 'It would suit you. Look, this emerald would be divine with your amber eyes. And with a figure like yours, you can show off so much of the fabric and all the hard work that went into it! Oh, you must, you simply must. Girls!' she calls to two children behind her, maybe around ten and plucking at threads of their own. 'Here, help me.'

'Oh, you don't have to –'

'No, no, I insist,' she says, dropping her weaving so abruptly the stone weight falls to the ground. She grabs at handfuls of accessories – scraps of linen to tie through hair, rope chiton ties and hammered peplos pins. One of the girls picks up the sheet of fabric and rushes about me before I can protest, tying the chiton over the one I'm wearing.

I catch Matheos's eye – not sure what to do. I cannot possibly let them do this and I have nothing to trade for it. But a fervour reminiscent of the priest's shines in the woman's eyes, and I'm so delighted at the enthusiasm – especially for this, for art and craft and design and beauty – that I'm not sure I can argue.

Matheos is too busy trying to suppress a smile, leaning against the edge of the stall and watching as the two girls rush around me.

'She's right,' he says. 'That colour was made for you.'

That colour is the forest incarnate, the foliage rising stark above us, sheltering us, lining the edges of our cottage. It is the colour of our home, a colour that makes me think of *him*, and

I am certain I am throwing the colour-matching off, flushing as I'm sure I suddenly am.

The woman tries to ply me with the whole stall.

'Take this!' She offers a woven bangle, then reaches for a matching necklace. 'And this!'

'No, please, you need something to trade!'

She blinks. 'Yes, absolutely I do. You're right. You're so very right.'

In the end, I leave with the green silk, a ribbon of the same fabric bound through my curls – letting the children toy with my hair until they're satisfied – and a thick woven shawl, given I neglected to pack any outerwear of my own. Or *anything* of my own.

Matheos gives the woman the skin of healing poultices and a handful of tools in exchange, even as she protests, until I say, 'We insist!' and suddenly she's nodding again, telling me I'm right once more.

We're not a stand away before she's back at the loom, ready to replace what we have purchased.

A few stands over we find jugs and pots, so many amphorae that I don't step any closer in case I knock one over. And every single one is inscribed with art, just like the Palace of Zeus on Olympus, small intricately painted pots so that mortals might bring art into their homes just as the gods do.

Matheos trades bundles of the food we have foraged for a small lekythos of oil for Korax, who has valiantly gone without on our travels, and who laps it up so gleefully I half expect a crowd to gather – this metal dog drinking oil out of a shallow bowl on the floor. But no one questions it.

And when we find the inn, the innkeeper simply looks at Korax and says: 'Sorry, we don't allow dogs – we hardly have enough time to do all our usual work, let alone groom and walk and feed pets.'

Matheos gives Korax an appraising look – like he would love it if it were an actual dog who needed all those things rather than an automaton.

I cover its ears and whisper so only he can hear, 'Do *not* say whatever you're thinking.'

Matheos snorts and turns back to the innkeeper. 'Very well. We can keep the dog outside. Two rooms, please.' Then, at the man's quizzical look, he adds: 'My wife snores.'

I jab him in the side as the innkeeper gestures for us to follow him.

'It will be nice to have a bed again,' Matheos says.

'It will be nice not to sleep beside an inconsiderate half-giant who steals the blanket.'

'Well, next time bring your own.'

Then the innkeeper shudders to a halt before Matheos has finished speaking, and his head jerks, snapping to me with wide-open eyes.

They flick down, right at Korax, and he frowns. 'I'm sorry, is the dog metal?'

'Yes!' I cry, delighted that another human has finally noticed. 'Why does no one seem to care about that?'

He looks from it to me and back. 'Well, how does it work? Did you create it? Are there more? What's its purpose? Why a dog?' I feel that familiar fervour building in his questions. They accelerate, beginning to blur like he cannot utter them quick enough.

I watch as it builds, as it burns within him, that spark I feel within me flaring in echo.

But this time I see the way he directs all of his questions at me, ignoring Matheos whom he was speaking to earlier, ignoring even Korax now, like I'm the only one who might give him those answers he's suddenly desperate for.

'Thank you,' I manage, voice low as a heavy comprehension dawns. 'We'll be fine from here.'

'Yes,' he says before I can even finish. 'I'd best be off!'

He runs so quickly down the steps I worry he might fall.

Korax, Matheos and I trail into one of the rooms, and I shut the door carefully behind me.

Matheos is looking at me like he's seeing me for the first time – or like he's come to the same realization I have.

'It's me. I'm the reason the humans are all behaving so strangely. I do something to them.' I snake my arms about myself, like I might hold myself together in the face of the horrific realization wrenching me apart. 'I *break* them.'

CHAPTER TWENTY-FIVE

'THE HUMANS ARE CALM AND disinterested. They only care about getting their tasks done and things being the way they're supposed to . . .' I begin, thinking aloud, stumbling forward only to start pacing around the small confines of the room.

Korax has immediately hopped on to the bed and Matheos looks about to tell it to get down. He'll lose that battle; I've let it on enough furniture that I'm sure its training is ruined.

Perhaps realizing that, Matheos sighs and turns to me. 'They don't care about much except their work. And then you speak and it's like something inside them ignites.'

'Or touch them!' I realize. 'The man that tried to move me in the crowd – he stopped and apologized and looked very confused about why he was doing it. It was because I was upset, and wanted him to. And the way all those people sprang apart to clear a path for me the moment I said I wanted to leave. I wanted the fabric, and suddenly that poor woman was trying to give me everything she had. That priest was different,'

I say, my steps quickening. 'I don't think I wanted anything from him, just . . . just for him to care. And then he did, but not quite in the way I wanted and, oh Fates, the innkeeper just now. One word from me and that curiosity that's always plagued me suddenly became his.'

Matheos crosses over to me and places his hands on my shoulders, halting my pacing. 'Firstly,' he says, 'if your curiosity has plagued anyone, it's *me*.'

'Matheos,' I growl – then jump a little, seeing my own startled expression on his face. 'Oh, this is strange. Normally it's me annoying you.'

'You don't annoy me, Pandora,' he says, and at my doubtful look he adds: 'Not in a way that I don't . . . tolerate.'

He's still holding me, his hands a heavy anchor on my shoulders, and when he speaks again his words are weighted too, slow and steady like he could calm me with their cadence. 'Returning to the point at hand, evidently there's something about you that the gods crafted to impact the humans.'

'Right. This pattern of theirs – punish Prometheus, then the humans. No wonder your brother didn't want me crossing that threshold – *I'm* the threat to the humans. I'm just some way for the gods to avenge themselves.'

'No, you aren't,' he says firmly.

But what if I'd let all those frenzies go unchallenged? What if those people had worked themselves up until they really couldn't breathe for the words spilling out of them? Or if I'd wanted something else, something worse, or if I'd accidentally said something careless? Just imagining the repercussions makes me want to run for the forest, to never risk contaminating the humans like this again.

'Pandora, you are so much more than whatever they intended,' Matheos says. 'If harming the humans was all the gods wanted from you, they would have sent you here directly. But they didn't, they sent you to me first.'

'For spite!' I determine. 'Because Prometheus told you not to accept a gift and you did. Just as they wanted you to be the one who left the humans with no attributes. And now when I hurt the humans in whatever way they've planned for me to, it was Prometheus's own brother who made it possible.'

His hands move, cradling my face, tilting my head up to him, and I realize I'm doing that thing where I think I'm looking at someone's eyes, but I'm actually a few breaths shy, catching them in my periphery instead. And when I do force myself to look at his eyes, even though I can hold this for only a few seconds, I see the intensity of the spiralling darkness, the brown deepening to pitch, and feel safe and solid and stable, like his gaze might hold me steady. 'There is nothing spiteful about you,' he insists.

'But who knows what I'm capable of?'

He draws in a breath and this close it is as though he inhales me, takes me in slowly and with great consideration. 'Maybe. If we're talking about potential, then very well, Pandora. Perhaps you have the capacity for all that you fear. But what I've seen is you bringing out passion and curiosity and kindness in people that didn't have much of it before. So if the gods created you to be a weapon in a war against humanity, forgive me for thinking we might be safe.'

His voice is low, intense, his face mere inches from mine so that his eyes dart across my face, like observing me all at once is not enough. My mouth dries with all the things I should say – things like *what are we doing?* And *what does this mean?* – but I can't risk breaking this moment between us. I feel like the tension is the only thing keeping me upright.

'Maybe your theory is correct and the gods intended us both to be tools in some plan, but haven't you already decided that we won't be? Maybe this *is* the threat to humanity that my brother warned of – but it's not *you*, it's whatever the gods are trying to achieve. And we're fighting against that, aren't we? If we are a move to be made then we will make moves of our own.'

I love that it is my words he returns to me. A reminder that I can trust myself, that I'm not defenceless in all this because I have so many skills at my disposal – and not all of them were gifted by the gods.

'Yes, yes, you're right,' I admit. 'So now we just have to work out what to do next.'

Matheos smiles, but there's something resigned about it, like there is bitterness in his answer. 'We use it. We make more of a scene, we distract the gods. And then, when they're looking over here, you sneak off to visit Prometheus.'

I bring my hand up, covering the one he still rests upon my cheek. 'Me?' He draws away, so it's only his hand caught in mine that keeps him from retreating. 'Matheos,' I push.

'You were right. It's a good plan.'

'It is a mediocre plan. I just suspect it may be the best one we have.'

'Well, I agree. If there is a chance, however slim, that we might keep the gods from knowing about the visit, a chance of keeping you safe from their potential wrath, then I will take it,' he says – voice catching. And then, lower: 'And honestly,

I don't think I can do it. All this way, every step towards this mountain. I came because Hesione told me to – but I can't . . . I just can't.'

'Alright.' I nod, trying to reassure him, but I'm not sure it will be enough – that perhaps anything ever will be. 'That's fine, I can go.'

'Maybe I'm like the humans and you make me better, too.' His voice is so quiet I can barely hear him, and his eyes are shut, those dark lashes shadowed across his cheeks. 'I think we can do this. We can figure out whatever they're planning and stop it. Prometheus will tell me it's not for me to think about. He'll convince me to obey him and play my part. But this doesn't feel like an overstep.' His hand tightens, pulling me closer, and I take that short step to him, just as his eyes open and lock on mine. 'It doesn't feel beyond me. Not with you.'

'Good,' I say. 'It's not.'

He pauses, allowing himself to linger in those savoured words. When he looks up at me, it is with a shade of the fervour I witnessed in the humans. 'If we are confident the gods created you for some plan of vengeance against my brother, then they didn't make you as a reward for my loyalty. You stayed, once, because we thought they would kill you if you didn't. But they wouldn't care. If your purpose is the humans, Pandora, then the gods can't think you've failed if you hate me.'

I wince, withdrawing a little myself now – a minuscule amount, but with him I count in breaths, and there are a few too many between us. 'I don't hate you.'

'But you could.' He draws nearer, closing that gap and more, reaching for me, his hands at my waist, holding me tight. 'You could pretend. So that if we fail, and the gods come for us, they will not even think to use you to get to me.' His eyes are eclipsed, his pupils swollen to near the edge of the iris, and those pitch-dark depths look endless – endless and aching. 'And then we could . . .'

'We could what, Matheos?' I ask, leaning on to the tips of my toes, a little closer still, my heart hammering so furiously I fear if I don't press myself against him it might burst free and find its twin beat itself. But I need him to say it.

'We could have everything.' He brushes his hand across my cheek, grasps my chin and tilts it up towards him.

Everything. That taut thread in my chest that draws me towards him, that would draw itself in knots so we might never detangle ourselves from one another. The crackling tinder of my heart yearning to be aflame. His heart beating against mine, his breath in my lungs, his hand in mine, his first words in the morning and his last thoughts at night.

Everything.

I do not wait for his lips to find mine.

I lean up, like I am yanked by that unseen thread, and I can feel the static between our lips, the air charged and expectant before our kiss finally sparks. Our lips glide against one another, warm and gentle until Matheos hums and it catches in his throat, and something in me pulses and our kiss becomes so debasingly needy as his tongue slides into my open, desperate mouth and –

Korax barks almost viciously.

'That damn machine,' Matheos growls.

This time I quite agree.

I take a half-step back, hoping this interruption is an easily rectifiable issue that will take no longer than twenty seconds and allow us to return to each other's lips without further hesitation.

It's not.

Matheos groans, staring furiously at the sunset bleeding across the sky like it's a personal slight against him.

'I was just about to pounce on you,' I whine.

'We need to convince the gods you despise me,' he says. 'If we're going to do this, we need to put on a show.'

'So what you're saying is that you *don't* want me to pounce on you?'

He turns his glare from the sunset to me, and somehow it's even more pointed. 'That is decidedly *not* what I am saying. In fact, please assume I am never saying that.'

I deserve monuments – no, kingdoms, *rivers of Hell*, I deserve a very throne on Olympus for resisting him right now.

With a sigh so deep it rattles in my chest I say: 'Well, come on, then. At least you've made it easy to hate you.'

CHAPTER TWENTY-SIX

W E READY OURSELVES QUICKLY AND I dress in my new emerald chiton, slipping off the dress I'd been wearing beneath. We instruct Korax to hide under the bed, hoping none of the staff will even conceive of someone breaking one of their precious rules.

As we reach the bottom of the steps, I grab Matheos's wrist to hold him back. 'Any boundaries in this facade?'

As soon as we are out of that door, any listening god might hear us.

'No,' he says, his gaze raking across me. 'Do whatever you need to do to convince them you despise me.'

'Nothing? So you'd be fine with me flirting with other mortals? I'm sure my disdain would be proved by sticking my tongue down someone else's throat.'

I have no intention – or desire – to do that but it feels like something we ought to discuss.

Matheos's nostrils flare at the thought, and the look he gives me is so covetous it feels indecent. But then he sighs. 'I'm terrified, Pandora. I cannot stress that enough, how deep this terror runs that the gods will take you and hurt you if they know how much I value you. Even a fraction of Prometheus's punishment enacted on you . . .' He reaches for the banister running along the stairs and curls his grip about it so tightly his knuckles pale. 'Do anything it takes. Fawn over other men, seduce other women, call me names, hit me – *rivers of Hell* – stab me if you must.'

'I'm not going to stab you,' I scold. 'It'd only be another job for me to stitch you up again.'

Matheos glowers, his grip not easing on the banister. 'Just do not leave them any doubt that you despise me.'

'Well, you need to hate me too if they're going to buy it. And I definitely do not give you permission to stab me.'

He looks affronted. 'I would never.'

'But you think I would?'

'I think you should at least consider it.'

'Look, we're overcomplicating this,' I say. 'It's the gods we're trying to persuade – so we just have to give them reasons they'd understand. I'll despise you for what Prometheus did – betraying the king I so revere – and you can channel the domineering disdain most of those gods harbour for their wives. Hate me for my humanity; I'll dismiss you as a Titan.'

'Alright.'

Something in his tone makes me look at him sharply. Is this it? The heart of all his reluctance? 'Does it bother you?' I ask, a little sadly. 'That I'm mortal and you're not?'

He glances down the hall, blinking, and I appreciate this is maybe not the best time to ask this. But I think I need to know, before we wield my mortality like an insult.

'Your mortality is bound up in who you are,' he says, voice solemn. I reach for his hand and he meets my gaze. 'I couldn't pick apart the boundlessness and vibrancy to find the mortal core in you. So, no, not in the gods-despising-mortals sense. But if you're asking if I've thought about the fact that one day you're going to die and I'll keep going on? Yes, Pandora, it bothers me.'

'I . . .' I don't really know what to say. I've only existed for a few months. Those stretching years feel like a yawning chasm, and I've been too busy reckoning with all I am to face who I will become.

'But,' he says before I can attempt to comfort him, 'this is a strange world. The rules for the gods' direct creations are often different – you might live longer. Or immortality can be granted, if we wished to seek it. Or I can simply come to terms with it, if you don't want any of that. All many options for a world where we have years together – but right now I'm distracted by the idea that we don't. That something is afoot that might halt our lives in their tracks, mortal and immortal both. And there's no one I'd trust more with finding out what it is than someone with mortal blood burning through their veins.'

I was worried the humans' proclivity for work might prevent us finding anywhere public to spend the evening, but tavernas bookend the streets – and I suppose that running them is still just another job for someone to fulfil.

I think about when I first arrived in Colchis, and how my first route to avoid the despair of Matheos's rejection was to keep busy, to find tasks and to work until I couldn't think any more.

It's a strange sort of kinship to find.

Not the one I was hoping for, but the sort that might make what we're about to do even more difficult.

We finally pass a taverna that looks tolerable – not so loud as to overwhelm me or make hearing difficult for Matheos, and not so quiet as to make the whole point of us being there redundant.

A woman plays an aulos in the corner, fingers deft and lithe on the twin pipes. I suppose I should be thankful some mortals consider art *work*, but then I realize it is likely only allowable because of gods like Apollo, Athena and Dionysus – you cannot be a god of crafts while withholding them from those you expect to worship you.

But the song is pleasant and the lighting is low, and a fire crackles in the corner. Matheos chooses a table at the back so he can sit against the wall with the noise coming from fewer directions. The chairs are uncomfortably narrow, with armrests that dig into my hips, but the moment we're seated, a boy hurries over to light a candle in the centre of the table.

It casts Matheos's face in a beautiful golden light, all its gentle contours and harsh strokes. I feel mesmerized by every tiny detail: the slight scar at his jaw, barely the width of a nail; the thick lines of his brows and the way the hair at the edges flicks out; the way his smile, which ghosts across his lips like he will allow only the barest twitch, always tugs a little more at the left corner than the right. He is lovely, as intricate as the workings of the automatons, and it is so difficult to believe no artistic hand moulded him from clay, too.

The light, the music, the two of us clustered close . . . I feel a deeper ache than the desire I've become so accustomed to.

I want him, suddenly and ardently, in every way the gods once promised.

'Isn't a romantic setting the opposite of what we were going for?' I whisper, forcing my hand on to my lap before I can reach across for him.

'All the better to cause a scene, I suppose,' he says, his eyes flicking around the taverna, and I assume he's looking for our audience, until he drops his gaze to the wavering candlelight and I realize he is simply not risking looking at me. Like he knows he won't be able to force the hatred we need to find if he does.

Then he looks up, and his eyes seem to catch on a table across from us. I follow them to where a group of people are sitting. They're clearly in conversation but it's different from what I've seen before – all animated expressions and rapid hand gestures. When I turn back to Matheos, he looks downright wistful.

'I've heard of languages like that,' he says softly. 'For people like me who have a harder time hearing, or who can't hear at all. They pop up in Deaf communities and, well, I've never had the people to develop one with.'

'Oh,' I say, because it feels like there aren't words in any language for what his isolation has cost him. Not just companionship but community, not just company but language itself. 'Maybe once this is over we can find one and learn.'

His lips press thin, and it's clear he is simply not giving voice to what he already believes is true: this will never be over. There will be no *after* point of the gods' vengeance.

'You have me,' I say. 'Kerkeis and Ione, too. We could make one.'

Not quite the same, not quite the full understanding he deserves. But something.

The corners of his lips twitch. 'I believe you normally start with a sign for your name.'

'Hmm.' I consider him only a moment. Then I bring one hand to the centre of my chest and lay another on my belly. 'This would be yours.'

His brows furrow. 'Why?'

Because *Matheos* to me conjures lungs incapable of holding air, a stomach that flutters and a heart startled to sudden gallop. 'This is where I feel it,' I say. 'When I think of you.'

His eyes meet mine across the flickering candle flame, and I'm not sure how I ever thought those features harsh. Right now they are gentle, made soft by the light and the way he's looking at me. 'I don't think that's universal, Pandora. It might not be quite right for a name. But maybe that could be our sign for . . . something else.'

I feel it all as he looks at me, that internal ache. 'Something else,' I agree.

The server returns then with an oinochoe of wine and a jug of water to mix it.

'So how do we summon the gods?' I ask, suddenly remembering our purpose here. Olympus above, this candlelight is dangerous. I feel the door behind me open again, more people shuffling through. Maybe some of them are gods in disguise.

Did Athena know the truth about me? Is that why she was so certain our passing through Tarsuras would attract attention? The effect I have on the humans, and all the gods drawn here to enjoy the show . . .

'Let's have a drink,' Matheos proposes. 'I imagine they might gather of their own volition – they do so love mortal entertainment, after all. Let's just give them some time to realize we're here.'

'We can order some bread and burn it in sacrifice, too – that might get their attention.'

As Matheos pours wine into my cup an idea coalesces.

'Wait, what if I had more than a drink?' I suggest, keeping my voice low. 'The humans would hate it – a drunk woman in public isn't how things are supposed to be – and you can be awful about it.'

Even beyond a distraction and cementing our ruse, between Matheos's embarrassment and my supposed hangover, it'll be reason enough not to question him being out alone tomorrow, leaving his wife in the inn to reflect on her actions. And in reality I'll be sneaking up to Mount Caucasus.

Matheos raises his cup, and as he is sitting with his back to the wall, so that everyone in here can see his face, he lets his gaze cut across me with a sneer. 'It's a good place to begin, but we're going to have to escalate it.'

I take up my cup and use it to hide my smile. 'Oh, don't worry, I have plans for that.'

The taverna soon grows crowded, full of people stitching scraps of fabric and repairing broken tools because evidently this is still not a place to simply relax. It's busy enough, though, that we can no longer speak freely. Anyone might overhear, as bodies crowd close to our table, as servers wander past, as the music dips and wanes.

I am loud, I am unsteady, I stagger on my return from the bathroom.

I slump unsteadily on to my hand, propped up on the table.

Matheos takes my cup away and I snatch it back. I've mixed the wine with three times as much water as I usually might, but of course no one knows that.

'Hey, I am *not* that drunk!'

'I didn't say you were.' He grinds the words out. 'But you might want to leave some wine for the rest of Colchis.'

I throw myself back in my chair with a huff.

'Well, maybe I should go spend time with the rest of Colchis,' I say. 'I'm sure there's no worse company in the whole land than the man sat opposite me.'

He casts me a withering look – and, honestly, it rather works for him, the disdain daring in the firelight. This is an act but it doesn't matter; I want to push it further. I want his attention, even at its worst. 'You're an embarrassment.'

'Me?' I demand, rising to my feet and letting my voice lift too. 'Gods, don't you have far too many things to be embarrassed about before we reach me? Personally, I'd start somewhere down there.' I give a theatrical wave to his crotch. 'And your inability to satisfy –'

'Excuse *me*!' The server has returned, another oinochoe of wine in his hand, though presumably on its way to another table. 'This is not behaviour we –'

I take the jug from him and pretend to drink straight from it. I suppose I could be doing all this for real, but that's a little Dionysian for my tastes. I remember the way the wine dulled my senses on Olympus, and I must be sharp. I only trust myself to pull this off if it is done with precision, carved the same way a gear in an automaton might be.

I cast my eye around. At least three people are watching me attentively – curious humans or gods? I catch a pair of grey eyes, but Athena is who I expected to be here first. Did she bring others?

And, oh Fates, I hope she appreciates the act. I am surprised to realize that her opinion apparently means enough to me that I need her to know it is one.

'Thank you!' I say, before the server can recover from his indignant spluttering. Then, louder, I shout across the bar. 'Now, who wants to dance?'

A moment before, the mortals had been locked in conversation. If they'd noticed us at all it was with disgruntled glares and hisses under their breath about propriety. But now they clamour, rushing forward, heads turning in my direction.

'I will!'

'It would be an honour!'

'Yes, let's!'

I jump back, reaching for the chair behind me. It is instantaneous, the change I cause. A roiling in my gut, a voice telling me that this is *wrong*, replacing their will with my own. It's how the gods behave.

But I can't afford to hesitate, cannot even let on that I notice the impact I have on the mortals, not with the potential for watching gods – so I take the nearest hand thrust towards me and offer a smile. This is what the gods made me to do, isn't it? To hide my discomfort behind facades. They taught me to deceive, to be irresistible despite myself, and I tell myself I will not do anything cruel to these humans. I can reckon with my reprehensible morals afterwards.

It's just dancing. But it's not.

It's not.

'I'm Pandora,' I say, to the man who reaches me first – and the other humans listen with rapt attention too. One word from me and suddenly they are locked in my orbit. I falter – and then I look at Matheos. His glare, his tense jaw, his beautiful, wonderful face and what the gods torturing me would mean to him.

I'm not sure he would recover – not again. There is only so far you can hurt someone before they break.

So I can pretend for him. And I can ask the humans to pretend for me too.

'Nikandros,' the man says. His hair is like thatch, golden and frayed, his eyes like the warm summer sky. He seems pleasant enough – or perhaps that's me making him so. Perhaps he's cruel, actually, and is kind now only because I want him to be.

'Nikandros, my dreadful husband is being terribly boring. Care to dance?'

A lyre has joined the woman playing the aulos, the two instruments a little jarring together, but quick and cheerful.

No one had been dancing before but since my call nearly everyone has taken to the floor and swings with wild abandon. Maybe they need this. Could the effects linger? I leave and they remember how to break their rules, how to have fun? Could there be some hopeful resolution to this awful thing?

Nikandros and I make it mere steps before Matheos is beside me once more, snatching my hand from the human's, his other on my hip as he spins me to face him.

'What do you think you are doing?' he demands.

'Dancing. I love this song.'

'You do not know this song,' he says, with a tired and weary edge.

'I do now!'

I try to turn back to the music but his grip tightens and he pulls me closer, so my hand rests on his chest. His thumb at my hip rubs a possessive sweep and he glares down from his full height. 'You do not dance with other men when the gods gave you to *me*.'

I scoff, pushing against his chest so that he stumbles back a step. 'Do not presume to tell me what to do, *Titan*.'

His eyebrows shoot up. 'Is that so, *mortal*?'

He sneers the word with just as much venom – and this is fun, actually. Now that it's just between us – the way even when we are faking an argument for Olympian spectators we still bounce off each other so easily.

'I wouldn't forget that fact,' he says, voice a low rumble beneath the music. 'That in a few years you'll be dust and I'll be free of you. You are nothing but a pathetic, worthless –'

'The gods *made* me, Epimatheos. Gods! The greatest beings in all the Heavens, and you're nothing but the brother of a disgraced traitor.'

'Better that than a being destined to decay.'

I turn from him, climbing on to the nearest table before he can begin. The mortals cease dancing immediately and turn to me, like they know I want their attention.

Dear gods, what did they do to me?

'Care to repeat that, Epimatheos?' I demand. 'I'm sure all the decaying beings in this room would love to hear more.'

The humans turn to him with murderous looks – though the moment I hope no violence will occur, the expressions soften a little. And from up here, I see them: the ones not turning, not dancing.

A white-haired man leaning against the bar.

The grey eyes watching me from the corner.

The curly-haired man smiling over a cup of wine.

A skittering in the rafters above and I wonder if there are more – gods hidden as rats and mice, as anything that might go unnoticed.

The music stopped the moment I climbed on this table and I pretend I don't notice the strange behaviour of the humans. That I do not realize I am the cause. As far as I am aware, my purpose is only to love Matheos.

And I'm failing – publicly.

'Get down,' Matheos snarls.

'What was that? Too afraid to repeat it? Surely you can't be *scared* of us mere mortals.'

Matheos's face is stony but his eyes are sparkling with amusement.

Fates, they'll never believe us.

It's too palpable, the way we chime together, are a team even in this. The humans begin yelling, snarling abuse his way, and he just looks up at me like I'm the only thing that matters, like this hatred he's faking is a twisted version of the true zeal beneath.

'I am not,' he says shortly. 'You mortals are weak, ignorant creatures that should have perished when King Zeus took fire from you. My brother was too arrogant to see it, so obsessed with his own might over the gods in the Heavens. I can only assume this is a punishment, too, to send me a mortal wife every bit as vapid as the rest of her kind. Now get down and cease this humiliation.'

The humans yell louder, fury sparking from them. Passion. *Oh, please let them keep it. Please don't let this be for nothing.*

Matheos steps forward and before I can react he has his arms about my sides, is hauling me into the air.

'Put me down!' I demand. Though I'm genuinely a little taken aback – at the firm muscles flexing beneath me, at the surety, at his body against mine.

'That is precisely what I am doing,' he hisses.

He deposits me on the floor without ceremony and as I go to speak he claps his hand over my mouth.

'That is enough.' He leans closer, spitting the words a breath away from me. Something in my chest burns, and his warm hand against my skin is the only thing keeping me from abandoning this charade and putting my lips to better use. 'As you so kindly pointed out, the gods gave you to me. They made you to be a wife and you will behave like one. You will obey me. That is the will of Zeus.'

I try to push him off me, but he is unyielding beneath my palms. Then he clasps both my wrists in a single hand and brings them down to my waist.

Finally, I reluctantly let the fight in me fade. I appear to accept my loss.

And the mortals cease hurling their abuse and fall silent.

'Do you understand?' Matheos asks.

I nod.

He lowers his hand from my mouth and I say nothing, just continue to glare at him with all the fake hatred I can muster.

'I've indulged this whim of yours to come to this hideous mortal town. I will not be doing so again.' He speaks slowly, and just as venomously as I hope my tense posture and clenched jaw convey. His hand slides to the back of my neck, forcing me to look at him – but it's gentle, a caress hidden in plain view, and our eyes meet with an urgent pull. 'You'll stay in the inn tomorrow, reflecting on your despicable behaviour, while I gather supplies. Then we are going home, where I will wait out your sorry existence.'

Each word is delivered with deliberate precision, and he gets a little nearer to me each time he utters one.

I forget everyone else in this taverna, forget all the watching gods, can focus only on the way each breath feels laboured, and how his own are so very close to mine, like we must share the air between us.

'Yes, husband,' I manage, my voice strained. 'Let's leave.'

His eyes dart across me. I wonder if I am flushed. I wonder if the desire encompassing me is palpable outside the two of us, and the tension threaded between us.

'Yes,' he says, his words laden. 'I need to get you back to the inn.'

He grabs my arm and pulls me along, pausing only to barter payment for the wine with the owners. I let my eyes fall to the ground like the perfectly chastened wife who knows she has pushed things too far. Neither of us looks back until we are out of the door.

It's not safe for us to drop our cover entirely, but we relax slightly, his grip on my arm gentler, and I fall into step beside him rather than trailing behind.

I itch with anticipation, which grows stronger with every

beat we draw closer to the inn. Once there, each step up the stairs towards our rooms thrums in my bones.

'My room or yours?' I whisper.

'I believe you mean our room or Korax's,' Matheos replies, turning quickly to flash a grin. 'Why do you think I got two rooms? I've had enough of the damn dog interrupting.'

By the time we reach the door I feel as though I might combust. The slow scrape of the key is agonizing, and I hope Matheos isn't expecting preamble – I plan on shoving him on to the bed the moment we cross the threshold.

But it is he who pulls me across it, slams the door and pushes me straight back against it, one hand still holding mine, flush against the wood, the other curling into my hair just like it did at the river.

Then his lips are on me, desperate and demanding, fingers clenching hard, his body pressed against mine. For a moment, there is the rough door behind me, the latch digging into my back, the sharp tilt of my head turned to face him.

And then nothing but the kiss, all-consuming.

Our hands become clumsy in their desperation – peeling off layers and running across skin, ravenous touch that is never enough. I kiss Matheos until the room spins, until my knees threaten to buckle – and even then he breaks it only to move his lips along my jaw, down to my collarbone, pulling at my neck right where I had his, where already I can see purple spots blooming on his golden-brown skin.

We finally break apart, panting, and I can't stop smiling.

'You must have been desperate to pin me against a wall,' I tease.

'Every minute since I did last,' he admits, eyes running

shamelessly across me. My chiton is thin, and the way he bunches it in the hand that lingers at my hip has it stretched across every curve and swell of my flesh.

'Evidently I should insult your manhood more often. Denounce your entire existence. Mock you before all who will listen . . .'

'Oh.' He finally drags his gaze away from my body, only to look deep into my eyes. His are swallowed by his pupils, his desire a demanding, esurient thing. 'I don't think you'll be speaking all that much for the remainder of the evening.'

'Get on the bed,' I command. 'I made some promises about pouncing that I would like to see to fruition.'

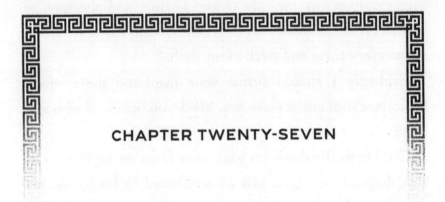

CHAPTER TWENTY-SEVEN

AFTER SO MUCH SEARCHING AND self-interrogation, to finally acknowledge my want, to give myself licence to want and want and want. And to not apologize for it, to give it voice – and taste and touch and feeling . . . I have never felt more settled in this clay-born skin.

We have so little time.

And we make the most of it.

We steal a few hours of sleep before the light wakes us, and I come to with Matheos's arm thrown across my stomach, our bodies curved together, like all the things we did last night did not bring us close enough.

I sigh, content to linger here a little longer, clinging to every second that passes. Matheos stirs a few moments later and turns, clipping his hearing cuffs on before leaning back to whisper things that have my toes curling all over again.

'You are the single most divine creature I have ever laid eyes on,' he says, voice strained – authenticity in the statement he once muttered in falsehood. Only now I do not think he did. I think it was always a truth – just one he was furious about.

'Do you think we have time to do it again before I have to leave?'

'No,' he admits. 'But I think we should anyway.'

'We were right. Lust forces very foolish decisions from us.'

'If this is our undoing then so be it.'

'So be it,' I agree, and turn to kiss him once more.

This time I do not let myself lie in his arms afterwards, do not crawl back into his embrace.

I wash in the bowl of cold water left at our door and begin tying up a chiton as Matheos scowls, as though covering my naked body is an offence. I roll up the hem to begin bandaging my thighs – the fabric barrier all I could do to stop the chafing on the journey here – and my skin smarts as I do, like it knows another long walk is ahead.

When I'm done, I lean back over the bed to kiss Matheos, soft and tender, unlike the urgent need of before.

'You'll need to leave first,' I say. 'Distract them so I can sneak out.'

'You shouldn't go alone,' he says, kissing my knuckles and looking up at me from where I perch above him. 'Take Korax. It will make me feel better to know you have some protection, even if it's utterly useless.'

He rolls off the bed then, washes and pulls on his own clothes as I pack a bag.

He leaves with a final kiss and a long, lingering look. 'Please stay safe. And . . . my brother . . . well. Tell him I don't regret anything. Trust me, he'll have plenty to say about this. In fact, as soon as he starts, please tell him I don't fucking care to hear it. I stand by my choice and he can stay chained to that rock until the Earth itself crumbles for all I care.'

'I don't think that will endear me to my brother-in-law,' I say, trying to pretend Matheos's indignant defence of *us* doesn't make my heart soar.

He kisses me once more. Like every time he commits to a last kiss he must take another.

And then he leaves, the door falling shut behind him.

Korax and I depart soon after, setting off on the dry dirt path that leads towards the mountains. My eyes track often to the cool grey clouds gathering in the sky, as though I might see an eagle swooping through them with bloodied beak and sharpened talons.

Korax's ears are pointed sharply up, alert for danger, but it walks close to me, its side brushing my leg like I might be the one to protect it from any potential threats.

We walk for hours through barren countryside and dusty roads, the incline steepening with every step, until the path fades and the mountain truly begins. We forge our way through brambled thickets and over crumbling rocks, on and on. Soon the coiled tangles of shrubbery peter out, replaced by twisting flowers with sickly yellow petals that bow towards the earth, too heavy for the twin blades they grow on. As I climb higher, they become denser, whole patches of them sprawling across the mountainside.

Every time I think we must nearly be there, we round a corner and the summit rises again, towering above us.

Occasionally, I think I must hear water, or can spy glimpses of a thin stream cutting along the mountainside – and then all at once the river is before me.

'Finally!' Kerkeis's voice rises from the water before she does, leaping out of it in one quick burst.

I half drench myself with the way I throw myself at her, colliding before she's even climbed from the stream's banks.

'What are you doing here?' I demand – but it is half a squeal, and quickly muffled by her hair against my mouth as I wrap my arms about her.

'Are you mistaking me for Ione, because I am certainly *not* a hugger,' she protests.

'Are you sure? Because I'm really very happy to see you.'

She gives a quick squeeze back – the closest I think I'll get to her admitting she feels similarly.

'Are we done now?' she huffs.

And yes, we are, so I draw back and repeat myself: 'What are you doing here?'

'Are you serious?' she asks, glowering as though she believes me intentionally obtuse. 'Half the ocean is talking about what happened between you and Matheos last night.'

'Pardon?' I breathe – because for one foolish moment there is only one thing I can think of that happened between Matheos and me last night.

Well, I suppose *technically* it happened three times.

'Your fight? The mob of humans you led against him? The first and last outing of the Titan and his mortal bride?'

'Oh. Yes.'

'Quite a show,' Kerkeis says. 'So much for remaining under the radar of the gods. But I assumed it meant you were both making your way here, so I thought I should probably ensure you don't die simply trying to climb the mountain.'

'But if the gods see you –'

'I'm well aware of the risk,' she says curtly. 'So let's not waste any more time. Where's Epimatheos?'

'Pulling focus elsewhere. And . . . he didn't think he could face it.'

Because he can't see the gore of Prometheus's torture, not while he blames himself. He cannot hear the snarling insults that will cut him back down to faithful obedience. He cannot face the reality of this, not while he lives its consequences.

It is braver, I think, to look inside yourself and know what will wound you, what will be unfathomable, and draw a line in the sand which you cannot cross, rather than plough ahead without caution.

And I want him to care. I want him to see himself as more than a thing to sacrifice.

'Good,' Kerkeis says, nodding quickly. 'I'm really glad he won't see this.'

It is slow, arduous and deadly. A steady climb alongside the water's edge.

A panic.

A fall.

A snarling rescue – water cocooning me as I plummet into it, plumes of it snatching me from the air just as the sharp rocks edge near.

And then to continue, up and around, rough stone cutting into my palms as I haul myself up.

Thankfully, it is not far, merely dangerous. As I finally heave myself over the last ledge, I collapse, panting for breath, and Kerkeis materializes next to me, similarly worn.

'Thank you,' I manage.

'That was exhausting,' she groans. 'I hate fresh water. It's so sterile and uninteresting and vapid. Even talking about it is tiring and I am never, ever doing this again!'

Korax clambers out of the stream without struggle and I am immensely jealous of the two of them for simply swimming up – though I can *hear* the churning current and know I wouldn't survive it.

'Alright, not much further,' Kerkeis says, nodding at the sloping mountainside ahead of me. 'The nymphs I spoke to came by chariot but they said it was just on from the source of the stream. I'll meet you back here, if that's alright. If it's already a risk then . . .'

'Then no need for you to be where the gods will almost definitely be watching.'

The sky bleeds past sunset into the dull bruise of dusk as we finally draw near, my thighs burning, every breath catching. Korax ambles slowly behind me, and I wonder if the automaton is actually weary – if it even can be – or Hephaestus just programmed it to behave that way.

And then at once I sense its imaginary hackles rise, and the dog stills, staring straight ahead, at the sharp curve we are approaching.

It is the only indication of what awaits us, and that alone disturbs me. I had expected grandeur in this punishment, Prometheus's anguish turned into an altar of Zeus's might. I thought I might pass carrion birds or mountain lions, attracted by the smell of his rich blood seeping into the rocks. And I'd expected Prometheus himself to be a monument somehow. His name is legend, his tale spun of such fine thread it was difficult to believe a man of flesh and blood might truly be chained here. In my mind I had made him a giant, whose very body spanned the mountainside, enormous and untouchable and perhaps able to bear all that heavy pain torn from him.

But when I turn that sharp corner, he is just a man – a fragile, broken one at that.

His limbs are emaciated with hunger, his frame hunched, pulling at the adamantine chains that bind him to the broken pillar set into the rock. They latch on to bronze bands at his wrists and ankles – then lace about his neck and his hips in thin, delicate ribbons that rub burning lines into the skin above the cloth tied about his waist – cloth so long past being stained with golden blood that it is a dark, mottled and hard-baked brown. A messy circle has been dragged through the dirt at his feet, barely visible for the flowers clustering there, fresh ichor staining their budding heads.

His hair is long and tattered, his shoulders sunburnt, his lips chapped. In the dark evening light, hours past his liver being ripped from him, only a shiny, irritated glare lingers across his side, so that I could almost believe the exposure the crueller punishment, the way this man is left to the whims of the elements, worn away by the wind and cold and burning sun as surely as the mountain itself.

'I had hoped the whispers of the earth lied, when they told me of your approach.'

His voice is clear and cutting, not the dry rasp I expected. And it is strong, despite the thin air and the chains looped round his throat. He doesn't look at me until he finishes – as though to raise his head takes energy he does not have to spare.

'I thought it better I came rather than your brother,' I say, taking a few steps closer. My stomach is in knots and I know it is not just the sight of him, but the sight of *him*. Matheos – written into his brother's features. The same slender nose, and brows like a sharp and halting line. The same shared history in the thick dark hair inherited from their mother, the war etched into the broad knuckles of a hand strengthened to wield a sword. 'I hoped it might be safer this way.'

'"Safe" is not a word you conjure.'

'Is there anything I can do?' I ask. 'Before we begin what I'm sure will be a comprehensive run-through of my faults and my need to stay away from your brother. Water? Food? Or . . . I have some medical supplies if –'

'I need nothing, Pandora,' he says wearily, and though malice lingers in his words he also sounds resigned, like these are motions he must go through. 'And certainly not from you. Do you think Zeus would chain me here if starvation or infection might end me before his torture drives truth from my lips?'

I can't look away. There is so much pain here, so much misery. And a testament, too, in this choice of punishment – a mountain almost impossible for a mortal to climb, but something the gods can see as they look out from the Heavens.

Prometheus is a warning to *them*, not to the mortals below. Defy Zeus, choose humans, and end up like this.

'You are crying,' he says, tilting his head to the side so that his tangled hair falls clear of his eyes. 'Why?'

'I'm sorry,' I say quickly, not sure whether it is an instinctive apology or the real pity for his pain. I hadn't considered how overwhelming this would be, and how it all just steals across me so that I myself am surprised by my damp cheeks. 'I just . . . You made us. And this is what they did to you.'

'I did not make *you*,' he says, staring with clear, unblinking focus. 'And yet you seem closer to the mortals I created than the ones the gods have allowed to exist for however many centuries now.'

'Really?'

'How cruel,' he says, smiling bitterly. 'Right there in your voice is the hope I imbued them with. Blind hopefulness, an ability to look past the darkness in search of the light. That was the first thing the gods stripped them of. And here you are, the woman who will take it from them forever.'

I pull my arms about myself. 'Is that the prophecy?'

Prometheus regards me for a long, lingering moment. 'I thought you might last at least a little longer before asking me about that.'

I feel chastened – even though his tone is amused rather than reprimanding. My time feels limited and crushing, but with all the questions in my mind, I could stay here for hours.

'I want to know,' I admit.

'I quite assume you do.'

'Maybe it's because the gods made me with that intent – to find it out. I'm not sure. All I know is I just . . . I want to know. And that want doesn't feel cruel or evil, just driving. But you think the gods created me for some awful purpose?'

'I know they did,' he corrects. 'You will be the downfall of humanity.'

I let the words settle, even though I knew they were coming. His warnings and everything Matheos has told me – I knew he would not care for me as Athena had hoped, even if I had nurtured the thought. But still, from him they feel a true indictment.

Here we are, supposedly: the originator of humanity and the inevitable bringer of its doom.

Like that forges some strange kinship between us, I ask: 'Why did you make humankind?'

He considers me. 'Because Zeus ordered me to.'

I shake my head. 'You love them. That does not come from an order.'

'I just named you the downfall of humanity, and now you would ask me about my love for them?'

It is difficult, to find common ground with a man who hates me. But then, he is not behaving as though he does. More as though he finds the doom I will likely bring simply something regrettable.

'I know you think me the ruin enacted on the thing you love. We can disagree on that, I suppose. But I just have so many questions.'

'You burn with them.'

I nod quickly, relieved he understands. 'I was brought into existence – and they made me so many things. I don't know what it means to be human in this world, to be a woman in this world, to be *me* in this world –'

'None of which are as important as what you actually *are* in this world: a tool of the gods.'

I scan the bronze chains that must surely cast their glare to Olympus. 'Well, aren't we all?'

He barks a laugh. 'I suppose that's true. I have questions too, Pandora. The gods have tried changing my mortals for centuries. What have they done now? The timelines are slippery things in this land – easy to see a future, difficult to know when it's come to pass. Are the mortals violent? Eternal children? Forever toiling? I suppose it does not matter which way the gods have chosen to bastardize my creations this time, stripping them of all that hope and curiosity they so happily gave you. I protected them as best I could – the core of them is untouchable. And still . . .' He drifts off, then stares me down once more.

'What I mean to say, Pandora, is that I do not hate *you*. You seem a wondrous thing – but that does not change what you are. And what the whispers of fate tell me you will do. Do you love the humans, as I do? Is that what drove you to this mountainside?'

I . . . do I? Mostly they were disappointing. But then I think of the glimpses I saw – the silk still draped across my skin, the passion for the gods of Olympus, the hand in mine ready to dance, the music chiming through the air, the art painted on to their pots and the curiosity I prised from them. And I think maybe if I do not love them, I love the potential of them.

And maybe I'd like to see what they – what *we* – become.

'Yes.'

He nods, eyes shuttering like he would linger a moment on that answer, and perhaps like he does not wish to see what will come of it. 'I made the humans, Pandora, because I had just survived a war. That changes who you are – it certainly did with the gods. They were greedy and bitter, their triumph made them grandiose, and I wanted to create something in their image without all that violence behind us. I made the humans to show the gods who they could be.'

'Oh.'

Because that would not please Zeus at all, the thought that he might learn lessons from lesser beings.

'Indeed. So he took fire, had my brother turn animals into predators, made each other something to fight, and the world something to fight against. But there's peace in there somewhere. A desire for it, at least. And you would drive them to quite the opposite, never-ending torment and –'

'But how?'

'I cannot tell you that, Pandora. To know would bring the gods' wrath tenfold, but if you cared for humans as you claim, you would leave this world now. You would run from these lands, hide from the gods themselves, and if you cannot, you ought to consider what you *would* sacrifice for your love of them, Pandora. For the good you hope you might achieve.

'You question the intention of your existence. But perhaps you should think on whether you ought to *exist* at all.'

A rock skitters behind us and I jump, neck smarting with how quickly I turn.

And there is Matheos, storming furiously from the shadows, each forceful step angry and quick until he is standing before his brother, forearm pressed to his throat, dagger clutched tight in his hand, blade shaking against Prometheus's cheek.

'Give me one *very* good reason that I should not use this.'

CHAPTER TWENTY-EIGHT

'WHAT ARE YOU DOING HERE?' I yelp, taking him in quickly. Matheos's cloak is dusty with travel and damp at the edges from wading through the stream. His hair is windswept and I notice – rather unimportantly, given the dagger he's wielding – that he's shaved. I also note my disappointment at that fact – I'd quite been enjoying the fine bristles.

'I came after you.'

'Sorry, let me rephrase: what are you doing here with a dagger at Prometheus's throat?'

Matheos turns to me, that blade not wavering. 'Well, it sounded like my brother was just trying to goad you into killing yourself, so I thought I'd rectify that problem.'

'We must all make sacrifices,' Prometheus says, unrepentant. 'This would never have been the one I would have chosen, nor would it be one we'd be discussing if you hadn't accepted this girl in the first place. Put the weapon down, Epimatheos. Hesione was supposed to be keeping you out of trouble. But once again it is my responsibility to tidy up the messes you have made. Last time I sacrificed myself – I won't allow you to sacrifice humanity now.'

Matheos's grip on the dagger tightens. 'And how exactly is Pandora going to doom us all? You always said the future was set and now you're saying it's shifted, all because I accepted a gift the gods gave me? If your futures are so fragile and changeable, why should I listen to a word you say?'

'You ought to stay out of matters you do not understand, brother.'

'I'm so sorry, Epimatheos,' I rush to interject before his anger can rile him into saying something else – potentially something that will damn him if the gods are truly watching. 'I never should have come here. And certainly not without discussing it with you.'

Matheos finally lowers the blade and steps back from his brother. He gives me a flickering glower – real ire glimmering. Then, at once, judging gods are remembered and here I am, taking responsibility. Now the best he can do is promise to punish me himself and hope that might be enough to appease any gods furious I am here. And if he wants to convince the Olympians that he hates me then threatening his brother on my behalf is something he needs to swiftly cover.

He seems to realize this – even if that glare is all too real, and he is evidently furious about placing the full weight of the blame on me.

'Oh, do not imagine that is forgotten,' he says coldly. 'But we will come to that later. My brother is right, I never should have accepted you.'

Prometheus watches us and it's clear he recognizes the

performance, his gaze darkening. 'Be careful, brother. You risk much here.'

'I've had quite enough of your worthless omens.'

'Prophecies are not set in stone, it's true. But I have reviewed the many threads of fate and worked to draw us down the one that offers the brightest future.'

'I'll have to imagine such brightness, given you've never offered me any glimpses.'

Prometheus lowers his voice to a hiss that may not carry. 'I have offered you as much as you need. One day I will be freed by a son of Zeus. And later, when Kairos is upon us, Zeus will fall.'

Matheos arches a brow. 'Sparse, as prophecies go.'

'You know I can't tell you everything,' Prometheus snarls. 'And there would be no point revealing it when this girl would drag us down another thread.'

'So the future *can* change?' I ask, treacherous hope bleeding into my voice again. But if that's the case, then I really might be able to avoid whatever doom is foretold.

'Of course the future can change,' Prometheus dismisses this – clearly frustrated at having to explain himself. I wonder if he ever has before. 'Why else would Zeus want the details of my prophecy? He wants to know how his fall will come so that he might change it. He's done it before. Metis . . . she was his first wife, you know. Titan of wisdom and mother of Athena. She never got that second child, the one prophesied to overthrow their father. Zeus swallowed Metis whole before he could be tempted to spawn another child with her.'

I can think of other ways to handle the situation. Kronos castrated his own father, for instance. That might be a useful solution.

'Still, there is time, there is time,' Prometheus continues, muttering to the ground now. 'Difficult to kill a Titan, that's the issue. Metis is still in there, somewhere. She flitted from his stomach to his mind and is responsible for every wise thought the man ever has.'

'Is that . . . is that what's going to happen in your prophecy? Metis is going to –'

'No, no. Her involvement is a possibility, certainly. One that could happen given time. But the destiny we are chasing will get him first.'

'And what of the humans?' Matheos asks. 'We just let them suffer in the interim?'

'Trust me, brother, this is the road of least suffering. Or it was – until Pandora came along.'

I fold my arms across my chest, staring this bound man down. 'Well, forgive me for thinking the least suffering is still too much. There must be something more we can do.'

'No. You would rectify one issue by causing another. You do not see the things I do, so listen to me instead: you must allow some evil, in order to reach the greatest good.'

'But . . . how? How do you just allow such terrible things to unfold? Surely your heart is not so logical, surely every good matters regardless of whether it is the greatest and –'

'You are living in an imaginary, idealistic world,' Prometheus spits, pulling at his chains. 'And it is at odds with the one the gods have created. One where the best-case scenario is being bound to a mountain to allow others to thrive. One where some deaths are better than all. Where the gods will wipe the mortals out and start again and it will still be better than the alternative of what you might do to them, to destroy them so thoroughly that wiping the clay clean cannot save them. If you wish to linger in the horror of that possibility then do so, but it will not save them.'

'You want us to let the gods . . . kill all the humans?' My voice is a whisper, too baffled to be aghast.

I'd thought he was telling us to allow the gods to keep picking off humans to harm and destroy. But he means us to allow the gods to annihilate them all? And to do so in the name of some future good?

'It does not matter – they will not succeed. Some will survive and repopulate the –'

Matheos gawks at his brother. 'That's still millions of deaths!'

'I am aware!' Prometheus snarls. 'That is the world Zeus has created. That is what I fight against, that is why I am bound here. But if we want to stop him then we must bide our time, and strike when Kairos is right. To waste your resistance at an inopportune moment is foolish.'

'Well, I do have a history of it,' Matheos counters dryly.

'To reach the promised thread you must traverse those you find unacceptable,' Prometheus insists. 'This is the greatest good, how Zeus falls –'

'Hold on,' Matheos interjects. 'When you say "the greatest good", is that what you mean? The fall of Zeus? Or saving the most lives?'

'The biggest threat to humanity is Zeus,' Prometheus seethes. 'Don't you see? Get rid of one, and you get rid of the other.'

And, oh Fates, is that what he meant, when he warned Matheos not to accept me? When he said the greatest threat was me crossing the threshold? Not to humanity, but to his planned rebellion . . .

Was it that I might stop the bloodshed he deems necessary?

'So, yes, I trust that path is our best course,' he continues, half to himself. 'If you had never accepted this girl into your life, you could have left those unsavoury decisions to those of us with the stomach for them, clung to your morals and maintained you would have made a better choice. But you're in this now, Epimatheos. So listen to me – get rid of her, don't let her near Olympus, and put her down if you must.'

Matheos steps closer to me, stops himself just shy of reaching out for my hand.

'But if the future can change,' I push, 'then we don't have to pick the best path. We can create a new one. You can't possibly see every potential outcome.'

'My answers lie in the Earth, Gaia whispers prophetic wisdom to me. The gods plotting in the Heavens may be shielded from her gaze but the truths she whispers are steadfast as the ground itself. The Heavens cannot alter them. The future wavers, but it does not break.'

He doesn't know. The thought hits me like a stone.

Oh gods, he doesn't know at all.

How much information does he have? Enough to make a show of it, to parade it and convince us he knows best. To have Epimatheos bow to his brother's wisdom in spite of his own doubts. To have even Zeus quaking with the fear of what he is shielding.

But it's a bluff. It's all a bluff.

Has he even seen anything of me? Or is foretelling our doom – and the role I might play in it – just another way to convince us all of his brilliance? To keep him from being written off and forgotten about on this mountain, to keep a sharp hint of threat.

The sun has finally dipped below the horizon, a dark so sudden smothering us so that we can hardly see one another against the jagged slope. We have already risked so much time here, and I feel the moment we realize this discussion must draw to a close.

'Epimatheos,' Prometheus pleads, his voice softening. 'You know that I know best. I have only ever kept you safe and done what I can for the mortals. Don't doubt that I am doing that once more.'

'No,' Matheos says coldly, the shutters down. 'All that I have heard here is that you are once again conspiring against the very gods who freed us from the oppression of the Titans. I want nothing to do with it. Goodbye, brother. I trust I won't be seeing you again. Come along, Pandora, we're going home.'

CHAPTER TWENTY-NINE

W E ALL BUT RUN FROM the mountainside, Korax hot on our heels, eyes aglow, and we don't risk talking again until we find Kerkeis with a bunch of those hideous, twin-stemmed flowers bundled in her arms, leaning in to drag a knife through another bunch.

'I never took Ione for much of a fan of flowers.'

'They love them, actually. Especially daffodils. They think they look like little dragons,' Kerkeis says, straightening up with a smile she can't quite hide from us. 'Epimatheos! You're here? How did you get up the mountain?'

He arches a brow. 'I climbed.'

'It's practically impossible!'

'I'm a Titan.'

'My point remains.'

'And my mother is an ocean nymph. I might not have your skills but the occasional fall into the river won't kill me.'

I scoff, remembering the last river and how that lineage didn't provide much help then.

'Ha, I knew you'd fall!' Kerkeis gathers up the flowers. 'Well, I'm relieved you survived.'

'You sound it.'

'What are these?' I ask, reaching for a petal. Although, from the way they sprouted around Prometheus's feet and trail down the mountainside – like spattered rain, like an eagle with blood dripping from its beak – I suspect they may spring wherever golden ichor touches. 'Or, actually, I think the better question is: what do they do?'

'They can heal most ailments,' Kerkeis says quietly.

'And why do you need flowers that heal?'

Kerkeis glances at the water, as though calculating how quickly she can make her escape. 'We might have been too good at sparking rebellion. With the horrific stories about Poseidon, we thought we ought to tackle him before we came for any Olympians. His own wife was the first to join us and, well, things are escalating quickly. Oceanus, Pontus, Phorcys, Nereus – they never fell to Tartarus like the titans of the sky or scattered like the primordial gods of the land. They've just been biding their time. War may flame quickly between the former kings of the sea.'

'Oh. Is Ione –'

'Fine. They're fine. Having the time of their life, actually, training hippocampi, convinced they might create an oceanic cavalry.'

'But these flowers are why you're here.'

Kerkeis twitches a smile. 'No, they were just a bonus. Now, come on, downstream is easier.'

It is, and at the other end we say a quick goodbye, not wanting to linger anywhere near here much longer. I make her promise she and Ione will be home when we get there. It is so dark now, night all-encompassing, and the long journey home stretches like a chasm before me.

I cheer up slightly at the foot of the mountain, where I see Matheos has tethered a horse and cart.

'Why did you come after me?' I ask, reaching for his hand – the only words I risk asking.

'You were gone for a week,' he replies, his fingers entwining with mine. 'Come, let's get away from here.'

What he doesn't say is that we still cannot speak freely, must wait until we are certain the gods no longer pay us any mind. But he still bundles me into the cart and kisses me gently beneath the cover of its wooden enclosure.

'You can sleep in the back if you want,' he says. 'I'll drive us for a little while.'

But I want to be by his side, even if all I can do is lean against him and feel his pulse flutter beneath his chest. A week, regardless of whether it was only a day for me, is far too long without one another. I think of time twisting like ropes about this land, shifting from mountain to town, and from town to forest, and then I gasp.

'What is it?' he asks, almost in alarm.

My answers lie in the Earth.

'Matheos, can you take us back to that ancient village in the forest? There's something I need to check.'

The first morning under the cover of the trees, I wake to the jostling cart and a painful crick in my neck. I bolt up as it trundles beneath me, kicking a blanket aside and scrambling forward, over the ledge, to rejoin Matheos on the bench.

'You were supposed to wake me,' I protest. It had taken me so long to agree to leave his side to sleep that us swapping over in a few hours' time was the condition of my agreement.

'You needed the sleep,' he says simply.

I hold a hand out for the reins. 'Give me those – you need to rest too.'

'Don't be foolish – no person of any reasonable height could possibly sleep back there.'

My glare is distinctly ineffective when it is *up* at him, and evidently he thinks so too because he meets it with a low chuckle and attempts a condescending pat on my head, foiled only by my elbow shoving into his side.

'If you can't fit in it, perhaps you'd like to be pushed off it instead.'

'With what upper-body strength?' he teases – and I gawk at the stolen line. But he smiles and adds: 'Good morning, Pandora.'

'You're in a disturbingly good mood,' I say. 'Is this where I ruin it by talking about last night?'

Matheos gathers the reins in one hand so he can reach for mine with the other. He brings it to his lips before holding it tight. 'I am in a good mood because I have spent the last week growing increasingly frantic over your disappearance. I will take whatever barbs my brother would hurl to have you back by my side.'

'You didn't exactly take them. There was definitely a dagger involved.'

'Yes – not something I've done before.' He takes a moment to ponder that. 'But I didn't hate it.'

I think of it now, the taut lines of his shoulders as he levelled the blade and the fierceness with which he threatened his brother, which is *definitely* not something I condone, even if it was to defend me and even if Prometheus did start the threats by trying to manipulate me towards self-annihilation and –

Fine. Apparently I'm condoning it.

'I didn't hate it either,' I admit.

Matheos drapes his arm across my shoulders, and I shift to lean against him a little more.

'Do you think he's right?' I ask. 'That the greatest threat to the mortals is Zeus?'

'Maybe. Or maybe he's finally broken under all this torture and his desire for vengeance has corrupted his love for humanity. Or maybe he's right, and letting Zeus do as he wishes this time will ensure more happiness in the long run. But regardless, that's the issue, isn't it? Prometheus expects my unyielding trust, when he was the one who followed Zeus into battle to begin with. Either he knows all, or he does not. Either the future is laid out ahead in all its possibilities and I need only obey him to find the most promising thread, or futures he cannot conceive of are possible too. And if that's the case, why listen to him at all?'

The horse and cart is a little quicker than walking, managing the journey to the village in just under a week.

We make campfires when we stop, spending whole evenings against the flames, and there talk turns from the gods and Prometheus to everything else: our hopes, our anxieties and all we might wish for in a gentler world.

We sit so close to each other we are practically on top of one another, until we are, whiling away whole evenings in our tent or before the fire or atop the cart, inhaling one another, kissing until the world swims, exploring each other until each freckle forms a well-known map of a beloved landscape, one I wish to traverse again and again and again.

I take note of the way Matheos finds familiarity with my body, too – the casual touches I am unsure he is even aware of. He toys with my hair when we lie beside each other, wittering on late into the night. He will come up behind me as I tend to Deinos – as Matheos has begun calling the horse – wrapping his arms around me, his hands resting on my hips as he holds me close – all intentional, obviously, but does he know that he always makes the same soft hum as he does it? Does he know he stoops to rest his chin on my shoulder, like the little groove was made precisely for this, to be a home for his affection, my body sculpted to be held? Does he know that there is a point each morning, before he is fully awake, when he stirs just enough to know he has moved apart from me in the night, and he shuffles closer, sighing as he finds me before his sleep deepens once more.

I have no idea we're approaching the ruins of the old village until we're upon them – one moment there are trees and next the barren meadow and its crumbling brick.

I do not even wait for the cart to roll to a stop, too thrilled at the thought of uncovering a mystery. Even if there is nothing there, that is something of an answer, and that will scratch the curious itch that just wants to *know*.

'Pandora!' Matheos calls, that beautiful mix of exasperated and amused that I often entice from him. He's still pulling the cart to a stop when I reach those evenly spaced stones marking out a tangled stretch of ground.

I crouch, brushing moss and grime from the rocks, but the engravings on them have eroded beyond recognition. Still, etched rocks and earth beneath my feet that just feels a little bit off? I know what I'm expecting, cannot see how it will help, but still I cannot shake the feeling that it will. If the answers are in the Earth, here is where I know I will find them.

I'm using a sharp-edged spoon to prise out the dirt when Korax runs over and pushes my hands aside with its nose, before its paws start tearing into the ground.

'Were you trying to dig with a spoon?' Matheos asks.

'When I first met you, you were eating eggshells.'

'You're never going to let that one go, are you?'

'One day, maybe, when you do something more foolish to replace it.'

He comes to kneel beside me in the dirt, his hand finding the small of my back like he cannot conceive of being so close without us touching.

Korax digs for a while. Whatever it is – if there is anything at all, it is buried deep.

When the dog finally stops, it steps back expectantly. And despite my need to know what is in the hole, I take the time to fill my spoon with a measure of oil which it laps up happily in reward for a job well done.

The hole is wide and deep – too far to simply reach into.

'I'm going to have to get in,' I say.

'You want to climb into a grave?' Matheos asks, because that is, surely, what this is.

'Will you help me?' I ask, holding out my hand.

He sighs before he takes it. 'I assume there's no chance you'll let me go instead?'

'No, I need to see this myself.'

'As expected. Very well, but you're defending me when Kerkeis yells at me for lowering my wife into a grave.'

'I'll protect you from the mean nymph lady,' I promise.

Matheos holds me steady as I lower myself down the slippery slope Korax has torn up, sliding the rest of the way in and trying to plant my feet at the edges, where I am less likely to crush anything important.

I can see something beneath the dirt, Korax having stopped just before it damaged anything. Clever dog.

I brush the mud and earth aside, revealing worn patches of material clinging to bone. I suspect it may once have been a burial shroud.

It comes into shape as I dust the dirt away – a skeleton, of course.

But other things, too – a decorative comb, a thin bracelet of hammered gold still encircling a wrist, shards of broken pottery.

I reach for one, imagining this person once buried with a jar or pot.

But there's engraving on it, and unlike the stones it is not worn away.

I realize what it is at once – because they do this, I know. I don't know how I know; it is simply in my mind like so many other things, wisdom placed by the gods. In some mortal towns where parchment is expensive and papyrus rare, they use scraps of pottery to vote or send their prayers at the shrines of gods like Asclepius.

Or to say goodbye.

Beloved mother.

I reach for another.

Missed sister.

And another.

Perfect daughter.

'Matheos!' I call, like he is not right beside me.

'What? What is it?'

'Help me up, please!' My voice is panicked and Matheos responds with the haste I would expect. But it is only the whirring cogs of my mind that cause the tension, as everything slots into place – and a horror too large to imagine dawns.

He grips me tight and half pulls me from the grave as I scramble up beside him. I open my palm, revealing the shards of pottery, the etchings marked upon them.

Matheos shakes his head, at a loss. 'I'm not with you. What puzzle are you seeing?'

'Kerkeis and Ione said for the Olympians and the rest of the world it had been centuries since the war, since you last walked through here. And look – it has to be, right? This is not a few decades' worth of decay; this town is in ruins.'

'Yes?'

'And Chronos's powers can only speed things up – like the way we race through it at our house, or the mountains. The inverse isn't possible. Which means those centuries can't have happened in the few months I've been in existence.'

He's still staring at me, still not understanding what I'm saying.

'I'm not the first woman, Matheos. Look – I bet if we dig up all these graves we'll find all that variety Ione said didn't exist among humans until I walked the Earth. And they'll have lived and died hundreds of years before the gods even thought to make me.'

And finally his eyes widen with understanding. 'Rivers of Hell, the gods want to kill all humans.'

'It's not merely a future threat. It's something they've done before.'

CHAPTER THIRTY

ONCE I REALIZE IT, IT is impossible to ignore. I always wondered why they gave me such stories. Did the gods want me to figure it out? Or were they so desperate for my adoration they never considered my realizing their contradictions?

Dionysus at the celebration after my creation. Dionysus who was born of a mortal woman.

Apollo was there, too – and he was shocked when Hermes told him I was the first woman. How did I not see it? The way Hermes hurried the conversation on . . .

And then – Aphrodite! Sending letters to Adonis, whose mortal mother she herself tormented.

And once those small threads are unpicked, nothing makes sense at all, down to the tiniest of details. Mortal women cropping up in the childhoods of the gods, in their first stories, in every tale they lived long before they thought to build me.

The answers were in the Earth, and they were in my head all this time.

The gods have tried changing my mortals for centuries, Prometheus said. And he said I would so destroy them that even *wiping the clay clean cannot save them.* Is that what the gods have done? Experimented with the mortals, created new batches and wiped out the old?

We uncover a few more graves, just to check – and find more proof, generations of families, children, those *others* that were not supposed to exist until I reshaped humanity away from a race of grown men.

And then the strangest thing of all: a skeleton of solid silver. It is the oldest of them, no scraps of fabric left to decay, nothing else to have survived, just the deepest grave and the thickest gathering of growth on the stones.

The day is warm, the exertion sweltering but I am cold to my bones, like if I cut deep enough I might find silver too.

'I wish we'd found this on our way to your brother,' I say. 'He might have cleared up some questions.'

'He wouldn't have,' Matheos says bitterly. 'He would just have berated us further for interfering. He built that house. He commanded I go there and stay out of it all. How furious he would be that we disobeyed.'

'Wait, he built the house?' I ask, my mind whirring once more.

But this time there is no answer waiting at the end of my contemplations. Just a frustrating unfurling of more questions.

'We can't leave them like this,' Matheos says. 'It's disrespectful.'

'Agreed.'

I scurry from grave to grave, ensuring all the shards of pottery are back in with the deceased. We toss handfuls of dirt into each before letting Korax bury the rest. I feel like we should say prayers but the last thing we need is those prayers reaching the ears of a god who might realize what we've discovered, so we sit in silence instead, and do not speak until we are in the cart and well away from the haunted village.

'How do you think they died?' I ask. 'Last time, I mean – not those individuals. If the gods wiped mortals out before and then created them all anew – or . . . maybe not? Prometheus suggested some would survive. Maybe that's what happened last time, maybe they annihilated most of them and experimented on the others. Maybe I'm just the first woman of this batch. I just . . . oh gods, this is horrible.'

'I don't know what happened,' Matheos says, eyes set dead ahead. 'And I'm not sure how we'll ever find out. Let alone in enough time to stop them from doing it again.'

We arrive home as night falls the next day. I feel heavy, like this despondent feeling settling within me is a physical weight for me to haul forth. Matheos takes my hand and I startle, lost in the repetitive churn of my despair.

I glance up at him, his face bright beneath the burning stars.

'We will stop this,' he insists, and it's so absurd – him being the optimistic one – that I laugh.

'How? They're gods.'

'And in my experience that has been their greatest shortcoming. They underestimate those who are not. They consider us afterthoughts if they think about us at all.'

I grip his hand tighter at that. 'Matheos –'

'It's alright,' he assures me. 'I have often found it a power, and I know I am not an afterthought to the people who matter.'

He looks at me with his own sort of heaviness, like the weight of all this has only made the thing between us more important. And I feel that, too, this need to cling to what we have because everything else is so enormous, and so cacophonous, that the two of us in its centre might be the only steady thing we can hold on to.

'You're my first thought, Matheos.'

He pushes my hair from my face so that when his nose wrinkles – *quite* adorably – it does not feel quite so dismissive. 'You should be your first thought. Please allow me to be the second.'

I consider. 'What about us? Can *we* be my first thought?'

He glowers, that stern brow furrowing in a way I was once unnervingly familiar with. 'That simply feels like a way of avoiding my suggestion.'

'I have better ways,' I say, and lean on to the tips of my toes to kiss his scowling mouth – but I still have to clench his chiton tight and pull him down to meet me.

The heaviness does not vanish but it shifts, no longer feels sad but poignant, like in the face of so much looming violence this affection matters all the more.

There is something so utterly and beautifully human about tending the soft flames. That maybe we cannot stop the howling gales to come, maybe we are not quite as powerful as that, but it matters nonetheless.

It matters that there is love here.

CHAPTER THIRTY-ONE

WE ARE DESCENDED UPON THE moment we cross the threshold – every automaton rushing to greet us, the birds landing on our shoulders and arms, nudging us with their heads to demand our attention.

'How was he?'

I jump at the voice, then freeze at the sight of the woman stepping through the door, a shawl wrapped around her shoulders – one that I myself once wove.

One I probably should have taken with me – but of course I simply ran when Hesione told me Matheos had left. And here she still is, waiting for our return.

My skin crawls at the thought of her making herself at home while we were gone, though I suppose I prefer it to the thought of her out there, scheming without us.

'I think we'd better discuss that inside, don't you?' I ask, breezing past her, and past Matheos too, like I cannot still feel the pressure of his lips, like I do not want to scream at this woman to leave us in blissful solitude.

The inside of our home is less suited for gathering in

than the courtyard – a handful of sparse chairs, all differing heights and styles. But what if the stars themselves can spy on us? Or Selene, sent to draw the moon and our secrets along with it.

'Please,' Hesione says as soon as we sit, looking at us both with an almost fervent need. 'I just need to know if he's alright.'

'He's not,' Matheos says bluntly, and I realize that he is nowhere near as all right with that fact as he has been pretending. 'He's suffering. But he's also indignant and righteous. He seems distracted from what they're doing to him. He's latched on to his fury and his determination that one day it will all be undone.'

Hesione tilts her chin up, lashes fluttering before she gives a curt nod. 'I suppose that's the best that could be expected. And did he say anything about what lies ahead?'

I squeeze Matheos's knee, trying to warn him off revealing too much. 'Have you met many women before?'

'What?' she asks, irritated. 'Yes, of course.'

'Recently?'

She glowers at me, and I can see her cycling through potential responses. That, yes, they were recent, or they were immortal women like her. But I can see the moment she understands that I know – and then as she decides what to tell me beyond that.

'Once,' she tells me. 'A long time ago, just after they imprisoned Prometheus on that mountain. A woman with skin so gold I thought her an automaton until she drew close. But I never saw another like her. Though I have heard rumours.'

Gold. Silver. Clay.

What is going on?

Korax chooses that moment to run in with tea balanced precariously on its back, its tail wagging so delightedly at being back home and in the role it knows that the liquid sloshes across the tray.

I reach for the jug and set it on the table before I speak.

'Prometheus said the gods wanted to kill all the mortals.' I only say it to watch her reaction.

To note that it is not one of shock.

'But you knew that.'

She bites at her lip, eyes flicking from me to Matheos.

'We are on the same side, Hesione.' He gives her nothing. 'Why won't you tell us what you know?'

She laughs, a little scornfully. 'Your brother was quite clear, Epimatheos. What you don't know keeps you safe, keeps you alive.'

'Keeps me in the dark, so he can wield the knowledge as power, you mean.'

Hesione blinks at him, then casts a withering glare at me, a half-smile on her lips. 'Your words, I assume?'

'Oh, my words couldn't possibly be said,' I say as I pour out the tea, 'within the confines of xenia.'

Matheos snorts, and I have to suppress a smile of my own.

'He's going to kill them and you aren't surprised – shall we return to that?' I ask, passing her a cup.

She narrows her eyes a moment, then shakes her head. 'I suppose if my husband trusted you enough to tell you that, I can share a little too.'

She waits as though I might thank her, but I just nod for her to go on and do not correct her that Prometheus's knowledge did not come from his considering me some sort of confidante.

'There was a race of men. That's what they always say, and at first I thought they meant it literally. Then I realized the gods just thought anyone who wasn't a man wasn't worth commenting on, but the others were there all the same. And, like Epimatheos, I felt if I got too close the Olympians would suspect I harboured the same love for the mortals as my husband did and might punish me too. So I kept my distance, but the rumours found me anyway. Mostly of the silver ones – childhood that stretched to a hundred years, all of humanity dependent on their mothers, and only a short time as adults before death snatched them. I'd hoped, despite what my husband had foretold, that that might make them harmless enough to the gods that they would leave the mortals alone. But it seems those humans had no interest in wasting their short adulthoods in worship of the Olympians, and Zeus . . . well. I don't know how he did it. But he put an end to them.'

My hand flutters to my mouth – and I don't know why it hurts so much. I knew this, didn't I? That the gods must have done something horrendous to eradicate the humans, and the women before me, and pretend I was the first. But to hear it now, and for such petty reasons . . .

'I don't think they make them fully anew each time,' Hesione continues. 'More that they alter the survivors and churn more of them out. Make them in the same shape Prometheus first did, but shift the material from clay to gold and silver – I even heard rumours of wood. And I suppose they're about to do it again.'

Matheos takes my hand from his knee and grips it tight.

'It's alright. It's almost over,' Hesione continues, though her words are more placating than reassuring. 'Prometheus said there would be five races – so if everything's on course, this will be the last. We just have to wait it out, because the time for Zeus to fall will come but we can't act while he is still so powerful. Don't give me that look,' she scolds – directing all her ire at me despite the fact Matheos is also glaring daggers at her. 'The only solace we've been able to find is playing a longer game while the gods seek instant gratification. Let them distract themselves with this pettiness; we'll bide our time and strike.'

'The mortal deaths are a pettiness?' I repeat.

'A convenient distraction?' Matheos adds, just as horrified.

Hesione's eyes flash. 'That is not what I said. You wouldn't understand, you're casting your judgement from a surface reflection, unable to even conceive of the depths below.'

'Help us, then,' I plead. 'Tell us.'

Hesione shakes her head and looks to Matheos. 'What did Prometheus say about the plan? Let us discuss it in private.'

Matheos glances down. 'There's nothing to discuss.' Hesione's gaze pins Matheos in place – and he does not cower before it; there's a rigidity that wasn't there before.

'Prometheus said the future would not change – that *the plan* of his eventual release and the Kairos point of Zeus's fall would still come.'

'That's not true,' she says slowly, and now her gaze shifts, weighted with disappointment like it is digging foundations, settling low enough that Matheos will be unable to lift it. 'The future was never merely going to arrive, we always had to sacrifice for it.' Her eyes flit to me with dawning realization. 'That's it, isn't it? He demanded a sacrifice you're unwilling to make. We knew all along that you shouldn't have accepted this "gift", and that remains our only option to get things back on track – to reject the gift. Reject her.'

Matheos remains calm but it's a stillness that bristles, rage seething beneath. 'I think the gods created a scapegoat for their will and my brother is foolish enough to believe it. Show me where in this grand game of gods and Titans one mortal girl is to blame?'

Hesione stands and casts a final, hateful look at me before turning back to him. 'We never should have entrusted you with any of this, Epimatheos. Your brother will be ashamed. Everything we've worked for, everything we've sacrificed, and you stand in defiance? I won't have it. As always, someone else is expected to repair what you have broken. Well, for once I hope you're prepared to deal with the consequences.'

She turns and sweeps from a room still ringing with her words, leaving only the fierce chill of them.

And the horror of all that has come before, and all that will surely follow after.

CHAPTER THIRTY-TWO

'**A**RE YOU ALRIGHT?' I ASK the moment she's gone.

Matheos worries his fingers through his hair, those thick black curls longer than I remember. It suits him, the messiness, the way it falls a little into his face and softens the sharp edges of his features.

He pushes it back as he turns to me, like he would not let a single strand block his view. 'Are *you* alright?'

'Me?'

'Of course. All anyone's told you is that you're not to be trusted, that you're little more than a way for the gods to catch us or a threat that has to be contained.'

'I ...' It had not really occurred to me to be upset. 'It doesn't feel great,' I admit. 'From Prometheus it hurt but only because my expectations were so high. He made humanity. He suffers for them. It is as you said: he is good even if he is also awful. Hesione, though? Well, I understand why you had reservations about me, and I can believe them from her too. But she was so busy being terrible to *you* that I was a little distracted.'

Matheos offers me his hand, pulling me to my feet and then forward, into his arms.

'I never noticed how they spoke to me,' he says. 'Not until they turned their cruelty on you.'

'Matheos, I –'

'I'm fine. I promise I'm fine, Pandora. But you . . .' He pauses, coiling a lock of my hair about his finger. 'You are the combined effort of a dozen gods.'

'That is indeed factually correct.'

He scowls, but presses on despite my attempts to ruin the moment. 'I am sure every single one of them had their own agenda and aims. I am sure many beings in this world want you to be a hundred different things, so they made you to bend and bow and break to make everyone around you happy. All their magic and all their ambition and here you are: the limitless potential of all that power.'

I'm not sure I understand what he is trying to say. But his tone is warm, his body close, and with all the intensity of his gaze I'm probably not thinking with full capacity.

'You are the closest I could come to believing the gods are capable of miracles.'

I can feel the chill in the air as he reaches to brush a lock of my hair from my face. I hadn't realized how much I needed kindness, not after everything and not when he is still not close enough.

'The gods may call you all the gifts and expect you to dole them back out in pleasantries and tasks. But please, Pandora, be selfish. Give yourself happiness, too.'

'I am happy, Matheos,' I say, taking his hand from my hair and twining my fingers through his. 'I'm really very happy.'

I lean up to claim his lips before he can kiss mine, to show him just how happy I am, and how I am even more so when I am with him.

He pulls me close like he would prove his happiness, too. His kiss is reverent, precise. Like an artist with a brush, he kisses me as though he is crafting a masterpiece.

He breaks away when I am short of breath, pushes a strand of my hair back behind my ear, his finger running along my cheek. 'It's come to my attention that I haven't had the opportunity to take your clothes off within these walls.'

I can feel my pulse thrumming in my throat, his touch a dial – everything under it accelerating, my breath catching, drawing in the scent of him. All other thoughts disperse and there is only him, and the ache in my gut that he conjures.

'If memory serves, you had many weeks of such opportunity.' I pout. 'You were just too busy being an arse.'

'Nevertheless, there are at least seven surfaces in this house I'd like to lay you down upon.'

'And so many walls,' I whisper, leaning into the hand trailing down my face once more, tilting my chin up as his hands curl into my hair. 'You love pushing me against those.'

'I firmly believe it's my gods-given purpose.' He breathes the words against my lips before crushing them once more, his kiss a heady thing, all its need and desire but all its desperation, too, the catch of teeth, the surrendering moans, like it is all too much and still nowhere near enough.

We are snatches: broken kisses as we tear at clothes, trails down collarbones before grasping each other once more, hands scrambling, barely resting before they are clutching again, like we cannot settle, are too busy wanting it all, needing everything at once.

He pushes me to the wall at last, drops to his knees, and, resting his head on my thigh as he looks up at me, says: 'You are not their ruination, Pandora. You are mine.'

I blamed the road, at first, for the way we could not keep our hands off each other. There was little to do, especially when the horse and cart meant we did not even need to pay all that much attention to navigating the forest. What better way to pass the time? It was exploratory, almost like those first days of figuring out who I was – to discover all the things I can do, all the ways I can feel.

But it's worse now we're home – this place transformed for the way it is truly ours now, for the way a future is so visible within its walls, even when the very future itself is under threat. *Us* has never felt so tangible a concept and we are both aflame with the possibility of it, fervently stoking all those palpable sparks and fires.

We fall asleep in the bed I made for Matheos, entwined with one another, and wake just the same, lying in each other's arms for another hour or so before we stumble into the kitchen to bake bread, which mostly involves me kneading dough and Matheos clinging behind me, pressing kisses to the crook of my neck. Rain pours in sheets, so impenetrable we cannot see the edge of the courtyard, so we dine inside, lasting only half the meal before I am on his lap, tasting the wine on his lips.

The rain never lets up, so a few hours later I decide it might be worth venturing out into it anyway.

'What is it?' Matheos asks, coming up behind me and placing a hand on my waist to look past my shoulder as I eye the downpour from the doorway.

'Prometheus built this house,' I say. 'And his answers are in the ground so . . .'

'So you want to dig again? Shall I fetch the spoon?'

I glower, eliciting a soft chuckle.

'There's something out there,' I say. 'I'm certain.'

'Have I just been a way to pass the time until you can get back to one of your beloved mysteries?'

'Oh no, don't make me choose. I thought you cared about my happiness. I'd like both, please.'

'I didn't say I was upset about it,' he says, the corners of his lips tilting with a smirk that feels decidedly intimate – like it is a challenge, a dare, something for me to resist. 'Quite the opposite – I hope you have more time to kill later.'

'You're insatiable,' I say, rolling my eyes and shedding my cloak so it cannot absorb the water. I venture out in only my chiton, the rain making it sheer and tight, so that when Matheos rushes to follow me I need only arch a brow at him to have him pointedly looking at my forehead and not a single inch lower.

'You wonder why,' he mutters.

The droplets cling and they are so cold I half expect them to crystalize into ice. Each one stabs as it hits, malevolent pinpricks that only spur us to move faster so that we might race back indoors. But it makes it easier to dig into the soft mud beneath the tiles. Matheos prises them up as I push the shovel in, Korax refusing to budge from the doorway. Given the way it's been gleefully jumping in rivers,

I do not think automatons rust in water – I suspect it's just a coward.

We spend hours searching and discover nothing, but maybe the answers lie deeper than we can dig or in the foundations themselves. Or, as Matheos says: 'It worked once. But I don't believe every answer to my brother's secrets lies beneath the ground. What exactly is it you're hoping to find?'

I hesitate, like sharing a theory would be to risk it. But Matheos has never shot down my ideas so perhaps they are safe with him. 'I don't believe time is warped across all of Colchis – and I definitely don't think a battle is to blame. I think Prometheus spread that tale to cover up whatever he did here, and whatever he's done to that mountain to mean our moments stretch to weeks.'

'So we're looking for something relating to Chronos?'

As he says that, my gaze catches on what should have been obvious from the start.

'I'm so stupid,' I say.

'Doubtful.'

'It's never made any sense,' I mutter, wading through the churning mess of mud and rock to the sundial at the very centre of the courtyard, a barely visible blur in all this rain.

There has been only the barest hint of daylight to shade it today – but even when the sun burns brightly, the arch of the house curves about it, enabling only a few hours when it might be in any way useful.

Unless, of course, that's not its purpose.

I fall to my knees beside it, running my fingers over every dent and groove. But they are only the marking for the hours, carved round the circular frame where the tall gnomon rises to throw its shadow, the thin rod angled across its centre.

I grab it and pull, hoping to lift the whole thing, but the fragile tip snaps off in my hand. Obviously – the base is a huge slab of rock. I am racing too quickly, keen to reach the end of the puzzle without considering the steps needed to get there.

'Well, it certainly won't work now,' Matheos says, surveying the flat disc of stone that remains.

'Help me,' I say, casting the useless rod aside and running my fingers round the edge for some sort of grip.

Matheos crouches beside me, wedging his fingers beneath the disc, and together we heave. It gives almost immediately, but it's so immensely heavy that I nearly flinch and drop it, crushing Matheos's fingers in the process. I feel the strain across my shoulders, my arms, my hands as I shift the weight to my palms until it finally tips over, crashing into the mud below.

And there, on its underside: the true markings.

A man at the centre, ringed by twelve segments, each patterned with a series of dots.

'What is it?' Matheos asks.

'I suspect the same markings Prometheus had carved into the dirt beneath his feet.'

I run my finger over the markings, realizing they're not stone at all. They're clay.

Bronze and gold hold magic best, but even clay can be imbued.

But Prometheus stood upon patterns drawn in the mud? Marks that – Oh.

All the metallic blood that drenched it, his power seeping into the dirt, those runes sparking to life.

But what *are* those markings? We consider them as the rain falls, each drop like seconds ticking away. But still it does not become clear.

'Let's draw a replica,' I suggest. 'So we don't have to stare at it in the rain.'

But it's so detailed that drawing it isn't an easy task to get right, and we don't have parchment large enough to convey precisely what it is we're seeing. So I stand in the rain, sketching it piece by piece, using my body to shield the tablet – the soft wax the only material that won't immediately be destroyed by the torrent – and then I race inside, passing it to Matheos who copies it in charcoal on to a wall, before taking up another and beginning on a new section.

Once I've got them all down, we shift the sundial back into place before a god can glance this way. Broken, it is little more than a circlet of rock, rising half a foot from the ground, a plinth in the centre of the courtyard.

Matheos finishes copying the tablets as I change into fresh clothes, clutching a himation about my shoulders for warmth. I emerge as he makes a final mark on the wall, glances at the tablet in his hands to check and nods, declaring it done.

He steps back, and together we survey the replica he has scrawled across the far edge of our reception room.

And for the first time since we tipped that sundial on its side, parts of it come to us.

'That's Capricorn,' Matheos says, stepping closer to trace the edges of one of the patterns. 'The half-goat, half-fish who aided Zeus during the gigantomachy. He set it among the stars.'

'Gigantomachy?' I ask, though it feels like something I once knew. The gods and all those tales of their might, steadily slipping from my mind.

'Giants. They attacked the Olympians after the Titans fell. The war was over before I even heard tales of it, though apparently these markings might be why.'

'Are they all constellations?' I ask, examining them closer. But for all the knowledge the gods gave me, they did not include the stars above. That is not the aspect of the Heavens they wanted me to know about.

'This one is.' Matheos nods at the one I stand by, then his hand covers mine and guides it over the marks he has carved. 'Pisces – the fish who rescued Aphrodite and Eros in the same war. See, this is the cord, leading to the tail, and this is where it loops.'

I shiver at the smooth roll of his voice, at the way he shows me the stars, and his warm hand over mine, his body pressed close. And in that moment I am so deliriously happy that I exist, that I have a hand Matheos can hold and a heart that always beats a little faster when he's around. And, too, I am so very envious of the gods in their Heavens. All that power and the very stars themselves at their fingertips. If I had their abilities, I would create such beauty, would take this joy inside my chest and set the world aflame with how brightly it burns.

How did they do this? Channel all of me into this form and still allow me to feel things so vast they surely cannot be contained, must shine from me as light or else ripple as waves through the air. How did they make me capable of such radiance?

'I don't recognize the others,' Matheos continues, oblivious to the way I must surely be glowing. 'But I've seen new stars appear before, normally followed by Kerkeis rushing to tell me some tale of gods and heroes.' He taps a few of the dots. 'These stars appeared long after my brother was chained to Mount Caucasus. So maybe others haven't appeared yet either. But they will.'

'They're prophecies,' I say, taking them in. 'Futures yet to pass.'

'*Time* yet to pass?' Matheos asks.

His words linger – because I don't want to say yes. To declare it would unravel a further puzzle. Are they simply predictions, or a way of binding magic in stone, or perhaps even an indication of where the magic actually lies? But I'm almost certain they have something to do with Prometheus catching and weaving time within our home, making it slow while the horrors the gods inflict race on.

But can we change it? Bring *us* into the moment and make *us* a part of this?

'Prometheus said that when Kairos is upon us, Zeus will fall,' I say, staring at the wall.

Kairos. A critical time. The right moment.

'What if . . .'

'Go on,' Matheos encourages.

'It's just a theory. One I have no idea how we would even go about testing.'

'There are few things in this world I would trust more than your theories.'

I take a breath, trying not to be too distracted by the way that makes something in my chest pulse almost intolerably.

'Kronos stole the power of Chronos, right? From the god of the same name. Every other power wielded by the Titans was re-allocated when they fell. Except for that one. There are the Horae,' I remember them alongside the Graces at my creation, adorning me with flowers. 'But that's not quite the same – personifications of seasons and hours? That's only a fragment of the same power, a way to make sense of it. But there's no god of time itself. So what happened to it? It wasn't like Kairos, too grandiose to be wielded by one person for long. So what if Prometheus found a way to take it – or some of it, at least – if it did indeed fragment?'

'He pockets it for when he needs it. He spreads rumours of the lingering effects of a battle to cover up what he took. And he uses that power to make time accelerate,' Matheos finishes my thought. 'It's how he survives the torture the gods inflict – he's speeding through it, through time. And so are we because of whatever he did here.'

So can we buy more time before the worst comes to pass?

We fall silent for a few moments – taking in the sheer expanse of the symbols on the wall. Every pinprick in each of those twelve segments feels charged, like by marking them down we have channelled the magic ourselves, even as it fades into the stone.

But it feels enormous, unwieldy, like even pressed into this pattern it surely cannot be contained.

'It's a relief, isn't it?' I ask, running my finger across one of the constellations etched into the wall. 'That more stars will come? That even with so all-encompassing a threat there will be more lights blazing in the sky, more stories for constellations to form, more people to gaze up and tell them.'

Matheos doesn't say anything. He just watches me, a glint to his gaze that I would mistake for longing if he didn't already have me so completely. So if not longing, then what, because it's wistful and taut, a need that must be quenched.

'Yes,' he says quietly. 'It's a relief.'

I expect him to turn to the stars but it's like he's forgotten they're there, as though I am the only thing worth marvelling at.

'It's fathomless, unreachable,' Matheos goes on. 'The gods and all their powers, shaping the very world around us. I thought I didn't care for it, needed only my tiny corner of its shores. Years of my life spent caring about the small, important things – when all along I had time itself etched within the foundations of my home. So maybe it's both: the small and the large, the close and the immediate. Maybe saving one means saving the other. But, Pandora, the only world I care to protect is one with you in it.'

'Matheos . . .' I step a little closer, but he stays resolute, like if he does not speak now he'll lose his nerve.

'That's what you are. In all your studies and examinations, to me you are each tiny detail. The way your eyes light up as you land on an idea, or the way you can't stand silence so your whistling floats down the halls, and the way you always press hardest in your final knead of dough like that's the one that counts. And you are the intangible: the way you perceive such beauty in the world, your every racing thought and the futures yet to unfold. You are everything.'

He still doesn't step towards me; he stands like the weight of all he is saying has grounded him in place. So I close the distance instead, reaching up, arms about his neck, pulling him down until our noses brush.

'And I love you,' he breathes, in the moment before he closes that final inch between us to press his lips to mine.

I inhale him, devour him, crush my lips against his with a desire that feels born of necessity, like without him I might never breathe again. He lifts me such that my legs have to catch round his waist so we do not stagger to the ground.

He stumbles back as he adjusts his angle on me until we are leaning against those stars on the wall, but what do they matter when our kiss contains everything the universe and all that time could hope to offer?

'I love you too,' I gasp. 'In case that wasn't obvious.'

He laughs, shifting his hold on me so that his hands grasp my thighs. 'I think you've made that pretty obvious.'

My fingers tighten in his hair, and I like that when he holds me like this, perched on the blades of his hips, I am taller than he is, by an inch or so, and I can pull his head back to where our lips can touch and I can hold him and feel him and revel in him.

Korax begins barking seconds before a knock pounds at the door – the door of the house itself, not the front wall – though the lights begin flashing all the same. Someone has already got past it – and Korax wouldn't be barking if it were Ione or Kerkeis.

Which is the only reason I don't ignore whoever it is and insist we continue.

Matheos lowers me down and I stumble a little, staggering down the hall until my legs remember how to work, shutting the door firmly behind us before we open the one at the front.

It's Hermes, smiling delightedly despite the rain that has his dark hair slicked tight to his reddish-brown skin. His winged shoes flap inches above the layers of mud.

Perhaps churning up the garden paving stones in the middle of an incessant downpour was not my finest hour.

'Hello, lovebirds,' Hermes says. 'I'm here to invite you both to Olympus.'

CHAPTER THIRTY-THREE

'**H**ERMES.'

'Yes, Epi, well done.' The god gives a well-worn sort of condescending grin, like it rarely leaves his face, like it's maybe not only Epimatheos he breaks it out for, and like maybe my fists curling at my side are an overreaction. 'It's me, well spotted. Now might I please come in out of this interminable rain?'

I push the door open a little further and step back, thinking of when I first arrived and how the gods trapped Matheos into letting me stay. And now, to leave a guest out in rain like this? Or to invite a predator into our home? Which threat is greater: the unseen curses of broken hospitality laws or Hermes, draping his cloak over a waiting Korax like the dog is a statue to be adorned?

'Are you remodelling?' the god asks, not caring to keep the sneering edge from his voice as he casts a glance back towards the torn-up courtyard. I turn back, checking the hall door is indeed shut, blocking our replica of the symbols beneath the sundial. We can't risk Hermes seeing it. What if he recognizes something we don't?

Worse, what if he's here because of it? It cannot be a coincidence, can it? All those weeks alone, and now a god at our door a mere day after we return from Tarsuras.

I need to disarm him. To reinforce that there is nothing to worry about.

I remember Hermes on Olympus and how much he enjoyed the give-and-take, and though I'm a little late in finding the right mask, now I readily slip it on.

'Oh Hermes, thank the Heavens. One more second alone with my husband and I'd do a lot worse to him than tear up his courtyard.'

Matheos joins me a beat later, snarling my name like it's a personal offence. '*Pandora.*'

'What? Going to yell at me in front of the gods who made me? Go right ahead, Titan, I'm pretty sure I know whose side they'll be on.' I hiss the words out like they scald, only so that I can turn to Hermes with a soft smile. 'Now please, tell me, how is everybody? I so fondly remember my time on Olympus.'

Matheos mutters beneath his breath like a whiny child: 'Feel free to return.'

I take a moment, ready to hurl something back – and realize my pulse is racing, exhilarated. My awareness of him beside me grows until every inch between us seems an affront and I realize it's this – the positioning of ourselves against the world, the con that only we know, the mere idea of any hatred between us being so laughable that we can manipulate it like this without ever once doubting it . . .

I love being on the inside, with him.

'Oh, this is *interesting*,' Hermes says before I can speak, leaning in close like he can see the tension thrumming between us. 'I thought this party would be quite boring, honestly. Father's in one of his gloating moods, which normally means he wants everyone to just shut up and listen to his stories that make increasingly less sense the more Ganymede refills his cups. But you two . . . oh, everyone's going to love it. Right, go on, go pack a bag or whatever it is both of you need for a visit to Olympus. I borrowed Apollo's chariot so it should be a quick trip up.'

'Party?' I ask, forcing a smile I certainly don't believe in – not least because I have not in any way prepared for this level of socializing and my brain feels like it's in free fall.

'Tonight,' he says, and I try not to wince. 'To celebrate all this.' Hermes waves a vague hand at the door he came through. 'His grand master plan of . . . what was it again . . . oh yes, rain. Ingenious. Fascinating. Wholly original.'

The master plan . . . No.

It couldn't be something so mundane. It's too horrific, a kind of evil I could not even guess at – that Zeus, king of the gods, conqueror of the Titans, who smote gods with his lightning, would be content to let the humans slowly drown beneath the rising floods.

'Father's been quite insufferably smug so most of us are hoping this celebration gets it out of his system.' Hermes might lose an eyeball if he rolls them back any further. 'Dionysus is bringing his strongest wines so I imagine we'll make it through with minimal teeth-grinding or bloodshed.'

'Oh, ah, how delightful! And he . . . he wants us in attendance?'

'My father loves an audience. As the representative of the humans, I expect he wants you grovelling in worship. I assume that won't be a problem?'

'No, no,' I rush. 'I'm just not sure I have anything suitable to wear, that's all.'

Hermes waves a hand. 'Whatever we made you in will be fine.'

Absolutely not.

'No one cares what you wear, Pandora,' Matheos snipes.

'Fine,' I snarl back, stalking from the room and not checking whether he's following.

He is, of course, pausing only to grab Stephanos and quietly instruct him not to let Hermes anywhere else in the house.

We wait to talk until we are upstairs and firmly away from Hermes – which involves venturing outside to the long walkway that connects the upper rooms, the rain slashing through at such an angle that the overhanging roof does little to protect us from the lacerating drops.

But when the door finally shuts behind us, I do not waste a moment.

'This is a trap, isn't it?'

Matheos leans against the wall, his body all artful slants as he regards me with a calm nonchalance that I am certainly not feeling. 'I would assume so, yes.'

I didn't need it confirmed, but hearing it makes the panic simmering in my chest claw at my throat.

'You think they're lying to us about the party? Trying to lure us to Olympus to punish us for visiting Prometheus?'

'Oh no,' Matheos says. 'I think there's a party. I just think we might be the evening's entertainment rather than its guests.

Or a part of it, at least. If it's to celebrate the eradication of the humans, then you're the human invited to watch and decry the gods' might and I'm there in Prometheus's stead to watch his beloved creations drown. Our suffering is a part of the show. Quite literally – didn't Prometheus imply you would be given a choice: something awful, or letting the mortals drown? I assume that will be the show. Forcing people to betray their own kind in favour of the gods is one of Zeus's favourite forms of entertainment. Or it might be even worse – if they know we've been conspiring against them, we might wish we faced the same fate as the mortals.'

He says this all with a nihilistic detachment – like it's set, and with nothing to be done he will simply lean back and watch it all happen.

'Right, and you're not climbing out of the window because . . .'

Matheos glances at the window without much commitment. 'Do you think we could run? That we could hide from the gods? I imagine that would only make it worse.'

'Will you stop being so infuriatingly calm about this?' I demand – because it's making me feel like I am doing this wrong, reacting incorrectly. My fear shot through with that damn lingering doubt that I'm not being all they built me to be – perfect and irresistible.

Matheos gives me a sharp look, one laced with surprise and a hint of hurt. 'Pandora, I'm terrified. But this is not my first time cornered by the gods. I know that the only hope we stand is to play their game and make the right choice – or the better one, if that's all you have left. But if you want to run, we can run.'

'No,' I say slowly. And not only because I agree that we would never make it.

Matheos's eyes narrow. 'No, absolutely not.'

'What? I thought you didn't want to run!'

'Not that. The look on your face. You want to take this awful situation and lace it with even further risk.'

'I'm not that readable!'

He waits, gaze expectant until I finally cave. 'But yes, I do think we could use this. If they're going to punish us for our insolence then at least they're taking us to the seat of their power first. We might last long enough to find out how they're killing these humans and stop it.'

It is the first break in his resolve I have seen, as he tears himself from the wall and shakes his head furiously, grabbing a bag and tossing it on to the bed to begin to pack. 'Olympus above, Pandora. Why is surviving never enough for you?'

I don't answer that – not least because I know he knows why. He survived. It was not enough for him.

'The party is a distraction. I could sneak away to Athena's library to research Kairos and Chronos or I can discover how Zeus plans on drowning the world and put a stop to it. I can do something *more* than march to Olympus simply because they told me to and face whatever it is they're planning on doing to us with the smile they carved on to my face. That's what's more than surviving, Matheos. Being a person and not their tool. We find a third option for whatever choice they try to force upon me. We fight back. We lie. We grovel and apologize and pretend wronging the gods is the worst thing we could ever conceive of, and while they're considering whether they buy it or not, we strike.'

'Well, on that part I agree,' Matheos says, calming a little, and I join him to gather my things. 'I am too stupid to know better and you are only mortal, so how could you behave as cunningly as the gods when they are so much more than you. And with how much we hate each other, how could they possibly concoct a worse punishment for us than being stuck in this house with one another for the rest of – No, you can't bring that.'

'What?' I scowl, having thrown a collection of our things into a sack.

'*That.*' He pokes at the red silk chiton hanging out the side of the bag. 'You cannot possibly expect me to keep up the ruse that I despise you and want nothing to do with you if you plan on wearing that.'

'You cannot be serious.' The very Heavens themselves are caving in, the gods are likely building the stage for our slaughter and he can't remain focused past one image of me in tight silk?

His gaze is steadfast, fixated in a way that normally results in his lips crashing into mine.

'I'm very serious, Pandora.'

I swallow – with great difficulty.

'I thought you said no one cared what I wore?'

'Believe me, I care very much whenever you wear anything at all – you being clothed always feels as though it goes against the very laws of the universe.'

I can't even look at him as he says this – knowing if I do I'll crumble, Hermes and all of Olympus be damned. The danger we find ourselves in, the adrenaline burning in my veins – all that heat is pushed between us instead. Forget running, we'll stay in this room until the rain crushes us, until the tides sweep in and the whole world washes away.

'You just told me you loved me, Matheos. I think we're doomed no matter what I wear.'

From the floorboards below, Stephanos gives a low rumbling growl.

'I think we'd better not leave Hermes alone for much longer,' I say, tying the bag up tight – red dress firmly included.

If he's going to look at me with disgust, I want to make it as difficult for him as possible.

In fact, if he's going to resist me, then I'm going to make sure it's the hardest thing he's ever done.

We step outside into blazing sunshine, the clouds having been swept away like a god's hand has wiped them clear.

Hermes glances up with a soft hum. 'I suppose he's holding off on that one, then. Right, the chariot is this way.'

The journey up is just as windblown and nauseating as the way down, and there's no time to admire the approach of Olympus – there are only the hazy white clouds in the sky and then the rocky mountain below, heaving beneath me as the world sways.

'Let me take you to the palace – I'm sure the Graces can help you get ready,' Hermes says while I'm still struggling to think straight. 'Do you want separate rooms or –'

'No,' Matheos says quickly. 'My wife will stay with me.'

And I appreciate the short bluntness of it, the way he does not offer a reason why so that we do not have to follow it with: 'Because we trust none of you.'

Hermes laughs. 'Ahh, I see it's another one of *those* marriages.

Perhaps less interesting than I expected, then. You'll find we're not exactly lacking in possessive, contemptuous unions on Olympus.'

I'm whisked away from Matheos the moment we step through the door of the palace, drawn down gilded halls that feel cold and hollow, like anything might await in all this emptiness, before being delivered into the hands of the three Graces who squeal in greeting and excitedly welcome me into their circle of preparations.

I try to calculate the time allotted to us, weighing it up against all I want to discover on Olympus. But I can't rush to Athena or rummage through Hephaestus's workshop – not while maintaining this act of a mortal who behaves only in accordance with the will of Olympus.

I'll have to wait until the party distracts everyone.

A bath is set into the floor that is larger than our courtyard, full to the brim with pink-hued bubbles and littered with pots laden with soaps and serums. The whole room is full of steam, and at the other side row upon row of dresses hang, tables are clustered with combs and jewels and the Graces sit braiding each other's hair until the moment I walk in, when they rush to take up my strands and declare it a veritable emergency.

Which I assume means my usual tumbling curls did not take well to the hurtling chariot ride.

It doesn't quite feel like they are pampering me for slaughter, so I can only assume that if Zeus does mean to make a show of harming me, it will at least be a surprise to these kind women who seem to care only for my comfort.

They introduce themselves as Thalia, Euphrosyne and Aglaea – the latter of whom takes a particularly keen interest in me, bringing up moments of my creation repeatedly, like they're fond memories for us all to share.

'Do you know Hephaestus wouldn't even start until he'd got the exact mixture of clay he wanted? He's so precise, isn't he? All that focus, the attention to detail? It's mesmerizing.'

I'm pretty sure Hephaestus is still married to Aphrodite, but it appears Aglaea's gunning to be my new stepmother.

Wait – is that ... Alright, interesting. I never really put much stock in the idea of parenthood given I didn't have any parents, but it appears I've managed to acquire daddy issues all the same. Between Hephaestus moulding me and Zeus sparking my existence with only a few words ...

Which were?

I blink, looking around at the golden beams and shining pillars of Olympus, letting their brilliance burn into my mind. I can half see the storeroom once more, the shambolic forge and scattered tools, the smell of baked clay lingering in the air. Zeus said something when he commanded me to be made. Two words, I think ...

But somewhere in the palace someone laughs, a high-pitched shriek that is nothing really, but it startles me enough that the thought slips from my mind entirely.

When we are done, the four of us gather before a huge mirror, surveying our efforts. My hair is piled in an artfully messy knot on top of my head, curls spiralling about my face – the sort of hairstyle you can imagine plucking out pin by pin. Strands of gold hang through my ears, dusting my shoulders. And then the red spill of silk begins, my chiton tied firmly about my waist, even though Thalia took one look at me, declared us about the same size and rushed to bring back an entire collection of gowns. At my doubtful glance she added, 'We can pin it at the shoulders to lift it up.' Because we might be similarly voluptuous but she's still a good head taller than me.

Maybe another outfit would have the same effect – showing off my every dip and the sensuous rounded glory it renders me in – but I want *this* dress, not only to tease Matheos with my beauty but to say that I know exactly what this dress does to him and I'm going to do it on purpose.

The only addition I borrow from their collection is a long, layered necklace that emphasizes the plunge of my dress.

The Graces are stunning, too, and we all shower each other with compliments in a way that feels simultaneously rote and beautiful. Like they are all scripted, but not without meaning – this ritual of kindness a precious thing in itself.

I think of when I first complimented the dress and the work that went into me, and how the male gods laughed. But if I'd stayed here, I might have suspected my purpose had something to do with this – this togetherness and reciprocity. Maybe that's why the men distrusted it; they fear camaraderie among us.

With mere minutes until Zeus's gathering, I thank them for their work, promise I'll see them later and rush to find Matheos.

I almost collide with him in the hallway, where already sounds from the gathering gods filter down to us, twinkling music playing behind. The ceilings of the Olympian palace tower above us, the halls so wide everything feels vacuous and thoroughly exposed.

Matheos startles, freezing at the sight of me, the only indication of any reaction a twitch at his jaw as his eyes trail down me.

'I thought me wearing clothes went against the laws of nature,' I tease, though it's not particularly easy when he too has spent this hour getting ready.

His chiton is a blue so dark it is almost black, like the ocean at dusk, its churning depths clashing against the dim rocks below. It hangs in long, elegant drapes that make him look taller and exaggerate the gentle muscles at the shoulders so that his waist is a drawn-in point. Gold cuffs shine at his wrists, the same burnished gold as the metal wrought around his ears. His eyes shine against the sparkle, the deep brown capturing every flickering candle flame and light bouncing off the metallic floor.

'By the Fates, we're done for,' he mutters, shutting his eyes and lingering for a moment on the thought of the impossible task ahead.

'Well, we knew that already, didn't we?'

Matheos metes out his gaze with small allowance. A careful sip, something to be savoured before a gulp can drown him whole. 'If the gods do mean to end us, at least this is my final view.'

'So, you look like that,' I say, keeping my eyes very open and taking in every inch of him while I still can.

'Yes, and you look like . . . that.' He gestures, shifting his focus to my hairline like he has risked too much already.

'And we have to pretend to hate each other.'

'Yes.'

'And on top of all of that –' I can barely manage the words, my mouth is so dry – 'we're now going to a party, which is going to be loud. So you'll be relying on lip-reading more than usual?'

'Yes.'

'So I have to pretend to hate you, my very hot husband who just declared a love that we're yet to celebrate, while you're staring at my lips?'

Matheos gives a half-nod, half-wince. 'Aside from missing the part where I'm having to be anywhere near you while you look like that without wanting to undo all the Graces' work in very short succession or mentioning the invisible blade the gods have levelled at our backs, pushing us towards this, then, yes, you've aptly summarized the numerous perils stacked against us.'

So much for using the party as a distraction while I gather my answers; I'll be too distracted myself to remember the questions.

'Alright.' I hear the tension in my own voice and wonder just how much we can convince the gods of our hatred when the energy between us is so excruciatingly palpable. 'Let's get this over with.'

We just need to convince them we are of no consequence. That we are petty, wrapped up in our own hatred. That we could never disobey them, would never even think about it.

Or, as I look at Matheos before me, I just have to convince them that *he* wouldn't.

'I'm very sorry,' he says, finally meeting my gaze. 'For the things I'm going to say about you.'

'You can make them up to me later.'

His smile unfurls, slow, deliberate and thoroughly wicked. 'In *every* conceivable way.'

Oh Fates, my knees feel weak and if I conceive of a *single* one of those ways right now I'm going to topple over.

Matheos offers me his arm and I take it quickly, thankful for someone to lean against. I stare down the golden, glimmering hall where the tinkling sounds of the gods celebrating mass slaughter chime. I feel my rage settle in my bones, the rigid set of my shoulders and clenched jaw. Let them read my anger as they wish, let them see it as nothing more than hatred for Matheos, and they will.

They do not need convincing, I am sure. They will believe I despise Matheos because they do, because anyone who is not an Olympian is unworthy.

We walk into the Great Hall, my fingers clenching Matheos's arm a little too tightly.

I feel as though I have fallen through time – the chattering gods, the melodic tunes gently strummed, the clack of heels on the golden floor, the laughter that catches at some unwound thread of myself. It's not panic, more an excruciating awareness of my existence, here and now and apart from it all, nothing out of the ordinary and yet it is *so very much*.

I do not want to drink to numb it again, I want to be sharp.

I drop Matheos's arm, even that contact a little overwhelming.

'Might I have a word, before we begin?' he demands, nodding to the side of the room and striding towards it before I realize what he's doing. He weaves away from the musicians, where most of the gods linger, clustered together, some already casting curious looks our way.

I can immediately breathe a little better. It's how I imagine a sudden plunge into the icy ocean, constricting and overwhelming, but now, a chance to acclimatize.

I can do this – can talk to people to distract myself from the noise, cling to the edges to avoid the mass of brushing dresses and accidental touches in the crowd.

'If you embarrass me tonight,' he says, not even turning to face me before he begins speaking, 'we leave. I will drag you out of here by your hair if I must. Being here is a *privilege*.' It's all very good apart from the way his eyes are boring into me. He might as well be elbowing me in the side and asking if I understand what he's getting at. 'So I suggest you behave, because we do not have to stay.'

My pulse skitters and, with it, my remaining tension eases. Because no, we do not have to stay.

I do not need to tell myself I can do this. Rather, if I cannot do this, that is perfectly fine – no failure, no loss, just a different course.

And if I want to leave, Matheos will come with me.

The gods will likely haul us back when they want us. We do not have to be among them to wait it out. We could find a quiet room, could decide to no longer convince anyone of anything and choose that if these are to be our last moments, we enjoy them in each other's arms.

'Do you understand?'

I roll my eyes – and it's not entirely an act. His words are sharp but I'm relieved no one can see his face as I can because it really is far from convincing.

I'm going to enjoy teasing him about it afterwards.

'Yes, husband, lord of my person, ruler of my existence, master of my – what was it again? Attendance at parties?'

'Watch your tongue.'

My smile is like a sharp lash, a devilish tease. 'Oh, I'm sure many people will be doing that for me.'

Matheos's eyes drop to my lips, and he swallows, his gaze flicking away as quickly as it landed.

I strut back into the party, ready to throw myself into this role – where I am just a girl who wants to have some fun, with a husband who finds my joy irritating and embarrassing.

I snatch a cup from a passing server, and take a tentative sip. It's dark and heady, which is a relief. Something that coats my tongue and lingers, so I might make a single serving last hours.

'The finest grapes in Naxos,' Dionysus says, appearing at my side and tapping the cup in my hand.

'Are all the grapes not fine in Naxos?' I counter, a wry arch to my brow and an intimate smile flashed in his direction.

A hand brushes the small of my back, comes to rest upon it as Matheos settles beside me. He stands closer than he usually might, possessive in his angling, as he gives a nod to Dionysus and greets him with a strange sort of flatness to his voice – a complex mix, and I realize Matheos is at once attempting his foolish Epimatheos role, awed at the gods and thankful for his presence among them, while also playing the fiercely jealous husband who still manages to despise his wife.

He comes across as petulant, a man who knows he has lost, who cannot possibly compete with the gods – and having nowhere else to take out that anger, directs it at me.

'Well, aren't you just an adorable couple,' Dionysus says, wry amusement written clean across his face. 'You're quite right, Pandora, no lacklustre grape has ever been grown on my island. Your wife has an acute palate, Epimatheos.'

'She should, she's sampled enough wine.'

'Yes, I heard about that little night out with the humans!' At this Dionysus sounds delighted. 'Aren't they fun? A shame about all this.'

And there's something I almost miss, too caught up in flicking irritated looks at Matheos – and that's Dionysus's anger, too.

How many gods here are outraged at what Zeus is doing?

And, more importantly, why aren't any of them trying to stop him?

Could I use their anger still? Perhaps not be so bold as to acquire allies but maybe leverage their fury to buy me the moment I need.

'Pandora, Pandora, Pandora!' Apollo sings, strutting towards us in a low-cut chiton, layers of necklaces draped so his skin flashes through, gold against gold.

Matheos's grip on me tightens – and I'm not sure it's part of the act, because the way Apollo so flagrantly lets his gaze wander about me, like he is consuming me piece by piece, has rage simmering in my veins, too. So much lust and not a drop of respect and still I force a smile for him, push a strand of my hair aside and say his name like I'm savouring it all the same.

'You don't mind, do you, Epimatheos, if I steal your wife for a dance?' The threat is not an undercurrent but a riptide, surging through his words. Apollo, council member and son of Zeus, one of the most powerful gods in the Heavens – and Epimatheos, a disgraced Titan. There is nothing Apollo might ask of him that he could refuse – he could take me to his bed if he were discreet enough to avoid catching the eye of Hera, queen of the gods and goddess of marriage, and then Epimatheos would simply have to swallow his rage.

Of course, I'd have several things to say about it, but if Apollo wishes to make his interest known, I'll happily use it.

Matheos turns to me and I see the question in his eyes – ruse or not, if I do not wish to do this, he will stop it and suffer the consequences.

But I grin and sigh: 'Oh, it would be so lovely to dance with someone who actually knows what they're doing.'

Dionysus snorts and Matheos shifts his supposed displeasure with Apollo on to me, the only place it could possibly land and exactly what these gods will expect. Heavens forbid any of them ever works through an emotion. Far better to take it out on the nearest human.

'Take her,' Matheos says, pushing me forward. 'And my thanks for a moment's respite.'

I turn to glower at him, his own look of contempt simmering back, and I feel that taut thread between us pull. I linger for a moment in the intensity of it, hatred I want to collide with, and smother that filthy look with need.

It's an echo of where we once were – the insistence of his hatred while it was very, *very* clear that the gods had not failed in their mission of making me irresistible to him – and now, fake or not, that tension resurfaces, a spark begging to flame.

Apollo takes my hand and guides me away. But it doesn't break the pull between us – instead I feel Matheos's gaze on me for every step I take, catch sight of him as Apollo places his hand on my waist, and he is looking right at me, unwavering and steadfast.

I force myself to turn, to look into Apollo's eyes instead, but I feel the heat of Matheos's fixation all the same.

'A tedious man, your husband.'

'Oh, let's not talk about him,' I say, fluttering my eyelashes and hoping it's not too much. 'I don't want to ruin my one night away from Earth. It's miserable down there.'

'Not enough,' Apollo snorts.

'No?'

'These mortals are placid and harmless, which is fine, I suppose, but it does take the joy out of punishing them when they just nod and say it's the will of the gods and all how it should be, before rushing back off to the jobs and tasks they delight in. If they're not distressed about it, what's the point? I think Father would love some more misery down there.'

'So what's he going to do?' I try to ask as though I am awed by the might of the gods, rather than disgusted and pointedly needing to know.

'Well, I imagine that's what he's gathered us all here to declare.'

'Oh, he didn't tell you first?' I ask, taking him in with a coy smile. 'I'd tell you. In fact, there's no god I'd trust more to be . . . discreet.'

He twirls me, catching my waist once more and drawing me closer. 'Oh, I am very good at keeping secrets.'

'And riling up a mortal beyond boring complacency.' I laugh flirtatiously. 'I can't believe your father didn't confide in you anything about tonight. You're his favourite son! And, well, I know we mere mortals shouldn't have a favourite god, but . . .' I duck my head as though to hide a blush.

Apollo puffs himself up just a little further at my flattery. 'Indeed, but then there's not much my father can hide from me.' He lowers his voice. 'He's tried wiping them out before, and making them anew. But he never gets it quite right. This time's different. He's planning a flood, yes, but he also asked Hephaestus to make something. Evils condensed, new emotions to flood the mortals with. Envy, greed, anger, pain – all the things that will make them *fear* the gods, drop to their knees and worship them as Father wishes. And, if they don't – well, I suppose he'll just try again with the next batch.'

I suddenly feel dizzy, and not merely from the dancing.

Thinking of every drop of rain below us and knowing it's the start of a new cleanse, to wipe out this batch of mortals and replace them with a new model more to the gods' liking.

How many times now?

Will they ever stop? Or will the gods' boredom always long for a new type of toy?

'He'll keep you, don't worry,' Apollo soothes, misreading my anguish. 'The others put too much work in. I think you're partly why he wants to start again – you've shown him how vibrant mortals could be with just a bit of tweaking. It's a beautiful evil – no one enjoys clearing out the old, but it will all be worth it when we can fill the world with something so much better. Dozens of women like you? Who could resist?'

Something thunders through me, some sharp, stinging bolt that makes my very bones vibrate, shudder and settle once more.

I drop Apollo's hand, the roar of the gathered gods sharp and drowning, the music too joyful – and what are we all doing here? Condoning all this – or at the very least pretending to?

'I'm going to be sick,' I blurt.

Apollo leaps back, disgusted, and I don't wait for his response before I am hurrying from the room.

People turn to me, watching me pass and whispering to their companions.

Matheos falls into step beside me, saying nothing until we are out of the room.

'What is it now?' he demands, glancing in the direction we came from, and I know neither of us believes we are fully safe to drop our act. 'Or did Apollo grow bored of you too?'

'Unlike some people I could mention, Apollo was perfectly satisfactory. I just don't feel well.'

He snorts. 'Mortal girl unable to handle the wine of the gods? Well, that *is* disappointing.'

I fix him with a glare. 'Just leave me alone, will you? I don't need you drawing more attention to me.' Go, *distract them* – in my mind I'm begging, chanting and pleading for him to understand what I need.

Recognition lights his eyes in an instant. 'How pathetically fragile,' he says, but still he takes my hand, and brings his other to my forehead, like he is gauging my temperature to drive home his point, but as he retracts it he lets it graze, just for a moment, in a soft caress.

I love you, I mouth, as Matheos's hand shields my lips from view. I cherish the words as I shape them – they're true and they're stable, a fixed mark within the churning currents of my thoughts. *A beautiful evil* – but not here, not now, not with him before me.

He closes in on me, a kiss that is fierce, unyielding and furious.

'The gods gave you to me, Pandora. And for as long as it is my misfortune to be married to you, you are mine,' he snarls. 'You will remember that.'

'Unfortunately there's not enough wine in the world to make me forget,' I hiss back, like I can't taste his choice of vintage – lighter, a hint of spice – on my lips.

'Go and sort yourself out,' he dismisses me, turning before he even finishes speaking.

And I set off down the halls of this empty palace, each footstep echoing sharply, each marble pillar identical.

But I know where I am heading like a lure is guiding me there, a whisper in my mind growing louder and louder until it is screaming.

A beautiful evil.

I need to know, once and for all, why I was created for this world.

So I will return to where it all began.

CHAPTER THIRTY-FOUR

THE WORKSHOP THEY MADE ME in was clearly haphazardly thrown together, all hastily assembled benches and scavenged tools. Certainly nothing like the real forge of Hephaestus, nestled deep in the Earth with its fires spewing forth over the slopes of Mount Etna.

This place is evidently designed for things to be made in secret, close to Zeus's overview. And if Hephaestus has been working once more, creating all the worst parts of humanity to flood the mortals with, I expect it will be here – in the room of my birth.

It's overflowing.

Parchment scatters the surfaces, covered in complex drawings and scribbled notes. Tools are lined neatly in racks on the walls, hammered metal in sheaths on benches, pots with materials stuffed to the brim. The smell is not unlike home, earthy and wooden with the drying pots and sawdust still floating through the air. I reach for a small clay jar, intrigued, and prise off the lid to find quicksilver sloshing about.

I slip it into my pocket – because surely stealing from the gods is the least of our problems right now, and there are so many things I could use it for, so many experiments I long to conduct. With enough study, I might even be able to make my own automatons.

I scan the parchment quickly – the meticulous sketches and detailed formulae. Notes on distilling magic, on forming something new, each a little different. I could spend years studying them – years I do not have.

And then, in the corner of the room, I see that amphora once more – and all my rejected parts.

The clay is hard now and, unbaked, it has cracked and crumbled. A finger fallen clean off the hand, hair balled into clumps, the eyeball riddled with grooves and lines, the breast caved in.

While I try desperately to unravel the mysteries of this world, and perhaps to save it, while I dance and kiss and laugh and cry . . . part of me is still in this place.

And it is *rotting*.

'I didn't expect you to come here.'

I jump, turning to find Hephaestus in the doorway, wearing a sleek grey chiton a few shades darker than his hair, which curls about his head, black strands flecked through it and peppering his beard too. A silver clasp holds his himation tight and he leans on his polished onyx cane as I regard him – then he steps forward, the door falling shut behind him with a heavy, final thud.

'I'm sorry,' I say quickly. 'I didn't mean to, I just –'

'Yes, you did,' he says softly, and offers a wavering smile.

'I was curious,' I admit.

'Well, you didn't get that from me. From any of us, I don't think.'

My heart is racing, and I don't believe it's from being caught where I should not be.

'Why am I here?'

He looks at me, almost uncertain, and when he speaks it sounds forced. 'You were curious.'

'Not *here*. Here – this world, all of it. Why did you make me?'

Hephaestus walks to one of the counters, the one where all that parchment lies scattered. Did I have a blueprint? I can hardly recall.

'Because Zeus asked us to.'

'A beautiful evil,' I say, because I remember now. *Kalon kakon,* he'd said, and there I was.

'Apparently.'

My fingers curl into my palms, tight enough to break the skin. 'But I'm just a mortal girl. I'm nothing to the king of the gods.'

Hephaestus arches an eyebrow. 'And that, I think, is the point. And the thing which terrifies him the most. That someone so inconsequential might prove themselves a threat. Humanity is potential power encased within the powerless. Better to kill them off before they find it, replace them with a weaker, more subservient form.'

And what if they did? What if the mortals actually did have the power to stop all this? The things they might do to the gods: chase them into the Heavens forever, keep them in the stars where they cannot hurt them. Where they cannot flood the world and drown them . . .

But Zeus took their ability to even care.

'Evil is relative,' Hephaestus continues. 'And evil to Zeus – well, it's interesting to consider.'

'But if that's the sort of mortal Zeus wants, why make me? I'm not exactly . . .'

'Subservient? No, you're not.'

I catch a glint in his eye, something he's not saying, but all I can think is that if he has sought loopholes within Zeus's words, than maybe I am one: his rebellion, the orders he has followed subverted.

But then again, this man has also built the horrors that will make millions of deaths all the crueller. So if I am his rebellion, I am surely a weak and ineffective one, and he is a coward.

'So if Zeus didn't want subservience from *me*, what did he intend?'

Hephaestus gives a small shrug. 'A threat for Prometheus, I think. To show that he could still get to him through his brother. Interesting, really. I've sent the boy plenty of things and no one ever seemed to read a threat into cogs and pipes. But evidently a woman sent straight from the king is a different kind of gift entirely. I imagine Zeus meant to imply that this time it's a beautiful wife sent to his home but next time it could be anything, so perhaps Prometheus had better tell him what he'd like to know before the real monsters find their way to Epimatheos's door.'

'That's not all it was.'

'Wasn't it?' he asks, eyebrow quirked, and my eyes sting. I do not know what is happening here, only that I feel so close to it all and still like I am being held back.

'No. Zeus didn't get half of Olympus involved in my creation for a mere calling card,' I snap. There is logic here, a puzzle. One I have spent so many weeks unravelling and putting back together. And now I am here, the resolution so tauntingly near. 'I'm part of his plan. Part of his punishment for the mortals, some torment sent for them and . . . Those things he's asked you to build. Pain, despair, misery, anger – all things the humans lack. The outrage I saw wasn't their own, it was yours. Rage flickering whenever something deviates from the way of things and the will of Olympus. Or . . . it's mine. My anger spread to them. The impact I have on them.'

'So . . .?' he prompts.

I take a breath, trying to find the patience to piece this together properly, but everything is racing far too quickly for that. I am so close to the answers and here he is, a man who might give me them; who clearly recognizes the chase, the hunt, that I am close to ensnaring them all. Perhaps it was he who gifted me this hunger – because I need to realize it myself. I need to *understand*.

I cross to him, and he watches as I snatch up the papers behind him. Not all of them are relevant, but I see it: the making of the evils the gods wish to unleash on the world.

Ways to distil them, isolate them, build them from scratch.

And an instability, in each and every one.

Hephaestus picks up a handful of stones from the side, smooth polished gems that he idly begins toying with. 'You're the first human woman. Well, of this batch at least. We have some more planned for the next – thought we'd try stone this time. But the collaborative efforts of the gods are far more powerful than what I can concoct alone. It all stems from you.'

I stare at the pages, the missing link – and then it clicks.

'Zeus never gets it quite right,' I say, remembering what Apollo said.

Didn't Prometheus himself say that core of the humans was immutable? No matter how many times the gods try to change them, they can't shift the truth of them.

I'm not like the other humans. Because, of course, how could I be, the first mortal woman shaped with the gifts of nearly every god in the Heavens.

I'm something else, not quite god and not quite mortal but something in between.

I'm a stepping stone, a bridge, a way for the gods to reach the mortals. Not a being but a through road to them.

'The impact I have on the humans,' I say. 'The way they all obey my will, the intensity of it –'

'It's too much for them,' he confirms. 'Because you were never meant to engage with them individually. You're supposed to alter them all.'

That's why Prometheus hates me – why he sees me as such a risk.

I look back at the pages, the evils. The missing components.

'These won't work without me,' I realize. Prometheus protected his mortals from the interference of the gods. So they created someone who could intervene, who was different enough that she might bypass his protections and warp them into the image the gods desired.

All this time wrestling with what the gods wanted me to do and it didn't even matter. I am not some tool through which they would enact their will, I'm their will incarnate, my very existence a threat to the mortals.

There's no satisfaction in the answers in my grasp, only

mounting horror. Only the breathless chase seen to fruition – and the hidden drop waiting at its end.

Hephaestus hums in agreement. 'Organic life is tricky to form, and the humans are complex beyond even my understanding. I was concerned, when Zeus requested you. But you came together quite easily. Your anima simply existed in a way I've never been able to replicate since.'

My breath catches. 'You've tried?'

Hephaestus does not confirm or deny this, he just adds: 'If you survive this, I'd very much appreciate you letting me run some tests.'

That's their plan? As with the mortals, they will simply try again if I do not work as they want.

I cannot quite fathom whether Hephaestus is thrilled to share all this – finding another who cares for the intricacies of craft and creation in the same way he does. Or if it is said with subtle menace, outlining who I am supposed to be so I will conform to it, reasserting himself as my creator.

But when he continues, it's with unnerving pride, like everything I am is his accomplishment. 'Altering the humans was an impossible feat – until now. Until you. Prometheus worked so hard to protect them from the worst we could do, but sending these evils through you confuses the source, lets those traits sneak past the mortals' defences because they register as human-borne.'

My stomach turns. I am right. They would have me betray the humans. They did not summon us here to punish our lack of loyalty but to test it.

I turn my attention to the pages in my hands, only so I can take a moment to formulate a response.

'Wait, what's this?' I ask, pointing to a symbol – one I know far, far too well, one I examined only this morning in my own home. A man in a circle, surrounded by twelve sections clustered with the stars.

It's not flat, though, not in Hephaestus's drawing. It's a wheel, complete with arrows denoting rotation.

Hephaestus leans forward to see what I am pointing to, and his expression falls with disinterest. 'My research into ageing. Without women to procreate with, the race of men never really grew old; they just died, then popped into existence anew. Aeon oversaw the process. I never understood why Zeus tasked him with it when everyone knew he had his eyes on becoming god of the zodiac. Zeus soon awarded that to him when he handed out the spoils of war, along with a medallion scavenged from the battlefield – etched with that very symbol. *Chronos Aeon*, as I have come to know it. I don't think Zeus even knows what power he gave away, just assumes it a dull symbol featuring Aeon's beloved constellations. A cycle. But those stars appeared, one by one. They have a start and an end – and I recognized that for what it was: the smallest scraping of Kronos's power, locked in a pendant worn by the Titan soldiers. Perhaps one day Aeon will make his own sort of time magic with it, but as it is? Linear time becomes a weapon to wield once more.'

'This is a weapon?' I ask, turning the page over. Is that what we have buried in our garden? Something to wield?

'In the wrong hands, all these substances are,' Hephaestus says almost forlornly, like he considers their weaponization a misuse. 'But a weapon is little more than a tool, Pandora. When Zeus ordered me to create old age, wanting some nonsensical prime for the mortals to lose, verity and agility to fade away, I thought of that symbol. If it was capable of scraping together the dregs of Kronos's scattered power, then couldn't I wield a portion of that power myself with the same symbol? Use it as the chisel to forge the ageing Zeus desired? Though we are yet to test whether I truly have made something work with the remnants of Kronos's mastery over time.'

The remnants? So maybe Prometheus didn't claim all of the magic, just shreds. Scraps that enabled him to survive. Maybe Aeon was given others. And here is Hephaestus, wresting some for himself.

New gears turn, that dread lifting – enough for hope to breeze through. Could we do the same?

'But if all Zeus wanted was a way to get to the humans, then why wait? If you just needed an intermediary to alter the humans, why send me to Epimatheos instead of straight to them? If all you wanted was to hurt Prometheus, making your own mortal to destroy the others would surely be enough without dragging his insufferable brother in.'

'Well –'

'I think that's enough.'

We turn, so caught up in ourselves – he in self-aggrandizing celebrations of his creations and abilities, and I in hoping I might find the clue to unravelling the plans they have formed – that we had not heard the door open.

And now Athena slides through, shutting it carefully behind her before looking right at me. 'It's been a while, Pandora. I think we're overdue a catch-up.'

CHAPTER THIRTY-FIVE

H EPHAESTUS'S HAND TIGHTENS A LITTLE on his walking stick, and his gaze slides from Athena back to me again with a swift but grating motion reminiscent of planing down timber.

'I made you for the challenge,' he says decidedly. 'For interest and for the art of the creation. Whatever anyone else intends from you – that wasn't why I did it. But you should know, Pandora, that sometimes an invention reveals itself to you, clay tells you what shape it should form. And such was the case with you – you were made with a will not my own, but of the creation itself.'

The gods gave me form, but I already existed – my anima wasn't made by cogs and machines. It was the thought, *kalon kakon*, and there I was.

Isn't that worse? That none of their love and skill matters beyond the beautiful evil I was born of?

Hephaestus turns to Athena. 'This won't work.'

'I know,' she says softly. 'Which is disappointing but manageable. Kairos isn't with us now, anyway.'

'What does that mean?' I ask, my voice a little curter than I'd intended.

Hephaestus doesn't answer, he just pauses at the doorway, voice soft as he adds: 'Please tell Epimatheos he's welcome to visit any time he pleases. I'll be in touch soon anyway – I have a mouse automaton I think he'll enjoy.'

The door falls heavily shut behind him.

Athena's gaze locks on to me with a fierceness that tells me I am going nowhere. 'It means that now is not the time for making moves. There is no opportunity to seize.'

No, she can't agree with Prometheus.

'Zeus is slaughtering the humans,' I snap. 'The ones that you claimed to care so very much about. If we don't act now, then –'

'No, Pandora,' Athena sighs, pinching the bridge of her nose like she is summoning patience from a barren reserve. 'Zeus is not slaughtering the humans. Now, why don't you tell me what Prometheus's prophecy is, and I'll tell you what's going on.'

There's something different about her, but I can't work out what. She looks different – her hair neatly curled and pinned, a slim ring of hammered gold encircling her neck, a thin chain belt where her usual sword should hang. Dressed for a party, not a war.

But that's not it.

'Prometheus didn't tell me the prophecy,' I say.

'Nothing?' she says sharply.

Oh – that's what it is. Her demeanour, stripped of kindness.

Kindness that was, I suspect, always an act. A manipulation. All this time seeing Hesione and Prometheus smother Matheos in their supposed love and care while telling him they were the only ones who could protect him, and I had not recognized it when Athena tried the same with me.

When she drove me to that mountain, to Prometheus, even asked me to leave Matheos behind . . .

She does not care for me; she just wants the prophecy.

I can't pretend it doesn't sting, an acidic bite at my core, and I have to clench my teeth to keep from lashing out in kind. At the very least, I have the satisfaction of seeing her efforts wasted. 'Prometheus said one day a hero would free him. He said Kairos would come for Zeus.'

'That's *it*?' She clutches the side, her nails curling against the countertop's edge. After a tense beat, she says: 'Alright, Pandora, you can go.'

The facade is dropped so suddenly that it wounds me far more than her original lies. I am not even worth manipulating now.

'You said you'd explain what's going on.'

'*If* you told me the prophecy,' she says, turning her stormy gaze upon me with an imperious sneer. 'You do not have the prophecy, even though I was so very clear it was needed.'

'Why? So you can warn Zeus?'

'*Please*,' she spits. 'I'm not in league with the man who imprisoned my mother within his own mind.'

The sudden hatred in her voice stills me. Athena is ordinarily so composed I half expect her every emotion to be calculated – but this is raw. I think of that prophecy: *Metis, Mother of Athena. She never got that second child, the one prophesied to overthrow their father.*

But was there something about the first child, too?

'You were born on the battlefield,' I say. 'So . . . your mother was fighting alongside Zeus before he grew to fear her?'

Athena straightens up. 'According to every account I can find, she was the mastermind behind it all. Kronos had imprisoned so many gods, snatched them when they were born, and she was the one who freed them. But Zeus took that credit, just as he took her and made her a part of himself – like a nymph turned current, she's little more than a spark in his mind. You know they call me a motherless goddess? They forget her.'

They do. Even my own mind, when I heard the names Epimatheos and Prometheus – I knew they meant *afterthought* and *forethought* but not what *thought* truly meant. *Matheos, Metheus, Metis.* She is the origin of the very names I speak but the gods gave me no knowledge of her.

'I advise him on everything,' Athena seethes. 'And he trusts me because I'm not the prophesied son of my mother. We are, always, the thoughts in his head or the voice at his side and still he declares his own might.'

'So help me stop him,' I say. 'If you despise him –'

'I will, Pandora. But not like this. I'd hoped maybe the time had come but it hasn't. We must tread far more carefully than this.'

'But how can you just let Zeus kill the humans –'

'I told you, he's not killing the humans,' she hisses. 'He's *threatening* to kill the humans. There's a difference – one that has you falling in line and enacting his will. He's proved he *can* flood the world, now he will consider whether to actually do it.'

I don't see how she can stand there, insisting she cares and glaring me down like I am somehow at fault for suggesting she help. So, I push again: 'And you're going to do nothing?'

'Nothing? *Everything* that has happened has been my doing. Zeus wanted to send you to the mortals as soon as you were formed to test whether you really did have the impact on them that we'd hoped. It was my idea to send you to Epimatheos first. I convinced Zeus it would be a greater insult to Prometheus that way. I hoped he'd drive you to his brother, that you could get the prophecy, but no, of course not. You're supposed to be irresistible, Pandora, so how did Prometheus resist telling you?'

I try not to flinch. I spent weeks despising myself for failing in my intended purpose. I thought I was beyond it – but here is Athena, someone I thought my friend among the Olympians, telling me that I have failed in the real thing she wanted of me.

The mystery solved, the failure apparent.

'You could have told me,' I say, though I'm not sure if this is truly what makes me angriest. 'You could have asked. I would have helped.'

She shakes her head. 'That would have been far too much of a risk. Do you not understand, Pandora? Do you not see in Prometheus why any way to even *slightly* weight the dice in our favour is worth taking? Trust me, or do not. But don't assume you are capable of standing against Zeus on your own.'

She turns her gaze from mine, back to the door, shaking her head like she doesn't know why she's wasting this time arguing with me. 'Just go back to the party. And when Zeus asks you to unleash those horrors on the mortals, say yes.'

Of course that's the choice. Make the mortals suffer, or let them die. And Prometheus would have me choose the latter. Would take their eventual repopulation over me breaking the core of them, and poisoning what it means to be human entirely.

'Do not arouse his suspicion, do not let him think a rebellion is afoot. This attempt might not have worked but there is more in motion – Amphitrite's uprising in the ocean is inspiring Hera to think she might be capable of the same. It's also got Poseidon setting his sights on a new throne altogether, and I'm sure I can coerce Apollo into joining us too – he never got over Zeus smiting his son Asclepius. Or I'll free my mother myself and let that second son be born. Or I'll find someone else to get that prophecy from Prometheus. I have options. But you've exhausted yours.'

'What? But I can help. We both want the same thing so why –'

'We all have our role to play, Pandora. Yours is one of obedience. To Zeus. To me. If you want to stop this, lower his suspicions. Do not give him cause to punish them all further. Don't be the reason your own people perish.'

CHAPTER THIRTY-SIX

A LL I WANT IS TO drag Matheos away from the party and tell him everything I've just discovered. But gods whisper as I enter, their eyes tracking my every step. And, as I walk in, I see Zeus. I do not know if it is because he is my creator, or because he is simply the king of the gods, but the room seems to orbit around him, crowds moving about him, and he remains still in the centre, his presence commanding, power radiating from him.

I scurry in the opposite direction – and see Matheos. He is less gravity than precision, my skittering pulse able to home in on him and no one else, to see him across the room and feel a lurch in my gut that draws me closer.

He's standing in a corner with gods I haven't met. A man in dark robes, which seem to be trailing darkness itself, is locked in conversation with a woman whose hair is threaded through with flowers. Matheos is standing a few paces away from them, talking to a silver-haired woman wearing a short hunting tunic and leather boots. It's a little slower, this cataloguing of the gods, than my last time in this hall. But after a moment their names slide into place, along with all the epithets and demands for worship. It feels quieter, though, an intrusive whisper rather than an urgent order.

Hades. Persephone. Artemis.

I cross quickly to Matheos, sliding in beside him and seeing the relief that briefly flashes across his face, before he slips his mask of indifference back on.

'Are you well?' he demands, attempting to hide his concern with irritation.

'Yes, thank you.' I nod.

'You were ill?' Artemis asks.

'Just nerves, I think,' I hurry. 'Everyone here is so lovely, but it's a bit overwhelming for a human brain to be surrounded by such beauty and power.'

They both face me as I speak, but it's Matheos's eyes I feel the most, locked on my lips, and even though I know it's because of the chattering crowds and blasting music, I still feel it in a way that lingers far beneath my skin.

Thunder cracks so loudly the chandeliers shake, lightning flashing through the room with blinding intensity. When it clears, the music is silent and Zeus has climbed the marble steps towards his throne at the end of the room.

He remains standing, arms outstretched and smiling wide. He is tall, his shoulders broad with hardened muscle, his skin weathered with faded scars and heavy armour. He wears the war within him, even in that flashing smile which speaks of victory. On the plinth he stands upon, he towers. He is monumental. And when he speaks, his voice booms.

'Welcome, everyone! And thank you for joining us as we celebrate a new age of man.'

The crowd cheers, as though Zeus is not achieving this new age by ending the last one.

Matheos and I join them, albeit a little late – and I suppose I cannot judge anyone else feigning their glee when we are doing the same. Besides, we're not the only ones. I can trace it now, in the crowd – dissenters. Athena clapping a little too tersely. Hera watching her husband with poise that feels too rehearsed. Hades' whisper of 'Please let me set the forces of Hell on him, just once', which is swiftly cut off by Persephone's sharp jab to his ribs and the accompanying forced smile.

In the buzz of the crowd, Matheos finds a way to slide closer to me. He does not hold me, not even in the possessive way he did previously – but his finger brushes against my hand, and somehow that secret, reassuring touch makes my breath catch. He must realize this is it, the moment Zeus asks me to do the unthinkable and harm the humans myself.

'We had considered starting completely anew, but won't you all agree we outdid ourselves with this one?'

The light shifts, stretching from Zeus's outstretched hand right to me. Matheos's breath hitches and the crowd parts. Some gods mutter, some clap and Hermes leads several in whooping loudly. But, oh gods, I feel that surging panic smothering me, that threat of being so overwhelmed my mind shuts itself down.

And even still, I find I am smiling and waving to the cheering gods and I am almost relieved for all these commands that tell me how I should behave when I no longer feel capable of acting the perfect role.

'Pandora, won't you come join me?'

Matheos's jaw clenches and I know I cannot say anything, not here. Not where they're watching.

But as I take that step forward, I bring my hands up. One to my chest, one to my stomach. *Something else.*

I have no way of getting a message across, but I hear his slight intake of breath as recognition hits, know he has got something from the sign. To me, that 'something else' right now is: *hope, a chance, Kairos yet to come. A way out, a third option . . .*

I wish he could stand with me, or that I even had Korax by my side, its tail slapping against my legs. Some sort of comfort against this feeling of being overexposed and woefully underprepared.

Zeus takes my hand and leads me up the steps at the front. As I reach the plinth the crowd erupts in cheers and applause.

'The humans of old were crafted by one man, who turned against us. Why should we trust any creatures built by him?'

Jeers now, and I know they're not for me – know they're likely not even felt but performed – but I still have to force myself not to wince in response.

'But look what we can do when we turn our hand to the matter. She is no fragile imitation of our splendour; Pandora is nearly as whole as an actual, real god.'

My smile burns.

I just need to get through this, and then I can escape with Matheos, run from this crowd, and we can figure it out. We have to. I cannot even consider the alternative: that we don't. That I have no choice but to obey Zeus in this.

And when I look up into the crowd and see Matheos, it is the only hope I need to keep that smile bright.

'Pandora, you've inspired us to enter this new age,' Zeus says. 'As a thank-you, we've crafted this – a gift for you to bring to your home, so that a piece of Olympus might reside on Earth in the household of our first mortal, a tie from our world to that of our worshippers. Are we not generous?'

He takes up a large clay pithos, the jar half as tall as I am and decorated with fine black drawings that tell tales I recognize – the gods in all their glory.

I am almost too late in realizing he is expecting a response from me, but I cover it with my shock and delight. 'I . . . So generous! My king, thank you!'

I fall to my knees – because this is what they want, isn't it? Mortals who share their tales and bow in worship. It's almost a relief to feel solid ground beneath me, to make myself smaller under their watching gazes. Not enough of a reprieve, but it dulls the sharp edge of panic.

Zeus nods his approval, turning back towards the crowd. 'I'd advise her not to open it, but we've established how unpredictable that human will of theirs can be. Isn't that the joy of them? That they may do as they wish – and face the consequences?'

I think of what Apollo said, about Zeus loving a show.

But I never wanted to be a part of it.

From the corner of my eye, I see Persephone take Hades' hand and slip from the room, hurried footsteps masked beneath the expectant breath of every other god whose eyes are piercing me.

Zeus places the jar before me and even though I know what it contains, there is something mesmerizing about it, and I reach out a tentative hand.

The clay is warm, a gentle hum beneath my skin, and oh gods . . .

I want to *know*. Want to prise that lid open and examine its insides, to see these blueprints come to life and take them apart just to see if I can.

I might resist opening for a day, a week, maybe even a month.

But I know myself – have spent so much time exploring who I am – and I was wrong. I am not that bin of discarded clay, I am so much more than what they made me to be, complex and curious and a dozen things they never intended. Things no one else will ever know as well as I do.

And I know myself well enough to be certain that I will absolutely open that jar eventually.

It's quite clever, really, offloading this moral responsibility on to me. No one will blame Zeus, not when it's the mortal girl who will bring evil to the world. Who cares how she got the jar if she couldn't do something as simple as resist opening it when she was clearly advised not to?

No wonder Prometheus didn't trust me. This is what Zeus always intended, a beautiful evil – a pretty thing to bring cruelty to the world. It's genius, and I should have known better than to think I could outwit the –

I nearly knock the jar over in my shock as the final piece falls into place, ringing as clearly as *a beautiful evil* ever did:

Metis is responsible for every wise thought the man ever has.

She's little more than a spark in his mind.

I look up at Zeus, still preaching to the crowd, and realize I am *not* looking at my creator – at least, not my sole originator. Because the last god to burst from Zeus's head was not only his child, but Metis's too . . .

I know now that the gods didn't make me, they just gave me form. It was a thought that birthed me.

But what if the idea of *kalon kakon* was never Zeus's at all? What if it was hers, the goddess of wisdom who he swallowed and trapped in his own mind? What if she saw an opportunity and took it?

And if that's true, then . . .

The prophecy. Athena mentioned a son, but Prometheus just said a second child, destined to overthrow Zeus. And he's the seer they're all desperate for prophecies from. What if Zeus just assumed it had to be a male god because, well, as Athena said, the women are the thoughts in their head and the voices at their side but never the threat standing before them.

What if *I'm* the child of the prophecy?

The jar burns hotter beneath my hand, and I pull away sharply, staring at it in awe.

What if there's still a way to stop this?

'Pandora,' Zeus says sharply, and I look up into his glowering face, skin worn with fine lines, eyes cold and hateful. While the puzzle righted itself in my mind, he was dismissing the crowd to drink and celebrate, and here I remain, on my knees before this enormous jar, its lid precariously perched so that the lightest knock might free it.

'Lord Zeus?' I ask tentatively, my fear smothering the words to a quiet whisper.

I expect him to tell me to rise, but instead he steps closer and clasps my chin in his hand, so that my head is tilted sharply back – like staring up at Olympus itself.

'I know you spoke to Prometheus,' he says, and my blood chills. I knew this was a possibility, but I did not think the gods would bide their time with the punishment. I imagined I had escaped, if they had not confronted me already. 'I hope whatever curiosity you held was sated, because any hint of further defiance will not be tolerated.'

I nod so quickly the whole room can surely sense my desperation.

'There is always something to be used as leverage, you see. Your husband found that with his brother. Going after Epimatheos wouldn't be as effective with you, I imagine. We all saw you in Tarsuras. Not his biggest fan, it appears. But, as I say, we all saw you in Tarsuras.'

He's enjoying this, his smile small and biting. 'I trust you know what's in this.' He taps the precariously mounted lid. 'And I trust you know what is expected of you. Choose your loyalties well and do it quickly. After all, as the people of Tarsuras know all too well, we have a second option.'

I pale, not wanting to understand what he's saying.

His smile grows, seeing the panic on my face. 'If you plan to drown the world, why not begin with the hardest part. With the right power, even towns perched at the feet of mountains wash away astonishingly quickly.'

It is only the shock that prevents me from screaming, the sudden grief like a hard, blunt whack.

Those people: the man I danced with, the innkeeper and his curious eyes, that woman and her poor children who dressed me so attentively and the priest with his devotion to the very god who . . .

Drowned.

The silver body in the grave, the deserted village. They'd done this before – *this*. Tarsuras's destruction was an experiment, the town whose fate now lingers above every other civilization on this Earth.

'Not that you'd know about it, of course. You'd be elsewhere. It would be such a pity to begin our new human era as we did the last, with the punishment of one who stood with the mortals over the gods who made them.'

There has to be a way to stop this . . . if I only have enough time.

'Don't set yourself against me, Pandora. You're not an opponent, you are a beacon. That is all you are, a post from which my lightning might be struck. You are an amplification of my might. And you are nothing without me. Embrace your purpose and open that jar.'

CHAPTER THIRTY-SEVEN

SOMEHOW, I SURVIVE THE EVENING.

I smile and laugh, I flirt with gods and sneer at Matheos, I separate my anxieties out so firmly it does not even feel like I am pretending to be fine and more as though, for now, they do not even exist.

Until the moment when, after the party starts to quieten and we can make our escape, Matheos leads us down to our assigned room, shuts the door behind us and turns to me.

'What did he say?' he whispers, confirming he's as suspicious as I am that we cannot speak freely even here.

'You didn't see?'

'I don't get every word when lip-reading. It's a useful boost when I can half hear someone in a busy room but it's definitely not enough to overcome distances and a man not facing my direction. But given the way he was behaving . . . I can assume it was a threat.'

'Oh. Well, thank you for explaining. And you're right: it was a threat. The jar is full of all the evils that Zeus wants me unleash on the humans. For it to work, I have to be the one to open it.'

'Evils?' he asks, keeping his voice low as though a god might be pressed against the door, listening at the crack beneath. Honestly, I wouldn't put it past Hermes.

'Ways to make the mortals suffer in the hopes their misery will bring them to the temples and altars of worship. Something about the way Prometheus built them means Zeus can never quite alter them how he wants, hence all the attempts from wood and silver and gold. But I think it's more than that. I think it's the same reason he gave me that jar in public and told me *not* to open it. He wants someone – and *something* – to blame. He can't position himself as the mortals' only hope if he's the one that brought them the misery. But if I take it back to Earth and open it when he's not looking, then he's the hero who advised against it.'

Matheos swallows. 'And I don't imagine Zeus is simply leaving opening that jar up to you.'

The words feel sharp-edged even on my own tongue. 'If I don't, he's going to drown the world. Just as he already did Tarsuras.'

Matheos takes the news like a glancing blow, a moment of lurching back, a slow wince and then he is back with me once more, the horror swallowed, the grief pushed deeper, in a place that will slowly wear him away rather than immediately consume him.

He reaches out his hand and I take it, let him stumble backwards until the backs of his knees hit the bed, and then we are upon it, facing each other, his head bowed towards mine and I can see the creases in the skin beneath his eyes and each heavy, repeated shuttering of his tired lids. I do not know how I'll ever sleep but all I want is to curl up with this boy and pause the world for a moment or two.

'Tomorrow I'll throttle Zeus myself,' he whispers.

'Of course, my love.'

He hums at the endearment and his arm snakes about my waist. 'But tonight, we'll just be sad.'

Being sad *with* someone, with *him*, feels comforting. It will not heal the hole carved within me, but it might make it ache less.

So I curl a little closer, leaning my head against his shoulder, and agree. 'Yes, let's be sad.'

The tears, when they come, roll straight down, sliding across my face into the pillows beneath us without a trace.

And even though I think it's impossible, I suppose my body recognizes the toll of the last few hours, and I am asleep before Matheos even leans over to blow out the candle.

It is Athena rather than Hermes who races us back home, piling us into her chariot where the gifted jar is tightly bound, the lid wrapped in firmly knotted strips. She is curt, polite. She pretends we do not know each other well, and that is fine with me.

I'm too busy watching her, trying to find any note of similarity between us.

Very little in the physical – she is tall and lithe with hard muscular edges, whereas I'm short and soft, with joyful roundness rather than her severe angles. Her hair is blonde to my dark tangles, her eyes grey to my terracotta brown, like the clay I originated from still clings to me.

But the deeper things – the sharpness of her gaze, the

way she fixates on the task at hand, her fascination with the world . . . it all feels familiar. Not quite enough to clearly label her my sister, but enough for me to mull the idea over again, to wonder if maybe the thought that crafted me wasn't really Zeus's after all. And if so, what that means for us now.

We squelch to a halt, the ground yet to dry and the mud sinking deep.

Wet with the same rain that washed away an entire town.

Athena deposits the jar on the only available point – the plinth of the sundial, rising out of the mud. She leaves all those leather cords lashed around its lid to hold it in place. I stare at it, and then at her. I have wondered so much about her and her motives – but now my thoughts lead where they haven't before.

How did she feel to be issued a decree to create a beautiful evil and then to discover that meant building a woman? Did she find it an insult? Or is she so wrapped up in appeasing Zeus she did not think twice about throwing her whole gender beneath the grinding mechanics of his will? Or is it as she told me: a way of lowering his guard? Of keeping him from suspecting her, or indeed seeing any woman as a threat?

Athena gives me a long hard look before silently turning and walking back to her chariot. As though she is daring me to resist opening it.

We leave it right there in the mud and rush inside.

I immediately run to my makeshift workshop, scattering pages and grasping a stylus to start scrawling all that I remember reading of Hephaestus's work.

I feel Matheos come in after me, sense him lean against the wall, but I'm wholly absorbed and he does not try to break it. Not until I finally finish and look up to face him.

'Well?'

'I have a theory,' I start.

He audibly sighs his relief and I look at him sharply.

'What?' he asks. 'They're normally correct.'

'I've been wrong before.'

'The odds still weigh in your favour.'

'Well, I'm not sure how we'd ever know with this one,' I say. 'But I keep thinking of that woman your brother mentioned – Metis.'

Matheos winces.

'Right, her. So Zeus tricks her into turning into a fly and swallows her when she does. But she's still pregnant. And eventually Athena bursts free from Zeus's head.'

'Sort of,' Matheos says. 'Prometheus had to cleave Zeus's head open mid-battle to free her.'

'I thought Hephaestus cut his head open?' I say as a story fills my mind.

'No, Hephaestus was only born because Hera was jealous of Zeus supposedly having Athena alone. She wanted to solely parent a child, too, in retaliation.'

'But Athena's mother is Metis.'

'And Hephaestus's father is very likely Zeus.' Matheos sighs. 'The gods need to stop shrouding their existence in their own sort of mythos. It's too confusing. Regardless, *someone* cleaved Zeus's head open.'

I shake my head – smashed skulls and torn-out livers . . . 'I can't believe I once stitched you up over a bear scratch.'

'Your worry was noted. And endearing.'

I narrow my eyes only slightly – all the fear I held in that moment prevents too much scorn, though he'd surely deserve it. I bring us back to the matter at hand. 'I think Metis might be my mother.'

I expect more of a reaction, but Matheos remains against the wall, arms folded, and one brow lifts.

'I existed before they gave me shape, existed from the moment Zeus commanded I be made. But what if it wasn't his command – what if it was hers? And if so, maybe that's it: maybe I solely belong to her. But if I'm his too, if it was some merging of their thoughts, then . . .'

'Then you'd be the second child of the prophecy.'

We stare at each other, neither of us wanting to say it.

I finally cave. 'It's a leap.'

'Perhaps one worth taking. But I've never cared much for prophecies, and I don't think it matters either way whether you're the one from the prophecy or not. So long as overthrowing Zeus is on your mind, I'm sure you'll find a way to achieve it.'

'So you agree, we should do something?'

The words feel dangerous, even here where they should be safe. But are we safe anywhere?

Matheos considers. 'I think you're going to resist opening that jar. And the gods aren't going to be happy about that. If we do nothing, they'll come for us – tear the rest of my brother's organs out, drown the humans, and find some punishment for us that we cannot even conceive of.'

'You're half right,' I say.

Matheos glowers. 'We are *not* considering Prometheus's solution.'

Oh, yes. My death. Kill me before I can open the jar and leave the gods to their backup plan of mass slaughter.

'No, that hadn't even occurred to me. I think I should open the jar.'

We fall silent, regarding each other as the wind tears at the walls and rain slams into stone and it is so very easy to imagine it is the gods howling to get in.

Matheos crosses to me, and takes my hand in his – and I didn't realize I was cold until I'm clasped in his warm grip. He holds me tight, lowers his gaze to mine and asks: 'Is there a version of this where we come out alive?'

I press my lips together, unsure of how honest to be. 'I'm working on it.'

'Alive *and well*?'

'Also part of the plan. Hopefully.'

His eyes dart across me, like he's looking for the final thread to connect it all. I don't expect him to get there, because I do not know what that thread is, until he says it. 'What was the command? What was it that Zeus said that made you?'

Is this where we break? Where he casts me out, locks away the jar, and scurries off to his brother?

But it's a fleeting thought, thoroughly illogical, an idea that can find no purchase. This is Matheos, a man who has made it clear several times over how resolutely he stands by my side. No words will make him leave me, even if commanded by the king of the gods himself.

'A beautiful evil.'

The words seem to swell in the air between us, and I watch them land. A flicker of fear sparking where I never thought I would see it.

He regards me for a moment, and when he speaks his words

are slow and deliberate, like he is holding himself back. 'And you think we *should* open the jar?'

'I think Zeus made me to bring pain to the mortals. But I'm not sure that the things in that jar *are* evils.'

A weapon is little more than a tool, Hephaestus said.

So if Zeus believes the contents of that jar a blade to wield against humanity, couldn't we find it a new purpose? Better, couldn't we turn it on him instead?

'Aren't you angry?' I continue, excited now as I feel the plan slot into place. 'I am – and you know what it's pushing me to do? Fight back. Envy? Doesn't seeing all that the gods have while we suffer force us to face the injustices of this world? All the misery in the jar might be what prompts them to stop thinking this is the way things are meant to be and fight for a better world. Zeus may think he's going to grind them into submission. But I think Zeus might have created his own undoing.'

Matheos's jaw tightens. 'Misery doesn't inspire you when you're powerless, it just crushes you. It shifts to despair, not hope. Trust me, Pandora, I've been there.'

I clutch his hand tight and draw him closer. I look up at him, hold him against me and say: 'That's what they're missing, and what we have to give them. *Hope.* There's strength in those numbers, Matheos – can't you see it? Maybe it's the workings of time etched through this house, but it feels prophetic, the humans chasing the gods back into the Heavens. But they'll never start the charge if they don't hope they can succeed.'

'We can't give every mortal in the land hope, Pandora. We have weeks at most before the gods demand to know why that jar remains shut.'

I pull the jar of quicksilver from my pocket and hold it up to him. 'Maybe we can. If the gods can make dozens of evils, couldn't we make just one good?'

'Hope is not powerful enough to make the humans rise in rebellion, Pandora. It is not worth opening that jar for. But if you don't, then . . .' He lets go of me, stepping back, tearing his hands through his hair. 'That can't be the alternative. It *can't*.'

'*Kalon kakon*,' I say quietly. 'That's what he said.'

'A beautiful evil.' Matheos nods.

'Perhaps. But both of those words are adjectives. Look at it from another angle and it means an *ugly good*.'

Matheos's eyes flick across my person, before locking on me with a degree of furious dismissal. 'Well, you're obviously not *that*.'

'I could be.'

'Decidedly not. The obvious aside –' he waves his hand across all of me – 'are we just going to ignore the context in which they made you? Of what they're trying to make you do now?'

'Zeus meant it that way, I'm sure, but maybe not Metis. If she seized her chance, took Zeus's desire for a beautiful evil and strung the words with secret meaning, then couldn't I be?'

'That's why you're not despairing,' Matheos realizes. He seems torn between disbelief and amusement. 'You're distracted by the mystery of it all. Focused on all these puzzle pieces which do not change the fact there is a jar the gods expect you to open, and misery to unleash.'

'It's part of the same problem. Maybe I'm not an ugly good, but opening that pithos could be. How ugly to release those evils, but if it spurs them into action then couldn't it be good, too? Maybe they won't fully riot against the gods but maybe they'll care enough to at least try to save themselves.'

Matheos takes a shaky breath. 'This is a terribly risky gamble.'

'But?'

His gaze moves level with mine. 'But it's the only one they've left us with. And you're the only one I'd trust to take it.'

Which is when the earth itself lurches beneath our feet and we are thrown to opposite sides of the room.

CHAPTER THIRTY-EIGHT

I CLIP MY CHIN AGAINST the table edge as I fall, and it tosses my head back sharply enough that I lie for a moment as the world continues to tremble. I hear things falling around me – pens and pots, my whole loom teetering without toppling entirely. Matheos hauls himself on top of me like he could shield me with his own body if the roof fell down.

'Don't, you'll get hurt,' I protest, wiping the blood from my chin.

'You're mortal.'

'And?'

'You're more finite – we've established this,' he says resolutely, clinging to a stubbornness I know I won't shift.

But after a moment the world around us stills.

'Hello?' a voice calls.

'Epimatheos? Pandora?'

Ione. Kerkeis.

And then it clicks: the rebellion in the ocean. Poseidon, king of the ocean. And all those other epithets unfurling in my mind, among them a key one repeated again and again: *Earth-shaker.*

We scramble to our feet and run to meet the nymphs at the door.

'What's happening?' I demand, as Ione rushes to my side to throw their arms around me.

'Zeus is throwing his weight behind Poseidon,' Kerkeis explains. 'They attacked the old sea gods this morning and the ocean's chaos. We might need a place to lay low for a little bit.'

Matheos arches a brow. 'Well, thankfully we have a spare bed.'

Kerkeis scowls – a little too pointedly for such a statement. Which also implies she knows exactly what that means – that since the last time we saw both of them, we might have stopped needing a second bedroom.

Matheos sighs and looks to me. 'Do you want to tell them or shall I?'

'I've seen you since this happened! And you said nothing! Nothing!' Kerkeis rages for perhaps the seventh time that evening.

'We were climbing an impossible mountain.'

'And what was the point of saving you if you couldn't use one of those precious minutes of salvaged life to mention that you and Epimatheos are fucking!'

'In love,' Epimatheos corrects.

'Fucking in love! Ridiculous!' Kerkeis throws herself back with a huff.

'Well, I'm happy for you,' Ione says, lifting their head from where it has been resting on my shoulder. Insisting they'd missed me, they'd settled beside me the moment they could, while Kerkeis apparently needed to face us both to yell at us appropriately.

'I'm happy for you!' she protests now. 'Of course I'm happy for you. But I can't believe you did all this without us. You should have waited!'

'Once again,' I say. 'Could we please return to the more important matter of crafting hope?'

Over the last few hours we've managed a small amount of productive conversation amid all the aforementioned shouting at us.

'I thought you wanted to sort time first?'

I chew on the edge of the stylus. 'I think so. It's a risk. If it works and we can actually manipulate Chronos enough to slow time rather than race us through it, we'd buy so much more time than we'd lose. I think we should try – but it's up to all of you if you think hope is the better thing to focus on.'

'Prometheus focused on time,' Matheos says, 'which suggests it's worth getting to grips with as a priority. We can't ask Hesione, though – she'd hate that we're trying to fight back ourselves rather than just letting things unfold as Prometheus has seen.'

'Honestly, let's look at time solely so Hesione can stop lording it over us,' Kerkeis says, but she tosses Matheos a sympathetic smile laced with rage that suggests she might throttle Hesione herself if she ever gets her hands on her.

A scowl forms between Ione's brows. 'Could we not just destroy the marks Prometheus made?'

I bite my lip, reluctant to admit: I don't know. It feels riskier than anything else we have considered. We don't know enough about Chronos and how to wield it to know what that might do. What if time fragments the way the broken pieces do, each of us jumping from point to point? Or if it makes the effect permanent? Even if time did not settle strangely in this land, there's some truth to what Athena said about the way Kairos and Chronos collided on the battlefield, and I suspect if we destroyed it at the wrong moment it might tear a whole thread from the timeline, warping time in pockets and loops.

'Maybe that's our last resort,' I propose.

Ione shrugs. 'Sure. Besides, the ingredients you'll need for hope will take us a while to gather, especially if we're sticking to rivers and avoiding going deep in the oceans,' they say, scanning my notes beside me. 'You can look at time while we source what you need.'

Right. Because I'm not a god, and I don't have their power.

But their magic is in the world around us. Bronze and gold hold magic best, Matheos said. Quicksilver is a start. So if we can extract power from where they've put it, we might be able to harness enough for something that feels so impossible.

These feelings in the hands of gods are embodiments, things so powerful they might become beings in their own right – hope and misery, dreams and strife.

In the hands of a mortal they are clumsy imitations with delusions of grandeur.

But Hephaestus summoned these same feelings from thoughts and ideas, pushed his own imaginings into the woes he distilled into that jar. And I do not need to imagine hope, not when I can feel it. So this mortal heart that feels things in excruciating depth might be the one point in our favour.

It's what's giving me such confidence in this plan: that I know as fundamentally as I know anything that hope in the hands of mortals is a powerful thing.

'We can get bronze from the remnants of the old forge,' Ione says, with a careful glance at Kerkeis who nods, lips pressed tight. 'There will be other useful things in it, too – given they made Zeus's lightning bolt there. Oh, this might be harder.'

But the look they give Matheos does not imply its rarity will be the problem.

'What?' he demands, reaching for the list and scanning quickly. 'The waters of the Lethe? I can write to Hades; I knew him a little in the war. He and Persephone left Zeus's gathering as soon as threats against the mortals were made, so for all we know they're working on their own plan to stop it. He's terrifying but not unreasonable, I'm sure he'd –'

'No,' Ione says, their voice honeyed, like they would imbue even this with warmth. 'The Caucasian herbs – well, there's only one thing that grows on Mount Caucasus.'

'Flowers,' Kerkeis explains. 'The ones you saw me gathering. Enormous, dual stemmed, can only be cut with Stygian blades . . .' Matheos stares unblinking, like he already knows what's coming. 'They grow wherever your brother's blood drops.'

Those flowers are evidence of the carnage. Of Prometheus's pain and torture. And a reminder that the man we saw was many hours past the worst of it.

But each new petal blooming is proof of his agony and to pluck them so mercilessly, to use them like they are a resource that makes the pain worthwhile . . .

Matheos nods, his eyes low as he grabs a stylus to scrawl a note on his page. 'Well, I'll ask Hades for some Stygian blades too, then.'

'Matheos –'

He doesn't let me finish – doesn't even let me start, really.

'We don't have time for me to get upset over this. I'll make a note to be sad later.'

Which doesn't strike me as particularly healthy, but with Olympus circling ever closer, presumably ready to break our door down and demand to know why the jar remains sealed, I fear he may be right.

'Alright. Stygian blades are also on the list, so thank you for getting them. I think we can manage the rest,' Ione says, scanning to the end of the list. 'And if we do – you can make this?'

No, not at all. The steps are fragile, the technique precise and the equipment almost as complicated to assemble as hope itself. In fact, I may run my wells of hope dry in simply assembling the equipment to make it.

'Hope? I think so. Time is trickier. But if Kronos was giving medallions to his soldiers then I think we can make necklaces of our own. Whether I can power them enough to override the magic Prometheus imbued the sundial with is another matter, but I can try,' I say. 'And I think at this point that's the best we can do.'

'It's all right if you can't,' Kerkeis says softly.

I turn to her, not thinking to hide my hurt. 'You don't believe I can?'

'Quite the contrary. I just don't want you breaking yourself to do it. We care about *you*, not your ability to defeat the gods' plans.'

'You *are* brilliant,' Ione adds. 'And that's not dependent on success. It would be wonderful if you could, of course, but you aren't letting us down if you don't.'

I nod, my throat burning. I once believed myself made to be loved, and yet so often I am overwhelmed by the sheer force of it.

'Thank you. I *am* going to do this, though.'

At least, I hope I can.

Ione and Kerkeis bring components almost daily, while I start work on my forge. There are logistical concerns, like how to burn fire hot enough to distil the elements, how to hammer with enough force to meld materials – but Hephaestus did not build these substances in his forge, he worked in a back room of the Olympian palace. So I believe this will work just as well.

'Evidence for Metis's involvement in your creation builds by the hour,' Matheos says, scanning the growing lab and placing tea beside me.

I'm focused on tightening a bolt on a stand, one that will hold a pot above a fire at the right distance to heat it properly, then Matheos hums, his fingers darting out in front of me, sliding a page I hadn't quite tucked away out into the open light.

My hand stills.

I don't realize I'm holding my breath, hoping that maybe he will not understand, until the moment he growls my name.

'Pandora, what is this?'

And then I find I cannot breathe at all.

'Something I'm working on.'

'I gathered. It's the *why* that I don't quite understand.'

I swallow. 'Prometheus imbued this house with some sort of magic around Chronos. Something that slows time for us, while it races in the world outside.'

'I'm aware,' he says this slowly, but there's an edge too, one that tells me he knows I am stalling and he is growing weary of it.

'Well, that's been great historically, but if we're looking to buy time to work on this, then reversing that would be convenient. We could achieve more while time outside slows.'

'*Pandora*,' he snaps, patience thoroughly frayed. 'That's not what I'm looking at here. Tell me what danger you think we're in.'

'Fine.' I finally turn to him, planting my pliers on the side with a little too much force. 'I'm hoping this works in the way we want – that the humans will rise against the gods, chasing them into the stars like I think they might. Even if it just enables them to fight for their own survival, great. Good. They'll survive. But we won't. Zeus will turn his rage on us. And if it only works a little, and the humans need years to gather the strength to overthrow them, then wouldn't it be great if we could not so much speed through this part, but simply jump to the next?'

'You want to remove us from this point in the Fates' tapestry and place us in another?'

'In effect, yes. Like what Prometheus is doing but . . . more.'

'You think that's possible.'

Yes. This one I am surer of. Those constellations, Prometheus's rending asunder of Chronos. It's replicable. I can feel the energy pulse, the magic of the gods – magic which is actually just a dozen different puzzles and intentions, redirected energy, and with the right focus point, the right symbol, actually within our grasp.

Matheos takes a breath. 'I appreciate the solution. But next time you suspect we are in such danger, please do feel free to inform me. And if it doesn't work, do not think I am allowing this.'

'What?'

'*This!* You trying to protect me. If our plan falls through and the gods come for us, know that you do not do this with my blessing. Sacrificing yourself is cruel to me, Pandora. I've had quite enough of it. So don't convince yourself it would be me that you're doing it for, it would be for your own selfishness.'

I scoff. 'Don't try to manipulate me into letting *you* sacrifice yourself for *me*.'

'But –'

'No, Matheos. Let's not argue about this. We know perfectly well that if it comes down to it then we'll both try to destroy ourselves to save each other, but rather than whining about it, I simply intend to be better at it than you are.'

Matheos narrows his eyes. 'Perhaps. But you're focused on manufacturing hope and warping time itself. I plan to dedicate myself wholly to saving you. If it's a competition, it's one you're ill prepared for. As I think we've established, my family are well versed in sacrifice.'

The challenge strings taut between us, and I feel the vehemence of all he feels: the anger and hurt, the love he would betray to protect, and perhaps this – because I feel it too – the dizziness and suffocation of such overwhelming stakes, of knowing the person you want to save is the one who might stand in your way. The intensity of knowing they want this as desperately as you do, and knowing if you succeed they might never forgive you for it.

It feels pivotal – like we are hurtling around this moment, balanced and equal and thoroughly precarious. Any tipping of these scales is devastating and irreparable.

Matheos steps nearer, his hand grazing my lower back, pulling me to close the little remaining distance. He glowers down at me like he would not wait for the supposed mortal rebellion, he might storm Olympus himself.

'I wish you'd never loved me. Not if this is what comes of it.'

'Alas.'

I tug him down by his collar at the same time as his hands grasp lower, hauling me up, and I leap, perhaps too aggressively because he stumbles back before adjusting his angle, and then my legs are wrapped around his waist and he is sighing into my mouth and, oh, thank whatever Fate conspired to give Titans such strength because I love when he holds me like this, like we cannot wait another moment to become entwined.

We kiss like we know exactly how precious the seconds we spend on it are, and choose to do it anyway. He is despair and desire in equal measure. And I am resolute, even more so now, that there cannot be a world without him in it.

He moans against my lips, his breath hot against my neck as he draws away, as he hisses in my ear: 'I'll show you sacrifice.'

Yes.

And I'll show him it in turn, as our contest shifts, both of us swept up and then persistent, all the things we would do for each other laid bare. He pushes me on to a workbench, shoving aside parchment and ink, drawing back until my legs lock tighter, pulling him right back to me, our hips harsh against one another.

We do not make it out of this room.

*

I draw a rough sketch but there's something missing, something I don't understand. The equations keep coming out wrong, no matter how many times I check the workings and formulae.

And I can't afford the time to be foolish.

I break the stylus in my hand and startle at the violence.

'What is it?' Matheos asks, coming up behind me to place a bowl of fresh berries beside where I'm sitting. His hand rests on my shoulder, pressing into a knot I'm unsurprised to find is there, given the way I've been hunched over the paper.

I lean back against him, sighing and reaching for a blackberry, only realizing as the tart juice bursts in my mouth that I can't remember the last time I ate anything.

'I love you,' I sigh, by which I mean in this moment I am so thankful he is here and looking out for me while I throw myself into this.

'I hope that's not the problem.'

I push the paper across to him. 'In theory this should work, but when I try to simulate it, it fails. The equations don't add up.'

Matheos glances at it. 'You haven't accounted for movement.'

I frown. 'How do you mean?'

'The sun falls and shifts across the sundial.'

I scoff. 'Sometimes.'

'Sometimes,' he allows. 'You said Hephaestus's page had arrows to mark rotation.'

'Right, but Prometheus's marks don't move. He just carved them into the dust.'

'He bleeds. His shadow moves across it.'

'Rivers of Hell, you're a genius. You're right.' I clutch the paper back. 'An external action, separate to the symbols themselves.'

Matheos presses a kiss to my hair before he leaves but I'm too focused on readjusting my notes to really notice it. Time marches on. That is what it does. A turn of the wheel, shadows moving across a dial, blood continuing to fall, a cog spinning.

And *there*. It works.

It works – and there is quite literally no time to waste in proving it.

I head to my workspace, shutting the door behind me with a sense of finality, like it might never open again.

And in it, I carve time.

I etch it into metal discs, all those symbols, the magic I lack as a mortal created from the quicksilver I refine, drying it into a fine dust to embed in each individual pinprick. It is delicate work – Prometheus set it into the very roots of this home and I'm crafting a counterbalance. Better, where he pressed it into clay, I'm moulding it in bronze. It's stronger, the magic more potent – potentially enough to override the laws he set into these foundations. But I begin too late, when the sun has already been drawn beneath the horizon – or, rather, when the dark clouds are tinged with a burnt ochre glow that decays into scornful black. I do not stop until the ink stain of darkness drains, the clouds lifeless and grey once more. I do not realize the chokehold the task has on me, that I cannot stop, cannot even look away, as though the magic has me in its grasp as much as I wield it.

Vaguely, I am aware of Matheos drifting in and out, talking, leaving food, the birds fluttering in to collect it when it grows cold. Korax curls at my feet like it would protect me from myself.

There is only this: each star to be formed – the perfect width, the precise distance from the next, the lenses to magnify the discs and the tools themselves, wire to carve, single-haired brushes with which to speck the distillation of the gods' powers, the slick glaze to seal it, and on and on. When one is finished, I begin on the next, chip at the edges, form perfect cog-like grooves.

The patterns lift, dance before my eyes, glimmer in the air and I do not know if it is the magic taking hold or my own delirium. But it is so clear: if the world is a weave and the future a tapestry, then time is the loom that holds it – wood and bolts, structure, levers and mechanics; a pull here, balance there, a cog that rotates against this edge turns this pulley here, and together it trundles on.

I'm merely increasing its capacity.

I bolt the discs together, turn each one to the precise moment that the circles layer over one another. I run a chain through the centre, finer than thread through a needle. My fingers tremble.

And the moment the final chain is taut, medallion held loose in fingers too weak to grip, I drop.

I do not hit the floor.

Arms, around me, *him*, petrichor and woodland with an aniseed tang.

How many hours? Standing here? Wielding magic it is not my right to understand, let alone manipulate. With what little strength I have left, I heave a chain around Matheos's neck, fumble at the one hanging about my own, and I try to concentrate, feel it wavering, my every thought gossamer-fine and slipping beneath the surface. Still, I scrabble at two of the plates, and shift them to the left, several degrees, as far as they might go.

Then the dark closes in.

I wake, bolt upright and immediately, so suddenly that Matheos jerks back, muttering curses. I almost collide with the medallion still strung around his neck.

I fumble for my own, calming when the metal brushes my skin.

'Olympus above, Pandora, you were snoring mere seconds ago,' he says, perching himself at the edge of the bed, leaning to press his hand to my forehead, which he must have been doing when I woke. 'I've never seen someone wake so abruptly.'

'I wasn't snoring.'

'Or wake so obstinately.'

I take his hand from my head and shuffle up so I'm sitting too, the blankets twisted about me, but both of us facing one another on the bed, mere inches apart.

I keep his hand in mine, and let my other trace the grooves of the medallion about his neck.

'It's dangerous,' I say. 'Last time anyone thought to string time as jewellery it was in the middle of a war. It should be able to manipulate Chronos, which is fine if used properly. And, Heavens above, if it breaks? I don't even want to think about what that would do to the world. Maybe I shouldn't have done this.'

'We'll be careful, and I'll tell Ione and Kerkeis to be too. I already gave them theirs,' he assures me.

I run my fingers over the etchings. They're so fine that if I had not carved them with my own hand, I would not have thought it possible – detail surely only achievable with the powers of the gods. Circles of metal, dials turned to a point.

It looks like it should work. It is identical to my drawings and, flipping mine over, I find that this one is too. I did not only create a perfect instrument of time, I did it several times over.

If it works, of course.

'It works,' Matheos says softly, like he knew it would be the first thought on my mind. Of course it would be – I pushed myself to the brink borrowing power from gods to create these things.

'How do you know?'

'You've been unconscious for four days. It was the same for Ione and Kerkeis, even though they swam further afield and far outside of whatever time-slowing powers that sundial has been wielding. It's been four days for us all. The medallions override it – time the same for us when we wear them as it is for anyone outside these walls.'

'Oh.'

I had known that might be their limitation – after all, Athena said that Chronos could only push time forward, not slow its pursuit. But still, some part of me had clung to the glimmering possibility that I was wrong – that she was wrong – and, if spun to their furthest reaches in one direction, they might be able to draw us to a steadier, meandering crawl.

After so long when our minutes equated to Olympian days and our grandest efforts were at a *distinct* disadvantage compared to theirs, I'd hoped we might not only snatch time from the cosmos, but pull it from the Olympians themselves to claw back some of the time we'd lost.

But evidently this steady, relentless beat is as slow as Chronos can go.

'Not what you wanted them to do?' Matheos asks.

'It's fine,' I say. 'It's more than I thought I'd actually be able to manage.'

But still not quite what I wanted. Which is irksome – an infuriating duality where I did not truly expect myself capable of achieving something that only the most skilled of gods with centuries of experience might, but am still irritated to fall short. Especially by so minuscule an amount. Especially when Athena herself *told me* this and I knew the limitation going in!

Then, that quiet, curious voice in my mind: *What about the other direction?*

If this orderly regularity is the slowest Chronos is capable of, what if I spun those dials to the right instead? How quickly could we go? Could we truly leap through time?

'It's brilliant,' he says, looking at me with the same fascination with which I regarded the medallions. 'You're brilliant.'

'You would say that – I was made to be perfect for you.'

'Pandora, with all the love in the world, you are absolutely not perfect for me.' He takes my hand and traces the lines there as he speaks, like he would sketch whichever path drew us together – finding the one that is not the gods and not their plan, but rather the path which might be about *us*. 'You're a dozen things I never thought to ask for and a dozen more I certainly don't deserve. We snipe, we bicker – we're not in love because we're some perfectly designed halves slotted together. I don't love you because I can't not. How did you put it? You aren't some thing for me to resist. I love you, intentionally and without reservation, because I decided to. We're not gods-ordained destiny, we're deliberate.'

My stomach swoops, a feeling like my skin is too tight – like the whole world is too tight. So, I take that hand holding me and draw him closer, let our lips meet, taste the sincerity on his tongue. He hums, a slight sigh, so gloriously content against me even with all that we are grappling with and the whole world hanging in the balance.

I am doing this for the humans, for the people just like me.

But, gods, I'm doing it for him too. It's different, I know – all that wiring in my mind is there to prime my love for service and usefulness. But I do not feel like I vanish here, I am not putting someone else first until I am so far behind as to disappear. Instead I feel pivotal, like I am centred precisely because this love means so much to me, he means so much to me, and it's my want, my need, to save him.

Matheos was right: it's selfish. And I want to be selfish a thousand times over.

Didn't he once ask that of me?

'You can do this, Pandora,' he says so earnestly that his belief alone could convince me. 'You can bring hope to the humans. You've already brought it to me.'

I press my lips back to his, quickly, like to linger will be to stay forever. 'I need to do it now, while I believe we really can.'

Matheos rises instantly, and offers me his hand. 'Put me to work.'

CHAPTER THIRTY-NINE

THE ROOM I'VE BEEN WORKING in is a mess, instruments strewn across the surfaces, new supplies from Kerkeis and Ione bundled everywhere, metal shavings littering the floor, and towers of parchment scattered with scribbled notes and meticulously detailed sketches.

'Do you have enough? Kerkeis and Ione should be back soon with rocks from Mount Sipylus if you need them.'

'I think this will work. No.' I allow myself a small smile. 'I hope it will.'

Matheos begins tidying but I draw him away and set him in front of a bench instead. He is used to pulling thorns from paws edged with razor-sharp claws, to stitching up gaping wounds in creatures with teeth larger than the needle, to slicing out decaying flesh and performing surgery on a forest floor.

Which is to say his hand is far steadier than mine – especially under pressure.

And hope is a delicate thing.

It can spark under varying circumstances, almost any, really.

But to be sustained? That is a precise mix – and we do not have room for errors as we craft it.

Not that we're crafting *hope* as such. We already have that, shining in our chests, singing at every beat. We just need something to pour it into – like the way my anima settled into the clay they shaped for me. We need a vessel. So here we are: quicksilver, Stygian iron, waters of the Lethe, ambrosia, nectar, Caucasian herbs, narcissi, anemones, asphodel, flowers of the Styx – it really is an awful lot of flowers. I have to check the list to confirm what some of these things piled high even are, the supplies long and bountiful.

And we need to drain each dreg of the gods' magic they hold, and turn it into something new.

An impossible task, and suddenly it feels so very foolish, all that we have set ourselves up to do. Why would this possibly work? And how can I expect to rival the gods?

But then I look at my notes, the curiosity that got me here, and broken down it does not feel so impossible – step by step towards impossible attainability. Mortals have been gifted godhood for their inventions – so why should I feel invention belongs only to the gods?

I boil the quicksilver, collect its steam, let it settle into liquid once more. Then I do it again and again, refining it each time. I look at the flickering flames and think of all the reasons the gods did not want hope in the hands of mortals, the power, warmth and comfort it holds. Power to be drawn and wielded . . .

The humans and their vibrancy. The tavernas and the bakeries, all those people whose lives revolve around making sure one another is fed. My own hands beating dough, tearing into the bread while it steams. Offering the first slice, to turn hope and love and happiness into a physical, sharable thing . . .

I simmer the petals, collect the vapour, run it through bronze pipes until it pools with the quicksilver. I etch letters into bone, into these fragments of the gods' creations, and, with slight hesitation, I finish with *kalon kakon* – because isn't that my hope incarnate? That if the gods dictate morality, then let me be an evil to them. Let me be that ugly good. Let that meaning spin and spin and spin . . .

Music – the quick pulsing beat of it. The desire to tap my feet, to dance. The priests in their temples and all their reverence, the indications of just how deeply they are able to care, of just how much hope they might hold within them . . .

I tip the shards into the pot and measure the waters of the Lethe carefully, pipette it in singular drops into the mixture – just enough to forget its origins, to leave it all a blank slate that might collect something new.

Kerkeis and Ione bursting through the door, that swelling feeling in my chest, that fear of taking a breath in case it could keep that hope aloft a moment longer. The way they rally round us, their comfort, the way they look at one another – so much feeling . . .

Matheos hands me the stems of the Caucasian herbs, can't meet my eyes as he does, and I feel hope swell there, too: that we might fix this one day, break his brother free, escape somewhere the gods can't reach. We are on the cusp of their power, after all – and there's a whole world stretching beyond those mountains.

I turn to the nectar and ambrosia, and Matheos heads to the door, muttering something about fetching the Stygian iron blades, about not trusting me with something so sharp for long.

I roll my eyes but I am revelling in it, in us. The teasing, the tenderness, the fires within us that only each other's touch can cool or stoke, the love in every beat of us.

I set the current mixture in a jar, etching the seal – we need the touch of the blades and –

'Stop.'

A familiar voice, harsh and commanding, bold with the expectation that she will be heard.

Hesione.

I jolt, just managing not to drop the jar – catching myself as I go to look and forcing my focus back to the work in front of me. Whatever is happening, it is not as important as carving the wax sealing the jar with markings of hope and etchings of belief.

'Pandora, put it down,' she snarls, like she can hardly speak for her fury. 'I mean it.'

I risk a glance – and wish I hadn't. The jar really does slip through my fingers, and though I catch it, my grip is too tight, smudging the symbols beyond recognition.

Hesione stands with Matheos angled before her, the point of a short sword pressed against his back.

My heart races, my thoughts spiralling to catch up: which steps do we still need to take, and can I do them subtly, can I stall, how much time do we need, and through it all the sharp, iron-hot sear of danger – of *Matheos* in danger. And confusion, all those variables accounted for and never whatever this is.

We prepared for every single god trying to stop us, but not her.

'Is this what you meant by fetching the Stygian blades? How did she get it off you?' I ask, hoping flippancy might distract her, while my thumb brushes over the wax, smoothing it so I might start again.

'She asked. She said the future was shifting, that whatever we were doing here was working and she wanted to be a part of it. Of course, I forgot my family are conniving, underhanded liars,' Matheos grumbles. 'Prometheus would be mortified, Hesione. Years of subtle manipulation and slowly chipped-away confidence and you reach straight for a blade the moment you don't get your way? Where's the nuance? Where's the skill?'

My hope flickers once more, knowing that Matheos can have a sword levelled at his gut and still be more irritated than fearful. Though I think he might be hiding that too.

'How dare you even speak your brother's name with all you're doing to him? Pandora,' Hesione says, trying to keep her voice calm, like she thinks that if she can control that, she can control everything else too. 'Put down that jar and come over here. We can discuss this.'

I turn my attention back to the symbols, picking up my stylus once more. 'Personally, I would have asked to talk before turning a blade on someone, but perhaps that's just me.'

'Enough. I really will hurt him.' Her grip on the sword shakes. 'I'll explain everything as soon as you stop. You must realize the gods are closing in on us. You and this foolish plan of yours are going to ruin everything. *Pandora*,' she says, so hatefully I feel a cold iron edge myself. 'Have I not made myself clear? Cease this.'

'Your leverage is a man I hate.' I shrug, as much as I can while continuing to etch the symbols into the wax. 'Telling me why might be more effective than threatening him.'

'Oh, don't even try me with that hating-one-another nonsense. You wouldn't have so corrupted him if it were true.'

Hesione bristles. 'And I think we've spoken quite enough already. This is a problem for a blade to fix.'

'Don't stop, Pandora,' Matheos says, voice harsh and urgent – markedly different to the nonchalance he has thus far been channelling while held at sword-point. It startles me enough that I look up from the patterns I've been marking – in time to catch him lower his voice to Hesione and demand: 'What are you going to do? There's two of us. And if you think I'm going to let you lay a hand on her then –'

His eyes meet mine, panic burning there as he cuts himself off.

And I understand what he has realized – what ought to have been immediately apparent, if it weren't for the jar in my hand and the blade at his back: that throughout, Hesione has seen only one solution to the problem of *me*. Only one way to get her husband's plan back on track.

And as she just admitted, what would conversation achieve that the blade in her hand couldn't do more effectively?

She too seems to realize that she just gave the game away, and her features harden, those narrow brows drawing down, harsh lips puckering in displeasure.

With a voice as brutal as the gods' justice, she says: 'Don't think I won't run him through first before I turn this blade on you.'

If she's reached such a state of desperation, to believe murder her only option, what difference is there really in two bodies rather than one? It's not just an aimless threat. She really would use that sword.

'Pandora,' Matheos begins, desperate, as for the first time in all of this I turn my attention to her and properly consider her ultimatum.

'What do you want?' I ask. 'Truly?'

She cocks her head, regarding me as her hand steadies on the blade. 'You know there are only two ways this ends. You either bring devastation to the mortals or we remove you from the picture.'

'There's a third option. This, what I'm –'

'What you're doing might draw us down another thread. You might buy a few years at the cost of our ultimate victory. We can't risk it. We never could. Epimatheos should have never let you through that door. But given he's a half-witted coward, I'm afraid it's on me to ensure you never walk back out of it.'

I clutch the jar tighter. This can't be it. We can't defy the gods only to be felled by the plans of a man they've already bound.

'You're right,' I say, trying to find that irresistible tongue I swear I was once capable of wielding. 'But you're not a murderer, Hesione. Give me the blade. I'll finish this myself. It is as Prometheus said: if I love those mortals as I claim to – as I *do*, and as he does – then I must be willing to sacrifice myself.' I take a breath. 'I always knew it might come to this. It's fine. Just let Epimatheos go.'

Her husband's name gives her pause, and Matheos's snarl of 'No, you can't!' must sound persuasive because she appears to actually consider my lies.

But her jaw hitches. 'If that's how you'd like to do this, then very well. But you're a fool if you think I'm giving up my leverage. So here's what's going to happen: you're going to destroy all of this. Break everything. Then you're going to take those cords binding those flowers and you're going to tie

Matheos here before coming with me. If you wish to finish this yourself, fine. But there's no need to give you a weapon, I don't think. Not when we can just as easily find some rope.'

A chill trickles down my back with every word, and as she finishes I feel it crystalize, gripping me like a vice. Caught and frozen, and at her mercy.

Still, there's potential here, right? Outside this room I can summon the automatons to subdue her. I'm not sure how quickly she'd be able to turn that blade on me, and who of the two of us might survive such a fight, but they're not the worst odds I've faced. She might be immortal but that Stygian blade is capable of killing either one of us.

'Pandora!' Matheos protests, as I consider it.

'Hush,' Hesione commands. 'Someone has to do what you could not stomach. As always, Matheos, we do this for you. We love you. You'll realize that one day.'

'I never doubted that,' he says, shoulders slumping.

But I catch his hands inching towards the blade she holds.

'Very well,' I say, meeting Matheos's eyes like I might convey my plan. His own gaze burns as though he would do the same, but all we seem capable of is urging each other towards trust.

I look to the equipment, wondering whether I can break enough of it to hide the jar within the wreckage, when Matheos turns, and snatches the sword – or tries to, at least. Hesione's grip is steadfast, wrenching it back towards her as they wrestle for it, her foot shooting out as he twists her wrist back. They stumble and I rush forward to help but before I can take another step, Hesione turns the blade sharply and jabs.

The sword pierces Matheos's side.

He howls, a shriek of pain so agonizing I feel it too, like that blade has wounded me instead. I stagger like it has. My heart thunders like it might beat for the both of us.

I grab at the edge of the table to steady myself. The blade is only buried an inch or so into his gut – a hesitant wound. Like we're struck, holding our breaths and waiting for whatever happens next.

Hesione takes the blade with both hands, holding it steady. 'You reckless, foolish boy. Don't make me push this in further.'

Matheos looks up at her, hatred pure and unfiltered burning in his eyes. 'Don't pretend I made you do any of this.'

And then he hurls himself forward, screaming as that blade slices through him to the hilt, and Hesione flinches, letting go as his blood bursts across her hands.

'What have you done?' she screeches, and I hate to agree with her, but I can feel his anguish in my bones, and I feel I must be screaming too as I rush forward.

The jar of hope smashes quickly against the ground as I run to him like I might help, when the damage has already been done.

I'm on my knees before Matheos. The ground is damp with the golden ichor that courses through his veins. Before I can tell him not to, he draws the blade out and his blood pulses hot and fast from the hole it had been plugging. I surge forward to cover it, pressing my hands over the gap and feeling his skin throb beneath. He hisses through his teeth.

'It'll be fine,' Hesione says quickly, as though to reassure herself. 'My husband manages perfectly well with his liver ripped out daily. He'll heal.'

She walks to my worktable like she would not waste another

second, and begins hurling jars to the floor while I flounder in Matheos's blood, spitting back: 'Prometheus's liver isn't ripped out by a Stygian blade.'

A sword cured in the river Styx. A relentless river, churning hatred, oaths sworn on its waters are unbreakable.

And wounds inflicted by blades set in its stream are unhealable.

At least not in any natural sense. It would take magic just as potent as the river itself.

It would take a god – and a powerful one at that.

'Why?' I ask Matheos urgently. 'Why did you do this?'

'Take away her leverage. Get the sword off her. History of sacrifice. Choose one.' Each option is a grunted gasp born of increasingly shallow breaths.

I scrabble for the remaining Caucasian herbs – a handful of stems and a small bud of petals.

'Eat these.' I force them to his lips.

'Not enough,' he gasps. 'Flowers born of Titan blood can cure mortal wounds, not our own.'

But he chokes them down anyway and I return my hands to his side like I can hold the ichor in myself.

'I had a plan,' I moan, seeing every scrap of hope I had shorn, in tatters.

'Your plan, I imagine, still carried the risk of her succeeding. I removed that possibility.' He glances at the sword in his hand. 'Quite literally.'

He chuckles but it's cut off by a sharp wince and he clutches at his side, his hand over mine before peeling one of them away and pressing the ichor-slicked sword into my palm. 'Pandora, you have to stop her.'

I cannot even think about her right now, not with Matheos paling by the second. Stygian iron, Stygian iron ... would stitches work? Cauterization? Or would it simply seal the skin shut while the wound bleeds beneath?

'Is this what your husband would have wanted?' I call, not tearing my eyes from all that hot, aureate blood. Maybe if I talk for long enough, a way forward will materialize. 'His brother bleeding out for his plan?'

Hesione doesn't even blink, just continues her path of destruction through my worktable. 'Don't be so petulant. Prometheus would understand, he always saw the bigger picture. You know what some of the men out there have begun decreeing, ever since the first human woman popped up? That the best thing for a woman to be is invisible, for no one to even know her name. It's better for us to be nothing than to be the hero. But here I am, managing to be both.'

'Prometheus *would* understand?' Matheos repeats quietly – and slowly. His every blink grows sluggish. There must be something I can do. I found a way to distil the magic of the gods from the dregs left in their creations – couldn't I use that to heal him? 'So he doesn't already. He doesn't know.'

'He knew what he needed to know and he trusted me with the rest, as you should have too,' Hesione says – then she takes a breath and squares her shoulders. 'I know you both just want what's best for the humans. I know you want to bring the gods down too. But the moment we tried to make this world even slightly kinder, Zeus turned to torture so gruesome it would serve as a warning to the rest of us. We're not cruel, Epimatheos. We don't act without reason. But the future is our only chance – it must be protected. This is never how I wanted this to go.' She locks eyes with me. 'Epimatheos is *not* the one who stands in our way.'

I swallow, running my hand down Matheos's cheek.

There's another way – maybe. A last chance.

But it's not one he'll like. Not when it's the very reason he let that blade strike.

'I'm sorry,' I say quietly, leaning my forehead against his for a moment, inhaling his breath and knowing he won't forgive me for this.

Then I hold the sword out to her. 'You have healing powers, right?' Matheos said that, once. That she blamed herself for Prometheus's pain. 'Heal Epimatheos and you can kill me.'

'No,' Matheos snarls, reaching clumsily for the sword, but his whole body wavers with the effort.

Hesione reaches for it too and I leap back as I scramble to my feet, putting distance between me and both of them. I clutch the sword close to my chest. 'Not until he's alright. The moment he is, I promise I'll give it to you.'

Matheos hisses through bared teeth, but he's losing the energy to even hate me for this.

'Fine,' Hesione snaps. 'But know that what I fix can be just as easily undone should you renege on this deal.'

Her gaze flickers to Matheos and for the first time I see doubt there. Perhaps even fear that she has gone too far.

'I never wanted this,' she says again, coming closer. 'I do love you, brother. I never wanted you hurt.'

I take another step back to make room for her, making the mistake of glancing down and seeing just how much golden blood I am coated in.

My stomach churns and it is only the fear of how much worse it is for Matheos that keeps me from vomiting. What if she can't fix this? What if it's every bit as bad as I fear?

'We're on the same side,' she repeats as she edges closer, like she thinks that is an apology.

'We're on the same side,' Matheos confirms, like he's finally accepting it.

She crouches by him, setting her hands on his side.

He does not even move quickly; he's lost too much blood. But she's so focused on the wound and I'm too busy waiting for her to declare it remedied that I do not see him remove the chain from around his own neck, only see him sling it around hers, and turn the dials all the way to the right.

She vanishes.

I scream.

'It works,' he says, with a satisfied nod, before slumping back against the wall.

'Matheos!'

'Is that not what you wanted it to do? To let us jump forward in time? I suppose that means she's our future problem, but you're mortal and I probably have minutes of life left so perhaps we'll get lucky and never see her again.'

'Don't say that,' I scold, rushing back to his side. 'You couldn't have waited until *after* she healed you?'

I'm so familiar with the dampness of his blood on my skin, so much of it that it's making my clothes cling to my frame, that it takes a moment to recognize the moisture on my cheeks.

I can't cry, not now, not at the end.

Not while he's dying.

'I finally make my own decisions and you're upset at the timing.'

'Stop joking while you're dying.' I practically choke on the words.

Matheos hesitates – a hesitation of laboured breathing and trembling pain. 'I'd rather not face the enormity of it.'

'Matheos,' I say, my voice breaking. I feel so utterly, debilitatingly helpless and this can't be it, this can't be how this goes.

'She couldn't heal me,' he says softly. 'Minor healing powers do not make her a god of medicine, which is the only thing that might stand a chance against Stygian iron. It wouldn't have worked, and I didn't know if I'd get her so close again. I was never going to let you give your life for mine.'

He raises his hand, wipes a tear from my cheek with a shaking finger.

His dark eyes swallow me whole, are levelled with such intensity – and such fear.

'I didn't mean it. When I told you I wished you'd never loved me.'

'I know.'

The corners of his lips twitch, the closest he can come to a smile. I'm saying his name, again and again, like I can plead with him to stay with me – but already his eyes are fluttering closed, his breathing slowing.

'No, no, no,' I mutter, sobbing now, whole-body heaves that are almost impossible to move through, but I fumble at the medallion around my neck and force it around his, shoving against those dials like I could reverse this, or at the very least freeze him in place until I can fix him.

But the dials won't budge. The slowest that time is capable of is the steady, inevitable churn towards the end.

I let it go and tear myself away to start scavenging in the scraps of Hesione's carnage. There must be something, surely. Some dregs of magic to summon, if not enough to heal him then enough to save him, not perfect, not without pain but – *Fates*, please – without death.

I find the shattered pot, the runes inscribed on it. Matheos's blood still coats my fingers and now the gold shines with the dark, gossamer web of the substance we created – the substance that was supposed to hold hope.

I've never hoped for anything more, and it is still not enough.

Thunder rumbles overhead, and suddenly Korax begins barking, its snarling shouts cutting through the deathly silence permeated only by Matheos's harrowed breaths.

A booming knock at the door, demanding and loud, like it is a step away from caving in. In the corners, lights flicker.

The gods are closing in.

I had not realized she meant so immediately.

I glance at Matheos, at the way his eyes have fallen shut, his chest barely moving. The shattered remnants of my hope, scattered around the room.

Broken. Defeated. Ready to surrender.

Fine. I'll do it.

I'll open that jar if they save him.

CHAPTER FORTY

'**SEE, YOU KNOCK AND PEOPLE** tend to answer, there's no need to – Oh, rivers of Hell, don't tell me you've killed him.'

The gods stare at me – or rather, they stare at the golden blood staining me.

Hermes seems the only one capable of speech – Athena's eyes dart across me like the ichor is an offensive puzzle to be solved, and Aphrodite physically recoils, which I suspect is from more than just the blood. My hair is a frenzied mess, piled atop my ahead, and I've been so consumed in making hope and altering time that I'm not actually sure when the last time I washed was.

'Heal him. *Please*. I'll do anything.'

Athena's eyes narrow. 'I am sure you would already do anything we asked without needing leverage. We are your creators, are we not?'

'Please,' I repeat, still crying, unable to think of anything clever to say, anything else that might persuade them. But is this not what the gods want of mortals? For them to beg and plead?

And every second we waste might be pivotal.

'Oh, let's not make this harder than it needs to be,' Hermes says, rolling his eyes to the Heavens. 'Asclepius's daughters took on his powers of healing after Zeus killed him, right? I'll have one of them snap their fingers and you can both explain what that *anything* will entail.'

He kicks into the air, the wings on his sandals fluttering to life and shooting him into the Heavens.

Athena regards me with a cool, steady gaze. 'He's not happy.'

Surely there is only one *he* that matters. And in my very short existence, it seems he is rarely happy.

'Consider this the final warning,' Athena says, risking a glance at Aphrodite before adding, 'For all of us. We made you, so we're all at risk if you don't obey him. We thought we might get here first and persuade you but it seems Hermes has happily accepted your bargain. Zeus will arrive shortly and he expects a ceremony of the opening. I trust that won't be a problem.'

So that's how she's couching this – as fear for those who made me and not that the merest hint of rebellion will have him looking for dissent everywhere.

'No,' I say hollowly, 'I don't think it will be.'

Does she not realize this is how he succeeds? By keeping us divided, too scared to unite and trust one another? Athena, Hesione, us too, I suppose – how many people in this world must be working to take Zeus down, through one route or another. The closest we came was trusting in Kerkeis and Ione, and their war in the oceans – how much bigger that could be, or have been.

But it won't, because we wouldn't risk too much.

I feel cold, like while Matheos bled I did too – the hopes I flung aside when I offered anything to heal him, any joy, any care drained.

I'll open the jar. I'll do whatever they ask – I just want this over. I just want to cling to Matheos and forget any of this ever happened.

Whatever anima they put in me feels broken.

'Pandora.'

But now that dwindling spark inside me flares at the voice behind me, and I turn without thought, like a cord within me has been yanked.

Matheos stands in the doorway of the room where so much destruction has happened. He staggers forward, still weak and dizzy, but the wound has stopped bleeding. In fact, through the gash in his chiton I can see no injury at all.

Hermes made good on our bargain, then. Which means I'll have to see it through as well.

Looking at Matheos, part of me wants to shriek with joy and part of me knows if I open my mouth I'll start crying again, so I just stand there, still and shocked until he is by my side, hand on my shoulder, turning to face the goddesses at our door.

'Hello,' he manages. 'I see my wife did not have the decorum to invite you in.'

Athena narrows her eyes. 'Oh, I see. You do realize she was just pleading for your life? This is all thoroughly dysfunctional, isn't it?'

'Love often is,' Aphrodite says, glancing between the two of us like she can see exactly what joins us.

'You would save a man who despises you?' Athena asks, wrinkling her nose in distaste – the only indication she gives that we are more familiar with one another than she pretends.

'Oh, I'm not so sure about that,' Aphrodite says, lips twitching in a smirk. 'Whatever is between these two is quite delicious. I hope Zeus lets them live – I want to see more.'

Matheos's fingers tighten on my shoulder and I don't know which part has caused his tension: the realization that I have begged for his life – and what I must surely have agreed to – or that the ruse we so carefully crafted to ensure they couldn't use one of us to get to the other has been thoroughly shattered.

He's alive.

He's alive and it's still not enough to fix my despair, to make me feel much of anything at all. I am here and I am nodding and I am forcing myself to look into their eyes and smile and say *yes, of course, whatever Zeus wants, whatever you wish, oh graceful goddesses who have created me* and I feel nothing at all.

More thunder rolls across the heavens – despite the sunshine, and the heat hissing against my ice-cold skin.

I reach behind me, feeling for Matheos, and when I touch his chiton I curl my fingers tight within it, where they cannot see. I need something to cling to, something to keep going for.

The chariot appears then, four horses dashing through the sky, hooves pounding into the air with thunderous claps.

'No time to change clothes, then,' Aphrodite says, like it's little more than a pity we are so inappropriately dressed – and not like it might be alarming to the king of the gods to greet him coated in resplendent, deific blood. 'You'll have to tell us all what happened – I do so adore a lovers' spat.'

As though I simply stabbed my own husband in the heat of an argument. As though that might be a brilliant story she would love to be told . . .

Truly these are not gods, but monsters.

The chariot lands within the courtyard walls, dragging through the mud, Zeus towering at the front, reins taut in his hands. He does not look around, does not even glance at the imposing umber pithos mere feet away. His gaze is locked firmly on me.

Hermes leaps out of the chariot first – and I hadn't even seen him until he does, hidden as he was by Zeus's enormous frame.

The king of the gods doesn't break his gaze to leave the chariot, just steps down like the drop is nothing, and stalks towards us.

He grins, but it's a cruel smile, and one laced with victory.

'Pandora,' he greets me.

Belatedly, I drop to my knees, pulling Matheos with me.

'My king,' I say quickly. 'Lord Zeus, it is an honour to have you in our home.'

'Epimatheos, all of you –' he turns to the gods – 'leave us. I would have words with our creation.'

The gods make to go, but Matheos doesn't. He stays beside me, hand at my back, resolute. Nearly dying has made him defiant, apparently – but what would we possibly gain from resisting? I refuse to lose him twice.

'Here, dear husband, let me help you up,' I say, rising. 'My apologies, Lord Zeus, Epimatheos was injured earlier today.'

Matheos's gaze is searching, and I try to tell him it's fine, that we're all right – just doing the best we can under impossible circumstances – trying to convince myself that if we refuse them, the gods will simply punish us and find some other way to torture the humans, so our involvement does not matter much at all.

But having felt little since Matheos was returned to me, it is that thought which makes something in my gut squirm.

I suppose the truth is, despite everything I claimed, when pushed I might sacrifice myself out of moral defiance, but I cannot bring myself to sacrifice Matheos too. That is how fragile my morals are, how quickly they cave. Knowing he will not let me do this for him, that we discussed this, that he told me firmly not to do it in his name – still I know I'll open that jar if it keeps him safe.

And I have already bargained his safety on this. The decision is made, now there is only a lid to prise free.

Matheos takes my hand, and I hate the doubt that flickers there, even as he trusts me and rises to his feet, offering one last concerned look, glancing at Zeus who glowers back, before retreating to join the other gods at the far end of the courtyard.

I watch him take his every step, like I might never take a single second of his existence for granted again. Zeus plants a hand on my shoulder and pulls me to face him, his expression moving beyond rage to something apoplectic that conjures thoughts of a town washed clean away, of smothering rain and of every cruel thought latched within that pithos.

'You have not opened the jar,' Zeus says. He makes his voice low but the power rolls through with a heaviness that feels crushing. I can only think of that voice issuing the decree that bound Prometheus to that mountainside, that detailed each instruction for what would happen to him there. 'I thought I was clear.'

'My apologies, my king,' I say quickly. 'I simply did not know *when* you wished for me to open the jar. I did not want to spoil your plans by opening it at the wrong time, and I've been looking for a sign every day since I left Olympus. And now here you are!'

He considers me, and I try to glaze my face with some appearance of sincerity but the lies aren't coming like they once did. They're there, somewhere, the roles I used to slip into – but I'm too exhausted to reach in and find them. I had no idea how much energy it took to pretend.

'You do not need to lie for Epimatheos, Pandora,' Zeus says finally. 'This is our fault. We made you to be his wife – we cannot blame you for obeying your husband as a good woman should. I always suspected he was a traitor like his brother before him. But do not worry. Once we have sorted this nonsense with the humans, we will deal with him and find a better match for you, a husband more loyal to your king's decrees.'

'No!' I say quickly, terror setting in. 'My lord, that's not . . . please don't punish him for my errors. It's my fault – I . . . I confess that I discovered what was in that jar, and how it will bring horrors to the humans and I, well, *I'm* human. I'm terrified of what lies within it, but I'm so sorry, my king, I never should have allowed my fear to stand before your will.'

I plead with wide-open eyes, praying my panicked lies translate as guilt, and when I'm done I duck my head as though ashamed. 'Please, punish me however you choose. It would be just.'

Zeus grunts as he considers, and I wonder if Metis is in there, persuading him to believe me.

I wonder if she's disappointed.

'Well, this defiance is something we will have to examine if we create another batch of humans,' Zeus mulls it over aloud. 'We'll have to tweak you somehow, too. It would be a shame to destroy the work of so many gods, but between your visit to Prometheus and your continued reluctance to follow perfectly clear orders, evidently someone failed at their part in your creation.'

I feel unravelled, like he has peeled the skin right off my body. That amphora of my decaying parts – how different am I, really, from those? Am I just as likely to be scrapped? Or else smelted and reshaped. And what of Matheos, once I am gone . . .

'It's a good thing we made so much of you, I suppose.' He lets his gaze crawl across me. 'Gives us space to whittle you down into something more . . . pliable.'

My throat tightens. I've never given much consideration to why they crafted me into this shape, only perhaps that, of the many ways a woman might be beautiful, this soft rolling abundance was the way they believed Matheos might prefer. But now I wonder . . .

The gods wanted a monument to their strength, just like Prometheus on that mountain. Someone who would always look up at them, yes, but a representation of their unyielding might nonetheless. A girl who embodied all their power.

And now I've spoken out, formed an opinion that wasn't theirs.

I've taken up too much fucking space.

So of course they want to drag me back, shrink me down and find fault with what was already perfect, because before they alter my mind, they'll reshape my body to suit. It is, after all, the first thing they picked and argued over and it will be the first place they seek to regain their control. They never even saw it as mine to begin with, always theirs – their creation, their canvas and their thing to deem worthy. 'Open the jar, Pandora,' Zeus commands, interrupting my spiralling thoughts. 'It is time.'

So long spent denying this truth of myself and fighting feebly against it. But I'm their tool, their play-piece, their beacon for the rest of humanity. I am nothing. I am a will to be bent under theirs.

Hesione and Prometheus knew it.

They were willing to kill me for it.

Maybe I should have let them.

'Yes, yes, of course, my lord. Thank you for allowing me the honour of unleashing all that is to come.'

CHAPTER FORTY-ONE

EUS SUMMONS THE OTHER GODS to come closer again, and they glance between us nervously. Will they be punished for the supposed fault I have revealed? Or do they fear I might have turned against them in my private conversation with their king?

Athena certainly glowers like she would ingrain my allegiance to them as my creators into my very skin.

Is this what they want of me? Someone to obey their every whim, to live up to all their expectations, to never move without one of them drawing tight the string?

It is hardly even a question; it is a truth. That is all any of them want of me.

'Pandora, surely you must be curious,' Zeus says, voice booming like it is part of the spectacle. 'You humans always are – to see how far a fall, how sharp an edge.'

'I . . . yes, I suppose,' I mutter – more lies, more performances. Why? Just so he can declare it was my own foolish human curiosity that unleashed such horrors, certainly no will of his own?

And then they'll haul me back to Olympus and cut open my mind. Erase me like my mother, if that is who she even is. Any trace of me just a palimpsest for what they would have me become.

I step towards the jar, those inscriptions and figures appearing to dance in the dappled sun, a dozen stories, myths and legends that track the might of the gods coming alive beneath their watchful gaze.

And within those stories, the weakness and folly of the humans beneath them.

Then Matheos steps up beside me. 'Blame us both,' he says to the baffled gods. 'This is what you want, yes? To hold human curiosity responsible for the horrors humanity will face? Well, blame it too on a man too blinded by lust to turn away such a cruel woman. Let the mortals once again be damned as much by my stupidity as their feeble resistances to their own impulses. It will be another lesson against the actions of my brother.'

Athena snorts as Hermes asks, 'Is he writing our messaging now?'

Zeus shrugs, smiling slightly like he's only mildly entertained by the whole affair. 'Very well, Epimatheos. You are proving your own point, I suppose, by so volunteering.'

Matheos's hand returns to the small of my back, guiding me towards the jar. And my hackles rise, my suspicion a difficult thing to contain as I step up and pretend this is all fine, that I am overjoyed to obey the will of Zeus with my husband in tow. But he nearly died to save me once, and I offered my own life for his, and I'm not convinced this isn't just another way to throw himself before the danger I am facing.

'Why did you do that?' I hiss beneath my breath when I am certain we are far enough away.

'So that I can stand by your side,' he answers. 'I let my brother take the fall. I'm joining you on yours – on ours.'

I turn to him, doubt still flickering. But something else, too, because where there is doubt, there is hope. Hope that he means this, that he is by my side, that we will make it through this.

'Matheos,' I say gently, reaching for his hand – and catching sight of my own.

The inky, pearlescent magic we'd contained in that jar, that I'd reached for the remnants of. There it is, glowing on my skin.

Hope.

The cogs of my mind whir, finally, pushing past the despair and connecting the threads that I'd thought were scattered. There is not enough magic here, not nearly enough – but there is something else, too. All those things we distilled, trying to replicate what had been made by the gods – when there are two things here made just as well by them.

The jar.

And me.

I'm a beacon.

I race the final steps towards the pithos, Matheos crossing to stand on its other side, untying those cords, loosening it all so I might set it free. He faces me over the top of the pithos. I touch its clay, rest my hands on the sloping sides and feel the heat of it. We may be able to shape this, may be able to do *something*.

May be able to *try*.

Matheos's hands cover mine, holding them tight. 'Are you sure about this?'

I glance at the expectant gods. What choice do we have? This – exactly this. To open the jar and still fight to defy them. To hope that one day enough people might do the same and it might make a difference.

To – if nothing else – give the humans a fighting chance.

I nod and he runs his thumb across my palm before he lets go, like he would savour one final caress. 'You're my hope,' he says. 'You always have been.'

Then I reach for the lid and I wrench it free.

CHAPTER FORTY-TWO

LIGHT BLASTS FROM WITHIN, CHURNING rays that shoot up so violently I have to hold the jar still. Matheos stumbles backwards from the force of it but I can't move, not once my hands touch the smooth clay sides; they seal in place and I feel the magic coursing through me too.

I close my eyes, try to focus on all the injustices, all the rage, all the things already churning through that clay and scattering into the air above. And within it, hope.

I only had it half right before – those moments of joy, those sparks of belief we distilled.

Yes. That's hope. But a hope that's gossamer-thin and easily spilled across the tiles. But *this?* This is true hope – a thing with teeth, a thing that can take a beating, *hope* that can be knocked down and bleed and surge once more. Hope a thing that can be pierced and wounded by all those evils and still survive, fierce enough to have them cowering in turn.

And it is hope that surges now, while wearing my husband's blood with the king of the gods raging mere feet away, hope that it might change – that we can make it change. For the humans to reject *the way of things* and hope for better, and make it so. To fight. To endure.

And to keep fucking going.

So: I hope.

I hope for a world where the gods are punished for the things they have done, where Ione and Kerkeis can swim wherever they like without fear, where men are not tied to mountainsides just for trying to keep people safe and warm, where Matheos and I can live quietly, at this edge of the world, and not have to ignore horrors to do so.

I think of Matheos and his smile, his hands on mine, the half-fond eye-rolls and the contented sighs, the hope in each and every one.

I push it all into the jar. It cannot fly free, not like the others. Not without that substance to give it shape and form. But that jar can be a vessel to keep it safe. And I can be its beacon, broadcasting it to the world, for as long as I live.

A heavy weight settles around my neck.

My eyes shoot open, my hands still locked in place.

Matheos, securing the medallion that shifts time around my neck.

'I win,' he says, brushing my hair from my face so that he can lean to kiss my forehead.

I gasp for breath, my voice breaking and desperate. 'What are you doing?'

I can't move – or maybe I could, if I let go of this hope and stepped away. But the humans need this, and as long as I'm here they'll have hope in their hearts. They'll have reasons to keep pushing, keep trying and not settle for *good enough* without hoping for more.

'You've given the gods a very convenient way to stop this when they realize what you're doing,' he says. 'Kill you, end hope. Frankly, I've had quite enough of that solution. Maybe this short burst will be enough – and if not, there will be hope in the future, where it might be safe. Because I'm not sure that it is here. And you certainly aren't.'

He reaches for the dials.

'No, please, don't!'

'I love you,' he says calmly, like he's not forcing me from his side.

'They'll punish you instead!'

He shrugs, the hint of a crooked smile on his face. On his beautiful, lovely face that I'll never see again – when I am still blood-drenched and far from over the heartbreak of fearing I might lose him. 'It's about time they did.'

He turns the dial and everything slows – the lingering moment between us, time stretching, dilating.

But the medallion only moves time forward – that's its very issue, it does not allow us to slow.

Matheos looks at me, and I wonder if he too knows of these precious seconds we have been awarded.

The critical moment. The time to act. The very reason time slows at a pivotal point, when it shifts not around the universe, but around us. Kairos.

'Break it,' I tell him.

'What? No. You made very, *very* clear how bad an idea that was.'

Yes, an appalling idea. An idea that could break time itself.

But why not try? The gods broke time when they shredded it and used it as a weapon. Prometheus warped it into protection.

So why can't we play the game of gods and Titans – we wished to be participants, after all. Let's take time and tear it. Not a moment and not a long unfurling line but a scrap of our own. A neat little loop: this time, this place. Us.

Time not a long reaching line but a power locked in orbit, our knot at its centre, radiating hope across centuries, millennia, all time. To not only give the current mortals hope but to imbue it across their timeline, to bind it with their humanity.

To take that first stolen fire and make it a true beacon.

'Colliding an invention of Chronos with a time of Kairos? It'll seal us in, trap us in time,' I explain. 'We'll become the new pivotal point. Completely closed and completely removed.'

Devastation is written across Matheos's face, and still he clutches the bundle of dials hung at my throat.

'We wouldn't just give up our future, Pandora. We'd erase our past. We'll never happen!'

'No – we'll happen *always*.'

He gapes, hesitates, and I know, I know exactly what is running through his mind because it would hurtle through mine too – do nothing and know the other is safe even if you doom yourself, or take the risk, take the chance, and *hope*.

'Time would break,' he says. 'Nothing would align, timelines would be torn to shreds and reset.'

'And there would be hope in every part of them, in every race of humans they ever try to wipe out!'

'But it would rewrite everything. It would take centuries until time righted itself.'

Centuries when nothing would make sense, when people might exist before they were born or waltz into one another's stories long after their bones were gone from this world.

'So? We'd be able to radiate hope across them all in a place where the gods can't stop us.'

And who knows how long we'd have, what length of loop we might rip out of time and trap ourselves within. The same year on repeat? The same decade? Century? But together, safe, away from all this.

Maybe.

It's ... at the very least it's a possibility. But so too is that loop not sealing but fraying – *disintegrating*. We would be at the epicentre of an explosion of time and doing little more than *hoping* we survive it.

But it's better than remaining here. It's a third option. A risk worth taking.

'Now, Matheos, will you please break that damn medallion?'

Kairos needs us to seize the pivotal moment, and we're floundering.

'How do you know this will work?' Matheos asks, and he's desperate, and I can see how much he wants an out, wants proof this might come true.

The light in the jar is spluttering, the last evils flying free. The moment the gods will act, will choose to stop us is coming ...

The moment that we cannot let escape us.

'I don't,' I admit, seeing pages of notes and all that time-tinkering rolling out before me. 'But I think maybe it already has.' All those inconsistencies, the stories that never made sense. Hephaestus or Prometheus breaking Zeus's skull – but maybe it was both. In different times, because that line is already beginning to fracture from the other manipulations time has faced.

But that time might already be splintering is no guarantee that we survive this. We might obliterate any coherent chronology and destroy ourselves in the process. We might, at best, survive as a whisper in a tale – an echo in the timelines we shatter.

Little more than a story – *if* they remember us at all.

I take a breath. 'It's just a theory.'

Matheos glances to the jar, and then looks to me. All his life, putting faith into the hands of people who misused it. I would be clutching it tight, not sharing it again so lightly.

But I see it, the way it pours from Matheos – my hope and his faith. And I see them collide, his belief in me and my longing for a better world.

He nods and I act, pushing my hope into that jar with every single thing I have.

The connection breaks, I can move, and I snatch the lid and hurl it on, throwing my body over it to seal it in place, to lock my hope inside where it will not falter, safe in this vessel of the gods' own crafting.

This is it: the end point, or the start of eternity.

I might never have the chance to say goodbye. I might never have to.

Matheos covers me in turn, his arms around me as he slips the chain about his neck too, binding us close, and with his hand still gripped tight on the metallic gears, he crushes them, breaks the soft filament holding them in place until the discs clatter to the ground beneath us. From me, not the jar or the dial beneath us, light explodes.

It is not darkness we fall into; it is luminescence.

Hope so bright it burns.

WE'LL NEVER HAPPEN

*T*IME BEGAN - THAT IS WHAT they will say.

They?

They are not here yet, only time, emerging into creation.

And with it, *inevitability.*

The clock that trundles on, the inexorable *next.*

Time and inevitability will split the world-egg in two and crack apart the universe, and then they will encircle the cosmos and rotate the heavens.

No, others will say – though, no, they are not here yet either.

It began with Khaos, the void at the dawn.

It doesn't truly matter what happened, only the stories that will be told. The world is chaos and inevitability, the press of time breathing down your neck.

We must peel away the enormity and make sense of the small slivers we can grasp – how we understand them and how we understand one another. It does not matter how came the world, only how we conceive of it.

In this world, the Titans will rise and fall like the waning moon and the gods crest soon after, thinking themselves invulnerable to the ebb of time. Some will know, a few among their number, with the mortals on the Earth below: all worlds turn and all suns must set. All cities fall. All nations fade. And the gods will weaken, too – of that there is hope. Hope to take the next step towards that inescapable horizon.

They follow the stories and the stories follow them: mother to child, brother to brother, letters across nations, lectured on street corners and chanted in temples. They all know, of course, that they were made of clay a long time ago. They'll tell a story of a girl with a jar – or, no, it was a box, wasn't it? Not that it matters much, anyway. It's only a story. They all have to be stories because nothing makes sense, the linearity a swooping tangle. And of course she never happened anyway; mortals were made together, in bodies with four arms that Zeus split apart for their pride. That's the story they've heard most often, at least.

But perhaps that's why they continue to listen to the story of the girl and her curiosity. The hope she kept trapped.

Because some will spend most of their lives looking for their other halves, the bodies they once lost – and think it's cruel of Zeus to take that from them. Vindictiveness in response to human pride? Hatred in the face of their happiness? Why not fire? Why not their creator, bound on a mountainside? They like the idea they are made of clay, too, purposeful and multifaceted.

And hope? There's a thought. There's a story that cannot die.

So one day, after years of war and anguish and chaos born anew, perhaps then the gods will be chased back into the Heavens. Everyone is so very tired of the age of heroes.

Let it be the age of quiet, of the ordinary, of love and of peace.

Perhaps not.

Probably not.

They cannot blame the gods for all their faults, of course.

But they can try to be better, try to build better.

That's where the stories lead them.

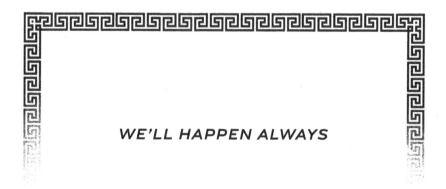

WE'LL HAPPEN ALWAYS

THERE'S ANOTHER STORY, THOUGH FEWER tell it.

On an island outside of time there is a girl and a boy and a dog that's not a dog.

They're happy, some say. Their love broke the cosmos, and now they're finally content, finally safe. They bake bread and tend the forests and the beasts within; there are nymphs there, too, and they trade stories and they are finally at ease to while away not-quite-eternity and not-quite-never.

Ludicrous, say the others, time was shredded long before their love sparked, they just stitched something from the pieces. And now they're working on something, a way to keep fighting. They have chiselled aeons and shattered chronology and now they are waiting for the right moment to slip from their knotted loop of time back into the linear weave.

No, actually, others argue, because it didn't work – they loved each other and they hoped for better and they tried to break time itself to be happy together. But it still wasn't enough. That is the moral: that sometimes love is not quite so powerful. That, sometimes, time persists even when you beg it not to. And sometimes hope is futile.

It doesn't really matter. It's a wavering sort of story, anyway. Fragments caught on the shore, written in a language long forgotten. It's not quite tangible, not quite real – it's a maybe. A possibility. A thing you can pray for, if it helps chase away the gloom. If it gives you something to cling on to.

We can hope they made it.

Because someone gave us the power to, once. Or never. Hid hope in a fennel stalk, or a jar, or within herself and dragged it to where the gods couldn't reach, ensured it would never be taken away.

Kept hope safe like a stolen flame.

Let it warm us through the darkness.

AFTERWORD

Hello, it's me again, the author!

Thank you so much for reading *A Beautiful Evil* – I really hope you enjoyed it. I just wanted to take a moment to discuss the neurodivergent characters within these pages – there are a few!

Specifically, I want to highlight Pandora, who doesn't have the language or framework within this fantastical ancient world to understand herself as autistic. But she is.

Her experiences are her own and they are individual to her character, but they are drawn from personal sentiments of feeling made wrong for this world – which you will have seen her navigate in these pages. As she comes to understand: there's no such thing. We are not made to suit a world but rather shape a world to suit us.

So if you've read this and resonated with her journey, I hope you also connected with the joy of coming to understand yourself. Please know that the world – and hopefully this story! – is so much more interesting for the variety within it.

Take care and I hope to see you again!

Bea x

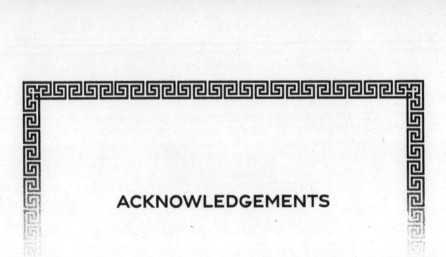

ACKNOWLEDGEMENTS

[Acknowledgements to come]

ACKNOWLEDGEMENTS

ACKNOWLEDGEMENTS

ACKNOWLEDGEMENTS

HOME IS WHERE
THE BOOKS LIVE

Discover your next read
on our TikTok channel @houseofya

Finished with this proof, but don't want to keep it?
Then read on . . .

If you love books, chances are you've got too many.
And, unfortunately, proofs you don't want can't be passed on*.
So what to do?

Burn it to keep warm? Great for local – but not global – warming. Plus, burning words and paper isn't a good look for a book lover.

Use it to prop up a wobbly table? Too thick. And you only need one . . .

Make a lot of paper aeroplanes? Scrunch the pages up for compost? Fun, or useful, but time consuming.

Alternatively, you could recycle your proof. Here's how:

Step One: if the cover, front or back, has any laminations, varnishes, or foils**, please tear it off and put it in your non-recycling rubbish.

Step Two: place the book in your recycling (after checking how your local recycling treats books at **recyclenow.com**).

That's it! Couldn't be easier.

If you'd like to be greener still (or reduce the strain on your book shelves), next time ask for a proof in a digital format. Recycling ones and zeroes is even easier.

We're making our books more recyclable

To find out more about our sustainability commitments including our journey to net zero, please visit greenpenguin.co.uk.

* They are not the final text and as such are available only for a limited time.

** These can contain metals and plastics.